The dying man stared at me with glass eyes in a skull face. "Listen," he croaked, "you think I'm raving, but I know what I'm saying. Get clear of this town now. Got no time to explain. Just move out."

I grabbed his shoulder, not gently. "Spit it out! Who are you? Why was he after you? Why did he shoot at me? Who was he?"

"All right," he was gasping. His face was that of a mummy who had died in agony. "I'll tell you. But you won't believe me."

"When the first quakes hit," he said, "they flew me in to Washington. Hell of a sight. The Washington Monument sticking up out of twenty feet of water, the Capitol dome down, a baby volcano building up where Mount Vernon used to be—"

"I know all that. Who was the man I shot?"

He ignored me. "Admiral Hayle came up with a plan. The South Polar ice cap was causing the crust of the Earth to slip. Send an expedition to the Pole, loaded with nuclear generator plant gear. We made our landfall. Lost men scaling the ice cliffs. Never even found the bodies.

"We reached our site, set up a base camp, and started in. We were sinking our shafts at the rate of about two hundred feet a day. On the thirty-first day, I had a hurry-up call from Station Four. They'd spotted dark shapes down in the ice. I went down to see for myself.

"They had widened out a chamber down there, thirty feet wide, pumps whining, the stink of decay. They'd smoothed off a flat place, like a picture window. They put the big lights on it. Then I saw what the excitement was all about. Rocks, tufts of grass, twigs. Looked as if they were floating in water. And way back you could see other things—bigger things."

"What kind of things?" I asked him, but he did not see me any longer.

"About forty feet away, a creature slumped sideways as though he'd leaned against a wall for a rest. Looked like the old elephant they had in the zoo at home, when I was a kid, except he had a coat of two-foot-long hair, reddish-black, plastered to his body."

"I know what a mammoth looks like," I said. "So you found one frozen; it's happened before. What makes it important?"

He moved his eyes to look at me. "Not like this one, they haven't. He was buckled into a harness like a circus pony. . . ."

—from *Catastrophe Planet*

FUTURE
IMPERFECT

KEITH LAUMER

EDITED BY ERIC FLINT

FUTURE IMPERFECT

This is a work of fiction. All the characters and events portrayed in this book are fictional, and any resemblance to real people or incidents is purely coincidental.

Catastrophe Planet (aka *The Breaking Earth*) was first published by Berkley in 1966. "The Walls" was first published in *Amazing*, March 1963. "Cocoon" was first published in *Fantastic*, December 1962. "Founder's Day" was first published in *The Magazine of Fantasy & Science Fiction*, July 1966. "Placement Test" was first published in *Amazing*, July 1964. "Worldmaster" was first published in *Worlds of Tomorrow*, November 1965. "The Day Before Forever" was first published in *The Magazine of Fantasy & Science Fiction*, July 1967.

A Baen Books Original

Baen Publishing Enterprises
P.O. Box 1403
Riverdale, NY 10471
www.baen.com

ISBN: 0-7434-3606-7

Cover art by Richard Martin

First printing, May 2003

Library of Congress Cataloging-in-Publication Data

Laumer, Keith, 1925-1993
   Future imperfect / by Keith Laumer ; edited by Eric Flint.
      p. cm.
   Contents: Catastrophe planet — The walls — Cocoon — Founder's day — Placement test — Worldmaster — The day before forever.
   ISBN 0-7434-3606-7 (trade pb.)
      1. Science fiction, American. I. Flint, Eric. II. Title.

PS3562.A84F88 2003
813'.54—dc21

                                                                    2003041678

Distributed by Simon & Schuster
1230 Avenue of the Americas
New York, NY 10020

Production by Windhaven Press, Auburn, NH
Printed in the United States of America

10   9   8   7   6   5   4   3   2   1

CONTENTS

CATASTROPHE PLANET

Chapter One

I held the turbo-car at a steady hundred and forty, watching the strip of cracked pavement that had been Interstate 10 unreel behind me, keeping a sharp eye ahead through the dust and volcanic smog for any breaks in the pavement too wide for the big car to jump. A brand-new six-megahorse job, it rode high and smooth on a two-foot air cushion. It was too bad about the broken hatch lock, but back in Dallas I hadn't had time to look around for the owner. The self-appointed vigilantes who called themselves the National Guard had developed a bad habit of shooting first and checking for explanations later. True, I had been doing a little informal shopping in a sporting goods store—but the owner would not have cared. He and most of the rest of the city had left for points north quite a few hours before I arrived—and I needed a gun and ammunition. A rifle would probably have been the best choice, but I had put in a lot of sociable hours on the Rod and Gun Club thousand-inch range back at San Luis, and the weight of the old-style .38 Smith and Wesson felt good at my hip.

There were low volcanic cones off to my right, trickling black smoke and getting ready for the next round. It was to be expected; I was keeping as close as the roads allowed to the line of tectonic activity running along the Gulf Coast from the former site of New

1

Orleans to the shallow sea that had been northern Florida. Before I reached Atlanta, sixty miles ahead, I would have to make a decision; either north, into the relative geologic stability of the Appalachians, already mobbed with refugees and consequently drastically short on food and water, to say nothing of amusement—or south, across the Florida Sea to the big island they called South Florida, that took in Tampa, Miami, Key West, and a lot of malodorous sand that had been sea bottom until a few months before.

I had a hunch which way I would go. I have always had a fondness for old Scotch, sunshine, white beaches, and the company of sportsmen who did not mind risking a flutter at cards. I would be more likely to find them south than north. The only station still broadcasting dance music was KSEA at Palm Beach. That was the spirit for me. If the planet was going to break up— all right. But while I was alive I would go on living at the best speed I could manage.

The map screen had warned me there was a town ahead. Just a hamlet which had once had ten thousand or so inhabitants, it would be a better bet for my purposes than a big city. Most of the cities had been stripped pretty clean by now, in this part of the country.

The town came into view spread out over low hills under a pall of smoke. I slowed, picked my way around what was left of a farmhouse that had been dropped on the road by one of the freak winds that had become as common as summer squalls. A trickle of glowing lava was running down across a field from a new cone of ash a quarter of a mile off to the right. I skirted it, gunned the turbos to hop a three-foot fissure that meandered off in a wide curve into the town itself.

It was late afternoon. The sun was a bilious puffball that shed a melancholy light on cracked and tilted slabs of broken pavement. In places, the street was nearly blocked by heaps of rubble from fallen buildings; hoods and flanks of half-buried vehicles, mud-colored from a coating of dust, projected from the detritus. The downtown portion was bad. Not a building over two stories was left standing, and the streets were strewn with everything from bedsteads to bags of rotted potatoes. It looked as though the backlash from one of the tidal waves from the coast had reached this far, spent its last energy finishing up what the quakes and fires had started.

Clotted drifts of flotsam were caught in alley mouths and doorways, and along the still-standing storefronts a dark line three feet from the ground indicated the highest reach of the flood waters. A deposit of red silt had dried to an almost impalpable dust that the ragged wind whirled up into streamers to join the big clouds that rolled in endlessly from the west.

Three blocks east of the main drag I found what I was looking for. The small street had failed even before the disaster. It was lined with cheap bars, last-resort pawnshops, secondhand stores with windows full of rusted revolvers, broken furniture and stacks of dog-eared pornography, sinister entrances under age-blackened signs offering clean beds one flight up. I slowed, looked over what was left of a coffee and 'burger joint that had never made any pretense of sanitation, spotted a two-customer-wide grocery store of the kind that specialized in canned beans and cheap wine.

I eased off power, settled to the ground, gave a blast from the cleaner-orifices to clear the dust from the canopy and waited for the dust to settle. The canopy made crunching noises as I cycled it open. I settled my breathing mask over my face and climbed out, stretching stiff legs. A neon sign reading Smoky's Kwik-Pick was hanging from one support and creak, creaking as the wind moaned around it. I heard the distant soft *buroom* of masonry falling into the dust blanket.

As I reached the curb, the dust lifted, danced like water, settled back in a pattern of ridges and ripples. I spun, took two jumps and the street came up and hit me like a missed step in the dark. I went down. Through a rising boil of dust, a clean-cut edge of concrete thrust up a yard from my nose with a shriek like Satan falling into Hell. Loose gravel fill cascaded; then raw, red clay was pushing up, a foot, two feet. There was a roaring like an artillery bombardment; the pavement hammered and thrust like a wild bronco on a rope. The uplifted section of street jittered and danced, then slid smoothly away, squealing like chalk on a giant blackboard. I got to hands and knees, braced myself to jump. Then another shock wave hit, and I was down again, bouncing against pavement that rippled like a fat girl's thigh.

The rumble died slowly. The tremble of the ground under me faded and merged with a jump of my muscles. There was not much I could see through the dust. A little smoke was curling up from the new chasm that had opened across the street; through the mask

I caught a whiff of sulphur. Behind me, things were still falling, in a leisurely, ponderous way, as though there were no hurry about returning what had once been the small city of Greenleaf, Georgia, to the soil it had sprung from.

The car was my first worry; it was on the far side of the fissure, a ragged two-yard-wide cut slicing down into the glisten of wet clay far below. I might have been able to jump it if my knees had not been twitching like a sleeping hound's elbow. I needed a plank to bridge it; from the sounds of falling objects, there should be plenty of loose ones lying around nearby.

Through the smashed front of a used-clothing emporium two doors down, I could see racks of worn suits of indeterminate color, powdered with fallen plaster. Behind them, collapsed wall shelves had spilled patched shirts, cracked shoes, and out-of-style hats across a litter of tables heaped with ties and socks among which tones of mustard and faded mauve seemed to predominate. A long timber that had supported the ends of a row of now-exposed rafters had come adrift, was slanted down across the debris. I picked my way through the wreckage, got a grip on the plank, twisted it free to the accompaniment of a new fall of brick chips.

Back outside, the dust was settling. The wind had died. There was a dead, muffled silence. My plank made an eerie grumbling sound as the end scored a path through the silt. I found myself almost tiptoeing, as though the noise of my passing might reawaken the slumbering earth giants. I passed the glassless door of Smoky's Kwik-Pick, and stopped dead, not even breathing. Ten seconds crept by like a parade of cripples dragging themselves to a miraculous shrine. Then I heard it again: a gasping moan from inside the ruined store.

I stood frozen, listening to silence, the board still in my hands, my teeth bared, not sure whether I had really heard a noise or just the creak of my own nerves. In this dead place, the suggestion of life had a shocking quality, like merriment in a graveyard.

Then, unmistakably, the sound came again. I dropped the plank, got the pistol clear of its holster. Beyond the broken door I could make out crooked ranks of home-made shelves, a drift of cans and broken bottles across the narrow floor.

"Who's there?" I called inanely. Something moved in the darkness at the back of the room. Cans clattered as I kicked them aside.

A thick sour stink of rotted food penetrated my respirator mask. I stepped on broken ketchup bottles and smashed cans, went past a festering display of lunch meat, a freezer with raised lid, jumped and almost fired when a foot-long rat darted out.

"Come on out," I called. My voice sounded as confident as a rookie cop bracing Public Enemy Number One. There was the sound of a shuddering breath.

I went toward it, saw the dim rectangle of a dust-coated window set in a rear door. The door was locked, but a kick slammed it open, let in a roil of sun-bright haze. A man was sitting on the floor, his back against the wall, his lap full of plaster fragments and broken glass. A massive double laundry sink rested across his legs below the knees, trailing a festoon of twisted pipes. His face was oily-pale, with eyes as round as half-dollars, and there was a quarter-inch stubble across hollow cheeks. Mud was caked in a ring around each nostril, his eyes, his mouth. Something was wrong with his nose and ears—they were lumped with thick, whitish scar tissue—and there were patches of keloid on his cheekbones. Joints were missing from several of the fingers of his clawlike left hand, which was holding a .45 automatic, propped up, aimed approximately at my left knee. I swung a foot and kicked the gun off into the shadows.

"Didn't need. . . . do that," he mumbled. His voice was as thin as lost hope.

I got a grip on the weight across his legs, heaved at it. Water sloshed, and he gave a wail as his head fell sideways.

It took five minutes to get him free, drag him up front where the light was better, settle him in comparative comfort on the floor with his head propped up on broken flour sacks covered with newspaper. He snored with his mouth slackly open. He smelled as though he had been dead for a week. Outside, the sun was glaring low through drifting smoke and dust layers, shaping up for another spectacular sunset.

I used my Boy Scout knife to cut away stiff cloth, examined his legs. They were both badly broken, but the bruises were several days old, at least. The last tremor had not been the one that caught him.

He opened his eyes. "You're not one of them," he said, faintly but clearly.

"How long have you been here?"

He shook his head, a barely perceptible movement. "Don't know. Maybe a week."

"I'll get you some water."

"Had plenty. . . . water," he said. "Cans, too. . . . but no opener. Rats were the worst."

"Take it easy. How about some food?"

"Never mind that. Better get moving. Bad here. Tremors every few hours. Last one was bad. Woke me up. . . ."

"You need food. Then I'll get you to my car."

"No use, mister, I've got. . . . internal injuries. Hurts too much to move. You cut out now. . . . while you can."

I sorted through the strewn cans, found a couple that seemed sound, cut the tops off. The odor of kidney beans and applesauce made my jaws ache. He shook his head. "You've got. . . . get clear. Leave me my gun."

"You won't need a gun—"

"I need it, mister." His whispering voice had taken on a harsh note. "I'd have used it on myself—but I was hoping they'd find me. I could take a couple of them along."

"Forget it, old-timer. You're—"

"No time for talk. They're here—in the town. I saw them, before. They won't give up." His eyes got worried. "You've got a car?"

I nodded.

"They'll spot it. Maybe already have. Get. . . . going. . . ."

I used the knife blade to spoon beans into his mouth. He turned his face away.

"Eat it, sailor—it's good for you."

His eyes were on my face. "How'd you know I was Navy?"

I nodded toward his hand. He lifted it half an inch, let it fall back.

"The ring. I should have gotten rid of it, but. . . ."

"Now take your beans like an old campaigner."

He gritted his teeth, twisted his face. "Can't eat," he protested. "God, the pain. . . ."

I tossed the can aside. "I'm going out and check the car," I said. "Then I'll be back for you."

"Listen," he croaked. "You think I'm raving, but I know what I'm saying. Get clear of this town—now. Got no time to explain. Just move out."

I grunted at him, went out into the street, recovered my plank, propped it with its end resting on the upper edge of the ravine that split the pavement. It was a shaky bridge; I went up it on all fours. As I was about to rise and step clear, I saw a movement ahead. My car sat ten yards away where I had left it, thickly coated now with new-fallen pumice. A man was circling it warily. He stepped in close, wiped a hand across the canopy, peered into the interior. I stayed where I was, kneeling on the plank over the dark fissure, just the top of my head above ground level.

The man went around to the driver's side, flipped the lever that opened the hatch, thrust his head inside. I shifted position, eased my gun out. I could not afford to be robbed of the car—not here, not now.

Instead of climbing in, he stepped away from the car, stood looking intently around at the ruined storefronts. He took a step my way, abruptly stopped dead, reached inside his coat, snatched out a small revolver, brought it up and in the same movement fired. The bullet threw dust in my face, sang off across the street and struck wood with a dull smack. Two more shots cracked before the first had stopped echoing—all this in perhaps three-quarters of a second. I hugged the board under me, dragged my gun clear as another shot scored concrete inches from my face. I squinted through haze, centered my sights on the black necktie of the man as he stood with his feet planted wide apart, frowning down the length of his outstretched arm. His small automatic flashed bright in the same instant that my shot boomed. He leaped back, bounced against the side of the car, went down on his back in the dust.

My breath went out in a long sigh, I holstered the .38, scrambled up to stand on the side of the riven street. He was lying on his side like a tired bum curled up for a nap, his face resting in a black paste of bloodied dust, lots of dustcaked blood on his shirt front. He was wearing a neat, dark suit, now dusty, new-looking shoes with almost unscratched soles. His age might have been anything from thirty-five to fifty. His eyes were open and a film of dust had already dimmed their shine. One hand was outflung, still holding the gun. I picked it up, looked it over absently. It was a Spanish automatic, nickel-plated. I tossed it aside, went through his coat pockets, found nothing except a small rectangle of paper stating that the garment had been checked by Inspector 13. Maybe that had been a bad omen. But then maybe he had not believed in omens.

His pants pockets were as empty: no wallet, no identification. He was as anonymous as a store-window dummy. And he had tried, without warning and without reason, to kill me on sight.

Back inside the store, the man with the broken legs lay where I had left him, staring toward me with glass eyes in a skull face.

"I met your friend," I said. My voice sounded strange in my ears, like an announcement beyond the grave.

"You're all right," he gasped.

"He wasn't very smart," I said. "Perfect target. He shot at me. I didn't have much choice." I felt my voice start to shake. I was not used to killing men.

"Listen," the skull-face said. "Get out now—while you can. There'll be more of them—"

"I killed him," I said. "One shot, one dead man." I looked down at the gun at my hip. "The world is coming apart and I'm killing men with a gun." I looked at him. "Who was he?"

"Forget him! Run! Get away!"

I squatted at his side. "Forget him, huh? Just like that. Get in my car and tootle off, whistling a merry tune." I reached out, grabbed his shoulder, not gently. "Who was he?" I was snarling between my teeth now, letting the shock work itself out in good healthy anger.

"You. . . . wouldn't understand. Wouldn't believe—"

"Try me!" I gripped harder. "Spit it out, sailor! What's it all about? Who are you? What were you doing here? Why was he after you? Why did he shoot at me? Who was he?"

"All right," he was gasping, showing his teeth. His face was that of a mummy who had died in agony. "I'll tell you. But you won't believe me."

"It was almost a year ago," he said. "I was on satellite duty on Sheppard Platform when the first quakes hit. We saw it all from up there—the smoke on the day side and the thousand-mile fires at night. They gave the order to evacuate the station—I never knew why."

"Pressure from Moscow," I told him. "They thought we were doing it."

"Sure. Everybody panicked. I guess we did, too. Our shuttle made a bad landing southwest of Havana. I was one of three survivors.

Spent a few days at Key West; then they flew me in to Washington. Hell of a sight. Ruins, fires, the Potomac out of its banks, meandering across Pennsylvania, the Washington Monument sticking up out of twenty feet of water, the capitol dome down, a baby volcano building up where Mount Vernon used to be—"

"I know all that. Who was the man I shot?"

He ignored me. "I gave my testimony. No signs of enemy activity. Just nature busting loose like nineteen hells. There was some professor there—he had all the facts. A hell of an uproar when he sprang his punch line, senators jumping up and yelling, M.P.'s everywhere, old Admiral Conaghy red in the face—"

"You're wandering," I reminded him. "Get to the point."

"The crust of the earth was slipping, he told them. Polnac, that was his name. Some kind of big shot from Hungary. The South Polar ice cap building up, throwing the machinery out of kilter. Eccentric thrust started the lithosphere sliding. He said it had slipped more than four miles then. Estimated it would hit an equilibrium at about a thousand. Take about two years—"

"I read the papers—or I did while there were any papers to read."

"Conaghy got the floor. Hit the South Pole with everything we had, he said; bust up the icecap. He scribbled on the back of an envelope and said fifty super-H's would do the job."

"They'd have loaded the atmosphere with enough radioactivity to sterilize the planet."

"No, might've worked. Propaganda. Scared of the Russkis, what they'd do. I missed out on the rest. They cleared the hearing room then. But I heard rumors later they'd put it to Koprovin and he said that at the first sign of a nuclear launch he'd hit us with his whole menagerie." The hollow eyes closed; a dry-looking tongue touched blackish lips. He swallowed hard. Then his eyes flew open again and he went on: "That's when Hayle came up with his plan. Secret force to be dispatched to the Pole, loaded with modified nuclear generator plant gear. There was a lot of resistance, but they bought it. He picked me to go with him."

I narrowed my eyes at him. "Vice-Admiral Hayle was lost on a routine orbital mission," I told him. "I never heard of any polar expedition."

"That's right—that was the cover story. Cosmic Top Secret. Operation Defrost, we called it."

"Sounds as though you were on the inside."

He nodded, a weak twitch. All his strength was going into his story. "We sailed from San Juan on Christmas Day. Two deep-water battlewagons, *Maine* and *Pearl*."

"They were lost with the submarine station at Guam."

"No. We had 'em. A dozen smaller ships, three thousand men. This was a major effort. New York was already gone, Boston, Philly, most of the East Coast, San Diego, Corpus—you remember how it was. Blue water over Panama. Hell, we spotted bodies floating a thousand miles at sea after the tornadoes. Surface covered with floating pumice as far south as Tierra del Fuego; new volcanoes there that made a glow in the sky six hundred miles east.

"Ice everywhere; a two-hundred-mile field of bergs broken loose from the cap. Looked like a lot of ice, but it was just crumbs. I saw those blue ice cliffs, rising two miles sheer out of the sea, peaks covered with black dust. That's a sight, mister. . . ." His voice trailed off; his eyes wandered from me, staring into the past—or into a pipedream.

"The man with the gun," I brought him back. "Where does he come in?".

"We made our landfall; lost our first men scaling the ice cliffs. Never even found the bodies. Treacherous footing. Used the new model laser-type handguns to melt a path up, then blasted. Took two weeks to get our gear ashore. Funny, wasn't too cold. Big yellow sun shining down on the ice, balmy breeze blowing. Gorgeous sunsets, but not much dust that far south. Ice looked fairly clean. We started inland in heavy assault and landing craft. Made two hundred miles a day. Our target was a spot Hayle had picked in Queen Maud Land—the Pensacola Mountains, under the ice. The plan was to cut the glacier at the ridge and free a couple of hundred square miles of it to move off toward the sea, with a little help from us. We were to bore sinks to the rock, and pump hot air down. Theory was we'd create a lubricating fluid layer at the interface.

"We reached our site, set up a base camp, and started in. I had the north complex—six drill sites stretched out over forty miles of glare ice. Things went pretty well. We were sinking our shafts at the rate of about two hundred feet a day. Couldn't go faster because of melt disposal. On the thirty-first day, I had a hurry-up call from Station Four. I went out on a snowcat. Trench—he was in command there—was excited. They'd spotted dark shapes down in the ice, lying off some yards from the shaft. Bad visibility, he said; the ice was as clear as water, but light did strange tricks down there. I went down to see for myself.

"It was a regulation-type mine lift, open-work sides. I watched the ice slide up past me—lots of dirt in it at places, strata two and three inches thick as black as your hat. We reached bottom. Trench had widened out a chamber down there, thirty feet wide, walls like black glass, damp, cold. Water dripping from the shaft above, puddling up underfoot, pumps whining, the stink of decay. He took me over to where they'd smoothed off a flat place, like a picture window. It was opaque—like polished marble—until we put the big lights on it. Then I saw what the excitement was all about.

"Rocks, bits of broken stone, tufts of grass, twigs. Looked as if they were floating in water, frozen. Swirls of mud here and there, all petrified in the ice. And way back—maybe fifty yards—you could see other things—bigger things."

"What kind of things?" I asked him, but he did not see me any longer.

"I told Trench to go ahead," the whispering voice went on. "Cut a side tunnel back. Sent word to the admiral to come down. By the time he got there we were sixty feet into the side wall. I'd had them steer for the nearest big object. He came down that tunnel swearing, wanting to know who the damned sightseers were who were diverting our resources into jaunts off into the countryside. I didn't answer him—just pointed.

"There, about forty feet away, a creature slumped a little sideways as though he'd leaned against a wall for a rest. His trunk was curled back against his chest and his tusks sort of glowed in the searchlight. Looked just like the old elephant they had in the zoo at home, when I was a kid, except he had a coat of two-foot-long hair, reddish-black, plastered to his body as if he was wet.

"Hayle damn near fell down. He stood there and gaped, then yelled at the crew to work in closer. We cleared the way, and they went at it. Water was sloshing around our feet, ankle deep; the pumps weren't keeping up. Air smelled bad. Lots of small items melting out; small animals, vegetation, black mud. He called a halt at ten feet. You could see old Jumbo now as if you were standing just beyond a glass cage. There was dirt caked on his flanks, and you could see mud still adhering to his feet. His eyes were open, and they caught the light and threw it back. His mouth was half open and the inside was dull red, and his tongue poked out at one corner. One of his tusks had the tip broken and splintered. They were yellower than elephant ivory, long and thin, and they curved out. . . ."

"I know what a mammoth looks like," I said. "So you found one frozen; it's happened before. What makes it important?"

He moved his eyes to look at me. "Not like this one, they haven't. It wasn't a mammoth! It was a mastodon. And he was buckled into a harness like a circus pony."

Chapter Two

"A mastodon in harness," I snorted, I was humoring him. "I suppose that implies that Antarctica was warmer once than it is now, that it was inhabited, and that the natives had tamed elephants. If the world weren't in the process of shaking itself to pieces, I'd find that pretty interesting, I guess—but still nothing to do murder over."

He lay there, his eyes shut, his chest rising and falling unevenly. His wrist was like a dry stick when I checked it; the pulse was fast and light. I did not know whether he was asleep or in a coma. Then his eyes opened suddenly. They were the only part of him that moved now.

"That was only the beginning," he said. His voice was fainter now, as though it were coming from somewhere far away. "We went on down with the main shaft. At seventy-three hundred feet, we came into a layer filled with artifacts like the Field Museum in Chicago before the lake got it. Wood, vegetation, planks, pieces of structures, paper, cloth items. Clothing in vivid colors, furniture, broken dishes—and some that weren't broken. Then we found the man." He stopped, and his face twitched. I waited and he went on.

"Short—not over five six, thick in the body, arms like a wrestler. Covered with hair—like Jumbo; pale, dirty-blond hair, and a face like your bad dreams. Big square teeth, and he was showing 'em. Thin lips, pulled back. He looked mad—plenty mad. He was wearing clothes—mostly straps and bits of brass, but well made.

And there was a gun in his hand—a mean-looking weapon, short, like a riot gun, with a big chamber. We tested it later. It blew a forty-foot crater in the ice on the shortest burst I could fire. Never did figure out how it worked.

"It was all pay dirt from then on. More of these ape men, more animals; then we saw the peak of what we thought was a mountain, rising up from below. It wasn't a mountain. It was a building. We melted our way down to it, forced a door. There was no ice inside. We wondered about that; then we decided that snowfalls had buried the buildings; and the inhabitants had evacuated, set up temporary camps on the top of the snow. But it kept snowing. In time the weight compressed the snow into clear ice. Probably there was some tunneling down to the city; we found what looked like old bores, flooded and frozen.

"I was in the advance party that broke into the tower. Terrible odor. Strange-looking furniture, mostly rotted, rotted rugs and wall hangings, some bones—men and animals. And one skeleton of a modern man with a broken skull. We got the idea the Neanderthal types were slaves. Maybe one of them paid off a grudge.

"There were plenty of metal and ceramic items around—not primitive. We were all pretty excited. Then—things started to happen. We heard noises, saw signs that somebody had been there ahead of us. Then men started disappearing. Found one man dead, with a hole in him. Hayle called topside for reinforcements. No answer. He figured the cable was broken. He sent me up with a couple of men to check on things, report what we'd run into. He was worried—plenty worried.

"At the top, Bachman and the other sailor stepped off. I stayed in the lift to run a test on the telephone. I got Hayle: he yelled something at me, but I couldn't make it out. Sounded like shots; then nothing.

"I started out to join the men—and it blew. I saw a flash; ice hit me in the face, and the car started to fall. . . .

"When I came to, I was still in the car, in the dark. It was canted sideways, half full of pulverized ice. I wasn't hurt much—a few bruises, but my left glove was gone, and my faceplate.

"I could see a dim glow up above. I went to work on the ice. It was like loose gravel. Maybe I should have gone down to check on the Admiral—but I didn't. I got to the surface the quickest way I could. The car had jammed in the shaft about ten feet down.

There was nothing in sight but ice. No sign of the camp, or of Bachman or the other men. And no signs of a big quake, either. Just a sort of crater where the tunnel mouth had been.

"It was eight miles to Station Three. My snowcat was gone with the rest. I took a bearing on the sun and started walking. Made it in just under five hours. Nothing there. Just a lot of broken ice.

"I took a break, rested, ate part of my suit rations. The coverall was keeping me warm enough. The batteries were good for another couple of hundred hours. I headed for Station Four. Half a mile out from it I found a motor sledge, loaded and fueled and footprints leading off to a ridge of ice, blood on the snow. I followed. It was Hansen, dead.

"I took the sledge, went on in. It was the same—just a stretch of ice. No trace of the huts, the equipment—or the men. The shaft was closed, obliterated. I used the radio on the sledge to try to raise Base Camp. No answer.

"It took me four days to check out the camps and get back to the coast. We'd left the squadron at anchor, sub-surface. I made it out to a tender—it was the closest to shore, and in shallow water. I got in and found her flooded. We'd left a skeleton complement behind. Three of them were there, dead, no marks on their bodies. I could have pumped her out, but I couldn't handle a two-thousand-tonner alone. I took a motorized lifeboat, stocked it with canned goods, and headed north.

"Seven days at sea; then I made port at a small Argentine town that had been a plantation village halfway up a mountain. It was a port now; a couple of hundred boats tied up to makeshift wharves, refugees everywhere. I tried to find a doctor for my hand and face—frostbite. There weren't any. No communications, either. I tried to pull rank on an Argentine gunboat skipper and nearly got myself shot.

"That night I went down to my boat with an armful of fresh fruit I'd gotten for my wristwatch. They jumped me as I was untying the dinghy to row out to her. I was lucky. The light was bad and the first one missed with his knife and I nailed him with a boathook. I shot the other one, and pushed off. Lots of lights on the beach by the time I headed out of the harbor, but nobody chased me.

"I made landfall south of Baton Rouge in four days. Played it cagey, brought her into a bayou mouth at night, kept out of sight behind flooded-out houses. Left the boat hidden and got into town. Tried to get a message off to a contact in Washington, but no luck. Chaos in the town. Famine was beginning to pinch then. All the refugees from the coast and from the fault areas farther west. Air like a foundry, soot everywhere, and more tremors every day.

"I took a car and headed east. Near Vicksburg a car tried to force me off the road. I fooled 'em; they hit instead. I went back and looked them over. Two men, dressed in plain suits, no identification. Looked about forty, fifty, might have been Americans, maybe not.

"Reached here on the third day—maybe a week ago. Saw food in here; then a quake caught me. Thought it was them, at first— like the ice shaft." He twitched his face in a ghastly grin.

"You think the polar expedition was wiped out by—whoever is chasing you?"

"You can stake your life on it!" His whisper was fierce. "And they're in town now. They're out there—looking for me. I was shrewd. I parked the car blocks away, meant to walk back. . . ."

"They're not there now," I reminded him, trying to speak gently.

"Searching the town," he said. "Won't give up. Find me in the end. And I'll be ready. . . ." He lifted his hand an inch, looked puzzled. "Where's my gun?"

"You won't need it," I started. "I'm going to take you—"

"They got it," he said. A tear leaked from the corner of his eye, ran down his scarred face. "Must have. . . . gone to sleep. . . ."

I got to my feet, fitted my mask back on. "Come on," I said. "Time to go." I got an arm under his back, started to lift him. He gave a thin cry like a stepped-on kitten. His eyes blinked, settled on my face.

"You take it," he said. "Show it. . . . them. Make. . . . listen. . . ."

"Sure, old-timer. Come on, now; got to pick you up—"

"Pocket," he gasped out. "Take it. Show. . . ." His jaw dropped and his eyes glazed over like hardening solder. I checked his wrist again. The last feeble flutter was gone.

For a minute, in the total silence, I looked at him, wondering how much, if any, of the wild story he had told had been true, and how much delirium. His pocket, he had said. I tried two, found only dust. There was an old-fashioned watch pocket under his belt that I almost missed. I stuck a finger in, felt something smooth and cool. I eased it out—a big, thick, round coin, just smaller than a silver dollar, with the tawdry yellow shine of pure gold. There was a stylized representation of a bird on one side; the obverse was covered with an elaborate pattern of curlicues that didn't quite seem to be writing.

I pocketed it, stood up—and heard a sound from the street.

Below the level of the glass- and plaster-littered sill where the front window had been was a scatter of glass chips and broken brick. I went flat on them, the gun in my hand without a conscious move on my part. The sound came again; the rattle of my plank bridge under the weight of feet. It was thirty feet to the back of the shop, through an obstacle course of fallen cans and broken bottles. I made it with no more sound than smoke makes going up a chimney, got to my feet in an alley half choked with flood-washed rubbish over-sprinkled with fallen stucco and drifted dust. It was almost dark now; the sun had sunk behind the dust clouds. I moved along silent-footed in the dust carpet, keeping near the wall to make my prints a little less obvious to anyone who might try to follow.

The street at the end was empty. I went along it to the corner, risked a look, saw a man in a dark suit come out of the store. He went to the plank, climbed up. The street was dark except for long shafts of blood red light striking across through gaps in the buildings. There were no birdcalls, no hum of insects, just the creaking from the man on the bridge, going carefully on all fours. He reached the top, stepped off. He must have found the dead sailor; that would satisfy him. Now he would be on his way. I watched him move off out of sight; then I stepped out, hugging the building fronts. I was not thinking—just reacting. It seemed suddenly important to keep him in sight, get the license number of his car; maybe trail him. . . .

I heard the click of metal and dived, hit hard on cracked concrete, rolled, came up among the folds of a dangling awning, heard the flat *crack!* of a gun. I could not tell what direction the shot had come from; the dust muffled everything, killing echoes. Feet were hurrying toward me. I heard a shout, an answer from above. The steps were slower now, passing by mere feet from me—

They halted, and I crouched, almost feeling the bullet crashing through my brain. It was not a time for indecision. I doubled my legs, launched myself from my hideaway in a driving tackle, hit him just below the knees—face-first. I saw a blinding shower of stars, and he was down, and I lunged, caught a swinging arm, drove a fist into what felt like his throat. He made a noise like broken pipes, kicked out, but I was across his chest now, my right hand on his throat. He pounded my back like a pal trying to clear my windpipe, then quit and lay back. I got to my knees, breathing hard. Blood was running down into my mouth, I squinted up at the higher section of the street, saw a head moving along away from me. He had not heard the skirmish—or had not interpreted it correctly. He thought his partner was still padding along the street, following whatever it was he had fired at.

Kneeling, I checked the dead man's pockets. They were clean. He wore no watch, no ring, nothing personal.

Steps were coming back. I saw, not thirty feet away, a silhouette against the streak of red sky under the smoke layer. The man looked at the plank, swung round, started down, twisting his head to look over his shoulder; dim light from below cast a ruddy highlight on his cheek. Then he saw me. His mouth opened and I jumped, caught the edge of the two-by-six, heaved it up. He went over without a sound, caught himself with one hand, held on, dangling, his feet working like a bicycle rider. I jerked the board hard, and he went down. It seemed like a long time before he hit.

Ten minutes later, not rested and not fed, operating on pure adrenaline, I was headed east along a dirt road with the autodrive on ninety.

Chapter Three

An hour after full dark I pulled into a one-pump motel-cum-café where a long-legged fellow with thin blondish hair and a mouth like a torn pocket met me at the door with a shotgun. He fueled me up, sold me coffee and a moon pie with a texture like vinyl tile, and accepted a well-worn twenty as payment. I felt him smiling craftily at his business acumen; the habits of a lifetime of penny-pinching are hard to break.

The beach came into view an hour later—a dark mirrorgleam reflecting the dirty clouds boiling along above. Trees and rooftops showed above the surface for a mile or two out; it had been gently sloping farmland before the ocean reclaimed it. The pavement slid off under the water without a ripple; I boosted my revs, rode my air cushion out onto it. It was not recommended practice—if you lost power you sank, but I was in no mood to go boat hunting. I poured on the coal and headed south.

It was a nice three-hour run on still water under a moon the color and shape of a rotten grapefruit. Once a patrol boat hailed me, but I doused my lights and outran him. Once I passed over a town that had installed one of the new floodproof all-automatic power systems. The lights gleamed up at me through green water like something from a fairy tale.

Just before dawn I hit a stretch of treetops clogged with floating wildlife. I threaded a twisting path through them, reached dry land as the sun came up reddish-black and flat on the bottom.

Tampa was a reeking ruin, a seaport town miles from the sea, surrounded by a bog of gray mud, left high and dry by the freakish withdrawal of the Gulf. Nothing there for me.

Early afternoon brought me into Miami. The beach was wiped clean—a bare sandbar, but the city proper still gleamed white beside a shore stained black by pumice and scum oil, and heaped with the jetsam of a drowned continent. Conditions were better here. There had been no major quakes to judge from the still-standing towers of coral and chartreuse and turquoise; maybe their hurricane-proof construction had helped when the ground shook under them. There was even a semblance of normal commerce. Police were much in evidence, along with squads of nervous-looking Guard recruits weighted down with combat gear. Lights were on in shops and restaurants, and the polyarcs along Biscayne were shedding their baleful light on an orderly traffic of cars, trucks and buses. There were fewer people on the streets than in normal times, but that suited me.

I checked into the Gulfstream—a lavish hundred and fifty-story hostelry that had known my custom in happier times. The desk man was a former Las Vegas man named Sal Anzio; he gave a two-handed shake and the twitch of the left cheek that passed with him for smile.

"Mal Irish," he stated in the tone of one answering questions under duress. "What brings you into town?"

"Things went a little sour down south," I told him. "The

Mexicans have a tendency to get overexcited when things go wrong, and blame it all on the gringos. Anything doing here?"

"Sure. Plenty of action. We had most of the regular spring crowd down here when the word went out. Most of 'em stayed on. A few tourists pulled out, but what the hell. We're doing OK. We got power, water, plenty of reserve food. Every hotel in town had their freezers stocked for a big summer trade. We're all right—for another six months, anyway. After that—well, I got a boat staked out. For a grand I can fix you with a spot."

I told him I would let him know later, took the key to a suite on the hundred and twelfth, and took the high-speed lift up.

It was a nice room, spacious, tastefully decorated, with a big double bed and a bath big enough to water a pet hippo in. I soaked off the dust of five days' travel, called room service for a change of clothes. I had a drink in the room, then, prompted by a vague yearning for human companionship, went down to the tenth floor terrace for dinner.

The best of the sunset was just past. Coal-black clouds rimmed with melted gold hung over the ink-colored sea like a threat. The sky was glowing yellow green, and it shed an eerie, enchanted light over the tables, the potted palms, the couples at the tables.

Off to the north you could see a dull glow in the sky—a reflection from the red-hot lava that was building a new mountain range across Georgia. The surface of the Gulf was a little odd too. The normal wave pattern was disturbed by an overlay of ripples set up by the constant minor trembling of the sea bottom. But the band murmured of love and the diners smiled and lifted glasses and to hell with tomorrow.

After a nice dinner of fresh scampi and Honduras shrimp accented with an Anjou rosé, I went down to the pleasure rooms on the third floor. Anzio was there, wearing his pale lavender tux and overlooking the tables with his version of a look of benign efficiency—an expression like Caesar's favorite executioner picking out his next client.

"Howzit, Mal," he checked me over with his quick glance that could estimate the size of a bankroll to the last half cee. "Care to try your luck tonight?"

"Maybe later, Sal," I told him. "Who's in town?"

He reeled off a roster of familiar ne'er-do-wells and the

parasites who preyed off them. I found my attention wandering. It was a nice night, a nice crowd, but something was worrying me. I kept remembering the man with the broken legs, and the silent, not overly bright boys who had come gunning for him—and for me. Three of them. All dead. Killed by me, a peaceful man who'd never fired a shot in anger until yesterday. But what else could I have done? They were out to kill—and I had beaten them to the prize. It was that simple. And yet it was not simple at all.

" . . . . people in town," Sal was saying. "Some strange cats, true, but rolled, Mal, rolled."

"Who's that fellow?" A slim chap was moving past in black tails and white tie, almost but not quite conservative enough to look a little odd in the fashionable crowd.

"Huh? I dunno." Sal lifted his chin in a gesture of dismissal. "One of those kooks in here for this convention, I guess."

"What convention?" I did not know quite what it was about the man's look that bothered me. He was bland-faced, fortyish, well groomed, quiet, wearing about as much expression as an omelet.

"This noomismatics bunch, or whatever you call it. Got the twenty-eighth and twenty-ninth floors. Biggest bunch of creeps you ever saw, if you ask me. No action there, Mal."

"Numismatics, huh?" Coin collectors. I had a coin upstairs—a heavy gold coin, handed me by a dying man with as wild a tale as ever curled a kid's hair at bedtime. He had wanted me to take it—somewhere, tell someone his story. Some story. I would wind up either kicked down a couple of flights of official stairs, or locked up until the birdies stopped singing in my ears. Mammoths under ice. Cave men in fancy pants, packing ray guns. The poor fellow had been raving, blowing his top in his final delirium, that was all. Nothing for me to get emotional about. The coin was probably a novelty piece, solid lead with a gold wash, issued to commemorate a tie for third in basketball scored by good old Pawtucket High in the hot season of '87.

And then again, maybe not.

Numismatics. They would know about coins. It would not take ten minutes to show it to one of them, get an opinion. That would settle the question once and for all, and leave me to get on undisturbed with the important business of providing for the needs of one Malcome Irish, late of the U.S. Navy and later still of the army of the unemployed, a healthy eater with a burning desire to experience the best his era had to offer—such as it was—with the least possible discomfort.

"Thanks, Sal," I said, and headed for the elevators.

The twenty-eighth floor was silent, somber under rose-toned glare strips set in the ceiling in a geometric pattern. Through wide double glass doors at the end of the corridor I could see a bright room where people stood in the static poses of cocktail-party conversation. I went along the pale, immaculate carpet, pushed through into a dull mutter of talk. Faces turned my way—bland, ordinary faces, calm to the point of boredom. A waiter eased over, offered a small tray of sweet-smelling drinks in flimsy glasses. I lifted one, let my eyes drift over the crowd.

They were all men, none very old, none very young, mostly in neat, dull-colored evening clothes, a few wearing sportier tartans or pastels. Eyes followed my progress as I moved across the room. A tall fellow with slicked-back gray hair drifted in from offside, edged casually into my path. It was either talk to him or knock him down—a smooth intercept. I gave him a crafty smile.

"I'm not party-crashing," I confided. "I'm not one of your group here, but I do have an interest in coins—"

"Certainly, sir," he purred; the corners of his mouth lifted the required amount, no more. "An amateur coin fancier, perhaps?"

"Yes, in a small way. Actually, I wanted an opinion on a piece I picked up a while back. . . ." I fished the big coin from an inner pocket. Light gleamed on it as I turned it over in my fingers.

"Probably a phony," I said lightly, "but maybe you can tell me for sure." I held it out to him. He did not take it. He was looking at the coin, the protocol smile gone now, lines showing tight in his neck.

"Don't get the wrong impression," I said quickly. "I'm not asking for free service. I realize that an expert opinion is worth a reasonable fee. . . ."

"Yes," he said. "I wonder, sir, if you would be so kind as to step this way for one moment. I will ask Mr. Zablun to have a look at your, ah, find." He had a trace of accent, I thought, a barely discernible oddness of intonation. He turned away and I followed him across to a limed-oak slab door, through it and down a step into a lounge with a look of institutional intimacy, like a corporation waiting room.

"If you'll have a seat for a moment. . . ." He waved a neat hand at a too-low chair done in fuzzy gray polyon, disappeared through a door across the room. I stood where I was, holding the coin on my palm. It was heavy enough, but so were all properly made gold bricks. In a minute I would probably get a withering smile from some old geezer with a pince-nez who would tell me my prize was inscribed in pig latin meaning "there's a sucker born every minute." I put it between my teeth, bit down gently, felt the metal yield. If it was gold, it was the pure article.

A door opened behind me and I jumped. I was as tense as a second-story man waiting for the down car. The bouncer was back with a short, plumpish fellow with artificial-looking black hair and a darting eye.

"May I present Mr. Zablun," the gray-haired smoothie waved a hand in a prestidigitator's gesture. "He will be happy to have a look at the piece, Mr. ummm. . . ."

"Philbert," I supplied. "Jimmy Philbert, from Butte, Montana."

Mr. Zablun's head bobbed on his short neck in a Prussian-type nod. He came across and held out a cluster of fingers. I poked the coin at them and he thrust it up under his eye as though he were wearing a jeweler's lens. Then he held it in front of the other eye, giving it a crack at the find.

He and Gray Hair exchanged a quick glance. I started to reach for the coin, but Zablun had turned for the side door.

"If you'll just follow along, Mr. Philbert," Gray Hair said. He waved that graceful hand again and I trailed the short man along a narrow passage into a low-ceilinged room with a plain desk with a draftsman's lamp shedding a cold light on a green show blotter. Zablun went briskly behind the desk, pulled open a drawer, got out a black cloth, a small electronic-looking gadget, a set of lenses like measuring spoons, began fussing over my trophy. If it was a hog-calling award, at least it was not obvious at a glance.

Gray Hair stood by, not saying anything, no expression on his face. There was a small window at the side of the office; through it I could see a red glare on the water from the rising moon.

Zablun was putting things back in the drawer now, being very precise about their arrangement. He placed the coin back on the desktop at the exact center of the pool of light, stood.

"The coin is genuine," he said indifferently. "Gold, twenty-four point nine five. Mint specimen."

"You've seen one like it before?"

"It is not a great rarity."

"Where's it from?"

"A number have come to light at Crete in recent years. Not so fine, you understand. Not uncirculated."

"A Greek coin, eh?"

"The actual origin is unknown. Where did you secure the piece?" His tone was as cool as a detective lieutenant running through his list of routine questions; it had that same quality of impeccable politeness, as impersonal as a traffic light.

"I picked it up in a poker game at Potosi a couple of weeks back," I confided. "I was afraid I'd been suckered. Ah, by the way, what's it worth?"

"I can offer you fifty cees, Mr. Philbert," Gray Hair stepped into the conversation.

"I don't think I want to sell right now," I said. "Makes a nice pocket piece." I reached, lifted the thick coin from the desk. "Just wanted to be sure I hadn't been taken."

"Perhaps an offer of one hundred cees—"

"It's not a matter of price." I showed them a breezy smile. "I took it for a ten-cee bet. I think I'll just hang onto it. Maybe it brings me luck. I've stayed alive lately; that takes luck today." I turned to the door. Gray Hair beat me to it, slipped past me, led the way back to a door that opened into the wide hall with the cream-colored carpet.

"How much do I owe you?" I reached for my wallet, still beaming the happy smile of a fellow who has lucked into something.

"Please." Gray Hair waved the idea of payment away. "If you should change your mind, Mr. Philbert. . . ."

"I'll let you know first thing," I assured him. He inclined his head; I sauntered off toward the lift. At the end of the hall I looked back. The lights were just going off in the big room. In the elevator I took out the coin, studied it carefully under the dome light. The metal was bright, smooth, unscarred. The little mark I had made biting it was gone.

Zablun had switched coins on me.

Chapter Four

Anzio was the kind of man who never let curiosity interfere with business arrangements. The fifty-cee note I passed him assured me free access to an empty suite on the twenty-ninth floor of the unused north wing, commanding a view of the full length of the main east-west block, with a set of 8x40 binoculars from the lost-and-found room thrown in. Another ten cees covered the services of an off-duty cop to loiter near the side entrance and report to me when and if the gray-haired gent—who was registered as R. Sethys—chose that route to leave the building.

Room service brought me a midnight snack. I ate it in the dark, watching the activities of the money men behind the dozen lighted windows on their two floors. Mr. Zablun appeared half an hour after I started my vigil, talking to a group who seemed to listen with monumental indifference. Men came and went, moving with unhurried gravity. They did not seem to be doing any drinking; no women were in evidence; no one even lit a cigar. They were an abstemious bunch, these numismatists. For that matter, they did not seem much interested in coins. I had a fine, clear view of their activities through the glass and steelprod walls, and not a glint of gold or silver did I see.

After a few hours of this sport, I left my post and went down to bed. I did not know what it was I was looking for, but my instincts told me to play a concealed hand, to lie low and watch. Mr. Zablun had not lifted my souvenir for nothing. Raising a howl when I discovered the switch would not have bought me anything, but a little judicious spying might net me something solid to work on. The theft of the gold piece did not lend any specific support to the sailor's story—Zablun might have palmed it for the gold in it—but on the other hand it had not been the nice, clean dismissal I had expected. Whatever the coin was, it had not come in a Cracker Jack box—and I had had ample evidence that there were men loose in the land who would kill to get it—

Or would they? There was no necessary connection between the dead man's story and the real reason for the hunters on his trail. For all I knew, he might have been an escaped maniac, and the men in the unmarked suits might have been CBI boys, with orders to shoot on sight. The shots they had fired at me might have been a simple case of mistaken identity; maybe they were not expecting anyone but Jack the Ripper in the ruined streets of Greenleaf.

And maybe I was Shirley Temple. No CBI man that ever packed a badge was as lousy a shot as the clowns I had gunned down, or as unschooled in the basics of alley fighting. They might, for reasons known to the inner circles of bureaucracy, wander around in suits with empty pockets and no labels—but even a Federal man moving in for a hot pinch would not blaze away at a stranger on sight.

It was a futile argument, and I was losing both sides of it. I switched off the light, punched the pillow into shape, and made myself a promise that first thing in the morning I would scale the coin out over the breakers and channel my efforts to matters of more immediate concern to my future—such as locating a serious poker game to replenish my reduced resources. I was picturing a succession of inside straights and four-card flushes when the phone rang.

"Mal—funny thing. Your stamp collectors—they're stirred up like an Elk's smoker tipped off to a vice raid. Your friend Sethys left by the front door two minutes ago; he's standing out on the drive in the rain giving the garageman a hard time about bringing out his car. Now, he says. Hell, it's probably buried in the stacks somewhere down on level four—"

"I'll be down," I told him. "Get me a car—any car—before he has his."

Six minutes later by my cuff-link Omega I slid into the seat of a low-built foreign job that Anzio had pulled around to the side in the shelter of a screen of hibiscus.

"For cripe's sake get it back in one piece, Mal," he hissed at me, squinting against the drizzle. "It belongs to some big oil bird in the tower suite—"

"If they nab me, I stole it." Another fifty cees changed hands. At this rate that game had better be soon—preferably with a couple of Maharajahs with just enough IQ to raise into a pat hand.

The turbos hummed at me when I touched the go pedal; there was plenty of power under the squat black hood. I eased her out, watched Sethys get into the back of a heavy maroon Monojag with three other coin collectors. They gunned off down the drive and I let them take a hundred-yard lead, then slid out behind them.

Old Miami was a town I had known well once, a lot of years ago. It had not changed much in the decade since I had last seen it—except for the recent scars of storm and flood. The high tides set up by the tremors that rocked the Gulf floor had swept it, east to west, half a dozen times, scoured away topsoil, lawns, shrubbery, felling twenty-year-old royal palms, sweeping to well-deserved oblivion the older, flimsier construction that dated back to post-boom times. But the main portion of the city—the famous two-hundred-story luxury hotels, the downtown streets of high-priced shops, the walled and remote residences, each on its manicured acre that made up the wealthiest suburbs north of Rio—they were unchanged.

I followed the Monojag along Flagler under the multiple spans of Interstate 509, west into a section of massive concrete warehouses and gaunt steel food-processing plants, the ugly spawn of the South American import trade that had been building to boom proportions before the onset of the catastrophes. Now they were run-down, rust-streaked, their yards grown high with rank weeds sprouted since the last high water a few weeks before. There were fewer polyarcs here; the Jag's headlights cut diamond-white swathes through flat black shadow.

My quarry was moving slowing now, creeping along at ten miles per hour. Once or twice the wan beam of a hand-flash probed furtively at a dark side street, flicked over a sign post. I kept well back, showing no lights, my turbos flicking over at minimum— just enough to keep my bumper rails off the blacktop. Ahead, the car stopped; I slid to the curb and grounded. Two men hopped out briskly, casting long, awkward shadows in the light of a block-distant pole. They ducked to confer briefly with their driver, shot a look my way which missed me in the shadows, then stepped off into an alley mouth. The Jag started up, moved quickly to the next corner, swung left. By the time I reached the corner—hanging back a little to give the ground troops time to put distance between themselves and the street—it was making another left turn ahead. I pulled to the curb halfway up the block.

I cracked the canopy, listened hard, heard nothing but the ancient song of the frogs, sounding complacent about the changes that had come to the area—their tribe had seen it all before, a hundred times. Out on the sidewalk I listened some more, heard car doors clack. It was a short sprint to the corner. Fifty yards along I saw the Monojag parked, doors open, a dim courtesy light from inside spilling out on the legs of two men, one of whom might have been my gray-haired acquaintance. They turned away, disappeared into what looked like a blank wall.

I did some mental estimating; their position was roughly opposite the alley mouth the first pair had entered. They were setting up a cordon—closing in on something—or someone.

But they had missed a bet—maybe. Back around the corner, where I had parked my borrowed Humber there had been a narrow air space cutting back into the monolithic Portland facades. I did not know where the alleys my friends had entered joined, but there was at least a chance that the side way I had seen intersected them. If so, their rabbit had a bolt hole. I dropped back and ran.

At the car, all was quiet. No hunted fugitives had dashed out from the dark crack in the wall; no shots and yells indicated a successful snatch somewhere back in the lightless recesses of the warehouse complex. There was not even a cheery drunk caroling his way home after a long evening with the daughter of the vine. There was just me, feeling a little fuzzy at three A.M., standing in the rain and wearing a trench coat over pajamas, and shoes without socks, looking from my borrowed car to the silent, faceless wall before me, and wondering just what it was that had seemed so important a few minutes earlier. For all I knew, Gray Hair owned the warehouse. Maybe he was a big importer, down checking on a report of mice. Maybe he was a member of the volunteer firemen, hot on the trail of an incipient blaze. If I was really interested in what he was doing, the small, shy voice of common sense was suggesting, why not walk up to him and ask him.

"Hi, there, Mr. Sethys," I would say. "Just noticed you taking a drive in the middle of the night, and thought I'd trail along and ask why. . . ."

There was a sound from the two-foot wide air space—a rustle, as of someone moving, stealthily. I moved over against the wall, one hand on the butt of my .38 like a good churchman fingering his crucifix for luck. I could hear breathing now—short, gasping breaths, noises made by someone who had run a long way and was about played out. Then I caught another sound—the hard clack of feet, running without much concern for who might be listening; confident feet, closing the gap.

I waited. Sound would carry in the confined space; the chaser and the chased were close, but it was hard to estimate—

There was a grunt, a muffled yelp, noises that indicated blows, lots of heavy breathing. The chasee had been caught yards from where I stood. Whoever it was, he was in the hands of Sethys' legmen now. I had poked my nose in—or tried to—but so far I was clean. I could slide back into my black leather seat and drift off into the night, and no one the wiser. Tomorrow I could get started on recouping my fortunes, and by this time next week the whole thing would seem like a bout of delirium. It was none of my business and if I was smart, it never would be.

I took two steps and slid into the narrow alley.

Ten feet away, a man stood, his arms clamped around a little slim fellow wrapped in a too-long coat. It was three jumps to where the tableau showed as a contorted black silhouette against the light from behind; I made it in two, caught the big boy by the collar, laid the flat of the gun across the side of his head. He kicked out, hit the wall as I pivoted behind him. My second swing caught him on the jaw. He lost his grip, slipped down into a half crouch, and I hit him again, putting plenty of power behind it, saw him sprawl out flat. Then I looked up—just in time to meet a big steel ball somebody had brought in to wreck the building with.

Fireworks were showering, pretty colors whirling around and round, round and round, and I was whirling with them, feeling ghostly bricks grinding into my face. I was remotely aware of a thin scream, the crunch of heavy feet across me, the impact of a mule kick in my side. Then I was clawing at a coarse-textured wall, blinking through haze at two figures who swayed above me in a strange and violent dance, swinging first this way, then that, locked in a close embrace. One of the dancers slipped, almost went down. I was on my knees now, creeping up the wall like a human fly tackling the Blue Tower in Manhattan, game, but a little discouraged by the long trip ahead.

There was another cry—a choked-off sob—and somehow I was standing, watching the close walls sway, under my hands. My mouth was open and drums beat behind my eyes; something hot and wet was running down over my chin. The back of a man before me was big, broad in a dark coat; the head was bent down, only the mussed hair on the back of the neck visible. I could not see the other dancer now.

I moved and my foot hit the gun. I grabbed it, went up on my toes, swung it down in a stiff-armed blow that had all my weight behind it. The impact was solid and unyielding, like kicking a watermelon. The big wide back twisted, fell away, and I was looking into a thin, frightened face, coal-dark eyes as big as black pansies—a woman's face.

A fan of light from a dropped torch gleamed on the rain-wet wall. I stamped on it, grabbed for her arm that was thrust out as if to push me away.

"Come on," I said blurrily. "Got a car—down here."

A trickle of blood was running down the high-cheek-boned face. She did not look much better than I felt. I yanked her arm, and she came, reluctantly.

"Let's go—fast." I set off at a ragged run. There might have been a shout from along the alley behind me; I was not sure, and I did not care. The object of the game was to get to the car before my legs quit on me, before the rocketing pains back of my eyes blew their way to the surface and took a piece of skull with them. That was enough for me to think about at the moment.

It seemed a long way before I came out onto the street, still holding her damp sleeve in one hand, the gun in the other, thinking about Mr. Sethys and his chums waiting there to greet me, but the shining, dark pavement was empty. I groped my way to the canopy release, popped it, half lifted my new friend in, swung aboard and kicked the car away from the curb before the hatch dropped. The Humber howled up to speed, bounced her side bumpers twice on the guide rail as I swung her into a well-lit cross avenue, then settled down to outrun whatever might be chewing up the pavement behind her.

They were waiting for me at the Gulfstream, three men in a cozy group by the waterless fountain beside the entrance to the big main drive, standing hatless in the rain. I slid the Humber on past, whipped to the right at the corner, gunned it back to sixty.

Six blocks from the hotel I parked in a half empty lot littered with fallen palm fronds. The woman on the seat beside me looked around quickly, then at me.

"We walk from here," I said. My tongue was too thick for my mouth. The pain in my head had abated to a dull throbbing, but I was dizzy as a weekend sailor in a sixty-mile gale. The hatch lifted and cold rain spattered in. I helped her out, took a minute to wipe blood from my chin from a cut lip, started off at a fast walk toward the lights of an all-night bar shining a cheerful mortuary blue through the smoke-tasting mist.

Inside, we took a table at the back near a door that ought to open onto an alley. I did not check it; I was not doing anything until I had downed a bracing dram. A thin, sun-scarred man with small eyes in nests of pale wrinkles came over, took an order for two double Scotches. So far, my lady fair had not said a word.

"Sethys must have a phone in his car," I told her. "Must have called in, told them what to look for. Or maybe he didn't. Maybe I spooked. Those three might have been off-duty waiters sweating out the last bus to the suburbs. Just as well. Don't know what I stuck my neck into. Good idea to fade out of sight anyway."

The waiter brought the drinks; I took half of mine without coming up for air. My drinking partner had hers in both hands swallowing. Then she choked, almost dropped the glass. From her expression I guessed that she had just discovered you do not chugalug hard liquor.

"Take it easy," I suggested. There was a glass of water beside her; I picked it up, offered it. She grabbed at it, sniffed, then drank, stuck her tongue into the glass to get the last drop.

"You're hungry," I said. The waiter was there again, holding out a folded towel.

"You missed a spot on the side of your jaw, buddy," he said in a voice like wind on hot sand. "Got a nice mouse working there, too." He flicked his eyes to my table mate, took in the wet hair, the oversized coat, the hungry look. I took the towel. It was cold and wet.

"Thanks. How about something to eat—hot soup, maybe?"

"Yeah, I can fetch you something." He went away without asking the questions; if you are lucky, you meet a few like that in a lifetime. I waited until the fat man getting up from the next booth had wheezed his way to the cashier, then I leaned across the table. The big dark eyes looked at me, still wary.

"Who are you, miss?" I kept my voice at a confidential pitch. "What was it all about back there?"

Her expression tightened a bit. She had nice teeth, even and white; they were set together like a soldier biting a bullet.

"I'm the fellow who butted in on your side, remember?" I tried out a small smile. "Any enemy of Sethys is a friend of mine."

She shivered. Her fingers were locked together like two arthritics shaking hands. I put my hand over them. They were as cold as marble.

"You've had a hell of an experience, but it's over now. Relax. I think we've got enough now to take to the police. Even in these times attempted murder's enough to interrupt the chief's nap for."

The waiter was back with two big plates of fish chowder on a tray, a couple of sandwiches on the side. The girl watched him put hers down in front of her, eyed the big spoon, then grabbed it with a ping-pong player's grip and dug in. She did not slow down until the bowl was dry. Then she looked at my bowl, I was watching her with my mouth open—a favorite expression of mine lately.

"Slow down, kid," I advised. "Here, try a sandwich." I picked up one of them—thick slabs of bread with a generous pile of ham between them—and offered it. She put it in her bowl, lifted the top bread slice, sniffed, then proceeded to clean out the ham with her fingers. When she finished, she licked them carefully, like a cat.

"Well," I commented, "maybe now we can get on with our talk. You haven't told me who you are."

She gave me an appealing look, flashed what might have been the hint of a smile, and said something that sounded like: "*Ithat ottoc otacu.*"

"Swell," I said. "That helps. The one person in this nutty world that might be able to tell me what's going on, and you speak Low Zulese—or is it Choctaw?"

"*Ottoc oll thitassa,*" she agreed.

"*Como se llamo?*" I tried. "*Comment vous appelez-vous? Vie heissen Sie? Vad Heter du?*"

"*Ithat oll uttruk mapala yo,*" she said. "*Mrack.*"

I gnawed the inside of my lip and stared at her. My head was throbbing; I could feel my eyelids wince with each pulse beat.

"We'll have to find a quiet place to hole up," I said, talking to myself now. "It might be a good idea to leave Miami, but to hell with that. I like it here. Mr. Sethys isn't going to run me out of town before I've had my play."

A medium-sized man in a dark suit had left his bar stool, sauntered over near our table. He stood six feet away, shaking a cigarette from a flip-top box, looking over the selections on the tape-screen box. He was thirty-five, give or take a couple of years, ordinary-looking, with sandy hair and a slightly receding chin. He seemed to be taking a long time with the cigarette.

"Wait right here," I said to the girl in what I hoped was a soothing tone. I stood, pushed the chair back. The man shot a quick glance my way, turned and went across to the door. I followed him through into the misty rain. He was already twenty feet away, walking fast, head down. I closed the gap, caught him by one shoulder, spun him around.

"All right, spill it," I said. "If you've got a gun, don't try it; mine's aimed at your second coat button."

His jaw dropped. He backed away, his hands up chest-high as if to fend me off. I followed him.

"Tell it fast, Mister. Make it good. This headache I've got puts me in a nasty temper."

He shot a look up and down the street. "Listen," he said in a choked voice, "don't shoot, see? You can have the wallet, and the watch—I got a pretty good watch. . . ." He fumbled at his wrist.

"Skip the act," I put plenty of snarl into it. "Who's Sethys? What did the coin mean to him? Who were the men tracking the sailor? And what was the idea of mugging the girl?"

"Hah?" He got the watch off, fumbled it, dropped it on the sidewalk. He was against the wall now, leaning away from me. His face was slack and yellowish.

"Last chance." I rammed the gun against him; he made a bleating sound and grabbed for it. I jerked it back and hit him on the side of the jaw. He covered his head with both arms and made broken noises.

"The wallet," I ordered. "Let's see it."

He lowered an arm to fumble it out of his hip pocket; I grabbed it, flipped it open. Stained cards told me this was Jim Ezzard, of 319 S. Tulip Way, insured by Eterna Mutual, accredited to the nation's oil dealers, a member in arrears of the Jolly Boys Social and Sporting Club.

I dropped the wallet on the pavement. "Where were you headed in such a hurry, Ezzard—or whatever your name is? What were you going to tell your boss?"

He was looking at the wallet, lying open at his feet, the few well-worn bills still in it. I could see an idea struggling for birth behind his face.

"You. . . . some kind of a cop?" he got out. "I—"

"Never mind what I am. We'll talk about you—"

"You got nothing on me." He was making a fast recovery, jerking his lapels back into line, working his jaw with his hand. "I'm clean as a cue ball all evening, you can check with the bar girls at Simon's—"

"Skip the bar girls at Simon's," I cut him off. "Turn your pockets out." He did, grumbling. They were full of the usual assortment of small change, paperclips, lint and canceled movie tickets.

"You guys are getting too big for your britches," he told me. "Getting where a guy can't stick his nose outside without some flattie—"

"Can it, Jim," I told him, "or I'll turn back into a bad guy."

I walked away, listening to his muttering get louder in inverse ratio to the distance between us.

Back inside the beanery, the girl waited where I had left her.

"Nothing," I said. "False alarm. I guess I'm getting hypersensitive to ordinary-looking men. They all look like they're carrying a hand-filed shiv and cyanide in a back tooth." She gave me her smile again—this time I was sure of it. She was nice to talk to, no back-talk, just a smile.

"Let's go," I took her hand, urged her to her feet. "We'll pick a second-rate house near here. We both need rest. In the morning. . . ."

Our waiter caught my eye, tipped his head. I went over. He went on arranging salt and pepper shakers on a tray, spoke from the corner of his mouth.

"I don't know if it's got anything to do with you folks," he said very softly. "But there's a couple fellers got this place staked out, front and rear."

The back door let onto a service passage, very old, very dark, very choked with overflowing garbage cans, heaped plastic cartons, weeds, and less savory reminders of the collapse of the municipal refuse collection system. I was getting pretty familiar with the back alleys of the city. This seemed like one of the less appealing in which to be cornered.

The girl stayed close beside me, scanning the dark path in both directions; even without words she seemed to understand the situation. She was nervous, but there was no panic in the way she watched me and followed my lead.

I kept to the wall, moved off easy-footed. The boy at the back door had been posted down near the street, according to my waiter friend. We might be stealing a march on him—or walking right into his arms, if he had changed position. The first warning I had was a gasp from the girl. She stopped, pointed. I saw him then— flattened against the wall a good twenty feet from the end of the alley. I pulled at her, and she resumed walking, keeping on my left, half a pace behind. My hope was that he had not noticed the momentary hesitation.

Ten feet from him, I started talking—something about the weather—which gave me an excuse to look away from him as the gap closed. Five feet, a yard, one more pace—

I spun, swung my fist backhanded, caught him just under the ribs in the same instant that he lifted a foot to swing in behind us. He doubled over and I kneed him, felt his nose go against my shin. Then he was down, twisting over on his back, one arm groping. I stamped on his wrist, saw the glint of metal as a small gun spun away, clattered against the wall. He lunged, tried to bite my leg. I got a grip on his coat, jerked him half to his feet, yanked the coat down off his shoulders, then held him by the arms.

"Get his tie," I hissed at the girl. I made meaningless motions with my head. She pulled the belt from her oversized coat, went to one knee, took two turns around his wrists and cinched it up as efficiently as a head nurse changing a diaper.

"Tell me about it, mister," I said into his ear. He kicked out, squirmed, spat at me. His mouth was working like someone's who had just gotten a big bite of a bad apple. Then his face tried to stretch itself around to the back of his head. The tendons of his neck stood out like lift cables; his legs straightened, thrust hard. Suddenly there was foam on his mouth. Then he went slack. His wrist when I grabbed it had as much pulse as a leg of lamb.

"I guess I wasn't kidding about the cyanide in the back tooth," I said to the balmy night air. The girl watched with eyes that seemed bigger than ever, while I checked his pockets. Nothing.

I stood up. "The Case of the Inept Assassins," I said aloud. "I don't know what the game is that's afoot, but I've got a feeling we're not winning, in spite of the impressive score we're racking up. They must have manpower to burn."

"*Im allak otturu*," the girl said. She was pointing at a rotted door standing six inches ajar, its lock broken by the frenzy of the man who lay dead at my feet. I pushed it open; across a littered room filled with dark shapes, faint predawn light glowed through dusty windows.

"It looks too easy," I said. "But let's try it anyway."

Ten minutes later, five blocks east of the scene of the skirmish, we found a sagging three-story house with a sign that read ROOMS—DAY, WEEK, MONTH, and a light on in a front window. The old rooster dozing at the desk looked us over like a sorority housemother checking for whiskey breath.

"Ten cees, advance," he challenged. I paid him, added a five.

"That's for that million-dollar smile, Pop," I told him. "Forget you ever saw us, and there'll be another one to keep it warm these cold nights."

"Cops looking for you?" he came back.

"Heck, no," I looked sheepish. "Her brother. Wants to keep her on the farm all her life. I plan to marry her and raise Scottie dogs."

He blinked at me. Then he blinked at her. His cheeks cracked and he showed pink gums in a sly grin.

"None o' my business," he said. He handed over two worn aluminum keys chained to rubber rings the size of airplane tires. "How long you folks staying?"

"A few days," I said, working my eyebrows to imply deep meaning behind the words. "You know."

"That'll be payment in advance every morning." The stern, businesslike look was back—we might be co-conspirators, but I need not get any big ideas about pulling any fast ones.

"I knew we could count on you," I said. We went around a louvered trellis set in a dry planting box, started up the stairs. At the landing I looked back to see him peering after us through a loose slat.

Chapter Five

The rooms were not much more than do-it-yourself partitions dividing what had once been somebody's grandmother's sewing room into two airless cubicles with built-in closets like up-ended coffins. The floors no longer lay as flat as might have been desired, and the faded wallpaper had not been an asset when new. There was a tiny bathroom between them with a rust-edged shower stall, a toilet with a cracked plastic seat, a sink big enough to wash out your socks in—just barely.

I took the cell nearest the stairs, just in case of funny noises during the night. It had a concave mattress on a steel frame, a chest of drawers with one drawer missing and a machine-knitted doily on top, a chair made of metal tubing with a red plastic seat with cigarette burns, a bedside table with a glass ashtray containing a cigar butt, and a Gideon Bible. There was an air conditioner unevenly mounted in the big double-hung window. I switched it on and it woke to life with a clatter like a broken fan belt.

"Luxury quarters," I told my lady friend. "And we seem to have the place to ourselves." I escorted her past the water closet into her chamber, appointed at least as handsomely as mine. She went to the bed, sat on it. Under the tan, her face looked greenish-pale. She was at the ragged edge of exhaustion.

"Here, get the wet coat off," I said. I took a stiff, yellowish towel from the bar in the bath, brought it over to her. She was sitting, watching me, fighting to hold her eyes open.

"Get out of the coat," I said. "You'll have a nice case of pneumonia in the morning." She did not lift a hand when I reached down, unbuttoned the collar that was turned up under her chin. I pulled her to her feet, undid the coat; she swayed against me.

"Another two minutes and you're tucked in," I soothed her. I flipped the coat back, hauled it free from her limp arms. It was an old trench coat, black with grease around the collar, torn and stained. She might have found it in a garbage can. I turned back to her with a snappy comment ready and found myself gaping at a skin-tight outfit of metallic blackish-green that reached from her neck to her feet, hugging a figure that would have graced a *première danseuse* at the Follies Bergere. She reached up, pulled the scarf off her head; coils of lustrous dark hair cascaded down. Then her knees let go and she folded onto the bed.

I straightened her out, used the towel to dry her face, then mopped my own. Looking down at her, I wondered if she were a Polynesian—or maybe a Mexican, or an Arab. None of them seemed to fit. She was a type I had never seen before. And she was young—not over twenty-five. Asleep, she looked helpless, innocent. But I remembered her in the dark alley where I had found her, battling the man who had sapped me, giving me time to get back on my feet. I had saved her neck—and she had saved mine. That was enough of a bond to keep me sleeping at her bedroom door for as long as she needed a watchdog.

I stumbled back into my own room, and do not even remember my face touching the pillow.

The rain was still coming down next morning. I lay for a few minutes, watching it drop from the eaves, feeling the ache along the side of my head beat at me as it had beat all night through exhausting dreams of running through knee-deep, blood-red water, with a pack of deadpan commuter types trailing me. My neck was stiff, the right eye was swollen and tender, and my upper lip felt as though I had a German sausage stuffed under it. I was not sure, but I thought I had a couple of loose teeth to complete the composition.

The bedsprings groaned when I sat up and swung my legs down, and I groaned right along with them. Now my hand was hurting; I looked at it. The knuckles were skinned raw. I had no idea where I had done that.

The connecting door to the bathroom swung back and I grabbed, came up with the .38 aimed at a slim female shape in lizard-skin tights. She did not jump; she gave me a hesitant smile, came on into the room, ignoring the gun. I had a strange feeling that she did not know what it was.

"Good morning." I put the pistol on the bed and stood. "Gamoning." She smiled a little wider. Her hair was pulled back, tied with a piece of string. The hunted expression was gone. She still looked like someone who had not eaten for three days, but in her own exotic way she was rather pretty.

Then what she had said registered. "You speak English after all!" The grin on my face made it ache in three new places. "Thank

God for that. Now maybe we can get somewhere. I don't know what you did to get Sethys mad at you, but whatever it was, I'm on your side. Now tell me about it."

"*Ot ottroc atahru*," she said diffidently.

"Back to that, huh? What's the idea? I heard you say 'good morning' like a little lady—"

"Gamoning," she said. "Liddalady."

"Oh," I felt my smile go sour on my face. "Like a parrot."

"Likaparot," she mimicked.

"Maybe it's a start at that." I put a hand on her arm. "Listen, kid, I've never even taught a pup to fetch newspapers, but if we work at it, maybe you can learn enough American to shed a little light on this farce." I pointed to my chest. "Malcome Irish."

"Akmalcomiriss," she repeated.

"Leave off the *akk* part; it's Malcome—Mal, if you prefer."

"Akmal." She looked confused—or maybe stubborn.

"OK; have it your way." I pointed at her. "What's your name?"

"Akricia," she said promptly, and inclined her head in a sort of formal gesture.

"Akricia," I said, and her face lit up in a real smile. "Suppose I call you 'Ricia for short. Ricia—nice name."

She looked flustered; two or three expressions tried themselves out on her face. Then she ducked her head. "Ricia," she whispered. "Mal. . . ." She nibbled her lip, then slipped a silver ring from her finger, held it out to me shyly, like a child offering candy. I took it; it was thick, heavy. "Very pretty," I said.

She seemed to be expecting something to happen. I thought of handing the ring back, but that did not seem to be indicated. I put it on my little finger and held it up. She smiled, took my hand between hers, and said something. I had a feeling we were now officially friends.

"Thanks, kid," I said. "It's a very nice present. Now let's get on with the lesson." I patted her hand—and suddenly noticed the grimy knuckles, the broken nails.

"Ricia, you need a bath. You slept in that leotard; it's time you got out of it and cleaned yourself up." I went into the bathroom, found a bar of green soap with hair stuck to it glued to a soap dish in the shower stall.

"You go ahead and take a shower," I suggested. "I'll get you some clothes, and I could use a change of socks myself." I pointed. "Take a bath," I turned the water on, pantomimed scrubbing my neck. Ricia nodded, looking eager. As I closed the door she was reaching for some kind of invisible fastener on the front of her outfit.

Downstairs, I explained my needs to our host, gave him money and added a five-cee note, the sight of which seemed to delight him just as much as if the bottom had not dropped out of the fiscal system. He pulled on a jacket that looked like something salvaged from a drowned man, made a big thing of locking the sheet-metal safe, set off at a fast dodder.

In half an hour he was back, rapping at the door with an armload of groceries, toiletries, and drygoods. He gave the room a sharp once-over, checking for rumpled bedding or other signs of dissipation, hovered as though ready to start a long conversation. I eased him out, hinting at more heavy tips in the offing.

Small sounds were coming from next door. I tapped, pushed the door open six inches and reached in with a paper bag containing soap with pink perfume, a comb, a toothbrush, a fingernail kit, a washcloth, odds and ends of cosmetics.

"Hurry it up," I called. "My hide is beginning to crawl around me."

I set the food out on the lace doily: bread, bottled cheese, canned meat, some fruit, coffee, a fifth of brandy with a blurry label. Ten minutes crawled past. There was a creak from the connecting door; it swung back and Ricia stepped through, looking as fresh and scrubbed as a baby on its first birthday—and dressed about the same. Her hair was done up in a striking composition on top of her head, tied with a red plastic ribbon from one of the cosmetic boxes. Her nails that had been gray crescents were pink and shiny. She was wearing just enough cologne to give me a faint whiff of florist shop—nothing else.

"Nice," I commented, trying to look as calm as she did. "A little unconventional, but very nice. Still, I think you'd better slip into something before I come down with hot flashes." I fumbled packages, dug out a little nylon nothings I had gotten for her, added a one-piece thing with a tag on it that said it was a playsuit. She accepted them with a wondering expression. I went through some ludicrous antics intended to show her what to do with them. She laughed at me. I could see a bruise along the side of her throat now that the dirt was gone.

Then she saw the food, tossed the clothes on the end of my bed, and went past me with a glint in her eye. The closed containers seemed to puzzle her, she picked up an orange, sniffed it, took a bite. She seemed to like it, peel and all. I just stood, gazing at the orange juice running down that fine, olive-hued figure, wondering just who—and what—the little creature was I had taken under my wing.

Ricia had an amazing ability to remember the words I taught her—and an equally amazing ignorance of the customs and appurtenances of society. The coffee made her wrinkle her nose; the potted meat made her gag. She liked the bread—once she accepted the idea that it was something to eat. Only the fruit seemed in any measure familiar to her.

In an hour she was talking to me—using sentences like "Ricia eat, Mal eat, good, no. Today, tomorrow, walk."

"We have to stay where we are until dark," I told her. "It's known as waiting till the heat's off. I'm sorry about the food, but there's not much available in the neighborhood. Miami's beginning to feel the pinch now. Even with nine-tenths of the population gone, the town can't run forever on what was on the shelves when the storms hit."

She nodded as though she understood. Maybe she did, maybe she was picking up more than I thought, the same way a child does—by listening and watching. She was sitting in front of the oval mirror over her dresser now, trying out different elaborate hair-do's.

Meanwhile, I was thinking over my plan of action—what to do when the time came to venture out from our hole. Going to the police was out now; there were too many bodies lying around town—to say nothing of the shambles at Greenleaf, Georgia—to invite close inquiry. Martial law was no joke. The looters and ghouls had seen to it that old-fashioned ideas regarding the innocence of the accused did not get in the way of quick and final disposition—usually by a firing squad. There was no time or temper to bother pampering criminals—or suspects—in cozy jail cells. I paced up and down explaining it all to Ricia.

"There are plenty of boats here, it's not like the foothills of Georgia. I can get something—a thirty-foot cabin cruiser would be about right. This fellow Sethys plays for keeps. Well, he can keep it. Maybe the sailor was telling the truth: maybe there are trained elephants under the ice. OK, they can stay there. My curiosity isn't satisfied, I'll admit—but it's cured. We'll head north and find a nice town in high country and weather this out."

"Sethys, no. Mal and Ricia, walk, today." She looked scared— or maybe just concerned, trying to understand what I was talking about, not able to express her own ideas.

"I wish you could talk to me, Ricia," I told her. "Who is Sethys? Why did he send his boys out after you? How did you get into that part of town in the first place? Where you come from?"

She shook her head, gave me a stubborn look. She understood all right—she just was not talking. I let it go. Maybe I did not really want to hear the answers.

It was twilight now, an eerie red and green time when the glare of the dusty sun lit up the room like a stage light, casting shadows across the crimsoned floor.

"I'm going out to see about picking up a boat," I told Ricia. "Don't let anybody in until I get back. And don't forget the gun." I laid the .38 in her hand; I had shown her how to aim and pull the trigger.

"Don't hesitate to use it. Anybody who breaks through that door is asking for it."

She gave me her second-best game smile. She did not like my leaving her alone, did not like the sight of the gun, but she was game, whatever happened.

Downstairs, old Bob, our landlord watched me cross the ten-by-twelve lobby.

"I see you're growing a beard," he snapped, as if he had caught me sneaking something out in a paper bag.

"You're a very perceptive fellow, Bob," I conceded.

"That what you come here for, figgered it was a good place to grow a beard?"

"As good as any."

"A disguise, like hey?" He was squinting at me, his voice lowered to a confidential tone.

"No, it's so my old friends will know me, Bob. Used to have a beard and shaved it off. Tried to hit one of them up for a small loan a few days back and he cut me dead."

"Hah?" Bob snapped his gallus at me. "Meant to tell you, raising the rates first of the week." He pushed his lips in and out, estimating what the traffic would bear. "Cost you fifteen a day, starting Monday."

"Fifteen a day," I nodded.

"That's day after tomorrow," he clarified. "You can have one more day at the ten cees."

"Hey Bob"—I leaned on the counter— "I should have told you sooner, maybe, but I wasn't sure I could trust you not to panic." I looked carefully around the room, frowned at the old-fashioned breakfront with glass-doored shelves loaded with bundled papers, stepped back a pace to peer behind the rubber plant. Bob followed every move.

"I'm with Greater Miami Bomb Disposal," I told him in the tone of a turf accountant imparting a hot tip. "The little lady's a medium-psychic, you know. Great help in our work. Lots of nuts loose in the city these days—couldn't make the readjustment when their farms went under, mother-in-law drowned, the whole bit— you know how it is. Not tough like you and me."

"What's that about a bomb?" Bob's Adam's apple was vibrating like a cello string.

I nodded. "Figured you knew what was up. You don't miss much, Bob. You've got enemies. Comes of being sharp, successful—like you. The word is it's one of those Chinese jobs—no bigger than a one-shot VD capsule but power enough to lift the roof off this place and dump the contents all over Biscayne Bay. I think we've got it pinpointed in the third-floor john; don't pull any chains until you hear from me."

"Here, you mean—"

"Keep it under your hairpiece, Bob. We're with you all the way. Should be able to let you know something by sundown tomorrow."

"Tomorrow? Me sit here with a bomb ticking someplace—"

"You're a cool one, Bob. Nerve like cast iron." I looked rueful. "I have to admit sometimes I get a little peckish, myself."

"Here, where you going? You're not leaving here without finding the thing?"

"Just stepping out for another pound or two of Indian cheese wax and a spare framitizer. Won't take long." I pushed on out the door, feeling a little lightheaded, aware of the stink of death and ruin and decay as the world shook civilization to pieces— and still, among the ruins, the little green weed of avarice grew and flourished. The emperors of the world were all dead, but the Bobs we have with us always.

It was a street that had once—maybe twenty years before—been a moderately prosperous avenue of not quite fashionable shops of the kind that catered to the middle-class tourist trade, offering lines of shoddy goods with mass-produced Miami labels to impress the folks back home. Its hour of respectability had passed long ago. Even before the disasters the cheap, bright cardboard and plastic had disappeared from the shop windows, the false elegance of the shop fronts had faded into the cracked pastels of neglect. Now, with the unswept debris of wind and flood and the litter of hasty departure drifted at the curbs and around the broken sidewalk benches and the rusting light poles, the muddy light of late twilight showed a dreary parade of boarded windows, hand-lettered signs tacked furtively on door frames, tall weeds fighting their way up between the jumbled hexagonal tiles that had once seemed gay. It was a poor address, but Mr. Sethys could look a long time and not find us here—if he was looking.

The coast looked clear. I turned up the collar of Ricia's grimy coat and set off toward a cross street on which a little traffic was moving.

It was a ten-block walk to the waterfront. I moved along at a moderate shamble, keeping a weather eye out for ordinary-looking men in conservative suits. There was little traffic, few cars parked at the curb. Miami had had plenty of warning, plenty of time for the citizenry to pack and head north in time to meet disaster head-on in the floods and eruptions that had wiped out the upper half of the state.

Most of the marinas were dark, heavily fenced and padlocked. I walked north, toward the run-down portion of the bay shore that had had its flush of popularity fifty years ago. Here there were rotting board fences, rusted wire mesh, a jungle of abandoned hot-dog and beer stands, bait stalls, faded signs offering fresh fish and shrimp, plenty of tall weeds, and an astonishing abundance of lean, wary cats who looked as though they had run out of mice and were living off each other.

About every third polyarc was still burning along this stretch; in between, the shadows lay across the street as black as powdered coal.

Off to the right a light surf slapped at the beach; there was a heavy odor of decaying sea things, salt water, and soot. I sniffed, caught the hot-iron odor of volcanic activity—even here, a thousand miles from the eruptions in Georgia.

A big concrete shed loomed up ahead; I made out the words NORTH BAY MARINE SALES in flaked paint along the side. The big main doors were shut, locked tight. Beside them a small personnel entrance swung idly in the fitful wind. Inside, the office was a mess. Papers were scattered on the two desks, on the chairs, on the floor. The drawers of the filing cabinet hung open, empty. An ashtray on a stand lay on its side, its contents spilled. Even the girlie calendar on the wall hung crooked on its nail. The odor of rot and dead meat was strong here.

An unlocked glass door lead through into the back. My feet echoed on gritty concrete; the sound rang back from corrugated metal and oily water. Three boats were moored in the dock—a pair of bright-colored sixteen-footers with lots of shiny fittings, one sunk to the gunwales, and a big, sullen-looking catamaran-hulled job, use-scarred, built for blue-water cruising. Aboard, I found a pair of Rolls-Royce Arthurs, a megahorse each, shipshape and ready to turn. Half a dozen heavy cartons were stacked in the stern—Air Force field rations, type Y, enough to feed a battalion for a week. A long, canvas-wrapped bundle was shoved down behind the cartons. I hauled it out, found a leather gun case. Inside were a .375 Weatherby and an evil-looking automatic rifle, about .25 caliber, with a spare magazine. I had never seen one before, but I knew it by reputation. It was the latest military model, and it could empty its thousand-round drum in one two-second burst on full automatic—a hail of steel that would cut a rhino in two. Someone had made some careful preparations for a getaway.

The cabin door was locked tight. I used a rusted fish knife I found on deck to pry the latch open. The door swung in, and the odor hit me in the face like a shovel. On the floor between the bunks, what had been a man lay on his back, his face a fright mask of empty eye sockets and a ragged mouth hole with yellow teeth showing in a snarl, the claw hands outspread. He was not so much decomposed as mummified in the intense heat of the closed room. The lean, blackened neck disappeared into a shirt collar, neatly buttoned but badly discolored. His blazer was well cut, expensive-looking; his deck shoes new. There were two large black stains on his chest, on the left side, above and below the heart. The artillery stowed aft had not done him much good.

He was amazingly light; I hauled him up the three steps, tilted him sideways to get him through the hatch, put him over the side. He slid down smoothly, disappeared. Then I went back to the stern and lost my lunch.

His preparations had been complete: there was a compact seawater converter, spare clothes, foul-weather gear, a well-stocked bar, even a rack filled with books. I had made a lucky find. Now to see if I could open the sea doors.

They were heavy metal panels, power-operated. I followed the leads, tried the switch. Nothing. There was a master switch below the junction box. I threw it, tried again. Still nothing.

Outside the water slammed and gurgled against the door, wanting in. I kept looking. It took me ten minutes to find the hand crank, folded back into a recess beside the left-hand door. I turned the crank; the doors groaned, started up. I cranked them back down, checked the boat's lines to be sure I could cast off in a hurry, then went back through the rifled office, stepped out into the dark street. There was an odd smell in the air—not just the stink of decay and volcanic dust, but a new scent—a choking odor like a pot boiled dry. Far away, thunder rolled and rumbled. There was a glow to the west, over beyond the city. I started walking.

A car came toward me, howling along at eighty or better, rocketed past, streaking north. Half a minute later another one shot by, then two more, neck and neck, like a chariot race. An instant later I felt the shock—a slow, inevitable sinking of the pavement under my feet, a pause, then a thrust upward. A ripple had passed over the city as if over a pond.

I broke into a run, fell flat when the next ripple hit, got up, ran on. Another car came into view, weaving across the road, turbos screaming. The next wave caught the car as it swerved wildly, going too fast for the narrow, rubble-strewn streets. The heaving pavement picked up the car as a breaker lifts a surfer, hurled it ahead in its long diagonal path. The car struck a brick warehouse, flipped on its back, hurtled along that way for fifty yards, then bounded high, exploded twenty feet above the street as I dived for a doorway. The shock brought bricks and shingles down in a long surf roar that seemed to echo long after the last shard of broken glass had tinkled from its frame. I stepped out, gave the boiling inferno one quick glance, ran on.

There were people in sight now, all running. Some ran toward me, others sprinted beside me. A wild-eyed woman darted aimlessly from one doorway to another. There were a lot of sounds: screams, yells, distant smashings and thumpings. The next tremor spilled people off their feet like a machine gun mowing down infantry. I rode it, jumped a drift of bricks that poured out across my path like a slot machine disgorging quarters.

A steady rain of debris was falling all around me. Ahead, a knot of half a dozen men darted toward me like comedians in a silent film, their footfalls and the yells from their open mouths lost in the background roar. I saw a man lying on his back in dusty rubble, the back of his head caved in, a woman tugging at his arm. A wrecked car lay on its side, its headlights still burning. Smoke churned from windows, backed by bright flames.

The next shock was worse. I went sprawling, came up to see building fronts toppling outward, crazily canted roofs sliding down into the street, truckloads of rubbish dropping like bombs among people—more and more of them running out now like excited ants, falling, jumping up and running, disappearing under clouds of brick and dust. There was a continuous crashing now like tanks battering through walls. A light pole ahead bounced twice, danced free of its mounting, hopped away ten feet before it fell with a back-breaking smash.

I saw my hotel ahead, a glimpse of dirty white stucco through wind-whipped dust and smoke, stained a dull orange by hundred-foot flames from a burning building across the street. Something blew up, and I felt the shock wave, the blast of heat against my face as small objects hissed past. Something ponderously heavy crashed down behind me close enough to send a hail of stinging concrete particles against the back of my neck. A length of wood, burning cheerfully, came arcing down, bounced away ahead of me.

The front door was gone. I took the broken steps in one jump, groped through dust past a tangle of fallen rafters. The breakfront lay across the counter, its papers spilled among broken glass. A thin arm poked out from under its edge; Bob had died at his post.

The stairs were gone, collapsed into shattered boards linked by a rope of worn carpet. Water was gushing down, staining bricks and plaster black in the gloom; pipes sagged in a graceless festoon. I went over a jumble of smashed furniture, pushed through the swinging door into a hall where the aroma of cabbage was still detectable through the smoke reek, went across a cramped, greasy kitchen full of broken crockery and dented pots. The service stair was there, at the back, almost hidden by the bulk of a toppled refrigerator. I climbed over it and went up.

On the second floor, things didn't look good: the passage was blocked by a jumble of two by fours and shattered plaster board. I pushed through a gap in the wall, ducked under cascading plaster dust, kicked the jammed door open, re-emerged into the hall ten feet from the open door to my room. Inside I found fallen plaster, toppled furniture, broken glass. A quarter-inch of water on the bathroom floor, trapped by the thresholds, danced with an intricate geometric pattern of ripples. I splashed through, calling Ricia's name.

She did not answer. The bed had collapsed; the mattress was spilled half off it, littered with plaster fragments. The chest of drawers still stood upright, its empty drawers pulled out. The patched Venetian blind at the window bulged with the weight of broken glass. The bottles and clothes that the late Bob had brought up a few hours earlier were scattered across the floor. I yelled for Ricia again over the roar of disintegration, jerked the closet door open, lifted the broken bed aside, found nothing but dust devils and worn linoleum.

Back in the other room, I shouted again, dug through the ruins of a fallen partition; nothing. Ricia was gone.

I stood in the middle of the room, trying to think in an orderly fashion, a neat trick in the best of times. I had told her to stay in the room; she had not done so. At least she had not died here. She was somewhere out in the street—and it was time for me to join her. I wove my way across the swaying floor, stepped into the hall and was looking down the barrel of a gun in the hand of the gray-haired man named Sethys.

Chapter Six

He was standing ten feet away, looking as unmoved as an undertaker figuring how much to mark up the florist's bill. There was a liberal sprinkling of plaster dust on his shoulders, a streak of something dark along his jaw; the slicked-back hair was a trifle ruffled, like a bird in a high wind. But the gun held steady as a tombstone. I saw his finger start to tighten—and the floor picked that moment to rock sideways.

Sethys staggered, put out a hand to catch himself; the gun went off, and the iron radiator beside me rang like a bell. Dust was spurting from the cracks between the dark-varnished floorboards. Sethys backed, braced himself with his feet apart, took careful aim at my second shirt button—

A section of the ceiling sagged, dropped suddenly, obscuring his view. He stepped sideways, started between the obstruction and the wall. There was a sound of tearing metal. Part of the fallen framing swung around, and a projecting stub of a broken joist stabbed out, caught him low in the stomach, thrust him back against the wall. He stood there, still neat, still unhurried; then his arms went out. The gun fell, bounced away and disappeared through a gap in the floor. He made a sound like a rusted nail being drawn from an oak plank. Then the rusting bulk of a radiator dropped out of the hole in the ceiling. When the dust cleared, Sethys lay face down, half under the radiator, with six inches of splintered timber projecting from his back.

It was no fun checking his pockets, but I did the best I could, brought out a much-folded map from inside his coat. A colorful spread published by the Oceanographic Institute at Woods Hole, the map showed the oceans of the world complete with bottom contours and the locations of ancient wrecks—as out of date now as last year's almanac. A mark on it caught my eye—a loose circle drawn around the island of Crete. It was a place that had been named earlier, by Zablun, the little man with the disappearing coin trick. It was an interesting thought, but just then another section of ceiling fell, close enough to seem personal. Research would have to wait; it was time to get out. I tossed the map aside and headed for the open air.

✧　✧　✧

The house was coming apart fast. I picked a path through broken walls to the stairwell, jumped down bare seconds before the ceiling let go with a sound like Golden Gate Bridge falling into the bay. The front of the building had fallen outward; I climbed across ruins toward the red glow of the fire across the way. The remains of the front door frame blocked the way; I started around, and a glint of green caught my eye. Something fluttered in the draft—a strip of cloth caught on the broken timber. I pulled it free, recognized the strange metallic fabric of Ricia's garment. It had been cut, not torn.

I wanted to think she had dissolved our partnership—run out on me when the going got rough, but a little voice back of my left ear said it was not so—and the strip of cloth proved it. She had waited—until Sethys showed up. His goons had taken her, while he waited around to clean me up when I arrived. For all my efforts, the girl was back where she had started.

I tossed the scrap of cloth aside and went on out into the roar of doomsday.

The boathouse was still standing; inside, my boat was floating high, looking ready and efficient. I got the doors open, saw strange, choppy whitecaps sliding across the black water—moving away from shore. The engines caught immediately; I backed the big cat out, brought her about, gunned toward open water. The big bow lights trained on the water dead ahead illuminated floating trees, half submerged roofs with shingles awash, the bodies of cows, a dead man. I rode out three big waves that overtook me, traveling fast from the west. They sluiced down over my deck like Niagaras, left me half drowned but still aboard. The boat did not seem to mind; she kept her transoms to the wind, came up purring smoothly as an outboard on a freshwater pond. The white crests of the big waves rushed on ahead into darkness. Behind me, the lights of Miami gradually sank down, winked out. I did not know whether I was losing the city over the horizon, or if it was sliding down under the waves. I hoped Ricia was clear—free or captive. Drowning is a bad way to go. I was remembering the scared, hopeful, trusting look on her face when I had left her alone the last time. She had put herself in my hands—and I was running out.

But damn it—what could a man do when the town was falling to pieces around him? I had myself to keep alive, too. I thought of the ring she had given me—some kind of token of trust. To hell with rings. I tugged at it; it seemed to tingle on my finger like a reminder of duties undone, faith betrayed. The harder I pulled, the harder it jammed itself against my knuckle. All right, I would get rid of it later, and forget the waif who had given it to me.

Meanwhile I had a course to chart. I could swing north, cruise the coast until I found a suitable harbor, rejoin the mainstream of human society—such as it was. Somewhere in the mountains I would find a nice town built on rock that had been stable for a few hundred millions years where I could ride out the cataclysm until the smoke cleared and the glow went out of the night sky and life picked up where it had left off. . . .

I was thinking about the girl again, about the cold-eyed men closing in on her, breaking down the door, dragging her away; hurting her—

Damn them! Damn her, too! Where would they be by now? Not in Miami—not if I was any judge of survivorship. Sethys had had a bad break, but his boys would be in the clear. As to where they would go. . . .

Crete, the name popped into my mind. Sethys had marked it on his map. Zablun had mentioned it; the coin came from there. I took it out, held it in the binnacle light. The dull gold winked at me; the figure of the bird with spread wings seemed to be poised, ready to leap off into flight to unknown lands.

Crete. It was not much to go on—maybe nothing at all; but the name seemed to tug at me. It was a long haul, but barring typhoons at sea, I could circle the globe on the supplies I had aboard. And it was not as though I had a destination. . . .

I flicked on the North Atlantic chart, checked the compass, and plugged in a course three points north of east. I was laughing at myself; I felt like a fool. But in an odd way, I felt better, too.

The route I had charted through the channel north of Great Abaco Island turned out to be a sloping ridge of black mud from which a salty ocean breeze blew an odor of broken drains. It was dawn before I found a clear passage north of Great Bahama, now a mountain range on a new subcontinent, a series of green peaks raised above rolling plains of stinking gray sands, shining in the ominous dawn. Far away on my port beam I saw shapes resting on the former sea bottom: the rusted hulks of drowned steamers, the gaunt ribs of wooden sailing vessels, sunk long ago.

Long, businesslike swells were passing in under my stern at fifteen-second intervals, rolling in on the long beaches with a sustained hiss like a forest fire. I quartered across them, holding my easterly course again. Four hours' run took me past the position from which Bermuda should have been a dark smudge on the port horizon. I could not sight it—either my navigation was off or another nice piece of real estate had gone to the bottom.

It was a long haul then, booming along at high speed across open water under skies that were as near clear as any on the planet. The sun was filtered to a flat red disc by a high stratum of stringy smog; a low haze layer carried the familiar hot-stone and sulphur odor. Five hundred miles at sea I was still brushing cinders off the map screen and picking them out of my mouth and eyes. The deck was crunchy with a drift of tiny black fragments of lava. I sighted drifting trees, boxes, rubbish of every description. It was like sailing on and on through an endless scene of shipwreck, but still it was the same sea I had always known. It had weathered other eras of planet-wide disaster, and when this was over, man and his cities might be gone, but the ocean would endure.

My rations were not bad—a big improvement over the cans I had been opening lately. There was smoked turkey, artichoke hearts, fresh-water prawns, plenty of Scottish wheat bread, a variety of fresh-frozen vegetables, even some irradiated apples. The small freezer yielded an ample supply of ice cubes to chill my whiskey, and my unknown benefactor's taste in wines left nothing to be desired: I had a chilled Dom Perignon with my gammon and eggs, a Spanish rosé for lunch, a Chateau Lafitte-Rothschilde with the evening's rare beef and crepes suzette. The diet kept me in a mild alcoholic fog, a state that had my full approval.

The boat's radio produced nothing but a crackle like New Year's Day in Chinatown, but there was a tape system aboard that boomed out Wagner and Sibelius and the jeweled sounds of deFalla and Borodin while the sun burned red across the sky, sank in a blaze like a continent afire.

The steady wind blowing through open windows had cleared the odor of death and decay from the cabin, but I brought up a folding bunk, clamped it to the roof of the deckhouse and slept under the open sky the first night. In the morning the drift of soot that covered me sent me below again.

On the third day the wind shifted to the south; the sky darkened with big black rain clouds; then the downpour started. It seemed to clear the air, though. By late afternoon the sun was out, looking more like its old self than I had seen it for months.

An hour before sunset I sighted Madeira, a misty rise of green far to the north of my course. At dusk the African coast was in view, looking normal except for an expanse of glistening mud flats that the charts did not show.

I sailed north during the night, passed lights that I identified as Casablanca and Rabat, reached Gibraltar at dawn. The famous rock was gone, and a new channel that I estimated at twenty miles wide stretched ahead into the open water of the Mediterranean. A fifteen-knot current poured out through the strait; I bucked it for more than two hours before I made still water under the cap above Tetuan.

The town looked peaceful—after four days at sea, I needed a drink ashore. There was a rough-and-ready wharf scabbed to heaped rock by the shore. I tied up to it, waved at a lean Moroccan who came down to stare at me.

"I need fresh water," I told him. He nodded, led me up the slope to a collapsing shed largely supported by a chipped Pepsi Cola sign. Inside, a fat woman with bracelets to the elbow gave me a warm Spanish beer across a bar made from a boat's mahogany foredeck, stood by warding off flies with a red plastic swatter. She talked to me in bad Spanish while I drank, telling me her troubles. She had plenty, but no worse than mine.

The man came in with two boys.

"Eesa nice boat, Señor," one of the lads told me. "Where you go een eet?"

"I'm headed for Crete," I told him.

They gabbled together for a while, using their hands to help them over the rough spots. I heard "Kreta" several times, and "Sicilia." Then the boy wagged his head at me.

"No sail to Kreta, Señor. No ees passage. Ees all"—he made lifting motions—"dry land between."

I quizzed them a little further, got a reasonably coherent story. Sicily was no longer an island; its southern tip now joined Cape

Bon, and its northern extremity was one with the mainland of Italy. So much for an uneventful boat ride. I gave them a fistful of worthless money, went back down and cast off. At the last minute the old man hurried down with a jug of vin ordinaire; I tossed him a package of cigarettes and pushed off.

They were right. I made it through the strait south of Sardinia dragging my keels, while the air grew fouler with every mile. Another half day's run over shoal water brought me into Naples harbor, still solidly at sea level under a blanket of smoke through which the glare of Vesuvius was only a bright haze. Wearing my respirator now, I tied up at three P.M. in darkness like an eclipse, within half an hour had sold my rig—no questions asked—to a quick-eyed man who looked like a Martian in an antique gas mask and the filthiest white suit on the planet. The deal was not good, but I got what I needed—a fairly sound-looking late model Turino ground car. I would have preferred to store the boat, but property not under armed guard was an ephemeral thing in Naples in the best of times.

I transferred two cases of rations from the boat to the car. The buyer got ready to protest when I took the cased guns, but I cut him off short; he chose not to argue the point. An hour later I was through the city, on the road leading east to Taranto. From there, my new business contact had assured me, I could ride the air cushion across some seventy miles of former sea bottom to the Greek mainland. He did not know about Crete, but his guess was I could make it all the way dry-shod.

The striking feature of the country—aside from the midnight pall from the line of volcanoes linking Vesuvius and Etna—was the absence of people. Even in Naples, they had been sparse; here there were none. It was easy to see why: even with the car closed and the filters going full blast, the air was as thick as a London pea-souper. I ploughed ahead, holding my new acquisition at fifty through the mountains, opened her up to a shaky ninety-five across the plains.

At a little town called Lecce on what had been Italy's east coast my Neapolitan friend's guess was confirmed: the Strait of Otranto was a rolling sun-hardened expanse of rock-dotted clay. The light was better here; the hills seemed to be holding back some of the smoke from the volcanoes. The crossing took two hours of eye straining through the murky twilight; then on higher ground I headed south, threaded a precarious route among broken hills. At sunset I reached a swampy stretch on the far side of which the island of Crete was a dim line of light. I found a sheltered stretch of former beach under a line of giant weed-covered rocks, pulled the car over and slept until dawn.

The Cretan shore was rocky, dry, parched, a landscape in Hell under the garish colors of sunrise seen through smoke. I found a road a mile inland, followed it to a town marked Khania on my map. It was an impoverished cluster of handmade hovels packed close along a cobbled street that led by a circuitous route up a hill from which I caught a sudden dramatic view of the modern city below, most of its church spires still intact, its streets busy with commerce.

There was a town square, a raised block, walled and turfed, where twisted dark trees brooded over benches and a small fountain from which no water flowed. I followed the imperative gestures of a small policeman in tan shorts, parked before a veranda-like promenade with chipped stone columns held upright by timber truss work. Small merchants hawked dubious wares on the cracked pavement, and busy pigeons, unconcerned by the unnatural darkness of the morning sky, flapped under the high overhang, or pecked among the hurrying feet of the shoppers. There was an air of hectic activity, like a beach town before a hurricane. The wind, from the north now, had a chill edge to it not native to these latitudes. The atmospheric dust was making its presence felt, now that fall was coming on.

There was a glowing neon rectangle suspended over the walk half a block from where I left the car. Inside, the long bar looked calm and dignified, like a judicial bench. A short, dark-faced man in a neat white jacket gave the polished top a swipe as I took a stool.

"Brandy," I said.

He stooped, brought a squat brown bottle up from under the bar, poured. I raised it to him, took a solid belt. It went down like cool smoke.

"That's Metaxa, Mac," the barman said. "You don't take that from the neck."

"My mistake. Join me."

He got out another glass, filled it. We clicked glasses and sipped.

"Just in from down south?" he asked me.

I shook my head. He didn't press the point. The door opened, let in baleful light, closed again. Someone slid onto the next stool. I glanced his way in the mirror, saw a square, sun-blackened face, pale hair in a Kennedy bang, a neck like a concrete piling. I felt my face breaking into a grin; I nodded to the Brooklyn Greek.

"A drink for Mr. Carmody," I said.

The man beside me swung around quickly; then a smile lit up his face like a floodlight. A hand the size of a catcher's mitt grabbed mine, tried to tear it off at the wrist.

We spent ten minutes remembering our past; then I shot a look at the bartender, busy at the far end of the bar. What I had to say next was private.

"I'm not here on a pleasure cruise, Carmody," I told him. "I'm doing a little amateur investigative work."

"Must be something big, to bring you this far from the joy circuit."

"Big enough. A friend of mine's been killed—or kidnapped."

"Know who did it?"

"Yes and no. I know who, I think—but not why."

"And you think you'll find out in Crete?"

I got out the gold piece, slid it across to him. He picked it up, frowned at it, flipped it over to look at the reverse. The barman was coming back.

"Nick's all right," Carmody said so softly I was not sure I heard him. He was squinting at the engraved bird. "This come from around here?"

"That's the story."

"How does this tie to your friend?"

"I'm not sure. But it's all I have to go on."

"Where'd you get it?"

"If you've got a few free minutes, I'll tell you."

He finished his drink with a flip of the wrist, stood. "Where you're concerned, pal, it's all free. Let's grab a table."

He picked a quiet position in the corner with a good view of both doors. Carmody had always been a man who liked to know who was coming and going. The barman brought refills. While we worked on them, I told the whole story, from Greenleaf to Sethys' last big scene in the collapsing hotel in Miami.

"I don't know whether she got out, or was nabbed by Sethys' boys," I finished. "If they got her, I'm pretty sure she's dead; that's the way they operate. But maybe not."

"This sailor," Carmody said, "you get his name, or rank?"

"No, but he must have been pretty well up the ladder—commander or better, I'd guess."

"Any holes in this story of his—holes you're sure about?"

"Aside from the idea of a Heidelberg man sporting a ray gun, no. The official story was that Admiral Hayle was lost in space, that the two ships he mentioned had been sunk in one of the early eruptions—but that could have been just a cover for the operation."

"What about his getaway in a lifeboat—possible?"

"No worse than my crossing the Atlantic in a thirty-foot cat."

"You knocked off three of these birds in the hick town; any reason to think there might have been more of them around?"

"I don't know. I didn't see anybody, no signs of a tail."

"Seems like this guy Sethys wised to you pretty quick; you think he was tipped?"

"Maybe."

"Could the girl have been a plant?"

I thought about it. "She could have been—but she wasn't."

"Any idea why they high-graded your gold piece and gave you one just like it?"

"Maybe this one's counterfeit." I clinked it on the table. Carmody picked it up, weighed it on his palm, fingered it, tried a fingernail on it. "That's gold," he said. He studied the design, frowning at it in the subdued light.

"I don't think I've seen one just like this before, Mal, but I think I can tell you what that bird is. A wild goose."

"Probably," I took the coin back. Nick came up behind him, soft-footed as a hungry lynx.

"How about it, Nick?" Carmody said. "Who's the man to see about old gold?"

"Hurous. Lives in a shack a couple miles east. He might know."

"Yeah, he might at that." Carmody looked at me. "Come on, Mal. Let's go pay a call before cocktail hour rolls around."

The road came to an end a quarter of a mile from the spot we were headed for; it was a stiff climb up a goat trail to the hut perched on a cliff edge under a lone olive tree. Hurous was home, lying on an iron cot in the shade of a one-vine grape arbor. He was sixtyish, unshaven, with small black eyes, a round, bald head, a roll of fat bulging a soiled undershirt packed with hair like a burst mattress. He sat up on one elbow when he saw us coming, reached under the cot for a nickel-plated .44 revolver as big as a tomahawk.

"Put the hog leg back where it was, Hurous," Carmody said easily. "It's a friendly call. A friendly business call."

"Yeah?" The man's voice was thick as a clogged drain.

"This is Mr. Smith. He wants to know where he could pick up some souvenirs. Old coins, for example."

"What you think, I run a souvenir stand?" Hurous lowered the gun.

"He likes big ones—the size of a five-drachma piece, say," Carmody amplified.

Hurous was looking me over like a skeptical buyer studying a secondhand slave. "Who's this fella?" He had the heavy accent of a tri-D spy.

"Mr. Smith, remember? He's a big man in the chicken business. Likes money with birds on it. He heard you might put him in line for some."

"Birds. What kind money got birds, hah? You try to pull my foot?"

"Show him a sample, Mr. Smith." Carmody flicked his eyelid in a wink. I got out my lucky piece, passed it over. Hurous let it lie on his fat palm; I thought maybe his puffed face stiffened a little.

"I don't see nothing like this before," he said. "Take it. You come to the wrong place. You waste my time."

Carmody reached for the gold piece, tossed it and caught it; the fat man's eyes followed.

"Mr. Smith is prepared to pay well for another like this, Hurous. Enough to set you up for the year."

Hurous' eyes darted a look at the blackened sky. "What year?" he growled. "Tomorrow maybe the whole island fall in the sea. What's a year to me?" He flopped back on the dirty cot, thrust the big gun under it. "You get off my place now, leave me be. I got nothing for you."

Carmody stepped forward, got a grip on the side of the bed's metal frame, heaved it over on its side. Hurous yelled, hit the ground with a heavy thump, came up reaching for his boot. Carmody scooped up the .44 with his left hand, dangled it negligently by the trigger guard.

"Let's not horse around, Hurous," he said genially. "Let's do business."

The fat man had snatched a slim-bladed dirk from its sheath on the inside of his shin. He held it point outward toward Carmody, the other hand spread as if it were a shield.

"I cut your heart out." He started around the end of the cot. Carmody did not move; he watched the man come, smiling lazily.

"You make a pass at me with that hatpin and I'll carve my initials on your jaw," he said gently.

Hurous stopped, stood, legs apart, his face a dull purplish shade. "You get offa my land." Then he said something in Greek. I had the impression it was uncomplimentary.

"Why get yourself roughed up?" Carmody inquired reasonably. "I didn't come up here for the view."

Hurous gathered in the bubbles at the corners of his mouth with a blackish tongue, spat at my feet. "Take this snooper with you."

There was a sudden move, a *pow!* like a cracked whip, and Hurous was lying on his back while Carmody stood over him, rubbing his palm on his thigh.

"Give, Hurous," he said.

The Greek rolled quickly, came to his feet, charged the big man head down. Carmody bounced him back with a casual swing of his right arm, followed up, twisted the man's arm behind him.

"We're wasting time," he said briskly. "Let's cut short the preliminaries. You spill or I break it. Clear?" He jerked the arm. Hurous yelped.

"Check around, Mr. Smith," Carmody said.

I gave him a look that felt stiff on my face, went inside the shack, looked around at stacked rubbish, broken odds and ends of furniture. The place smelled like the locker room at the Railroad Men's Y. I poked at a chipped teapot, lifted the lid on a cigar box filled with scraps of paper and pencil stubs, went back out.

"If there's anything in there it will have to stay there," I said. "Let's go, Carmody."

"Last chance before the fracture," Carmody twisted Hurous' arm another three degrees. The Greek went to his knees, made a noise like a rusty hinge.

"Rassias," he squealed. "Fisherman."

Carmody pushed him away, watched the man pick himself up painfully.

"What's his address?"

Hurous was working his arm experimentally. "Ten cees," he said.

I got out my wallet, handed over the paper money.

"He got a place out west of town," Hurous said. "Ask the fishermen, they tell you. You know you almost bust my arm?"

Carmody broke the .44, took out the chunky cartridges, tossed them away, dropped the gun on the ground.

"Let's go, Mr. Smith," he said.

Back at the car, I gave him a sideways look.

"You're a hard man, Carmody."

He gave me a one-sided grin. "Hurous and I are old pals. He sold me to the mainland police once. He didn't even get a good price. I was clean as a hound's tooth, as it happened. He's been waiting around for me to call ever since. Expected me to cut his throat. Old Greek custom. They can't figure us foreigners out. Right now he's counting his money and laughing. I had to bend him a little; he figures this squares things."

"Swell," I said. "If there's anything I don't need it's a new enemy."

Chapter Seven

Down by the shore that curved away west of town there were wooden shacks, strung nets, beached boats, weather-beaten docks that seemed to sway with each wave that splashed up around the barnacle-ringed pilings. We left the car up on the road, walked down across gray sand to a group of men gathered around one overturned boat. They watched us come up; none of them showed any signs of joy at our arrival. Carmody greeted them in Greek, made what I judged were a few remarks about the weather which netted him reluctant nods. Then I caught the name Rassias. The silence that fell made their previous taciturnity seem noisy. One man crossed himself when he thought no one was looking.

"Maybe the smell of money would help their memories, Mr. Smith," he suggested. I took out my usual ten-cee note; nobody reached for it. Carmody talked some more. The men looked at each other, at their feet, out to sea. Then one of them waved an arm;

another plucked the note from my fingers. They closed ranks, moved off toward what I suspected was the nearest bar.

Carmody nodded toward a lone shack, almost out of sight around a curve of the beach.

"That must be it."

"I got the feeling Rassias isn't a big favorite with them."

"They're afraid of him. They didn't say why."

I pulled the car along the road, turned off on a track that led down through the dunes, pulled up behind the house. It looked a little more substantial than the others; there were some new boards across the back, and a meter on a pole attested to the presence of electric power. We walked around to the front; a wharf led out across the mud, projected fifty feet into the water. A solid-looking thirty-foot boat was tied up beyond it.

"Looks like Rassias is in the chips," Carmody noted. He rapped on the door. Nobody answered. He tried the knob, pushed it open, looked inside.

"He's out."

"Not very far out," I said. He followed my look. A thin, wiry man with a cloth tied around his head had appeared on the dock. He wore a black turtleneck sweater, vague-colored pants that fitted tightly from the knee down to bare feet. He was smoking a brown cigarette in a long black holder.

"What you want?" he said in a low, husky voice.

"You Rassias?" Carmody called.

"That's right."

"My name's Carmody—"

"I know you, mister."

"OK. This is my friend Smith. He's looking for something; maybe you can help him."

"He lose something?"

"I understand you might be able to tell me where to get a gold coin of a certain type," I said. Rassias thought that over, came along the dock, jumped down to face us. He studied my face, wrinkling his nose at the smoke from the cigarette.

"Come inside." He walked away and we followed.

The cabin was fitted up with a neatly-made bunk, wall shelves, a newspaper-covered table, chairs. A big shiny tri-D set occupied a place of prominence at one end of the single room; a two-tube fluorescent fixture hung from weathered ceiling beams. Rassias motioned us to chairs, sat down across the table from us. He crushed out the cigarette in a sea-shell ashtray, blew through the holder, tucked it away.

"You been talking to them. . . ." He motioned with his head to indicate the town.

"They don't talk much," I said. "I'm hoping maybe you can be of a little more help."

"Help how?"

I got out my magic gold piece, the sight of which struck people dumb. "Ever see one like this before?"

Rassias glanced at it.

"What's in it, mister?"

"I'll pay for whatever you can tell me."

"Why?"

"I'm paying for information," I pointed out. "Not selling."

"You could take a walk," Rassias said. He spoke English with a unique mixture of Greek and Cockney accents.

"I've had my walk," I said. "This is the end of the line."

Rassias nodded. "Always me," he said. "Always it's me they come to with their dirty work. Why me?" He leaned forward. "I'll tell you why me. Because I'm Rassias, and Rassias is not afraid." He leaned back, looking unafraid.

"Good, then you're not too shy to tell me what you know about the coin."

"I've seen a few like it," he said flatly. I waited.

"Talk it up, Rassias," Carmody said. "Mr. Smith hasn't got time to sit here and play twenty questions."

"Mr. Smith can get in his car and tootle off," Rassias told him.

"Where did you see these coins?" I cut in. I had an idea Carmody's weight tactics would not buy anything here.

"Right here." Rassias held out a hand lumpy with calluses.

"Where did you get them?"

"They was paid to me."

"Who paid them to you?"

"A number of gentlemen." Rassias smiled crookedly. He had good teeth except for a gap at the side where a left hook might have landed once.

"What were they paying for?"

"My services."

"What kind of services?"

Rassias pointed with his chin in the general direction of the Mediterranean. "I own a boat. A good boat. Fast. Reliable. I know these waters—even now."

"You took them somewhere?"

"Sure."

"Where?"

Rassias frowned. "Out there," he said, and pointed again with his chin.

"How about getting a little more specific, Mr. Rassias?" I suggested. "I told you I'd pay for information; so far I haven't gotten any."

Rassias laughed; I thought I detected just a faint note of nervousness. "I answer everything you ask, Mister. Maybe you don't ask the right questions."

"I want to know where the coin came from."

"All I know is, they pay me. I don't ask no questions." Rassias wasn't laughing now; he wasn't even smiling.

"You know where you took them."

"That's right. I know."

"So?"

"I tell you, maybe you don't believe." His English was getting worse. He sounded worried now.

"Why wouldn't I believe you—if you're telling the truth?"

Rassias shifted in his chair. He wiped the back of his hand across his mouth.

"OK," he said, speaking in a flat, businesslike tone now. "They come here, say can I take them out, twenty kilometers, twenty-five kilometers. I say sure. Why not? They nice-looking gentlemen, dress good, speak good. From Athens, maybe, businessmen. They want to go then, same night.

"An hour out, one fellow, he comes back to the wheelhouse, stands by me, tells me steer right, steer left. I don't know where he goes, but what's that to me?

"Another half hour, he says, 'Stop here.' OK I stop. This man says to me, go below, in the cabin. I argue, but I go. You say why? I say why not? They pay me plenty, OK. But I know something they don't. Sometimes out working deep for scampi, I set the automatic steering, I go below, get a little rest. But I want to know what is up ahead. I don't want no collision. So I rig up the mirrors. I can lie on the bunk and I can see the foredeck and the sea off the bow.

"So I watch the mirror. Down below I got also a gun, you know? Maybe I have to use it, if these nice gentlemen start some monkey business. But I see them go forward, and I see them go over the side. In their nice suits. All of them. Four men, all go over the side.

"I come up on deck quick. In those clothes they drown. I got a life preserver. I put on the big deck light. But it's nothing. I don't see nothing. All I see is black water, a light sea running, good moon, stars. But no passengers. They go over the side. And they don't come back."

Carmody whistled. "What is it, some kind of crazy suicide club?"

"You tell me the name, I don't know. They hire me, they pay me, I take them out. They want to go over the side, that's their business."

"How long ago was this?"

Rassias looked wary. "I forgot."

"In the last month, say?"

"Maybe. Maybe longer."

"And you never saw them before?"

"No—not before."

"What does that mean?"

"I saw one—after."

"What did he do, wash up on the beach?" Carmody wrinkled his forehead.

Rassias pointed at the door. "He came there and knocked. I let him in."

"This was after you took him out and he jumped overboard?"

"A month later."

"They must have had a boat out there—"

"No boat. Nothing. A man in those clothes, he couldn't swim ten yards. I stayed half an hour that night, working the deck light. Nothing."

"But he came back."

"He came back."

"What for?"

"To rent my boat. He had two friends with him. He paid in advance." Rassias grinned. "For this kind of business, it is always the pay in advance, you understand."

"You took them out too?"

"Sure. It's what they pay for. To the same place."

"How do you know it was the same place. You said—"

"I know. By the smell of the sea, by the wind, by the ripples on the water, by something here"—he pointed at his chest—"that makes me the true sailor. I know."

"And what did they do this time?"

"It was the same. I go below, and they throw themselves into the sea. But quietly. This time I waste no time with the deck light. I have a quiet smoke below; then I come back."

"And they paid you in coins like this?" I picked up my trophy.

"I tell them no paper money. For this work, gold! But the second time, I raise the price. I told him, if the police hear about it, finish! I don't tell them, but—word gets out. You know—" Rassias twitched his mouth in a half-smile. "They all know about my cargoes that go out and never come back. They too don't talk to the police. What for? Who are the police? Who knows the police? Pouf!" He dismissed the police with a downward sweep of his hand.

"Some tale," Carmody said. "Wonder how much of it's true."

The sailor looked at him from the corners of his eyes.

"You think a little bit, mister," he said softly, "before you call Rassias a liar."

"I haven't called you anything—yet," Carmody grunted. "You have any proof you didn't dream the whole thing?"

Rassias smiled a quick smile, got up and went to a box on the shelf, came back and spread half a dozen bright gold discs on the newspaper that covered the tabletop. I leaned over to study them, picked one up, there was a tiny depression in the gold, just to the left of the bird's beak: the mark of my tooth. It was the coin the sailor had given me—the one Mr. Zablun had switched in his neat little office on the twenty-eighth floor at the Gulfstream, a week earlier.

"I had more," Rassias was saying. "I sold a couple."

"A month ago, huh, that last run?"

"Sure."

I swung from the floor, caught him on the cheekbone; he went down hard, came up with a knife ready. I yanked my .38 up, held it on him. Carmody started a move, checked it.

"Forget it, Rassias," I cut him off. "Can you find that spot again?"

"Sure." He looked at the gun, rubbed his face. "Inside a hundred meters, same spot." His eyes probed at me like scalpels. "Why?"

"I'm going out."

He laughed. "Maybe I was a little off on the date, OK. My boat's for hire. You pay, I take you out." He got to his feet, put the knife away.

"We won't need your boat," Carmody said. "My boat. You pilot her."

Rassias thought about it. "Cost you one hundred cees," he said. Carmody looked at me. I nodded.

"OK." Rassias showed me his teeth. "Your boat, my boat, what's the difference? I go."

"Tonight?"

"Sure, tonight."

"Meet us at nine o'clock at Stavros' Bar, Rassias," Carmody said. "That sound all right to you, Mr. Smith?"

I said it did; Rassias said he would be there. Outside, Carmody gave me his sideways look. "You got a little rough yourself."

"Yeah. A hundred cees is a nice tab for a look at a piece of sea water. Money's free, where I come from."

"What do you expect to find out there, a bottle with a clue in it?"

"I'd settle for that."

"Face it, Mal, this kid you found in the alley is dead."

"Probably."

"OK, it's your game." We went back to the car and drove into town.

Carmody's boat was a handsome thirty-eight-footer, equipped with more electronic gear than a Navy picket. Rassias followed us aboard, prowled it from one end to the other while I stowed my gun case. He came back, grinning at Carmody in the yellow light of a carbide lantern set on a pole on the wharf.

"She's nice, mister. When you die, you leave her to me, OK?"

"You know how to make sail?"

"Sure, what you think, I'm one of these gasoline sailors?"

"We'll take her out on the diesels. When we're half a mile from target, we'll shut down and ride the breeze in."

We cast loose and edged across the bar, then Carmody threw power to her and the big boat put her stern down and headed out.

"You know this is a nutty idea, don't you?" he said over the thrum of the big engines and the shrill of the airstream. "You ever used scuba gear before?"

"A few times."

"A swell way to drown."

"As good as any."

"You sound bitter, pal."

"What's there to be bitter about? Half the world is under water and most of the rest is choking to death on volcanic gas. Every building on earth over two stories high is piled in what's left of the street. The only government still operating is what a few towns here and there have managed to keep alive at gunpoint—and just to liven things up, a pack of madmen are running around loose picking victims out of a hat. But I'm still breathing, so what do I care?"

"The girl must have meant a lot to you."

"I hardly knew her."

A stiff westerly breeze was blowing cool salt mist against my face; underfoot the deck trembled and thudded like something alive. Out here, at night, it was almost possible to imagine that back on shore life went on, music played, people laughed, sang, went for walks in the woods, took picnic lunches to the park secure in the knowledge that the ground would not break apart under their feet, that the worst natural disaster they were likely to encounter was an unexpected shower.

But that dream was gone forever—or for my lifetime, at least. Man, the bright young primate, had had it lucky for his first million years. There had been a few brief eras of planetary upheaval in his time; the legends of flood and hellfire attested to their impact on the race memory. But, by and large, he had had a long vacation in which to evolve, build cities, invent culture.

And now the vacation was over.

It was nothing abnormal, as events in the life of a planet went; you had to expect an age of mountain raising, sea draining, continent breaking now and then. It was only the egotism of man that had made him imagine it could not happen to him. Now it was happening—and when it was over, future generations would tell the story to their surviving young down through the centuries, and graybeards would sort through the rock strata chipping out coffee pots and fossilized spare tires and make beautiful theories to account for it all.

But we were here; we knew: A planet is a strange and fearful place for fragile living creatures.

✧   ✧   ✧

Forty minutes' run nearly due east, Rassias came back from the prow where he had been standing straddle-legged in the blue glow of the bow lights watching the water.

"Time to break out the sail, Captain." He was smiling as if he were pleased with the whole thing, happy to be here, eager for the fun.

Carmody cut the throttles back. "You sure?"

Rassias shrugged. "If you got no confidence, why you pay me?" He went forward, set to work hauling the tarpaulin clear of the sail locker. He finished, gave a wave; Carmody pushed a button. The telescoping mast rose up, pivoted into position; the sail shook itself out, took the wind, came taut with a soft boom. The sound of the engines died and I could hear the hiss of water, the sigh of air through the rigging. We rode in darkness now, running lights off.

"I'll go below and dress out," I told Carmody. In the cabin I stripped, pulled on cotton longjohns, then the cold-suit; rigged harness straps so that the air tanks would ride comfortably. The mask was one of the new all-in-one type—a flexible plastic helmet with a 180-degree glass window. I got it on, adjusted the air flow.

Up above, a whine started up; a moment later Carmody came down, checked me over.

"We're in position, according to Rassias," he said. "I've set the gyro anchor to hold us on the spot." His voice sounded tinny through the inductance pickups. "The bottom's at thirty-five fathoms out here," he added.

"Fine. I'm ready."

Up on deck, Carmody showed me the controls—a few simple knobs that regulated the breathing mixture, a bigger one that controlled the power unit.

"Remember this one." He tapped a flat lever set in a small panel above my right knee. "It's a wake-up shot if you begin to go woozy down there."

"I've got plenty to keep me awake."

"Sure. Remember it anyway." He took a small canvas case from a locker, clipped it to my belt.

"Tools," he said. "There's a little cutting torch, pry bars, special stuff. Maybe you'll want it."

"I'm not going down to crack a safe."

"Why are you going down, Mal? What do you expect to find down there?"

"If I knew, I might not have to go."

"I ought to go with you, but I have to keep an eye on our boy. Embarrassing if he pulled out and left us."

"It's all right."

"You don't have to go, you know. You could forget the whole thing. I need a partner."

"Thanks. I've got to play the hand I drew."

"This is no card game, pal—but every man to his own kick."

It was a fine night, as nights went nowadays. The sea was flat, moving in slow swells; there was no moon, no stars. The odor of volcano was a little thicker than it had been ashore. Carmody pushed another button and a chrome-plated ladder ran out astern. I climbed the rail and felt the tug of the water at my legs.

"Say something every now and then, old buddy," Carmody's voice sounded in my ear. "Keep in touch."

"I will. Don't go 'way."

"We'll be here, pal."

The surface closed over my head and I let go and sank down into utter blackness.

Chapter Eight

There were sounds: the wheeze of my breathing, the tiny hum of the recycler, the creak of the belt against the foam suit. I touched the power switch, felt the instant thrust from the water jet mounted under my back tanks. The glow of the depth meter and attitude indicator on my wrist was barely visible through the cloudy water. I held them close to my eyes, maneuvered into the recommended face-down position by working my ankle fins.

There was a stiff current flowing. Carmody had told me that the Mediterranean was still falling by half an inch a week, pouring out through Gibraltar to equalize the difference in levels created by the upthrust of the Sicilian bridge. The land-locked eastern portion in which I was now having my dip was feeding the flow through subterranean channels. I faced myself upstream, assumed a forty-five-degree downward angle, and concentrated on holding my stance.

At seventy-five feet I eased off power, studied the depths under me. It was like looking at the back of your eyelids in a dark room. The water was cold here; my bare hands ached. I thrust them into the heated pockets on the sides of the suit, twisted over on my back to look up. There was a barely perceptible lightening of the darkness there—or maybe it was my imagination.

My position indicator said I had drifted a hundred yards from the boat; I swam level for five minutes to get back on target, then started down again. The pressure was beginning to bother me a little now; I ignored the pins-and-needles sensation back of my eyes, bored on down to a hundred and fifty feet.

This time I needed a longer rest. Breathing against the pressure of the sea was hard work at this depth. There was still nothing in sight. A lot of unwelcome thoughts were running through my head: sharks, a plugged air conduit, seasickness. . . .

That was not buying me anything. I blanked off the nagging instinct that told me I was a land animal a long way from the open air, oriented myself, and went on down.

The glowing needle on my left wrist quivered past the hundred-and-seventy-foot mark—the deepest I had ever dived, back in the clear water off Bermuda under a tropical sun shining out of a sky full of fluffy little clouds like freshly scrubbed lambs. It was a nice thought; I held on to it, rode it down past the two-hundred-foot mark.

Time for another short break. I was breathing hard, listening to a roaring in my head like a fast freight making up lost time in the Channel tunnel. The water seemed warmer now—or maybe my hands were getting numb. It was harder than ever to see my instrument faces; I had to hold them against my nose.

I started below. Thirty-five fathoms, Carmody had said; my faceplate should be scraping bottom now. I waggled my feet, swam down another yard—

Something moved and I shied; it was a waving frond of weed, glowing faintly with marine phosphorescence. I was on the bottom.

I drifted down, felt my legs touch yielding ooze. The tall stand of kelp held its position; there seemed to be no current here. Standing upright, I did a slow three-sixty, staring through blackness, saw nothing but the ghostly weeds. They moved with a pleasing grace, disturbed by my intrusion among them. I had the thought that if I relaxed, hung absolutely still, they would forget

I was here. I would sink slowly to the soft muck of the sea floor, and there I could rest, and watch the slow dance of the glowing ribbons, and—

A phrase popped into my head: "The rapture of the deep." I tried to move, almost gave it up as too much effort, then kicked out, beat at the water with my arms to shake off the lethargy that was wrapping around me like a warm blanket. I kept it up for what seemed like a long time, then hung in the water, breathing hard.

My depth gauge read two hundred and twelve feet. A high, singing sound had joined the other noises in my ears. The glow of the instrument face seemed to be sliding away from me, a tiny light glowing in the big dark, and in a moment more it would be gone. It did not seem important. I let it go, and suddenly in its place were colors, flowing around me like a molten rainbow, and as they flowed they sang in a high sweet voice, and I was flying through space at a fantastic speed and the singing voices were all around me, escorting me through pillars of cool fire toward that attainable place seen only in dreams where the soul would dance naked in golden sunshine—

But first, there was something—something that had been important, once; something I was supposed to do.

I groped for my knee, felt a square button against my fingers, pushed at it. It moved. I felt a sense of relief at a tiresome chore done; now I could turn back to the colors and the song—

There was a sharp pang in my throat, a sensation like hot wires jammed up my nose. My head jerked and I took a deep breath to yell, choked instead. I kicked out, flapped my arms, got my feet under me, looked at my watch. I had been floating head down, blacked-out for nearly fifteen minutes.

The singing was gone but the thud of my heart was loud enough to make up for it. Darkness was all around me; even the weed was gone now. It had been a wild venture to start with, and nothing I had seen down here made it look any more promising. It was time to go up, shake hands all around, and head back to Stavros' for a couple of stirrup cups. Carmody was a good lad in spite of his informal methods of making a living. I could throw in with him; we could head for the South Seas where the living was easy, and forget this forlorn chase.

I reached for the power control to start my ascent and found myself looking at the soft, green glow of a light shining steadily through the murk.

My depth gauge said I was at two hundred and one feet now. I stroked with my feet, moved toward the glow, found myself sliding past; I was back in the current. The water was clearer here. A school of small silvery darts hovered nearby; light glinted on their sides as they shot away. I used the water jet to work back upstream to the source of the light.

It came from a round cave mouth like a four-foot-high section of sewer pipe lying in a trough in the mud. Ten feet inside its mouth a baffle stood half open; the light came from beyond it. I swam into the opening; beyond the disc that half blocked the passage I could see the tunnel fading away, light reflecting along its sides. There was room at the side of the baffle for me to pass; I turned on my side and eased through into the passage.

A slight current thrust me back through the barrier; I used more power to push upstream. I could feel a heavy thumping through the water, like a whale's heartbeat. The tunnel curved gently, leading off to the left and trending downward. I thought about Carmody, slouching in a canvas chair on a deck two hundred feet above and an unknown number of feet west, chewing on his pipestem and checking the watch on his thick, hairy wrist. I had forgotten all about calling in; by now he had probably decided the sharks had me. I checked my watch; it had been thirty-five minutes since I went over the side.

The current seemed stronger now. I put the jet control knob all the way over, made headway against turbulent currents that slammed me against first one side of the tunnel and then the other. Ahead, the light was brighter; I made out vertical lines silhouetted against a brilliant glare.

Up close, the lines resolved into a set of louvers, each a foot wide, standing half open. I got a grip on one, held on against a stiff flow that tugged at me hard enough to make my shoulder ache. The pressure was increasing by the second. Inside my helmet, a fine sweat prickled on my forehead. If I let go now, I would be tossed downstream like a chip in a millrace—with the baffle waiting at the end of the line to break my back. If I held on until my arms gave out, I would hit even harder. I felt like a blimp's ground crewman who has forgotten to let go of the rope.

There was one other possibility; I got a grip with the other hand, hauled hard, pulled myself forward between the louvers. The tunnel curved upward sharply ahead. Working hard, I got my shoulders through, then my chest. The water pounded at me, as heavy as falling pianos. My legs came through, and I braced them, stood up, reached for the rim of a circular port above through which the water sluiced down in a cascade that broke, turned to churning white, fell away abruptly to a splash, then a trickle. Under my feet, the heavy metal slats rotated suddenly, came together with a solid snap that sounded as final as dirt hitting a coffin. If I had been thirty seconds slower getting through, I would have been sliced like a salami.

I hauled myself up and through the manhole, looked around at a room the size of the main roulette salon at Monte Carlo, ringed with stumpy spiral-carved columns. The walls looked like ancient, discolored stone, broken by half a dozen rectangular openings that might have been windows once, blocked up now with rough masonry and black mortar.

I looked for the source of the light, saw strips set into recesses in the ceiling, glowing a cold blue. There were massive items of furniture here and there—stone benches, a stone table, what looked like a birdbath with a pipe projecting from it. Through a coating of black on the floor, I could make out traces of a mosaic pattern.

The thumping had stopped now. My faceplate was frosting over. I pulled the helmet off, snorted at a stink of decay thick enough to shovel. Still, it was air. I went across the room, found a flight of slimy steps leading up. At the top a heavy door swung open when I pushed on it, and I stepped through into what looked like a junk dealer's attic.

It was a big, square room, stacked, heaped, packed with statues, pots, tall clay vases, wooden chests, bundles, bulging sacks of scuffed leather, odds and ends of spidery chairs, massive benches, carved screens. There was a slim statuette that must have been brass, lying on its side nearby, next to it a dark red bowl with black designs of women and sheep, beyond that a carved cat with a long body like a rail fence and bits of stone for eyes. Under everything there was a drift of broken potsherd, rotted wood fragments, the glint of small bright objects half buried in the rubbish. Where the floor was visible, it looked wet.

A path of sorts led through the collection to an alcove in the opposite wall where water trickled down steps leading up to a massive door made of wide planks bound with brass strips. I had my foot on the bottom step when the door rattled, swung open.

I stepped back into a recess between a statue of a squatting deity and an upturned two-wheeled cart. The legs of a man came into view, moving awkwardly under the weight of a wooden chest the size of a foot locker. He reached the floor, paused, looked around, then turned and shoved the box back on top of the nearest heap. He turned my way then, stood wiping his hands on a piece of brown cloth with beads along the edge. I held my breath and pretended to be a shadow.

Ten slow seconds ticked by; then he took a step my way. My disguise had not worked. I put a hand on the grip of the spear pistol at my right hip and waited for him. He stopped a few feet away, looked me over, then said something in what might have been Greek.

I shook my head. "No kapisch," I told him. "I was just waiting for the cross-town car."

His expression did not change; it looked like something carved on a wooden Indian. He was dressed in thick, olive-drab trousers and a tan shirt with shoulder straps, both badly worn and dirt-stained.

"Who ordered you to this section?" he asked in a tone like a tired cop making a routine license check.

"I came here on my own," I told him.

"Where is your leader?" He had some kind of accent, but I could not place it.

"I'm the leader," I came back. He was a little too far away to reach without taking a step. I debated whether to try him now, or wait for him to move in a little closer.

"I was not informed," he said. He dropped the cloth he had been using on his hands and made some sort of gesture with his fingers.

"Never mind the excuses," I said. "You can go now."

"Those instructions are not explicit," he commented. "To where am I instructed to go?"

"Where would you like to go?" My upper lip was getting sweaty now; the nutty conversation was getting on my nerves. I wished he would either flash his badge, let out a yell or make his play. Instead, he stood there, looking thoughtful.

"I would like to return to my room and sleep," he stated.

"Swell. You do that."

He turned his back and headed for the steps. I watched him go, then stepped out after him.

"Maybe before you go to sleep you'd better show me around a little," I called after him. "I'm new here."

He was on the steps, looking back at me. "What do you wish to see?"

"Everything."

"Your instructions are not clear," he stated.

"Just show me around, I'll decide what to look at."

He hesitated. "I know," I said, cutting him off before he said anything, "that's not explicit. Just start showing me things as we come to them."

The door opened into a hallway better lit than the room below. It smelled of moldy cucumbers and iodine, with an overlay of river mud. The floor was made of large stone slabs, between the joints of which water oozed. There were discolored cracks in the rough-plastered walls, and more water trickled from them. We passed doorways, blocked with tarred brickwork, likewise damp-looking. It appeared the place had sprung a number of leaks.

The passage made an abrupt right turn, ended at a metal wall with a circular door that looked as massive as a bank vault. My guide gripped a two-handed lever, pulled it out, turned it to the left; the port swung in. He ducked, stepped through, with me close behind.

We were in a wide corridor, brightly lit, with smooth walls, a polished floor, fresh-smelling air. A few yards along, we turned into a spacious room with a mosaic floor as bright as neon, and mural-covered walls showing men and women in short white kilts throwing sticks at birds rising from a swamp. In the far corner of the room, near a wide doorway with a gold lintel, a man sat behind a long marble-slab table, working over papers. We went across to him.

"I require your help," my guide said. The man looked at him, past him at me, got to his feet. My guide stepped back, waited for him to come around the table.

"Seize him," he said in an unexcited tone and lunged for my arm. I gave him the back of my hand, spun around in time to meet his partner with a wild swing that connected somewhere in the vicinity of his right ear, knocked him over the table as the other man landed on my back. We went down together and I twisted as I fell, heard his head hit hard. I rolled clear and he slid off on his face, out cold. The man behind the table was on his knees, fumbling with a little gold whistle hanging on a cord around his neck; I grabbed for it, yanked his head hard. It hit marble with a dull sound and he went down bubbling.

I was breathing hard, listening to surf booming way back in my skull. I still had not gotten my wind back from the swim up the sewer pipe. The place was silent now, except for two sets of hoarse breathing; then I heard footsteps coming along the hall—more than one man. Various ideas ran through my head, none of them good; two bleeding bodies are too much of a burden for any bluff to carry.

The gold-ornamented door caught my eye. I jumped the secretarial type lying half under it, tried the big handle. It turned, and the door opened with a squeal as I pushed through and closed it behind me.

This time the passage was wider, higher, floored with red flagstones, lit by chandeliers hanging at five-yard intervals. Along one side were columns supporting arches, like a Gothic cloister; all the openings had been smoothly cemented in. There was a wide, open door on the right ahead. I went along to it, turned in to a roomy apartment fitted out with modern factory-built furnishings, rugs, framed pictures. The place was in a state of chaotic disarray: papers and odd garments were heaped on tables, scattered over the floor; dirty dishes were stacked on the arms of chairs, on a wide buffet, on two carpeted steps that led down to an open archway. There were dark stains on the rug, the glisten of water along a crack in the patterned wallpaper.

From the corridor I heard the scrape of the big door, a mutter of voices. I was in plain sight from the apartment door. I went down the steps, through into the next room, almost choked on a reek of garlic and stale bedding. Against the left wall, a vast, bloated bulk of a man lay spread eagled on a four-poster just smaller than a hand-ball court, propped up on a heap of gold-tasseled pillows. He stared at me fixedly with small, protruding eyes in a brown face that looked too small for the big, hairless skull. The massive jowls quivered; a voice like a rubber doll squeaked something at me.

"Keep quiet," I ordered. I yanked the spear pistol from its sheath, moved over against the wall beside the bed, out of sight from the doorway.

"If they stick their heads in here, I'll put a bolt through your neck. Do I make myself clear?"

The bulging eyes bulged at me a little harder; otherwise he made no sign that he had heard me. Maybe he was deaf; maybe he did not understand English. Either way, the weapon in my hand should have given him enough of a hint. The voices were coming from the outer room now.

"Tell them to go away," I hissed at him. "In English."

He heaved his chest—an effect like a wave rolling inshore—and shrilled, "Go away!"

Steps approached the door, soft on the carpet. Someone spoke, no more than six feet from where I stood flattened against the wall. I measured the distance to the rolls of fat around the reclining beauty's neck.

"Go away!" the Minnie Mouse voice squealed. "Go away instantly."

The voice outside made a final comment and the steps retreated. I waited until the silence had stretched out to breaking point, then let out a breath I did not realize I had been holding. The big man was watching me as if he expected me to do something astonishing at any moment and he did not want to miss it.

"You are not of us," he piped suddenly.

"Who is us?"

"How did you come here?" he came back.

"I followed a trail; this is where it ended."

"That is impossible," the hairless head wobbled in agitation.

"It's happening. Talk it up, big boy. I'm a long way from home and my nerves are shot. I could get violent at any moment."

"I have a great deal of money," the tiny voice stated, sounding calm now.

"In gold pieces?"

"Whatever you wish. I will summon one who—"

"You won't summon anybody. Who were the lads who paid Rassias to bring them out here?"

The purse mouth worked. "I can give you power—"

"I've got all the power I need." I took a step, poked the triangular point of the foot-long harpoon against his throat. "Who are you? What is this place? Who are the silent lads with the quick guns?"

He squeaked and flapped his hands against the dirty silken sheet.

"Ever met a man named Sethys?" If the name startled him, he did not show it. He kept the eyes glued on me like gold stars on a stripper. I stepped back, looked around the room. It was like the sitting room outside—an unwholesome combination of luxury and dirty socks. There was a closed door across the room; I tried it, found it locked. Beside it was a tall wardrobe, it opened and I looked in at suits, coats, hats, shoes, all on the same gargantuan scale as my new chum on the bed. A table beside the wardrobe was stacked with newspapers, soiled clothes, scattered coins—none gold—more gravy-stained dishes. I dumped them off, checked the drawer, found bits of paper, a gold fountain pen of antique design, envelopes, a bottle of purple pills. The chest of drawers yielded folded underwear, chicken bones, an expensive-looking wrist watch, an empty bottle. I did not know what I was looking for, but I was not finding it.

Fatty was watching every move. The sheet was thrown back from his chest, exposing an expanse of tough-looking brown skin like a hairless walrus. He had one hand out, fingering the top of a carved chest beside the bed; he pulled it back when I looked his way. I went over and lifted the lid. A heap of metallic green cloth lay on top of folded linens. I was reaching for it when he made a noise like a strangled chicken and lunged for me.

I jumped, but not quickly enough. One fat hand caught my gun hand below the wrist with a grip like a hydraulic vise, yanked me to him. I twisted far enough to get a hip into his belly, put my elbow in his eye, and socked him on the ear as hard as circumstances permitted. It was not enough. He screeched like an insulted elephant, made a grab for my neck, got a handful of shoulder instead. I brought a hard chop down on the bridge of his nose, hit him across his well-padded throat, got a thumb into the other eye. He dropped the grip on my shoulder, heaved himself up for another try at my throat. This time he made it. Fingers like bolt cutters dug in. I braced myself, picked a spot just behind the corner of his mouth, put everything I had into a right-handed chop that snapped his head sideways hard enough to bounce it off his shoulder. His eyes went dull; he shuddered and went limp.

I dragged myself to my feet, checked my major bones and joints. I was a little surprised to find them all intact. When Big Boy got started, he was full of surprises.

I picked up the green garment, shook it out. It was an overall, cut to fit a medium-sized female. There was a tear down the back, and another on the right sleeve. I laid it out flat on the side of the bed, smoothed it. A piece was missing from the torn sleeve— a piece that would be some six inches long and half an inch wide— just the size of the strip I had found at the door of the collapsing hotel.

Chapter Nine

He came to five minutes later, made a couple of convulsive flops, steadied down when I touched his side with the razor-sharp spear point.

"Where is she?"

He looked at the garment in my hand. His face worked like fudge about to come to a boil.

"I cannot tell you."

"Too bad." I rammed the spear medium hard; blood started from the cut. He jerked away and I prodded him again.

"You used up all your good will with me when you put your thumb in my neck," I told him. "Get her here or I'll pin you to the mattress and go looking for her myself."

"You must not kill me," he chirped. He seemed very serious about this. "I must not be touched, damaged, or caused pain."

"That's understandable—but life is full of disappointments. I can give you five minutes."

"I will give you other women—as many as you like—"

"Just the one, thanks."

"I need this woman," he insisted.

"For what? Why did you bring her here?"

"I require a mistress—many mistresses—"

"All the way from Miami?"

"She caught my eye; I desired her."

"Let's have the truth. It's less taxing on the brain."

"I have told you—"

I poked him; he jumped, made a half-hearted grab for the pistol. I shifted position, caught him on the hand with the point. He gave a squeal like a stepped-on rat, rammed the hand in his mouth and made sucking sounds.

"Call one of your boys and have her brought here; then tell them to go away. You know just how to do it—nice and easy."

He made gobbling noises, pointed to a large button set in the carved headboard.

"I must use this," he choked out.

"Go ahead. You know the rules."

I watched while he thumbed the call button; faint crackling sounds started up. "Yes," a voice said from across the room. I looked across at a small tri-D screen from which a face was staring.

"He cannot see us," the fat man whispered in a hoarse yelp.

The man on the screen said something in a strange, staccato language. My host replied in kind. I kept a little pressure on the spear point to remind him of our arrangement. The face went away and the screen winked off. Fatty whined and flopped his hands on the bed. There was quite a bit of blackish blood spattered around on the sheets now from the punctures in his hide. I must have been pushing harder than I thought.

"When the woman is brought here, you must go away," he piped.

"Get her here; I'll take it from there."

He lay on the bed, looking at me. From time to time his chest heaved in a shuddery sob. I checked my watch. It had been five minutes since the call.

Suddenly, there were footsteps in the outer room. I moved back against the wall.

"Just the girl," I whispered through my teeth. Fatty chirped orders. There were sounds of a scuffle; then Ricia stumbled through the doorway. She was dressed in a shapeless gray sack, bare-footed. There was a small cut on her forehead. Her hands were trussed behind her. She looked at the man on the bed with an expression of mild distaste, and said something haughty in the same language she had used on me. He flopped his hands, pointed at me. Ricia took a step forward, saw me and stiffened—then smiled like the sun breaking through clouds.

"Akmal!" She took a step my way, then faltered, looked at the fat man. He spoke to her in what sounded like her own tongue.

"Tell her I'm getting her out of here," I snapped. Then, to her: "It's all right now, Ricia. We're leaving." I went to her, cut the tough cords binding her wrists. There were deep red marks where they had been. The fat man was talking—speaking persuasively, waving his hands.

"That's enough," I cut him off. "Let's go, Ricia." I took her hand. She hung back, spoke sharply to the fat man. He answered. She snapped an order at him. He rolled the bugged eyes at me.

"You will be caught," he said. "They will kill you. The woman commands me to say this to you."

"Sure." I looked into Ricia's face. She smiled again, tentatively. "It's good to see you again, kid," I told her. "Let's travel." I went to the head of Fatty's bed, used the spear point to dig the call button out of the wood and poke the connecting wires back in out of reach.

"I need one more thing of you," I told him. "A diving outfit for the girl."

"I know nothing—"

"Better try." Another jab—a hearty one. He yelped.

"Perhaps—at the lock. Yes—I remember it now. It has been many years—"

"Where's the nearest exit?"

"There." He pointed at the locked door beside the wardrobe, "Follow the passage. The lock is there."

"Where's the key?"

"Press the head of the carved dragon."

I tried it. The door slid back; I looked in at wet floor stretching off into darkness. Ricia was beside me.

"Mal—no walk. Bad," she said.

"I don't like it too well myself, but if we don't find the lock I'll come back and cut him a new mouth under those chins." I gave Fatty a last smile to show him my morale was up, took Ricia's hand, and stepped through. We had gone about ten feet when the light narrowed down, went out. My dive for the closing door was a yard short and a second late.

"Mal!" Ricia's voice was a gasp.

"I'm all right, just stupid. I guess Tubby had a button I missed." I got to my feet, groped my way to her, put an arm around her shoulders. She shivered, clung to me. My hand light was still clipped to my belt; I flashed it over the door. The inner side was smooth, with no nice dragon heads to push. I leaned on it; it was like leaning against the First National Bank.

"No joy here, Ricia. I guess we keep going." She gave me a grave smile and took my free hand. Together we followed the passage. Forty feet along it turned right and ended in a cul-de-sac where a doorway had been walled up.

"Swell," I said. "End of the line. But maybe there's a door we missed." We went back along the route, studying the walls. They were smooth masonry, unbroken except for a few floor-to-ceiling fractures through which water seeped to add to the slosh underfoot.

"We'll never punch our way through this, kid," I said. "I think we'd better have another look at that door."

I checked it over from edge to edge, from threshold to header. There was not even a pinhole to work on. It seemed to be a slab of solid metal.

Ricia was holding the light for me. She reached out, touched the case Carmody had clipped to my belt.

"This?" she said.

"Burglar tools," I said. "They're no help if I don't have a lock or hinges to work on." I unsnapped the case, lifted out a plastic box, opened it; the light winked from polished metal. "Jimmies, pinch bars, backsaws—everything the well-dressed burglar needs."

I was looking at the small cutting torch, no bigger than a can opener. It was something special, Carmody had told me; it used a new mixture of gases developed for working the material used to line rocket exhaust tubes. It was intended for nothing heavier than cutting cables, but this was not a time to be particular.

It took five minutes of experimentation before I got a steady white flame burning, another five minutes to find a setting that nibbled a pit in the metal.

"At this rate we won't need to make any social engagements for a while," I said over the crackle of the torch. "I'll try for a hole big enough to get my hand through. This spot should be just about opposite the dragon's left ear."

Ricia stood by me, watching as the glow spread. The pockmark in the hard metal widened to a half-inch pit. Suddenly sparks showered and molten metal welled out.

"Luck," I said. "I've cut through into a softer layer."

Ricia put a hand on my arm. "Mal, listen!"

I listened, heard nothing but the snap and pop of the flame.

"Bad men. Here." She pointed at the door. I shut down the torch and at once heard a dull pounding.

"Sounds like they're beating on the door."

Ricia looked up at me, said nothing.

"Why the hell would they pound on the door? All they have to do is push the dragon's head."

Ricia pointed to the glowing orifice in the door. "Broken," she said. "No dragon's head."

"Could be—I must have cut a wire." My lips felt as dry as blotters. "I had a wild idea they might stay away for a while, but it looks like Big Boy was a couple of jumps ahead of me all the way."

Nobody contradicted me. I stood there, watching the glow fade, feeling the glow of forlorn hope fading along with it. Ricia crept in close, put her head against my chest.

"Sorry, kid." I stroked her hair. "I guess you might have had a better chance if I'd kept out of it. They hadn't murdered you yet; maybe they didn't intend to. . . ."

"Better here, Mal."

"Yeah, if you're lucky, they get the door open and take you back; if not, you starve where you are." My fingers touched the smooth skin of her throat. Before I would let her starve, I would have to kill her myself—choke her or break her neck. She would understand what I was doing, and smile at me as I touched her.

"No!" I slammed a fist against the door. "Come and get her, you lousy killers! Tear that door down—"

"Mal. . . ." Ricia's hands were on my face, around my neck, her lips against mine. Slowly the roaring died down in my head. I leaned against the wall while she talked to me, soothing me like you soothe a restless animal.

"If I could rig a trap for those zombies," I said. "Something that would blow. . . ." I stopped talking, feeling a thump in my chest that meant that hope, down for the count, was picking herself off the canvas for another try.

"Mal, what?"

"Nothing. An idiot idea. But it might—just might be something. . . ."

She held the light again while I set to work, digging the flash metal away from the hole I had cut. The door was hollow, filled with a perforated honeycomb of light metal under the quarter-inch covering of stainless steel.

"So far so good." My fingers had developed a gross tremor, like a dipso groping for his first drink of the morning. I used the spear head to saw a strip from Ricia's cuff, wrapped it around the nozzle of the torch, fitted it into the hole; then I thumbed the control full over. The gas mixture hissed softly, pouring into the hollow interior of the door.

"This part is guesswork," I told Ricia. "These capsules at the base of the handle store the gas in liquid form; I don't know how long they'll feed. And I need to keep a little in reserve."

Ricia was sniffing. I sniffed, too, caught the sour lemon smell of the gas.

"I guess she's full." I removed the torch, plugged the hole with the scrap of cloth, then propped the torch on the floor, using the tool kit to support it in a vertical position.

"I'll light the torch and let it play on the door. When the metal gets white-hot—well, we'll see what happens."

A moment later the blue-white flame was sputtering against the metal, eight inches from the bottom edge of the door.

"Let's go." I took Ricia's hand and we ran for the end of the corridor, ducked around into the shelter of the walled-off cubicle at its end.

"This will probably be a dud," I said, talking to hear myself. "There won't be enough gas there to ignite, maybe. Or maybe it'll go *pop!* and blow the plug out."

"Yes, Mal." Ricia patted my hand.

"Or maybe nothing will happen at all. Maybe the torch will go out. Maybe—"

Ricia took my hands, placed them over her ears. I smiled a crooked smile at her. "Good idea," I said. "Just in case—"

A club struck my head, slammed me back against the stone wall like a mouse riding the clapper of a giant bell. I seemed to be flying end over end, while bright pinwheels whirled all around me like Independence Day in Texas. I groped, found rough masonry under me. I could taste blood in my mouth.

"Ricia!" I felt my throat vibrate with the yell, but all I could hear was a high, insistent singing, like a stuck siren. Then I touched her hand; I caught at it, pulled her close, felt over her face and body for wounds. She was limp, out cold, but I could feel her breath on my face; she was alive. I yelled her name again, but nothing could penetrate the siren tone that filled the darkness as water fills a well.

Something cold was washing up my side. I found my hand light, switched it on. Muddy water was swirling around the corner, foaming, bearing a litter of floating debris.

"Must have knocked a hole in the wall," I felt myself say. I groped my way to my feet, caught up Ricia, got her over my shoulder, stepped out past the angle of the short passage. At the far end, light glared through a ragged opening like a paper hoop the trick dog has just jumped through. Dirty water poured toward me in a white cataract, carrying papers, small objects, fragments of shattered wood. I waded upstream, climbed through into the room beyond.

The fat man was gone. The bed lay like a crashed balloon, the mattress split wide in a welter of soggy cotton and coil springs, the headboard collapsed over it, the canopy of dark brown silk sagging above, dirty water tugging at its corner. By the steps, a man lay half-submerged, trails of pink blood swirling away from him. Another man lay on his back across the shattered wardrobe, his face and chest torn into blackish-red jam. Major fragments of other men bumped along in the current.

"They must have been standing in front of the door when it went." I towed Ricia across through shin-deep water, up the steps into the sitting room. A wide crack had opened across the left wall, through which water jetted in a translucent sheet halfway across the room. I ducked through it, reached the outer passage, stumbled over broken stones crumbled from the walled-up arches, reached the open door into the lounge with the marble table. The two men whose heads I had cracked were gone; the bright mosaic floor was a rippling pattern under a foot of water. Through cracks in the murals, more water flowed.

"That blast must have been the last straw," I mumbled aloud, hearing the words ring deafly inside my head. "The place is breaking up."

By the time I reached the closed hatch through which I had come on the way in, the stream was knee deep, awash with feather fans, wood carvings, papers. I grabbed the big handle, yanked and twisted, then calmed down, tried to remember my guide's technique. He had pushed the lever in, turned it to the left. I did the same, and the heavy metal port swung toward me pushed by a vast gush of water that knocked me off my feet, washed me twenty feet downstream. Somehow I kept my grip on the girl, got my feet under me, waded back, climbed through the hatch. The water surged and boiled, eddying around a large mahogany chest wedged in the passage.

I got a foot on it, started over, saw two men fifty feet downstream, hauling at what looked like another hatch like the one we had just passed. One of them looked my way, pointed; the other went on with what he was doing. The pointer grabbed his arm and the other fellow pushed him away, kept working. Abruptly, a red light went on above the port as it swung out. I laid Ricia out across the top of the heavy chest, vaulted over it, lifted her again, half swam, half waded along to the port. Both men had disappeared behind it now. I reached it just as it started its swing inward, got a grip on its edge, braced my feet, hauled back.

Pain exploded in my hand; one of the boys was pounding my fingers. I fumbled left-handed, freed the spear pistol from my belt, aimed it past the edge of the door, and fired. There was a grunt, then threshing sounds. The door gave a foot, and I caught a glimpse of an interior like a section of sewer main, bright-lit, with a second port dogged shut on its opposite side. A locker mounted against the wall was open, and a man, half into a leathery-looking frogman outfit, was crumpled against it, three inches of blue steel bolt projecting from a bloody patch just below his ear.

I just had time to note the purplish color of the face of the man holding the door against me when something bright flashed up, swung down at me, and I ducked, took the blow across the top of my head, felt myself going back and down. Churning water closed over my face.

For what seemed like a long time, I tumbled, feeling the burn of water in my chest, the dim, ghostly blows of the walls and floor against me as the racing water hurled me along. Then somehow I was swimming, my face above water, my ears popping from the pressure of air compressed between the rising flood and the passage walls. I yelled for Ricia, then saw her dark hair afloat on the surface, swam a few floundering strokes, caught her and lifted her face clear. Water ran from her nose and mouth. Her face was a dim yellow in the faint light.

The water swept us along, dunked us rounding a bend, then hurled us down a slope into a log jam of floating chairs, tables, statuary, paper, rubbish. I took a sharp crack on the head, a gouge in the side before I caught a big box bobbing in the flood, got my back to it to fend off the flotsam. The ceiling was no more than five feet above the water; I recognized it as a room I had seen before.

The water was rising fast. There was no more than thirty inches now between the discolored bricks of the ceiling and the roiled surface of the water. My head seemed to ring with a clear, steady note. My arms ached from the effort of holding Ricia's head above the choppy ripples. A sudden lassitude swept over me; it would be so easy to relax, slide down under the black surface and let it all go.

I thought of Ricia, the trusting squeeze of her hand just before the blast that smashed her unconscious—and pictured her waking here, choking alone before those last seconds before the long blackness.

There was an abrupt change in the flow of water around me; I felt, rather than heard, the deep-toned thud of machinery. A new current stirred, pulled me toward a newly formed eddy at the center of the chamber. Down below—submerged under ten feet of black water—the louvers would be open now. Somehow, in spite of the broached walls, the pumps were working, forcing the inrushing waters out through a hundred yards of tunnel, to the open sea bottom. How much longer they would operate was a question.

There was no time for me to weigh the alternatives. I poured the water from my breathing helmet, pulled it over my head, snapped it in place. Then, with the unconscious body of the girl tucked under my arm, I let go of my support and slid under the surface.

Finding the big drain was easy; a swift current sucked at me, swept me to it, slammed me hard against the open louvers. I twisted over on my back, lowered my feet through the narrow gap between slats, pulled Ricia after me. I could see her face, a ghostly pale blue in the murky water. All around, floating objects bobbed and whirled. I grabbed at a helmet, jammed it somehow on Ricia's head. It was going to be a long haul to the surface if we ever made it.

The flow took me down, under the curve of the tunnel's ceiling. I brought the hand light around, shone it through the water; the narrow beam faded out six feet from my face.

I cracked the jet control, slowed our motion. Water hammered at me, tore at Ricia. We crept along, past yard after yard of monotonously unvarying gray wall—and then suddenly the dark barrier of the baffle was looming up in front of me. I steered to the right, held Ricia's limp body close to me, shot past the open valve and out into the murky turbulence of freedom.

✧   ✧   ✧

I groped over the slight body in my arms, tried to find her wrist, to check her pulse, but my hands were clumsy with cold. In the beam of the hand light, an immense and curious fish swam close, shot away as I waved an arm. At one hundred feet, I felt a twinge in my left elbow, then a sharp pain at the base of my skull. The rapid ascent was equivalent to explosive decompression—a trick that could transform a healthy man into a broken cripple in a matter of seconds. It would have been nice to spend a couple of hours in a timed ascent.

I bent my arm against the pain in the joint, read the depth gauge. Fifty-one feet, forty-six, forty, thirty-two—

Pain like a hot knife seared the back of my right leg, clamped my ankle in a vise of agony. I held on, forced my eyes open against pressure that was forcing them from their sockets.

I shot clear of the surface, fell back in a cage of pain that wrenched at every joint in my body like a farmer wringing the necks of chickens. I got a quick flash of lights bobbing across the water, then found the jet control. I steered with my legs, aiming for the glitter of the chrome-plated ladder over the boat's stern, caught it, held on, while a red haze shot with lightning closed down over my brain. Then a hand was on my arm, hauling at me.

"Ricia. . . . get her—decompression chamber. . . ." I could feel my tongue slurring the words. Then her weight was gone from my arm. Hands hauled me up over the rail and onto the deck. Warm air struck my face as the helmet was pulled off, all in a silence broken only by the high hum that had rung in my head since the explosion. My eyes were balls of white-hot pain, spikes driven into my brain.

I made a move to get up, and the hands lifted me. Then I was on my back, feeling a deep hammer of air against me. I groped, found the cold curve of Ricia's cheek. Quite suddenly, the pain eased, like a thorn pulled from a wound. I took a breath, tasted the metallic flavor of the air, almost laughed as I realized that for an hour I had forgotten the odor of volcanoes.

Then the smell and the lights and the pain faded, and I sank down into regions of warmth and forgetfulness.

Chapter Ten

Consciousness was a long time returning, like an old soldier who has forgotten the way home. I was aware of the pain in my head first, then of other pains. My eyes hurt with a burning, purple agony. I opened them against pressure, saw the light in the ceiling of the decompression tank as a blurry puffball. I tried an arm; it seemed to work all right. I used it to push myself up to a sitting position. Ricia lay on her face beside me, wrapped in a blanket. For a heart-stopping instant my hand against her lips felt nothing; then a faint breath of warm air came. She was breathing.

I got to my feet, crouched under the low curve of the tank. My right knee was swollen and numb. I put my face close to the pressure gauges on the wall, made out the shape of the long needle resting square on 14.6 PSI. It would be safe to open now. I went to the closed entry hatch, tugged at the handle; I was as weak as watered booze. I started to hammer on the wall to let Carmody know I was up and around, but something stopped me. I stood with my fist raised, wondering what it was.

Then I got it; the boat was wallowing in a cross-chop. We were still at sea. My watch said twenty minutes till five—nearly seven hours since I had started my swim. What had Carmody not run us back into port, gotten Ricia to a medic? And why was the boat drifting, broadside to the swell?"

I tried the handle again; this time it budged. I brought it around in a full turn to release the pressure latch, and the door popped free, swung in half an inch. I looked out at gray dawn light, the bleached teak of the deck, and the lower legs and feet of a man lying face down six feet from me. I eased the door shut, reached for the spear pistol; it was gone—lost in the scramble through the sewer, no doubt.

I let five minutes go by, the slow way; then I cracked the door again, took another look at the legs. My vision was like steamed glass, but they looked like Carmody's rope-soled shoes. The boat was silent, except for the hum that was still with me. Maybe I was deaf, the thought hit me. I held my fingers to my ear and rubbed them together; I could faintly hear the sound.

I stepped out, keeping ducked behind the decomp tank, closed the hatch behind me, looked over toward the man on the deck. It was Carmody, all right, and he was very dead. Twenty miles from land, the flies had already found him.

Rassias was forward, lying on his back with his head in the scuppers, shot through the right eye. Near him there was a patch of rusty-looking blood on the scarred deck, a trail of blood leading to the rail. Someone with a hole in him had gone over the side.

I had been moving carefully, barefooted—but not carefully enough. The back of a man's head appeared just as I turned, coming up from below. I dropped to a crouch, moved in close to the deckhouse, crept on back until I could risk a quick look. He was standing two feet away, looking back across the stern. In another half-second he would turn; I could tell by the set of his shoulders. Before he could move, I jumped. My bum knee gave under me and I missed his back, slammed against his hip as he jumped aside. I hit the deck hard, rolled, came up facing him. His gun was out, coming down to an aiming point six inches below my chin. He had a thoughtful, intent expression on his face, like a billiards champ lining up for a two-banker.

"No. Keep this one alive for the present." I heard the call through the hum. A second man came up from the gloom of the cabin. I blinked, trying to get a clear view of his face. I was not sure, but I thought I had seen him before—maybe in Miami.

The fellow with the gun lowered it, tucked it away. He looked like a schoolteacher—a medium-sized, medium-aged man with thinning hair, a little plump around the middle, dressed in a rumpled tan suit. The other had the carefully mournful expression of a coffin salesman. His suit was a dusty black. They stood looking at me for a moment, then the gun handler turned away.

"I will find ropes to tie him with." He spoke flawless English with a faint foreign flavor. I had the feeling he could do the same in twelve other languages.

The man who was watching me stood like a bored commuter waiting for a bus. He did not smoke, did not scowl, did not twitch. He just stood there. He looked easy to take. I sat up slowly and his hand flicked, brought out a gun.

"Take off the belt," he said flatly. I unbuckled it, heavy with gear.

"Throw it over the side," he commanded. I was looking straight up the barrel of the gun. He must have been the one who shot Rassias; he liked eye shots. I did as he told me.

"Take off the suit," he said.

I got to my feet, moving very slowly, unzipped the cold-suit, pulled it off, not without a certain amount of groaning. My bones felt as though they had been taken out and pounded.

"Throw it away." I bundled it up and tossed it over the rail. That left me my underwear and my natural dignity.

He put the gun away; I was harmless now. The other fellow came back and told me to lie down. I did. I was in a cooperative mood this morning. It was chilly on deck; I shivered while cold, smooth hands took three turns of half-inch nylon around my ankles, cinched them up tight enough to hurt, knotted the rope. Then I rolled over on my face while they did my hands. They walked away, left me lying face down on the deck in a puddle of ice-cold water.

I flip-flopped, pulled myself aft another yard, twisted over for a look. The two men stood together by the deckhouse, staring out over the port rail. The boat wallowed, drifting with the wind. Carmody lay where they had left him, attended only by the buzzing insects, one of which flew back to check me, decided not yet, and went away.

A steel storage box was bolted to the deck two feet from my head. I hunched my way back until I could see behind it. The canvas-wrapped gun case I had brought aboard was still there. I tried the ropes on my wrists; they gave a little; nylon is no good for some jobs. I could just touch one knot with my fingertips. I teased it, got a few strands started. Half a minute later the knot bulged, flopped free. Another five minutes and I was rubbing my hands together behind me, trying to work the stiffness out of fingers as cold and insensitive as frozen fishsticks.

The boys up front were ignoring me. One was pointing, and I followed his finger, saw a big, dark-painted boat coming up fast off the port bow. Sunlight winked from a big searchlight on its foredeck, and there were bulky, tarpaulin-covered shapes that would be deck guns. It looked like a revenue cutter on a business trip. My boys did not act worried; they stood indifferently, waiting for it.

I slipped a hand over behind the box, dragged the gun case toward me, unsnapped the flap, got a grip on the butt of the nearest weapon, pulled it half out, froze when the schoolteacher looked my way. I flopped, faked a futile effort to sit up. He watched me for a moment, went back to watching the boat. It was close enough for me to hear it now; the big engines were throttled back, growling as she swung past, coming around to the upwind side. She looked bigger than ever, up close—five hundred tons at least. There were half a dozen men at the rail. One of them shouted, and the coffin salesman waved a hand in a stiff gesture. The faint hope that the law had arrived died.

Both my keepers had their backs to me now. I snaked the gun clear of the case, brought it over into my lap. It was the Weatherby .375 repeater, a good gun for an elephant. I had loaded it before the trip. Lying on my back, with the gun on my chest, I snicked off the safety, raised my head far enough to sight, lined up on the schoolteacher's back, and squeezed off a round. The recoil hit my right cheekbone like a baseball bat, and my target leaped forward, went down out of sight. The other man whirled, bringing out his gun. I swung the sights over, found his face, fired again, caught a glimpse of a red explosion where his head had been.

Men were running on the deck of the cutter. I saw a bright flash, heard a ricochet whine past me. I dumped the Weatherby, hauled the gun case out, stripped it from the chrome steel and black plastic of the big military high-speed job, jacked the lever over to full automatic and dived for the shelter of the rail.

Shots were hitting all around me now; one ploughed a dark streak in the salt-bleached deck near my face. I spat splinters, poked the snout of my gun out through a hawse hole, took aim at the gunboat's water line, and squeezed. There was a roar like a gut-shot tyrannosaurus, but my gun was a sweet weapon. Except for a mule kick straight into my shoulder, it rode as smoothly as a cap pistol, poured out its magazine in one furious burst that hammered against my dulled ears like a cotton-padded alarm clock, and was abruptly silent. I dropped it and rolled right, heard the dull spang of bullets hitting the steel spray shield by my head. Looking forward, I saw paint chips from the rail, splinters shower from the deck. They were laying down a barrage like a battalion of infantry.

I hugged the deck and waited. Shots kept hitting around me; one smacked metal an inch from my face, punched a finger-tip-sized dent, scattered paint dust in my face. I could see the Weatherby lying ten feet away; a bullet had gouged the stock. If my try with the burp gun had not done the job, the cutter would be looking up alongside in another few seconds.

I watched where the shots were hitting; I was not sure, but the fire seemed to be falling off, the gouges in the deck moving away, getting longer, as from low-angle fire. I inched back to the hawsehole, risked a look. The cutter was hove to, a hundred feet off the starboard bow. Her high, sharp prow was toward me. I could not see the side I had fired a thousand rounds of armor-piercing slugs into, but there seemed to be a slight list to starboard.

The shooting stopped suddenly. I watched as men swarmed around the forward deck gun, pulling the canvas cover from it. It was time to try for the elephant gun. I made it in a dive, rolled, scrambled for cover. Nobody fired.

I crawled along the deck to my loophole, lay flat behind it, drew a bead on the man on top of the .88 millimeter. The report was a flat crack. He went down like a blown-over scarecrow. A shoulder was showing to the left of the gun. I shot at it and it went away. Someone was running across the deck, I led him two feet, fired, missed, and he ducked out of sight. Another fellow popped up, reached for the breech lever; I knocked him flying. The cutter was definitely listing now. She had swung around, showing her port side. Nobody was moving near the guns.

When the cutter was a hundred yards away, I fired my last two rounds, heard them ring off the gun's shield, then snaked across to the deckhouse and down the two steps to the cockpit. I tried the starter. The diesels groaned, fired, caught. I kept low, swung her away to port, opened the throttles and she put her nose up and dug in. I worked the wheel hard, putting her into sliding turns to left and right, but it was a full minute before the first round from the cutter's gun fountained ahead, a wide miss. She fired twice more, then gave it up. When I came up for air, the cutter was a mile astern, very low by the bow, wallowing in the swells.

The lopsided orange sun of morning was glaring across the water now, painting red streaks on the waves. I corrected course to put the sun at my back, set the automatic pilot and went aft to the decomp tank to see about Ricia.

She was awake, looking wan and thinner than ever, but she smiled when she saw me, said something in a voice too faint to hear.

"Sorry, kid," I said. My voice sounded strange in my ears, like a bad recording playing in the next apartment. "I can't hear you. Too many loud noises too close to my eardrums lately. How do you feel?"

She shook her head, pointed to her ears. She was as deaf as I was. I put a hand against her forehead; she seemed to be about the right temperature. Her pulse felt good, strong and steady.

"I'll get you some soup." In the galley I opened a can, boiled water, fixed up a tray with toast and a glass of orange juice. She almost sat up when she saw it, but I could tell the effort hurt. I propped her up on cushions from the cabin, spoon-fed her. She ate like a starved kitten. When the soup was gone, she lifted an arm that seemed too heavy for her, touched my face. I saw her lips move, but all I caught was "Mal." Then she touched her eyes. There were dark lines around them—bruises, from blood vessels broken by the sudden pressure drop when we surfaced. I got her to move her arms and legs; they seemed all right.

We had both been lucky. Aside from a few more spots no more painful than bad sprains, we had survived the bends in good shape. I wanted to move her to the cabin, but at the moment I was not up to lifting anything heavier than a soup spoon. I tucked her in, checked to be sure the ventilator was working, went down into the cabin and collapsed on the bunk.

When I woke, I had the feeling it was late afternoon. I got my feet on the floor, tottered over to the wall mirror. The face that peered out at me looked like something they keep in a cage at second-rate carnies and feed live chickens to, four shows a day. Both eyes were purple-black, swollen almost shut. There was caked blood in my hair, in the black stubble across my jaws. What showed of the rest was a dirty gray.

I sluiced my head in cold water, then hot, got out Carmody's razor and shaved. The shower could wait until I had checked on Ricia. She was awake, showing a little color in her cheeks now. I made more soup, brought her hot water and soap and a comb, then went back down and used up a tank of hot water on myself. Carmody's clothes were a little large for me, but I rolled the cuffs of a shirt and a pair of denim pants and went up on deck to do what had to be done.

Carmody was heavy; it took me five minutes to get him to the rail and over. I saw one arm flash for an instant above the water, as though he were waving good-by. He had been a good man, and he had died helping me, no questions asked. I hated to deal so callously with his body, but it was hot out here and Ricia would be coming on deck soon.

Rassias was easier. Afterward I used a bucket of salt water to wash down the deck. The flies seemed annoyed; they buzzed angrily around my head while I worked. I finished and the sun shone down, red and sullen, on a shipshape deck.

I checked our course and position. We were holding due west, and in another hour I would be sighting the coast of Africa south of Tunis—unless it had dropped out of sight since the last time I had passed this way. Ricia was still stretched out on the floor of the tank; it was the coolest place on the boat, and the air was clean. The same unit that pumped it up to pressure filtered and chilled it.

"We'll be in port soon," I told her. "I'll get a doctor there and in a few days you'll feel fine. Then we can head somewhere— wherever you like. We've got plenty of supplies for a long cruise." I did not say anything about the leaky palazzo on the sea bottom; it was already beginning to seem like something out of a fever dream. As far as I was concerned, the score was about even. I had gotten Ricia out and saved my own neck. I was sorry about Carmody—and Rassias. But they were dead, along with a lot of odd little men whose role in life I would never discover now— and did not want to. Ricia and I were alive. My modest ambition was to keep it that way.

An hour after noon I sighted a long brown line rising out of a sea as flat as a ballroom floor. Fifteen minutes later we were threading our way into a harbor choked with wreckage like a vacant lot filled with junked cars. One of the typhoons that had swept the area had caught a lot of shipping in port.

We tied up at a quay that showed some signs of life—stacks of red-painted fuel drums, a floating crane, piled crates, half a dozen lounging men who caught the bow line, made it fast. I had already told Ricia I would leave the boat just long enough to find a doctor. I jumped down on the pier, flashed a ten-cee note, asked who spoke English. A fellow with a mustache like a GI shoebrush pushed through, took the ten, showed me a set of teeth like broken earthenware.

"I speak, you bet. You want woman?" He was the kind of linguist who shouts to make his meaning clear, which was a break for me.

"I need a doctor," I explained.

He nodded vigorously. He had a rag tied around his head like Gunga Din. "Best doctor, fix you up good, you catch something from woman." He led me up the wharf, across a noisy street of white dust into the mouth of a narrow way that snaked around an outthrust angle of ancient masonry, narrowed still further into a covered stair between mossy walls. At the top, I caught a glimpse of him darting into a doorway across a courtyard of broken brick. Halfway to it, I realized something was wrong.

It was another fifty feet to the doorway; to the left of it was another arch like the one I had come in through. I kept going, at the last moment whirled left and ran for it. It was a nice try, but useless. A small man in a dirty brown suit stepped from my sanctuary, spread his arms. I hit him full tilt, kept my feet just long enough to see the club the fellow behind him swung at my head before all the lights went out.

Waking up this time was bad. I had not felt too well before the latest crack on the skull; now I hurt all over again, from the soles of my feet to the lump over my ear. The throbbing in my head should have been audible at fifty yards and the pain in my stomach told me I had been retching even before I came to. I seemed to be lying on a bench in a room that was hot and close.

"How do you feel?" an indifferent voice said from somewhere in the surrounding misery. I got an eyelid up, looked at a neatly dressed fellow with thin hair parted on the center line, a face like a brown prune, a scrawny neck I would have enjoyed squeezing.

"Like a pulled tooth," I said. My tongue was as thick as a pastrami sandwich, but I could hear myself a little better now. Maybe I would recover my hearing in time to listen to my own last words.

"Where is the woman?" Prune Face asked. I got the feeling he did not really care how I felt after all.

"What woman?"

Someone on the other side of me made a sudden move, was checked by a bark from Brownie.

"Now you're playing it smart," I congratulated him. "Any more rough stuff now and I'll be singing in a heavenly choir instead of into your brown, shell-like ear."

"When you have told me where you have left the woman, your wound will be attended."

"Which one?"

"The woman whom you abducted. Do not waste our time."

"I meant which wound? I've got a variety."

"Your boat has been searched. Since she is not aboard, it is apparent that you put into port and placed her ashore. It will save us time and trouble if you will state where this took place."

"Sure. Why should I make trouble for myself over a slip of a girl? I made a high-speed run over to the mudflats off Athens and dumped her over the side. A nice walk to shore."

"You are lying."

"That's right."

"Where is the woman?"

"You're not cops?"

"That has no bearing on the question."

"Like hell. If you're cops I'm not admitting anything. You might call it murder and make trouble for me."

"You are already in trouble. But we are not police."

"OK. I dumped her."

"Why?"

"She didn't want to play."

"Play?"

"Do I have to draw you a picture?"

"You abducted the woman for this purpose?"

"Why else?"

Prune Face conferred briefly with two other voices which floated around behind me, out of sight. The language they used sounded like Chinese to me. Maybe it *was* Chinese. Whatever it was, it did not seem to be a clue.

"Let me attempt pain techniques," a new voice said in English.

"That is not practical."

"He would survive long enough to speak."

"Not this type. He will die. There is no time for experimentation."

Someone said something in the other language but Prunie cut him off short.

"No," he said in a tone of flat finality. "The decision has been made. Take him to the courtyard and cut his throat."

Chapter Eleven

Fatigue is a wonderful thing. They had to wake me up five minutes later—or maybe later than that; I did not check my watch—to get me to my feet, walk me along a white-washed galley with one side open to a stormy sky, down crooked stairs to a rectangle of hard-baked mud surrounded by lofty, cracked walls. The whole proceeding did not interest me much. As soon as they let go, I sat down hard. Somebody issued orders in a flat voice, like a bank examiner asking for the books, and businesslike hands pulled me to my feet again. It seemed that around here you only got your throat cut standing up. I wondered if the knife would be sharp, if it would hurt much; but the questions seemed academic. I had the feeling that must come to the stag at the end of a long run, an almost grateful relief that it was all over.

The hard hands on my arms bothered me. I made an effort, got my knees locked to take the weight. The walls seemed to be going around me in a smooth procession like the view from a merry-go-round. Dust choked me and I coughed. The sun was hot in the enclosed space where no breeze could move. The pleasant lassitude was wearing off while they talked, on and on. Suddenly I was shaking. I started to fall and my escort grabbed my arms again. In another second I was going to be a very sick man.

Then the hands were hauling at me, and somehow my legs were moving, and they were taking me away. It got shady and almost cool, and my feet scrabbled, trying to keep up. There was daylight again suddenly, and I hit my head on something and the pain pierced the fog long enough for me to get a glimpse of a car's interior, all gray leather and inlaid Circassian walnut. Someone shoved at me, and I was wedged in between two fattish men who smelled of sweat and curry. I felt the car start up, jolt a couple of times pulling out across rough ground. A voice that I had heard before was talking: " . . . . the instruction of the Primary."

"This one is of no importance. The space—"

"That is my decision."

Then it all dissolved into a glowing fog and I let go and sank into it. . . .

✧   ✧   ✧

. . . . And awoke to the same old nightmare of hands that hauled
me, made me walk with legs like broken soda straws down stairs,
across pavements from which the heat of day glared, along echoing
boards with the slap of water near. Then there was the smell of
sea water and corruption, the lift and surge of a boat, the grumble
and roar of engines, and spray that fell on my face in an irregular rhythm. Voices spoke around me, sometimes in English, sometimes in French or German or Russian, sometimes in dialects I
had never heard before, weaving themselves into strange dreams
of pursuit and revenge. My arms and legs and back ached with
a screaming fatigue that was almost, but not quite enough, to shatter the drugged semi-consciousness that I clung to like a lost child
hugging a teddy bear.

And then I was in a cool place, dim-lit, and the hands were
lifting me, and I was lying on my back and cold indifferent hands
were touching my face, my scalp, and there was the sting of cold
steel against my arm and the sounds and sensations whirled away
into a blackness filled with lights that swirled and died and I slept.

Someone was prodding my foot. I opened my eyes, saw a pale-
faced man in immaculate whites standing over me. He had soft
features, rimless glasses that caught the light, tufts of ginger hair
over each ear.

"Your food is here," he said briskly. "You will feed yourself."

I caught a whiff of meat and vegetables from a tray on a cart
by the bed. Beyond it were the plain white walls of a small room,
a brown dresser with a square mirror, the corner of a narrow
louvered door, another door half open on the stainless-steel bathroom fittings. I was still dizzy; the bed seemed to lift under me,
pause, drop gently back.

"Where am I, in a hospital?" I was surprised to hear my voice
come out in a high-pitched whisper.

"Sit up," the man in white commanded. I got my hands under
me, pushed, and my attendant shoved pillows down behind me.
Then he lifted the tray and placed it across my lap, supported
on four wire legs. I did not wait for further urging—my stomach felt as hollow as Yorick's skull. My arm was a little heavy,
but I managed to get a grip on the spoon, dig into the stew.
Someone had left the salt out, but otherwise it was just what

my tissues were screaming for. I ate it all, while the orderly stood by, saying nothing. When I had finished the last bite, he lifted the tray and disappeared without looking back.

I dozed some more, had another meal, watched the reddish light fade into gloom. I had a vague feeling there were things I was not doing, but I did not want to think about that just now. I had a bed, food, and solitude. For now, that was enough.

Light glared abruptly. The door thumped open and a man with a wrinkled brown face came through it, walked over to stare down at me. It was a face I had seen before, in unpleasant circumstances.

"Will you tell me where the woman is now?" he asked in the tone of a hash-house waiter taking an order.

"What woman?"

"The woman you abducted—you know quite well what I mean."

"You've got a one-track mind. I thought you were having my throat cut. What happened, lose your nerve?"

"My instructions were overruled. You are to receive special interrogation. You will save yourself from acute discomfort if you speak up now."

"Don't scare me; I'm a sick man."

"You are quite recovered from the concussion. Your scalp wound has been dressed and drugs have been administered to hasten healing of the decompression damage. You are now able to withstand prolonged questioning."

"How long have I been here?"

"I will answer no questions."

"You want answers, don't you?"

"Yes. Where—"

"I said how long have I been here?"

He looked at me; wheels seemed to be turning behind his unremarkable face. "Three days."

"Where am I?"

"Aboard an ocean-going vessel."

"Bound where?"

"I will answer no more questions. Now, where did you land the woman?"

"What woman?"

"You implied that you would cooperate if I answered your questions."

"I'm tricky."

He turned and walked out of the room and I noticed the sharp *snick!* of the lock behind him. He had told me more than he thought. Three days had passed and they had not yet found Ricia. The decompression tank on Carmody's boat was a home-built job; at a glance it looked like what it had started life as, a five-hundred-gallon auxiliary fuel tank. If you did not know about the hatch at the aft end, you would never think to look inside for a sick woman. From what I had seen of the deadly little men who were hunting her, they were curiously lacking in the imagination department.

But even if they had not found her, that did not mean she was in the clear. She had been as weak as a new-born fawn when I left her. Assuming she had lain low, weathered the search, let herself out of the tank—then what? She had no clothes but an oversized coverall, no money, could not speak any language she would be likely to encounter in North Africa. And she was still a sick girl, lacking the cozy comforts I had been enjoying.

That was the kind of thinking that can break you out in a cold sweat, while producing no useful results. I had done my best, and it had not been good enough. At least she was not in the hands of these reptile-blooded goons. I would have to settle for that for now.

Meanwhile, I had problems of my own. Prune Face had said we were aboard ship; that was something to check. I pushed back the sheet, discovered I had no clothes. I swung my legs over the side and stood up, swaying a little, but feeling better than I had expected. The medicine was doing its job.

It was a long walk to the porthole eight feet away. I made it, looked out at swift-moving dark waves, the reflections of lights shining somewhere above. The story checked, as far as it went, and it ended right here.

I went back to bed puffing like a mountain climber. When my next meal came, just after daylight, I ate it all and asked for more. My waiter this time was a lath-thin lad of about eighteen with a pulpy complexion and the dead, unquestioning eyes of a carp. He shook his head to my question, reached for the tray. I grabbed his wrist.

"I want more food, Bright Eyes," I told him. He pulled, and I held on.

"Bring me more chow or I'll raise hell."

"You have had the meal prepared for you."

"The Big Boy wouldn't like it if I raised hell, would he? He might think you were at fault. In fact, I'll tell him you were. I'll tell him you made a deal with me and then reneged."

"That is not true." He did not seem very strong; weak as I was, I held him.

"*You* know it's not true and *I* know it's not true, but the Big Boy won't. He'll believe me. I wouldn't be surprised if he had your throat cut. That's what he does with people he doesn't need."

"I will tell him it is not true."

"Don't you care if he kills you?"

The boy thought it over. "I have not yet propagated," he said.

"Tough—and you never will—unless you bring me some more of this nice breakfast slop. You can work it; just ask for it."

"Very well. Let go of my arm."

I dropped his wrist, leaned back and watched the little bright lights whirl round and round. This was a funny bunch I was mixed up with. I had met some cold fish in my time, but never before whole schools of them.

He came back in ten minutes with the food. I ate it—not that it was good—then gave the boy a nasty smile.

"If I tell old Prune Face you brought me more rations than you were ordered to, he'll dump you overboard without waiting to cut your throat."

"You will tell him?" The kid stared at me.

"Not unless I have to. All I want is the answers to a few little questions. Like where's this tub bound?"

"I can answer no question." He reached for the tray.

"Better think it over," I said. "What will it hurt if I know where we're going?"

"I can tell you nothing." He took the tray and turned to the door.

"Think about it. I'll give you till lunch time. If you don't answer my question I'll yell for the big shot and tell him the whole story. He'll see to it you never propagate."

He hesitated, went on out. I flopped back and watched the door close behind him.

He was a little late with the lunch tray. I waited until he had placed it just so, then braced him.

"I have learned where we are bound," he said. "If I tell you, you will not report my deviation from instructions?"

"I won't tell him about the extra bowl of gruel."

"Our destination is Gonwondo."

"Where's that? Somewhere in Africa?"

"No."

"Come on, don't stall me, Junior. Where is it?"

"We sail south for nine days."

"South? We've passed Suez?"

"Yes."

"Nine days south—that takes you past the Cape, out into open sea. There's nothing down there but icebergs and penguins. Unless...." I stopped babbling and stared at him. He stared back.

"Sure," I said. "It figures. Antarctica."

I did not push my new contact too hard. The evening meal went by with no quiz session; he watched me but did not comment. When he was gone, I climbed out of bed and paced the cabin until the singing started up in my head again, then slept like a corpse until breakfast. When I was almost finished with the mess—like a soupy oatmeal—I looked up and caught the boy's eye.

"Who runs this ship?"

He made an uncomfortable motion. "We do."

"Who are 'we'?"

"*You* are not one of us."

"Who are you, then?"

He gave me the cold eye. I tried a new tack. "Why are they after the girl?"

"I know nothing about a girl."

"What do they expect me to tell them?"

"I cannot speak of these things."

"Ah-ah, I'll tell Prune Face all about how we're going to dock in Antarctica in nine days. He'll be annoyed with you. Your only chance to propagate is to tell me what I want to know."

He was getting a glazed, resigned look. He turned, started for the door.

"Hold it," I called after him. "Think about it before you put your head on the block. What does it matter if you answer a few questions? As soon as we get there, I'll know where we are, and I'll know how long it's taken. What's the big secret?"

He turned to look at me. "My instructions are to speak no more than is necessary."

"For you, boy, it's necessary to speak to me."

He had to think that one out. "Yes," he announced. "That is true."

"They aren't shanghaiing me halfway across the globe just to ask me where I hid the girl; they could beat that out of me and we all know it. If she's not clear of where I left her now, she never will be. So what's the real interest in me?"

"I do not know."

"Find out."

"That is not possible."

"I said find out."

The fish eyes blinked at me.

"I will try."

He had news for me at lunch. "You will be taken to the hidden place for questioning."

"About what? And why don't they question me here?"

"You will tell them how you knew the location of the Secret Place. There are machines at Gonwondo which will force you to speak."

"Machines, huh? Thumbscrews? The iron maiden?"

The boy made motions indicating large size. "Great machines. They have no name."

"All right, you're doing fine, Junior. I think you may get to propagate after all, if you keep it up. Now I want to know all about the landing procedure: where this ship will dock, what kind of country, how far inland they plan to take me—the works."

"I know nothing of these things."

"Sure, but you can learn. And, by the way, you can spread the word that I'm pretty weak. It's all I can do to make it to the head and back."

He took the tray and left. I put in another half hour of pacing, then tried a few arm-swinging exercises. The soreness was going out of my joints gradually; the right knee was the worst. Aside from a little lost weight, shaky hands, and a tendency for my head to ache, I was pretty well recovered from a harrowing weekend.

At the evening feeding Junior gave me a little more data: we would drop anchor offshore and go in by landing craft. It would be a half a day's run over land to the Hidden Place.

"How big are these landing craft? How many men will they carry?"

He did not know. Junior had a lot of objectionable qualities, but curiosity wasn't one of them. When he left this time, I checked the door. The lock was not much—just a thumb latch that had had the lever removed from the inside. I pried a strip of walnut veneer from the edge of the bureau, used it to jimmy the mechanism, then jam it open. I eased the door open, took a quick look out, saw a narrow passage, red lights gleaming on polished wood paneling, closed doors. There was no sound but the thud of far-away engines. It looked like as good a time as any for a little scouting expedition. I slid out, barefooted it along to the next door, reached for the knob, then rattled my knuckles on the panel instead, ready to run at the first sound. No response. I pushed the door open and stepped inside.

It was another bare little room, with a bare mattress on the bunk, bare hangers in the closet. I ducked out, tried the next, found it locked. So were the next three.

The last cabin on the right was a big room with two beds, a wide closet with more empty hangers and a dusty felt hat on the shelf. The bedside table yielded hairpins, a pencil, some hard chewing gum. The dresser drawers were empty. In the bathroom I looked into an empty medicine cabinet, a laundry box with one sock forgotten in the bottom, a paper carton on the floor that had once contained soap. A slot beside the sink caught my eye; I poked carefully with one of my hairpins, lifted out two reasonably rusty double-edged blades for an old-type manual razor.

I dumped my loot in the hat, made it back to my cubicle without getting caught. Finding a hiding place gave me a little trouble; I tucked it all under the mattress finally, dropped on the bed and panted like a mile runner. I was not as strong as I thought I was.

I made my next foray after midnight, had a bad moment when feet clumped past in the hall while I flattened myself against the wall of a four-man cell forty feet along the corridor from my own room. They faded out and nothing happened. I resisted the impulse to dash back and pull the covers up to my chin, checked the closet instead. The shelf and bar were empty, and in the darkness I almost missed the coat wadded into a ball and kicked into a back corner. It was a heavy, dark-blue waterproof, much worn and blotched with salt-water stains. It was a few sizes small for me, but better than nudity in a pinch. Nobody nabbed me getting to my room with it. I spread it under the mattress and went to sleep to dream of dramatic escapes in which overcoats, chewed gum, and bare feet played vital roles.

Junior seemed to be even more listless than usual the next morning.

"Cheer up," I urged him. "You're a cinch to propagate now; I'm not asking any more questions, so all you have to do is carry on in your usual light-hearted fashion."

He did not answer. I did not like the beaten look on his face. He was going to need his morale boosted to shape him up for my next demands.

"Yes, sir, Junior, you should follow my example: *you* have propagating to look forward to—that's more than *I* can say. I don't suppose I'll last long once those machines get their gears on me."

He gave me a furtive, almost puzzled look. That was better than no reaction at all. I pursued the line I had taken.

"Yep, there you'll be, propagating like mad, and I'll be feeding the fish. You'll be way ahead of me, Junior. I never propagated myself, but I'm sure that to a fellow with an interest in that sort of thing, a family is hard to beat.

"You have never propagated?"

"Not even once."

His mouth opened and closed. "You are aware that your existence will soon end," he said. He seemed to be talking to himself, not to me. "It is for that reason that you behave as you do."

"I guess you're right."

"Even now, you weaken when you should regain your strength. It is because your hope of propagation is lost."

"You've put your finger on it, Junior," I encouraged him. "Whereas you—"

"I must inform my Secondary of these conclusions," he said abruptly, and started for the door—the first time he had turned his back on the tray. I whipped the spoon under the sheet and called, "Just a minute, Junior, don't do anything hasty. You want to think this thing all the way through first."

He hesitated, with his hand on the doorknob.

"If you tell him, he'll want to know how you found out. He'll discover you've been talking to me, and the next thing you know, *skrtt!*" I made a slashing motion across my throat.

He thought that over. "That is true. But it is my duty to report this information."

"Your duty to whom?"

"I must report to my Secondary." He turned the knob.

"What about propagating?" I was just stalling now; the situation had suddenly slipped out of hand. If I could get him close enough to jump him, I might be able to brain him and then sell the Big Boys a story that he had fallen and cracked his skull. If he reported our little talks, my last hope of pulling a surprise was gone.

"Yes, I have also the duty to propagate. . . ." His voice sounded a little faint; I followed up my advantage.

"Sure, it's your duty to propagate! And that's a higher duty than this other thing. You've got to do everything in your power to succeed in propagating! Spilling the beans to Big Boy right now is the worst thing you could do!"

"I must report to my Secondary—but I must also propagate." Junior's loose lower lip was working like a worm on a hook. I had a feeling his wiring would burn through any moment.

"But there's a solution," I said.

"What is the solution?"

"First propagate; *then* tell your Secondary!"

Again the pause to consider. The lip was limp now, catching its breath. Junior gulped hard. He was a very upset lad.

"The information will be of no value unless—"

"Details," I cut him off. "You're going to report, just as soon as you've attended to the more important duty of propagating. That's all you need to think about."

"Yes." Junior was almost brisk now. "That is all I need to think about."

That night I made a reconnoiter beyond the end of the corridor, following a fore-and-aft passage that ended in a companionway leading up. At the top, I found a small room where clothes hung on pegs. I helped myself to a wool cap, a set of formerly white dungarees, a pair of knee-high plastic boots, turned to start back down and heard voices coming closer. There was a dark corner at the end of the hanging clothes. I slid into it, much aware of my pale, bare legs showing below the garments.

Feet clumped up the stair; grunting voices spoke to each other in a strange dialect. I practiced not breathing. An outer door opened and icy, blustery wind whipped the skirts of a plastic slicker against my legs. Someone came in, stamping his feet. The closing door cut off the howl of the wind.

"There is much ice," a new voice said.

Someone answered in the gobbling language they had been speaking before the interruption.

"The Primary directs that the landing craft be brought on deck tomorrow."

More gibberish. The tone suggested a half-hearted complaint.

"It will be necessary to conduct the transfer within the ice field. The vehicles must be available for prompt landing."

Again the reply, this time a long harangue. The English-speaking one cut it off with a curt order: "See that the vehicles are in place on Number Two hatch within twelve hours."

There were a few mutters, then sounds of feet thumping down the companionway. I waited five minutes, then ducked out and reached my cabin just as voices sounded at the far end of the passage. There was no time to hide my new finds. I tossed the bundle into the closet, leaped for the bunk, got the sheet up to my chin as the door banged wide. Junior was there, with a fattish, middle-aged man with wide-set pale eyes and thin lips like a chimpanzee.

"What has this one told you?" he asked me. He did not sound as though he cared much.

"Told me?" I registered the astonishment. "Nothing. He wouldn't even give me the time of day. I figured the damned fool couldn't talk."

"He did not speak to you of our destination?"

"You must be mixed up. I talked to him about our destination. I know what it is, too. You fellows can't fool me."

"What is our destination?"

"Australia," I said promptly. "Only place it could be."

"This one said nothing to you of. . . . other matters?"

"How could he? He doesn't speak English."

"*Verstehen Sie Deutsch?*" he said quickly.

"Huh?"

"*Est-ce-que vous parlez français?*"

I frowned darkly. "Don't horse around. Talk American."

"You speak only English?"

"Why not? It's the best language there is. I—"

"And you are certain this one told you nothing?"

"Look, I tried to get him to tell me his name; he wouldn't even do that."

"Why did you wish to know his name?"

"So I could call him by it."

"Why was it necessary for you to call him by a specific name?"

"That way he'd know who I was talking to."

"But if he were alone here with you there would be no possibility of confusion."

"That's why I call him Junior."

"Explain that."

"He knows I mean him, because he's the only one here."

The wide, pale eyes blinked at me, the apelike lips twitched thoughtfully. Then both callers turned and walked out. I stared at the door after it closed, wondering what sort of idiot's conversation I had stumbled into. Then I remembered Carmody, lying on deck with his face blasted away, and Rassias, and the blank look on Sethys' face as he turned his gun on me, and the others—all the way back to Greenleaf, Georgia. If they were maniacs, they were of the homicidal variety.

My next meal was brought by a new man who looked like a CPA retired after forty years with the company.

"What happened to Junior?" I asked him. He did not seem to hear me. I let it pass, ate my bowl of mush and watched him leave. On the way out he checked the latch, seemed satisfied, went on. I had not liked him much. Maybe he was a plant, sent in to see what kind of questions I was likely to ask. Maybe Junior would be back on duty for the next meal. I hoped so; I had plans for him.

But again there was a new face. This one could have belonged to a small-town mail carrier. I did not say a word to him, and he did not break the silence. After dinner, I did my regular stint of pacing. Nobody interrupted me; no feet passed in the corridor. I had an eerie sensation that they had all left the ship, that I was here alone—but I did not stick my head out to find out. Instinct said this would be a good time to lie low and play dumb.

✧　　✧　　✧

Sometimes during the night I was flung awake by a tremendous rumbling crash that nearly pitched me out on the floor. I hit the deck expecting to see green water pouring through the door, but aside from a few running feet in the distance, there was no reaction. It was an iceberg, I decided. Half an hour later there was another impact, not as bad as the first. I listened at the door, heard a few shouts, some distant thumps, more feet. The ship seemed to be coming to life; we were arriving somewhere, two days ahead of Junior's schedule. It was time for me to make a move.

I dug out my odds and ends of garments, used the blanket from the bed to wrap my feet before putting on the boots, pulled on the coverall, the coat and the wool hat. I tucked my other things away in a pocket—the hairpins and spoon and razor blades, not forgetting the Wrigley's Triple-mint, listened at the door to be sure the coast was clear, opened it and stepped out into the muzzle of a machine pistol in the hands of Prune Face.

Chapter Twelve

There were two other men with him; all three wore gold suits, snow boots, and unfriendly expressions. My stomach went as hard as a washboard, waiting for the impact of the slugs.

"Walk ahead of me," Prune Face said, and motioned with the gun. I followed instructions. We went along corridors, crossed a lounge, pushed through a vestibule, stepped out into a scarlet glare of sunlight on ice and a blast of cold air that struck me like a spiked club. The gun jabbed again, and I went along the deck toward the stern, passing up little groups of men standing silently, looking incuriously across at the ranks of giant ice towers stretching away to the shimmer of the glacier face some five miles distant.

A hatch cover was open on the fantail; a deck crane rumbled, lifted a squat, fat-tired vehicle from the hold, swung it out, over the side. Landing nets were rigged, and men were scrambling over the rail down out of sight. I watched, acutely aware of the gun aimed at my ribs. The sub-zero wind cut through my clothes like swinging axes. I turned to my keeper.

"You want to get me there alive, don't you?" My face was stiff and the words came out blurred. Prune Face just looked at me.

"It must be thirty below out here. I'm practically naked."

Prune Face spoke to one of the other men; he went away, came back five minutes later with a blanket. I wrapped myself like Sitting Bull, but it did not seem to help much.

Prunie watched closely until the last of the men were over the side—ten minutes that seemed longer—then motioned me to go. I went across, detoured around a massive deck fitting like a generator housing, saw a man lying on his back with his eyes open. He was dressed in white trousers and a coat caked with frozen blood. It was Junior, and his dead eyes gazed at the sky, emptier than ever now.

"I guess he won't propagate after all," I said.

"This was a defective. He would not have been permitted to propagate in any event." Prune Face sounded almost indignant.

At the rail, I looked down at choppy, dark-blue water twenty feet below. The long, mud-gray shape of a landing craft wallowed against the side of the ship. Eight or ten men were huddled in rows in the bow; three of the large-wheeled snowcats occupied the center of the boat. One man stood in the stern, looking up expectantly.

"Descend," my guardian angel ordered.

"My hands and feet are too numb for climbing," I pointed out.

The gun jabbed me hard enough to bruise a rib. I went over the rail.

The landing net rigged to the side was coated with ice. My hands were like a couple of iron hooks. I groped my way down, fell the last few feet, hit hard, was shoved to the bench by the fellow I landed on. Prune Face and his two boys squeezed in beside me, and we pushed off. The big, ugly machine pistol was lying across the knees of the man next to me with its snout pointing at my hip bone, but it did not interest me any more. I was wrapped up in my arms like lovers meeting, while the chill cut into me like butchers' knives.

Someone was going to be very upset with Prune Face, because long before we picked our way across five miles of iceberg-filled water, I would be dead of exposure. I turned to tell him so, and my elbow accidentally struck the gun. It fell off on the floor, skidded away. The fellow who had been holding it jumped up, went after it. Prune Face whirled my way, came half to his feet—

There was an ominous grinding sound, and the boat trembled,

lurched sideways, riding up on a submerged ice shelf. The man reaching for the gun took an extra step, went over head first into the water without a sound. Prunie had started a lunge in my direction; I leaned back, palmed him hard as he fell past; he made a nice splash. The third man went for the gun, got it, thrust it out over the side to Prune Face.

The boat shuddered, slid down off the ice shelf it had struck, sent a soaking surge of water over the side and the man with the gun. He went back on his haunches, sputtering. The same shock knocked me off the perch, sent me flat on my face in the sluice of ice water surging in the bottom of the boat, up against the side of the nearest snowcat. I scraped floorboards, worked my knees, reached the cat's door handle, pulled myself up and in, then caught the door, slammed it behind me. A glow of warmth started up from a perforated panel a foot from my face: an automatic heating system, activated when anyone entered the car. It was a good thing. I could not have crawled to the driver's seat to push a button.

For a long time I just lay, hoping they would not haul me back out into the cold until they had picked up the men overboard. Some feeling was coming back into my hands. My ears and nose felt as though little men with pliers were working on them; I sat up, the stiff clothing scraped me like sheet metal. My toes were thawing now, a sensation like a claw hammer pulling at them. I wrung out the thawing clothing as well as I could, began chipping melting ice from the blanket. The flow of hot air from the register was as dry as only super-cooled and reheated air can be; in ten minutes it had sucked the moisture from the coverall. They still hadn't come for me. They thought I had gone over the side with the others.

I risked a look out the driver's window. No one was in sight in the stern except a man I had not seen before, standing by the bench looking back toward the ship, which was half-hidden behind ice floes now. Keeping low, I slid forward to the driver's compartment, looked over the controls. It was a standard Navy Grumman VIT model, with a couple of megahorsepower and a thousand-mile range, fueled and ready to go. Nothing but the best for Prune Face and his chums. I went back to my heater, huddled up against it to soak up all the warmth I could before they found me.

An hour later the landing craft scraped bottom and the engines growled to a stop—and still nobody had yanked the door open and hauled me out into the cold. I eased back up beside the driver's padded bucket seat, looked out through the clear patch on the fogged double-glass window. A crew was working at the side of the boat, undogging the cable releases that locked the side panel in place. It went down with a heavy clang that I heard even through the insulated car. Two men in cold-suits splashed over it, waded a few feet to a pitted surface of rotten ice that shelved away toward the cliffs, looming close now. There was vibration through the floor; the snowcat at the end on the right of the lineup moved forward, tilted down across the ramp, wallowed forward and up onto the ice, streaming water that froze in crusted stalactites. The one beside me started up, sat puffing fumes from a tall stack on its side, then lurched forward. Not until then did the idea hit me.

I swung around, flipped the door locking lever down, then climbed into the seat, looked over the panel, flipped switches, pushed the starter button. The diesels churned, popped, then caught and roared unevenly before they settled down to a smooth rumble. The second car was having difficulty; it seemed to be jammed between the ramp and the ice shelf. I threw in the drive lever just as the door handle clattered. Fists were hammering the side of the car; I steered it down past the stuck cat. I gunned it when I hit the water; and a big bow wave came up and over the glass, started the automatic wipers racing. There was a heavy shock as the clawing front wheels hit the ice, hauled the car up, a forward surge as the rear pair got traction.

Visibility ahead was not good. I could see a stretch of uneven ice, a dim streak that might have been a trail across the foothills of tumbled bergs. Someone was still pounding at the door. A man ran out from somewhere, cut across in front of me waving his arms. His face rushed toward me and I felt a slight jar and he disappeared and I gunned my engines and steered for the pass.

The track that led up through the broken ice twisted and doubled back, threading a route among slabs of transparent blue ice the size of apartment houses. I tried to keep one eye ahead, one on the rearview mirror, a trick that produced two close calls in the first hundred yards. On a badly banked curve, the car skidded, slammed stern first against an ice wall, rocked as fragments rained down on it; then it churned free and kept going. Behind me, a minor avalanche started up, blocking the route—a nice break for our side, I thought, until I saw the prow of a snowcat appear through the clod of ice chips less than fifty yards behind me and coming up fast. I kicked the throttle to the floor, and devoted my full attention to steering.

The road mounted swiftly toward the blue-black ice face rearing up to an unbelievable height—two miles, the sailor had told me, a lifetime ago. My road turned hard to the right, paralleled the foot of that impossible cliff, then veered left and I was in purple gloom that deepened into blackness, howling upward along a ridged tunnel that threw back a million flashing reflections in the beam of my single headlight. The sailor had said that Hayle's expedition had melted a path to the cliff top. Unless my guess was no better than my luck, this was it.

The going was a little better here. The speedometer said I was doing sixty-five, but it seemed faster. The cat bounded and hammered across the uneven surface, and I held on and rode her. The headlight of the car on my tail splashed in my mirror; he was sticking to me like a California driver. Then a pinpoint of red light danced ahead, swelled into concentric rings that raced toward me, expanding into a glare of purple twilight and I was out of the tunnel, racing across a red-stained emptiness stretching to the far horizon.

My first concern was to put distance between myself and the landing party down on the beach; the second was to shake the eager party on my tail. For an hour I held the cat at the best speed I could manage without flipping her on the ridges that the wind had cut into the surface of the snow like oversized sand ripples on a beach.

The boy behind me was moving up, careless of the rough ground, closing the half-mile gap I had built up. He swung wide to the left, came up abreast, then cut in to ram me. I swung hard right, gunned the cat, swerved left again. He barreled past my stern, came around in a shower of ice, overhauling me on the right now. We were both doing eighty now, over ice rough enough to jar the fillings out of a back tooth. He swung in behind me, closing in. Now he was giving me a choice: I could either break my neck racing him on the broken ground, or let him ram me from the rear. Or maybe, if I timed it just right, there was a third choice. I gauged the distance—fifty feet, twenty-five, ten. . . .

I hit the accelerator for everything it had. The cat lunged forward, and when it hit eighty-five, I hit the brakes and cut the wheel hard to the right, held on as she spun end-for-end, hit the throttle again and leaped off almost at right angles to my previous course. He shot past me, cutting his wheel hard. For a hairy second it looked as though he would go over, but he caught it, came on again.

This time he paralleled me, keeping twenty feet offside, I let him come alongside, inch a few yards ahead. When he swerved in on me, I was ready. I braked, swung to the right. My cat skidded, caught itself, then hit a freak bump that straightened her out just as I hit the pedal, I had a fast glimpse of the other car rushing in at me; then I hit, felt my car going up and over. I covered my head, rode out a shock that nearly snapped my neck, another, then went whirling off into an explosion of stars.

I was not out, just stunned. For a minute I could not understand why my head felt so heavy. Then I realized I was hanging upside down in my seat harness. I got a grip on what was left of the panel, unsnapped buckles, fell ungracefully to the crumpled surface that had been the car's roof. One door was sprung half open and bitter wind was whirling ice crystals in around me. I kicked at the door, got it open, crawled out into a glazed, porous surface of frozen snow. There were new ruts cut in it where the car had skidded; fifty feet away the other car sat, right side up but with the top crushed like a stepped-on top hat. Bright, pale flames were flickering somewhere inside. I ran to it, limping pretty badly—my weak right knee had gotten a nice twist—tried to get the door open, gave up and ran around to the other side. The door was open here; the driver was lying on his face half in, half out, not moving. From the angle of his left leg, it was badly broken. I grabbed his arm, hauled him clear, turned him over. He was one of the men who had been with Prune Face when he came for me with the gun—the one who had not fallen overboard.

The wind sawed at me; I could feel my frostbitten ears and nose beginning to burn again. I got a fireman's carry on the man, staggered across to my car, got inside and dragged him after me, wedged the door as nearly shut as I could. It was not warm here, but it was at least a shelter from the wind.

My playmate made a bubbly sound and opened his eyes. I waited until he had blinked a few times, gazed around and let his eyes rest on me.

"Why were you chasing me?" I asked him.

"To catch you," he said in a ghostly whisper.

"Here we go again. Look, pal, I've been brought a long way for something; I want to know what."

"It. . . . so ordered. . . ." His eyes were still open but while I watched the faint spark died from them. I grabbed him by both shoulders, shook him.

"Answer me, damn you! You can't die yet! I have to know. . . ." His head lolled against his shoulder. I let him fall back, took a deep breath, shivered.

"OK, Irish, here you are, free as a bird," I said aloud. "Nobody within fifty miles. You can go where you want to go, do what you want to do. . . ."

I was looking at his cold-suit; he was smaller than I, but I was prepared to make a few concessions.

It took me fifteen minutes to strip the suit from him, shove the pale body out onto the ice, wrestle out of my own makeshifts, and force myself into the tight, plastic-foam coverall. The boots were too small; I had to keep the flimsy ones I had. When I finished, I grabbed the emergency ration pack from its rack and crawled out of the wreck. I felt like a sausage packed into an undersized skin, but, except for my feet, I was warm enough.

The other car was still burning. As far as the eye could see across the twilight, it was the only break in the monotony of ice. The sun had set; the sky was an ominous, sulky violet—clearer than most of the world's atmosphere, but still nothing to get out the Brownie for. Back on the coast, the boys would be painstakingly following along my trail, noting every little break in the crust, every minute trace of a passing wheel. It might take them a few hours, but they would be along. I could creep back inside the car and make myself comfortable, and in due course they would arrive to take me back. They would not be too upset about my attempted escape. Nothing seemed to make them mad, any more than anything seemed to make them happy—or scare them, impress them, tire them. And then they would take me on to their Hidden Place just as they had planned all along.

That was the thing that bothered me most about these

cold-eyed men. They were like a tide rising on a beach; you could fight and struggle and even mow them down with machine guns, but they simply kept coming. They were not very bright, not very strong, but in the end they had their way.

But not this time. They could follow the trail, and they would find the burning car, and the other one, and the dead man, but not me. A man on foot would leave no more trail on the ice than a fish did in water. If I kept up a good pace, I could be ten miles away in three hours. And if they found me after that, I would be frozen too hard for even Junior's big machines to dig any answers out of.

I picked a direction at random and started walking.

It was not easy going. The ice underfoot was as hard as Manhattan pavement, uneven as a rock pile, slippery as oil. I fell and got up and fell again. After what seemed like a long time I looked back, saw the two cars just a long rock toss away. The smoke from the fire streamed away to the left like a marker beacon; I should have taken the time to damp the fire out, but I was not going back now.

My feet hurt for a while, then went big and warm, as dead as fence posts. I stumped on, the wind more or less at my back, watching the sky ahead slowly fade into deeper shades of purple and burgundy and gold. I must still be several hundred miles from the Pole, I thought; farther south, the setting of the sun was a weeks-long process.

Maybe the theories were right; maybe Antarctica was moving north, dragging the whole crust of the planet with it to the accompaniment of quakes and typhoons and rivers of lava, forcing new mountains up where the skin was compressed as areas moved poleward, opening vast new chasms where the lithosphere was stretched to span the increasing planetary circumference of equatorial regions. It was as good a theory as any.

It was the price the world had to pay, periodically, for its unique, life-giving structure. It wasn't like the Moon, or Mars, or Jupiter's satellites—a cold ball of solid rock. It was a living, pulsating complex of molten core, inner and outer mantles, thin crust with continents floating on seas of magma, oceans of free water, ice caps, an atmosphere dense enough to support hurricanes, ice caps that grew and waned—and all infected with that strange disease called life. Life thrived on change, variety—and periodically, life paid the toll. Nature always had her checks and balances, and now man knew another of her rules: a world where life thrives is by its nature a planet of catastrophe.

I was lying on the ice, resting. I did not know how I had gotten there; I did not remember lying down. It was very comfortable, except for the weights strapped to my feet. A faint glow twinkled far away across the dark ice. It was the burning car, still faithfully marking the spot. And here I was running for my life.

No, not my life. That was already forfeit. Running for my death—a private death, unassisted, with no cold, indifferent little men with bland, unremarkable faces grouped around to poke and probe and question, question.

I rolled over, got my dead feet under me. It was hard to balance, but I made it. I seemed to be standing on stilts. My legs ended at the calf. There was no pain, just the annoying sense of dead weight, dragging.

Something hit me in the face. It was not painful—more like a mattress falling from somewhere. I groped, felt ice under me, got up and went on. It was almost full dark now, the sky a blue-black wall where here and there stars winked between black cloud strata. If I kept on long enough, I would reach them, and then I could walk through rose-covered gates into a garden of sun-warmed grass, where I could lie down among flowers and sleep.

I awoke with a terrible sense of duty not completed, of a voice urging me on—to what, I could not remember. Pain crouched like a tiger on my chest, I tried to move, and my arms and legs stirred reluctantly, as though I were frozen into a block of ice.

Ice. I remembered walking, falling, walking on, while the sky turned black and stars gleamed just ahead. There was a star shining now, a steady yellow glow across the ice. It looked close—almost close enough to reach out to. All I had to do was go on—just a little farther—and I would reach it. It was so near, and I had come so far, it seemed a pity not to go on, just that little way. I got to hands and knees, tried to stand, went down hard on my face; pain knifed through the fog that had settled behind my eyes. I tried again, got to all fours, blinking at the light. It was a strange sort of mirage; I was awake now, aware of where I was, what I was doing. . . .

What was I doing?

Sure, I remembered now: I had been driving fast all day, and just at dark the curve had come on me unexpectedly, and the car had gone over and down among trees, and I had been thrown clear, and then the police had arrived, and there had been an ambulance, and lights, and a smell of neoform. . . .

No. That was wrong. The wreck had been a long time ago; before—

I remembered mountains shooting fire into the sky, and a storm, like a bombardment out of hell, and a city where the buildings lay shattered in broken streets, and a dead man who gave me a coin and the flies had buzzed, buzzed around me as I lifted him over the side. . . .

That was not right either. I could not remember what had happened, but that was not important now. What was important was the light, shining serenely through the darkness. . . .

I was walking. There was something wrong with my feet, but it was only necessary to move one leg, and then the other, being careful not to fall, and not to think, but just to walk. . . . walk toward the dancing yellow light that seemed always to recede before me, beckoning me on. . . .

I dreamed I was crawling across a vast ice field. I was all alone on the southern ice cap of a strange planet whirling silently through space and eternity. My enemies pursued me, but they were far away, and only some blind force made me crawl, moving my hands and knees like parts of some broken machine in which I was somehow trapped. It was an unpleasant, painful dream. I tried to open my eyes, but I was still crawling, watching the light that swelled and blurred ahead. I laughed at the idiocy of it—lying comfortably in bed, dreaming of ice and pain, and, aware that I was dreaming, not able to end the dream while the light beckoned me on. It was strange how the pain in the dream was as real as any other pain. Perhaps all pain, all life, was a dream, an endless creeping progress across an untamable phantom wilderness toward a goal that always glimmered out of reach.

But the light looked so close now, so real, a pale rectangle of yellow radiance casting a golden pathway on the snow. Just a little farther, a few more agonizing yards. . . .

My arms moved, without my willing them. My legs had quit now; I dragged them behind me like a broken-backed dog, clawed another yard ahead, and then another, and the glowing doorway was close now, close enough that I could feel the toasting warmth flow out in a wave from it as it opened for me.

For an instant, a part of my mind stirred awake, recognized the mirage. But what did it matter whether my golden door was real or not? I had attained it, and passed through, and a warmth more marvelous than the diversions of emperors washed over me like a benign wave and carried me with it out into an endless sea.

I had recently developed a habit of wincing when I opened my eyes, ready to tally up my latest aches, breaks, and contusions, and review the events that had led up to them. This time was different. There was a mirage bending over me—a young face framed in glossy black hair; a face that smiled, and a soft hand that touched my cheek.

"Maliriss," Ricia said.

Chapter Thirteen

For a while after that I paid no attention to the passing of time. Ricia tended me like a little girl with a new doll while fever burned through me like a magnesium fire, faded away into a sort of soft haze in which I was half aware of being fed, bathed, soothed when the pain in my feet flared up and I ran from faceless men who pursued me with silent shouts through rivers of molten lead.

Then one day I was sitting up, eating soup with a spoon, and looking at two massive bundles of bandages that were my feet.

"I don't know where to start," I said to Ricia. "I don't know where the nightmares end and the delusions begin. I don't know where I am, or how I got here; I don't even know who you are. And you don't know what I'm saying."

"Yes, Mal, know," she said. She was nodding, looking pleased.

"You understand me?"

"Listen, Mal, learn Engliss word, many."

"Kid, you're a wonder." I caught her hand. "Look, maybe I've gone soft behind the eyes, but the way I remember it, I left you in a hotel room in Miami; a little more than two weeks later, I was hiking across the South Pole. The next thing I know—this!"

I waved a hand to take in the bed, the room, the whole incomprehensible universe. "Did I imagine the whole thing? Am I in Miami now with the DTs and a case of trench foot from taking long walks in the rain?"

"No, Mal. Gonwondo, here."

"Gonwondo—that's what Junior called it! He said they were taking me to something called the Hidden Place—" I broke off. "But to hell with that. I'll chew through that later and sort out the facts from the fancies. What I really want to know is—how did you find me?"

She smiled, shook her head. "No, Mal. I find, no. You find me."

"I found you?"

"You come to me, Mal. Close now, we." Her eyes looked soft and dreamy. She took my hand, lifted it, touched the ring she had given me. "This call you to me, Mal."

I blinked a few times, feeling like a kid who's just flunked his IQ test. "Sure," I said, "it's a nice touch of sentiment, girl, but I'm talking about taking a stroll ten thousand miles from the nearest town and running into an old friend. How did you know—"

"Mal, no too many word. This call you, Mal. Believe." She looked at me with a worried expression, like a fond mother waiting for the baby to say "Bye-bye."

I patted her hand. "All right, Ricia. I'll believe."

In a few days—or perhaps "sleeps" would be a more precise term, since the windows stayed an opaque black—I was up and hobbling around the apartment. The frostbite had been the rough equivalent of second-degree burns, but Ricia had applied various balms with curious odors, and the healing was rapid.

There were four main rooms: the lounge, where I had found myself, just inside a heavy, vaultlike door; a dining room with a big, low table; the bedroom and an adjoining bath with a twelve-foot square sunken pool, and another spacious room that I dubbed the library, not that there were any books in sight. The floors were a hard, lustrous material with overall patterns in soft colors that varied from room to room. The walls seemed to be made of the same composition, with an eggshell finish that subtly and unpredictably changed colors.

The furniture was comfortable, but oddly proportioned, curiously put together from colored hardwoods with bright fabrics.

There was music, too—haunting, not-quite-familiar tones built to a scale that seemed to have too many notes.

Ricia produced our meals from a well in the center of the big table in the dining room; there was no kitchen, no pantry, no heating plant, no doors. From somewhere, she got clothes for both of us—a loose sort of sarong for herself, a short robe with loose sleeves for me. They seemed to be new each morning. I asked questions and she showed me a closet that seemed to be empty when I looked inside. But the next morning, there were our new clothes again—not that Ricia was scrupulous about wearing them. She seemed to be as comfortable nude as otherwise.

It was an easy routine: I slept, woke, ate, lay on my bed and studied the pictures on the walls, the hangings with their stylized representations of stick figures hunting dragons, the bowls in which the food popped up on the table, the food itself. The menu consisted of variations on a theme resembling sukiyaki, with large, shallow glasses of what seemed to be bland, faintly sweet wines.

"Where does it all come from?" I watched Ricia open the lid and lift out a hot meal. "How is it prepared? And what is it, anyway?" She laughed and told me to look for myself. I used the silver chopsticks to stab a bite-sized piece of meat from the bowl in front of me.

"It's good," I said. "Well marbled, tender, nice flavor. It's a little like pork and a little like beef, but it isn't either one."

She smiled, made motions like someone strewing confetti in the air, put two fists in front of her nose and swung them out in a grand gesture.

"Sorry—the sign language is worse than the other," I said. "I'll just eat in ignorance."

On my first day up, I explored the apartment, ended in the room I called the library. It was a plain room furnished with seats along one side. The walls, I discovered, were lined with what looked like sealed storage cabinets. There were no latches, no handles to turn, no drawers to pull out. I tapped, got a hollow ring. Ricia was following me, looking a little thoughtful.

"What's all this for?" I wanted to know. "I can understand the rest of the place, but this stumps me."

She took my arm, tried to guide me back toward the doorway. "No, Mal, not now look. Too much tired still."

"I'm not too tired to be curious."

"Not talk now. Mal—"

I took her by both arms, gently but firmly. "Listen to me, Ricia. You've been putting me off for a week now, and I've gone along because—maybe I didn't want to dive back into troubled waters myself. Let's stop kidding each other. There are things I have to know, and you can tell me."

"Mal—sick, you. Rest."

"First," I continued, "I want to know how you figure in all this. Who are you, Ricia, aside from being my ministering angel? Where did you come from? What do you know about. . . . them?"

She stiffened, looking into my face.

"Better, Mal forget." She looked at me appealingly.

I shook my head. "Not as long as I'm alive."

She gave me a long, tortured look; then her shoulders drooped. She nodded slowly.

"I think, Mal, these are ones our legend tells of. The under-men, hide away deep in earth; but when bad time is come, then they appear. Sometime, take woman away to burrow deep in earth, do evil thing with her. Old man never see again."

"Fairy tales aren't—" I started.

"Live long there, in hidden places. And wait. Old men say, when bad time come, then again under-men come among us. Bad time here, now, Mal. And they are here."

"Legends," I said. "Folk tales. But these killers aren't pipedreams, Ricia! They're here, now! And they have a special interest in you. Why? There must be something you know that would shed a little light on this."

"Mal, under-men everywhere now. Take all place, make men slave. We stay here, quiet, live, forget."

"I wouldn't make a good slave, kid. I'm a little too used to independence. Don't hold out on me now. I have to know. What more can you tell me about them—and about yourself?"

"No, Mal, not think this thing. Rest, get strong."

"Sure, I'll rest—as soon as you've told me what I need to know."

Ricia looked sorrowfully at me. Then she sighed. "Yes, Mal. Better no, better stay here, happy and alone. But you are man; you must ask, and not rest." She led me to a chair. "Sit, look now. I show many thing."

✧　　✧　　✧

I started to argue then went along, sat in one of the too-low, too-wide chairs. She went to the wall, twiddled things out of sight. The light in the room dimmed to deep gloom. A glow sprang up in the center of the room; I could not tell where it came from. It grew, resolved itself into misty shapes that grew solider, became a scene of sun-bright plains stretching away to wooded hills. Something moved at the center of the picture—a tiny, distant point that grew, became the bobbling form of a galloping animal. In the foreground, trees swept into view as the camera panned.

From the dappled shadows of the foliage, a man stepped out, trotted forward, away from the camera. He was a tall, dark-skinned, handsomely built fellow, dressed in close-fitting black. His black hair was cut short; he was carrying what looked like a weapon in his right hand. He was running fast now, angling out across the path of the approaching animal. I could not tell yet what the quarry was he had marked out, but it was big, even at half a mile. It was not a horse; the legs were too short in proportion to the body. I had about decided it was a big bull bison when it changed course, veered away to the right. I got a good look then; it was a black elephant, running like a trotter, right legs, then left legs, his trunk curled up between a pair of tusks that would have looked good over any mantle in town.

The lone hunter changed course to intercept the big bull. The camera followed, holding on him at about a hundred yards. He was racing along full tilt now, his head back, his legs pumping like pistons. The shape of the lumbering elephant was growing fast; his head swung around—an oddly shaped head, rising to a peak between the too-small ears. Then he was braking to a halt with all four legs, swinging around to face the man who was coming up fast now. The trunk went up—it looked shocking pink against the dark body—and the mouth opened. There was no sound, but I could almost hear the bellow of rage that went with the expression.

The man came on, while the shape of the animal grew—and grew—and grew some more. The hunter looked like a child against the tusker that towered up over him to a height of at least sixteen feet at the shoulder. And I was close enough now to see that I had made a mistake: the hide wasn't black; I was looking at a heavy coat of long, shaggy hair that hung down far enough to brush the grass tops.

The hunter had dropped back to a trot. Now he was walking, no more than fifty yards from the mountain of flesh that stood with its trunk still up, its yellow tusks curving out and away, two tiny reddish eyes watching every move. It swung its head restlessly from side to side, and again the mouth opened in a silent trumpet.

At fifty feet, the man stopped. He brought the thing in his hand around, lifted it, and I saw it was a horn with a flared mouth. At once the hairy elephant dropped his trunk, lifted it again to sample the air. The hunter moved forward, stopped when the trunk curled high. He blew another blast, and again the monster rocked back, swung his head from side to side, watching the man come on steadily until I thought he was going to climb a leg. He had the horn up again, and I sensed somehow that he was blowing softly on it now, crooning some kind of mammoth lullaby to the big fellow who stood over him like a mastiff over a mouse, rocking gently with one foot raised clear of the ground like a field dog on point.

A full minute passed. I could see the wind stirring the grass, the fluffy shapes changing form against the hills in the background. The man was swaying and the elephant followed the motion with his eyes—the camera was that close now.

Quite suddenly, the man lowered the horn, made a smooth gesture with his right hand. The immense animal took a step backward. The man walked in, holding his hand out. The restless trunk curled out, touched the hand. A moment later the man was stroking the massive organ that could rip a hundred-year oak nut out of the ground with one tug. Then he reached up, caught a tusk, pulled himself up and an instant later was sitting just behind the big fellow's head.

The mammoth did not like that much; he stepped sideways, shaking his head, and the man went flat, holding on the round, naked-looking ears. For half a minute the mammoth curvetted ponderously, while his trunk curled up and over to touch the man, as though not quite sure now how he felt about the proceedings. Then the man sat up, kicked his heels against the beast's neck, and the ten-ton mount swung off at a brisk walk as though that was what he had intended all along.

The picture faded into a bright mist and I let out a long breath.

"What in the name of Phineas T. Barnum was *that!*" I called to Ricia.

"Look," she said. "More see."

The mist was taking shape again; this time it showed a view from fifteen feet above an avenue paved with glazed and colored bricks, laid in patterns that reminded me of the floors in the apartment. Dead ahead, the vast bulk of another shaggy elephant swayed, moving placidly down the center of the street. There was a gilded howdah strapped to his back, and under the fringed, peaked canopy a woman sat bolt upright, her arms folded. She had a beautiful, straight back, quite bare; the skin was a tawny olive color that gleamed in the sunlight. Her hair was blue-black, arranged high on her head in an ornate style woven through with strings of bright beads. Along the avenue, people with dark skin and barbaric costumes waved their hands and smiled as she rode past.

The buildings behind them were elaborate with bright colors against gleaming white, like something a fanciful baker might have made from colored sugar. Ahead, the avenue widened into a broad plaza faced on the far side by a building that went up into the clear sky like a lone skyscraper. The wide steps in front of the building were packed with people in fancy headdress.

When the elephant was a hundred feet from the steps, he stopped, went heavily down to his knees. The girl rose, slid down to the ground. She was wearing nothing but beads and loops of white silk fore and aft, but she had the figure for it. She raised her arms and turned around, and I said, "Hey. . . . !"

She looked enough like Ricia to be her sister—or at least her cousin.

The scene faded, took shape again—this time showing a grassy slope above cliffs with white breakers churning at the bottom. A thing like a dragonfly rested at the top of the slope. It started moving slowly, coasted down the hill, lifted off just at the brink, soared out in a wide curve that swept it past the camera's vantage point, and I saw a man crouched in a frame of sticks and wire, his hair tossed by the wind, grinning from ear to ear. A second glider had launched itself now. It shot outward, climbing in a steady updraft, bucking and pitching. Abruptly one wing crumpled, folded back; the broken flyer dropped, spinning lazily, struck the sea far below with a lazy explosion of white water that made me wince.

Another picture was taking form; this time a gay-colored boat was mooring to a long jetty; it had a short mast, an open deck with a small deckhouse. Men stood on the deck, waving to those on shore. A plank was run out, and crewmen came across, leading what looked like a captive gorilla; then I caught a glimpse of the wide, pale face, the swift-darting eyes, a startling pale blue. It was a man, hairy as a sheep dog, with his hands manacled before him.

The show went on and on. I saw men with glittering short swords hack at each other in an arena decked with flowers; a giant tiger walking on a leash held by a girl who was the twin of the mammoth rider; a view from a balcony across a city that sparkled on a mountainside; an interior shot of a wide room with a polished floor where men bent over a long table with an array of glittering apparatus, a vaulted chamber that might have been a powerhouse.

When the misty sphere faded and the lights came up, I patted my nonexistent pockets for a cigarette I had not had for weeks.

"What"—I had to swallow—"what was it? *Where* was it?" I looked at Ricia. "*When* was it?" My voice came out in a dry whisper.

"My home," Ricia said. "My people." A look of desolate loss swept across her face, and she lifted her chin above it. "Gone, now. All dead, my people. Only me, now."

I hobbled into the dining room, lifted the cover of the food well, grabbed the wine glass as it popped up, drank it off. It did not change anything, but it was something to do to span the whirling seconds while my mind tried to find a floating straw to grab at. I had a second, then turned; Ricia stood there, looking concerned.

"Rest now, Mal," she put a hand on my arm. I took her hand.

"Sorry, girl, I've had my rest. We talk now." I led her into the lounge, sat her down in a chair, took the one beside it.

"These movies you just showed me: they were. . . . real?"

"Oh, yes, real, Mal."

"They were made—here, on earth?"

She looked surprised. "Yes."

"Where? What country?"

"Gonwondo, here, this country." She pointed to the floor.

"Yes, but—"

"Not ice, that time, Mal. Beautiful land, my Gonwondo."

"Antarctica—before the ice." I was shaking my head. I did not hear a rattle.

"Mal, how long time?" She looked anxiously at me.

"God, I don't know, Ricia." I tried to remember what I had read on the subject. "The generally accepted figure is a few million years; some theorists say a few hundred thousand—and some say only ten to twenty thousand years. But from what I saw—mammoths and cave men—and if that cat wasn't a sabertooth, I'll turn in my junior woodsman's badge—that means anything up to a hundred thousand years, anyway."

"What is hunditausen?"

I took five minutes off to explain the numbering system to her. She looked at her fingers and large tears leaked from her eyes. She wiped them away impatiently and said, "Thousand, hundred thousand, same. All dead."

"These were your ancestors?"

She shook her head. "No. My people, my city. Ulmoc name. Me I am here, I ride Holgotha, I walk these streets, I see these sky."

"How?"

"Here, Mal." She pointed to the bedroom. "Long sleep. There is"—she made smoothing motions with her hands—"roof. Breathe"—she breathed deep—"sleep-air. Come, show—"

I followed her into the bedroom. She touched a spot that looked just like the rest of the wall to me, but a table like a morgue slab tilted out. A gray steel cover was hinged above it, with tubes leading to it.

"Lie here, Mal. Roof come down, sleep-air inside, cold, cold. Sleep long."

"But—what for?"

She looked stricken. "Bad time come, Mal. Sky turn from blue to black, sun red. Earth shake. Ice come from sky, many day, thousand day. My. . . ." She shook her head. "Too many word, no, Mal. You wait, teach more—"

"Go ahead, you're doing fine. Your what?"

"Man, woman, old—me." She pointed at her chest. I shook my head. "I don't get that, but go ahead."

"My. . . . old man. Take me here. . . ."

I grinned in spite of the excitement pounding in my ears. "You're getting the hang of the vernacular now. Go on."

"Many people go in boat, thousand boat. But my old man, no. He is fear—for me, not he. I must sleep, wait, I must do, Mal. I say good-by, lie here. Darkness come."

"I can't say that I blame him. Those boats didn't look like anything I'd want to go to sea in."

"Have more boat, Mal. Big, big. But many bad thing, other land. Holgotha, Otucca, beast-man. He fear for me, Mal."

"Sure. So you told your family good-by and. . . . died." I pictured her, lying alone in the dark and the cold, while the world circled the sun and cultures rose and died and the ice built up above her.

"Not die, Mal. Live on, and one day—wake."

"Then what?" I asked.

"I think soon old man come back. Very sick, Mal. Long time here, so sick. Long sleep no good. But house good, help, tell me what to do—"

"The house told you what to do?"

"Yes, house. Very wise, know all thing. Say to me, do that, I do, soon well. But old man—"

"I'm afraid you lost me."

"Come." This time she took me to the library, to the small niche at one side with a seat in front of it. She sat down, put her hands flat on the foldout tabletop.

"*Iklathu ottraha oppacu madhali att,*" she said, as well as I could make out.

"*Optu; imruhalo soronith tatrac. . . .*" a hollow voice rasped in a monotone. It went on, reeling off words. When it finished, Ricia said, "*Accu,*" and stood up.

"You see? House say ice falling above now; tomorrow, warmer; ice become water."

"It's some kind of automatic weather-report gimmick?"

"House know *all* things, Mal. Not house here—great house, there." She pointed.

"It's tied in to another machine? Some kind of recorded information service?"

"Not know too many word, Mal. You see, not talk more now."

"What woke you up?" I cut her off.

"Ice go, make water, above." She pointed at the ceiling.

"The ice was melting, and the. . . . machinery. . . . was set to bring you out of it when the thaw started?"

"Maybe, Mal." She looked doubtful.

"Don't mind me, kid; I'm just talking to hear myself think. Anyway, you woke up; you were sick, but you recovered. Then what?"

"I must go, find old man. Take sea clothes, small food. Much ice above, but house make way through. Much water, soft ice, hard to go with sled. . . ." She described what sounded like a self-propelled surfboard that she used to cross the slushy ice to the spot where the city had stood. There was nothing there but ice. She headed for the coast; she had decided to follow her father and the others. After a couple of days of cruising along the beach, she found a boat—a derelict, thawing out of the ice. She broke it loose, hoisted a sail and headed north.

Her story was halting, vague, interrupted by the frequent need to act out a missing word; but I got the picture of days of sailing, living on food concentrates and fish. Her sea suit—the green outfit she had been wearing when I found her—kept her warm enough. From her description, it was a lot more efficient and less bulky than my cold-suit.

She steered due north, missed the coast of South America by a few hundred miles. She had steady winds and fair weather—but no landfall. She had started to believe the whole world was flooded when she sighted islands—maybe the Azores. They had been evacuated, of course; she found no one there. She set off again, followed the wind. It brought her into the South Florida coast ten days later.

She saw the lights of Miami, landed the boat, went looking for people. She found them—but no one understood her language. Everything was strange: the people, the buildings, the animals—cats and dogs. She was hungry, but without money, nobody would feed her. Then one day a man came up to her and spoke to her in her own language.

She was overjoyed; she followed him. He led her into a dark alley and tried to kill her. She broke away, and ran. Three days later, in another dark alley she met me.

"It's a swell world," I told her. "You went under while the crust was going through contortions, and woke up in time to catch the next show. In between we had a few thousand years of nice weather, but you missed it. OK. Now, what about the men that tried to kill you. Any idea why?"

"No, Mal. I think first, nice friend. Then—choke me. I"—she acted out a punch to the jaw and a knee in the groin—"run away."

"Good for you, kid. But think: you must have some idea who they are, why they tried to kill you—and me, and the sailor. What about Sethys? The name mean anything?"

"No, nothing, Mal. Strange men."

"But they spoke your language."

"Spoke, yes." She nodded vigorously. "Speak strange, but understand."

"All right, there's one obvious tie-in—the sailor visited Antarctica; he swore the little men sabotaged the expedition and followed him. And you say they speak a language that was used here, sometime in the remote past. As for why they chased me, I walked into their conference in Miami and showed them the coin. A nice piece of strategy, that."

"Coin?"

"A gold piece, money. Like this." I rummaged in a drawer, found a stylus and pad, sketched the design on the coin as well as I could from memory."

"Gold," I amplified. "Yellow metal."

Ricia nodded suddenly. It was a gesture she had gotten from me. "This is *grisp*, for. . . ." She waved her hands, unable to express the function of money in pig latin.

"He said he picked it up here—in a building frozen in the ice. Sethys recognized it. He switched coins on me. I don't know why."

"Mal, swish?"

"Changed—he took my coin and gave me a different one."

"Yes, yes!" She looked excited. "Coin like ring, Mal. But bring him to *you*!"

"What does that mean?"

"Mal, wise men, my people, make ring, make little thing inside ring." She groped for words. "You, me, ring. . . . together."

"What is it—magic?"

"Mal—ring made for woman, give to man. It call man to woman."

"You don't need a ring for that."

"Sethys have same thing, in coin. Give you, call him to you."

"In other words, as long as I carried the coin, he had a tag on me." I snorted. "And I thought we were hidden away at Bob's place like the bankroll in grandma's sock."

"You have *grisp* now?" Ricia caught at my arm.

"No. I guess I left it on the boat. Now, let's have your story. How did you get clear? You were a sick girl when I left you. I thought—"

"Yes, Mal, I sick. Lie, wait, long time, two days, night. Feel better, wait, dark, go off boat. Think one thing, go to home, away from strange men. I look Mal, find man—strange man talk my language."

"You went looking for those killers?"

"How else I get thing I want? Know him, now, not afraid. Get man alone. Fool man, learn many thing. Go to place of machine sail in air—"

"The jetport?"

"Yes. Find other man, take me in machine, sail in air long way."

"What happened to the first man?"

Ricia made motions graphically depicting a knee in the back and a broken neck. "Strong, me."

"My God, and I was worried about you."

"Come to place," she went on. "Johannesburg. Buy boat."

"Buy with what?"

"Dead man, plenty *grisp*."

"And then?"

"Sail south; come to Gonwondo, come here, to house."

"On foot?"

"Sled still there, Mal, same place."

"You must have some sense of direction, kid."

"Not need; have ring too." She smiled and held up her hand, showing me the ring, the twin to the one she had given me. "Easy find sled; call to ring. Then come here, to house, wait. I know maybe Mal. . . . dead." She put her hand on mine. She had a nice way of touching me, as though she could transmit her meaning through her fingertips.

"But if you alive, you come. I know maybe long time; think maybe go back on cold-bed; but wait, and soon you come."

"OK, I'll pass that for now. That leaves us with a few large questions still unanswered: who are they—Sethys and his gang? What do they want? Why did they try to kill you, then kidnap you? That place under the water—"

"Yes, Mal! Old place; long-ago house, like this—but water come, wise men fix, hold water back, I think."

"Yeah, it looked like a hurry-up job. But there was a lot of know-how there. These wise men of yours must have been first-rate engineers. But what was the idea of grabbing you in Miami and taking you there? If they wanted to kill you, why didn't they do it in the hotel?"

"Not want kill, Mal. Old man, evil and ugly, want. . . . use me."

"Use you? For what?"

"For son." Her lip curled.

"You don't mean. . . ."

"He talk, make much question. I talk, no. Then he tell, I make son for him, many son."

"That old devil couldn't even roll over in bed."

"Mal—very strange, old man. Son very important. Say many strange thing. . . ." She shook her head impatiently. "No too many word, Mal!"

"All right, you're doing fine. Forget him; his playhouse broke up; he's probably washing ashore on a mud flat about now. But we still don't know what it is these fellows want."

"Mal, you tell, sailor here, Gonwondo, find *grisp*. . . . in house." Her eyes were bright with excitement. "What house, where?"

"He claimed they'd found a city under the ice."

Her fingers on my arm hurt. "Mal, city—*my* city! Ulmoc! Still there!"

"It couldn't be; these glaciers move. They'd have scraped the rock to the bone. If there had been a city, it would be in small pieces now."

"But, Mal, sailor have *grisp*."

"There is that." I rubbed at my chin. "Hell, there's no point in trying to be logical. Maybe the snow fell and turned to ice and the mountains held it in place so it couldn't slide."

"Yes, Mal! Mountain! Every side! Ulmoc in. . . ." She picked up a bowl from the table. "Like this, Mal."

"Maybe it's possible then. Maybe he really did find a buried city. And"—I snapped my fingers—"Junior told me something called the Hidden Place; maybe this was what he meant!"

Ricia looked at me anxiously, watching my lips as though she could read them. I got up, stumped painfully up and down the room. "They had to be headed somewhere. It could have been some kind of in-gathering; that ship was loaded with them. Maybe this is their big annual get-together. If so—" I smacked a fist into my palm. "Ricia, how far is this Ulmoc place from here?"

"Why, Mal?" She stood, looking worried.

"That's where the answers are."

"Mal, no! Stay here, safe, warm! Sick, Mal. Rest!" She was close to me, her face turned up to me. Her eyes looked big and dark enough to dive into and get lost. This was one of the days she was wearing her chiton, but I was suddenly acutely aware of her feminine nearness.

"You act as though you really care." I tried to make my voice jovial but it came out cracked.

Her hands crept up my chest to my shoulders. "Yes, Mal, care." She kept her eyes wide open when I kissed her; her mouth was soft and startled under mine. Afterward she touched my lips with her fingers. "Care much, Mal. You stay, forget strange men."

"I'm not an invalid any more; at least I won't be in a few more days. I can't sit here, hiding like a hunted rabbit. For now, they've lost me—but they'll find us some day; they're that kind of boys. This is my chance—maybe my only chance—to slip up on their blind side. If this is the place my sailor friend was talking about—"

"Stay!" She threw her arms around me and squeezed hard enough to hurt. I patted her back, feeling like I had sneaked in under false pretenses.

"Listen to me, I think I may know a back way in—if the shaft the Navy dug is still intact. I can take your sled, go in at night, do a fast reconnoiter, and get out again before they know it."

"They kill you."

I took her arms and eased her back far enough to look at her. Her eyes brimmed like overfilled teacups. "Think about it for a minute. These baby-faced killers wiped out a couple of hundred men—Hayle's whole outfit. They hunted the lone survivor down and would have killed him, if he hadn't died first. Then they went after you. My guess is they recognized who or what you were—and that meant things to them. And last but not least, they killed Carmody, and Rassias—and made a nice try at me. It was nothing but dumb luck that I got clear. I'm a guy that will go the long way around to miss trouble every time, Ricia, but I can't duck this. If those lads are holed up just over the hill, I have to go see."

"Mal, take boat, go back, your city. Tell wise men all things, bring many good men."

"There's no one to tell. Hayle's expedition was the last gasp of organized government. There's nobody to get another. And if there were, I'd be laughed into the chuckle ward with my story. I have no proof—not even the coin. Nothing!"

"Say to friends, tell all things—"

"If our guesses are right—if they're there—I can get proof, I'll have something to show, then. Maybe there'd be a chance of getting away from here and organizing something. Maybe in Denver; I heard the Air Academy was still holding something together." Ricia was watching me, shaking her head.

"No, Mal," she whispered. "Safe, here."

"Could I operate your sled?"

"No!" She looked stubborn.

"Then I'll walk."

We argued the point for another hour, but in the end she went dull and rigid-faced and agreed to help me get ready.

Chapter Fourteen

Eight more days went by before Ricia led the way up the sloping, jointed tunnel to the surface and we stood together in purple twilight on the frozen slush surface twenty feet above the buried house. I was dressed in a blue-black shimmery suit like her green one; it was as light and comfortable as cotton, and kept out the bitter cold like a brick house. Ricia had supplied me with boots that seemed to be made of a sort of tough felt; inside them my feet were still a little tender, but warm enough. I had gloves and a cowl that fitted over my head like a hood of a parka. As a sample of Gonwodon science the outfit was impressive. I took Ricia's hands between mine.

"I won't get hurt, kid. Just a fast, sneaky look around, and then out; just long enough to pick up something more convincing than a few bruises to prove I ever met these boys."

"It will be dark soon. Time to start," she said woodenly.

"Yeah, just show me the sled and I'll be on my way."

She went past me, used a small pick on an ice-crusted mound. I helped her; in five minutes the sled was clear. It was flat, about the size of an air mattress, with a hooded panel at one end. It did not look like much. Ricia knelt by it, twiddled things; it made a singing noise and lifted itself six inches from the ice. There did not seem to be any airstream coming from under it.

"How do you make it go?" I came to Ricia's side. She swung onto the sled.

"Get on," she said in a dull voice. I climbed on behind her. She leaned forward over the controls.

"I can't see a thing from here," I said. "Better let me get up there."

"It is not necessary," she called back to me. "I am going with you." She had learned a lot of English in the past week. Maybe I should start competing with Berlitz when the world calmed down again.

"Not a chance, girl. You're going back down in that nice snug burrow of yours and sit tight until I get back."

She swung around to face me. "I am not afraid for me—only for you."

"My God, Ricia, this isn't a chicken contest! I'm going in there because I have to!"

"I have to also."

"You're not going."

"Mal"—she leaned against me—"I will operate the sled, and help you dig; it will not be easy to uncover the shaft. And inside—how will you know the way, if I am not there? This is my city; I know its streets."

"Its streets are solid ice now; I don't need a guide. I'll play it by ear, and—"

"No." She was smiling at me, looking impish. I wondered how I could ever have thought she was anything but beautiful. "We will play it by *my* ear."

"What's that supposed to mean? I'll have enough on my mind without looking out for you too."

She pointed to a button set behind her ear like a hearing aid. "This is linked to the house library. It will speak wisdom in my ear."

I was in no mood to be impressed. The closer I got to bearding the quiet men in their Hidden Place, the less I liked the sensations it engendered under my ribs. I wanted to get it over with in a hurry now.

"Sure, your wise men were clever as hell. But we aren't trying to break the bank on a quiz show. Now just slide off of here like a good girl."

"You do not understand. This"—she touched the button—"is an instrument of the most fine. . . ." Her English still slipped a little under pressure, and she still had an exotic way with her words sometimes.

" . . . . will detect sounds, sight, hidden things; all these it will relay to the library, and the library will advise us."

"Swell, the voice of conscience in your ear, ready with an oracular saying for every emergency."

"Even now it tells me things." She had a faraway look in her eyes, as though she were listening to a distant drummer beating out a rhythm I would never hear. "It says men are abroad even now; ten. . . . *sarads* away, there—" She pointed out across the dark ice.

"All right, let me have it then." I was humoring her. "Maybe it will direct me to the civic booze supply; I'll probably be needing a drink."

"No, only I can use it." She looked triumphant. "It speaks in my language, not your English."

"Go below, Ricia!" I took her arm, tried to ease her over the side. She resisted; she *was* strong. I got my leg under me to lift her and her eyes met mine.

"You would have me wait alone *again*, Malcome?" she asked softly.

I was holding her by both shoulders. I looked at her and thought about her waiting down there, if I did not come back, and the days going by and lengthening into years.

I let my breath out in a long sigh. "All right, kid. Let's get going. I want to finish this caper before the sun comes up."

Ricia held the sled six feet above the ice, raked it along at a speed that made bob-sledding seem sedentary. It was a good forty-mile run, I estimated; we made it in under an hour, the last few miles at a fast crawl.

We came up over a slight rise, down across an open stretch that showed up pale in the light of a few stars that had found a crack in the cloud layer. It took us half an hour, while Ricia pored over instrument faces, to find a pit scooped out in the ice like a crater dug by an air burst. Ricia maneuvered up to it, settled in and cut the switch.

"This looks like the spot," I told her. "It's just as the sailor described it."

"Grand Tower of the Sun is here, Mal." She jumped off the sled, pointed to the ground at her feet. "The master steerer of the sled is centered here."

"Was that the tall building I saw in the picture?"

"Yes." She paused, listening. "Library tells me they are here," she said in a low, tense voice. "This is their Hidden Place—my city of Ulmoc!"

"Well, it's not hidden any longer. Let's see what we can do about clearing the shaft." My feet crunched loose ice in the hollow. I used the pick on it; it was a solid mass, thawed and frozen again. Ricia came up with a metal tube like a flashlight, aimed it at the ice. Water bubbled, boiled away from the cavity that appeared.

"You're full of surprises," I said. "And I was going to try it with hairpins and chewing gum."

"I do not know those tools. Are they better than my heat gun?"

"They're pretty versatile, but for a job like this you can't beat specialization. You're doing fine."

"Mal, you use too many words you have not taught me."

"I use too many words, period. I get gabby when I'm nervous." I watched while she cut a deep slot across the ice, then another beside it. I picked at it, broke a fifty-pound chunk loose, tossed it aside, and Ricia went to work widening the hole.

An hour later, six feet down in a slushy pit of porous ice, there was a sudden hollow crunch and a slab dropped from under us. I grabbed Ricia with one hand, the edge of the pit with the other. There was a hole in the floor of the excavation now; through it, the corner of a metal cage showed.

"This is it; that's the car the sailor was caught in." Ricia kicked more ice away, cleared the top of the car. There was an access door, frozen shut. I used a pick to lever it open. We dropped down inside the six-foot square cage. It was half full of ice forced in through the half-open door. I used Ricia's light, set now for a pencil-thin beam. It showed me an unbroken drop into a blue-black well that dwindled away to darkness far below. The cables suspended from the bottom of the car fell away in lazy loops.

"This is the end of the line for you, kid," I said. "There's only one way down, and that's via the cables. You wait up on top, by the sled."

"I will go down."

"Listen, girl, sliding down is easy—maybe. Coming back up is another thing. I can't climb a rope and carry you."

"I climb very well. Now we must go down, or go back together."

"You're not easy to discourage. Maybe I'm glad, at that." I squeezed through the door, dropped down until I was holding on to the door sill, swung my legs out and tangled them in the cables, lowered myself a few yards hand over hand. The ropes were a nine-gauge synthetic fiber, no bigger than my little finger and slippery with ice. They quivered as Ricia swung out above me.

"Stay close," I called up to her. "If you slip, I'll stop you."

"I will not slip," she said coolly. I grunted, got a loop of rope around my leg as a brake, and started down.

I tried to keep track of distance but gave it up after the first hundred feet. At any moment I expected to slam against a blockage in the tube or come to the end of the cable. My arms got tired and then numb, then ached again. I called to Ricia and she answered, sounding calm and a lot less winded than I was. Then my feet hit a sloping surface of loose ice. A moment later Ricia was standing beside me in what felt like a small cave hollowed out of the ice. She flashed the light around on glassy black walls—and stopped on a surface of gray stone with a tall narrow niche fronting on a tiny balcony railed with twisted iron.

"Mal, it is"—her voice broke—"the Grand Tower. . . ."

I put an arm around her shoulders, stared at the ancient wall. "Skyscrapers under the ice," I said. "I don't think I really believed it—until now."

She went to the niche, stepped over the railing, disappeared into darkness. I followed. The light showed us a tiny room with a narrow bed with carved head- and footboards, a squat table with an open drawer, rotted scraps of rug, a doorless opening in the opposite wall. There was an odor of suppressed corruption, like a cold-storage vault.

"This is where he found the coin." My voice was as hoarse as a sideshow barker's. Ricia was already at the doorway, flashing the light on a wall with blotchy painted murals.

"The ramp is this way." She led me along the hall, past doors closed on secrets preserved in deep freeze for an unknown number of millennia. A part of my mind told me that I was walking through a greater treasurehouse than archaeology had ever dreamed of, but the other part kept my hackles raised and my muscles tensed for a fast jump—in either direction.

We reached the ramp. It was wide, like a grand staircase, and wound down in a sweep around a central well. There was no guard rail. I took the lead, hugging the wall.

Five floors down, I saw the first sign of recent occupancy—a cast-off carton marked *U.S. Navy—One Ration, Type Y-2.* For a moment it gave me an almost comforting sense of human companionship. Then I saw the fellow who had been eating it.

He was lying on his face, ten yards along the corridor. I turned him over carefully; it was like handling a dummy in a store window. He was in good shape—a little dark and withdrawn-looking, his eyelids sunken, his cheeks drawn in—but the bitter cold was an excellent preservative. He was wearing a heavy parka and thick boots laced to the knee. The can of potted meat was still in one hand.

"He didn't die of starvation," I said. My voice seemed to echo like a shout.

Ricia pointed. There was a tiny black spot, almost hidden in the fold of the parka.

"Burn gun," she said. "*They* did it."

"What's a burn gun?"

She held the light out. "Like this, but more strong. It kills."

I unstrapped the forty-five from the dead sailor's waist, buckled it on. "So does this. Let's go."

Two levels lower we found two more men. One was a Navy rating lying curled on his side with his face frozen into an expression of agony like a tortured pharaoh and six burns that I could see without moving him. The other was a soft-looking fellow of perhaps fifty, with a round, oriental-looking face. He was dressed in a quilted suit and felt boots. There was a large bullet hole in his chest. "Pay dirt," I said. "This is one of them. He's got the look." I went through his pockets, found nothing. There was no gun on the sailor's body.

"How many floors are there in this building?" I asked Ricia.

"Eight tens. . . . and three," she calculated.

"Where would they be most likely to hole up?"

"They would take the rooms nearest the kitchens, would they not?"

"Unless they're living on concentrates. They didn't strike me as lads who cared a lot about creature comforts—except for the fat one they called the Primary."

"I think they could be anywhere. There are many apartments here. Only on the lowest floors are there rooms not suitable for sleeping—storage rooms and offices and spaces for the heat engines and other things."

"All right, we'll push on."

At the next floor, Ricia touched my arm. "There is warmth coming from there. . . ." She pointed along a dark corridor.

"I don't feel it."

"The library tells me." Her voice was a tense whisper.

"Let's take a look." I unholstered the gun. Ricia adjusted the light to cast a barely visible pink glow over the floor ahead. I eased off, breathing with my mouth open. Ricia walked beside me, silent as a shadow. We passed open doorways beyond which I caught fleeting glimpses of dark furnishings of strange proportions.

"Close, now," Ricia breathed at my ear.

"Better douse the light."

"Wait." The light dimmed to a sultry glow, went out. Something touched my hand.

"Fit this over your eyes," she whispered. It was a sort of visor, feeling like smooth plastic. I clamped it over my head without asking questions. Now I could see a bright puddle of radiance on the floor ahead from Ricia's light.

"Infrared," I told myself. "That's some bag of tricks you've got there, girl."

We moved on. Two doorways down, Ricia touched my hand. "In there."

I moved up beside the arched opening, listening hard, heard nothing but the blood beating in my ear.

"I think your library's got an overactive imagination," I whispered. "Why would—"

Ricia put a hand over my mouth—too late. Something stirred in the darkness—a sharp, sudden movement. I jumped back, pushed Ricia behind me. A heavy body slammed the wall where we had stood an instant before. The gun was ready in my hand, but I didn't want to use it. I stepped in, swung and connected with something as bristly as a bear. It grunted and clawed at me and I kicked it away, just as Ricia's light found it. I froze, staring at a tall, rangy man, bundled in grimy gray cloth and matted fur, his face pale and hollow-eyed in a snarl of beard. Blood was running down the side of his jaw, and he was showing his teeth in a snarl that could have been either pain or rage.

"Hold it—" I started. He did not wait to hear the rest. He swung wildly, missed, then kicked me hard enough to chip bone. I rushed him, slammed him back against the wall. "I said hold it, damn you!" I got out between my teeth. "We're on your side!"

He went rigid, blinking almost at my face. He was breathing hard between his teeth.

"Give us some light, Ricia," I snapped. The eerie glow of infrared brightened to an honest pink. The man I was holding squinted his eyes, stared into my face. Then he relaxed, let out a long, shuddering breath.

"Thank God," he croaked. "Addison got through. . . ."

The room he had fixed up for himself smelled like a Hudson's Bay store just before the fur ship arrives. There was a rough pallet of rotted cloth and odds and ends of clothing in one corner, a pile of Navy ration cartons beside it. He was sitting against the wall, limp as a scarecrow now that the excitement was over.

"I've gotten careless lately," he nodded toward his meager effects. "I used to keep it all hidden, but they never come up here any more. They think I'm dead; I was content to keep it that way. A waiting game, that was all, until you got here." Even talking was an effort for him. I wondered how he had gotten the strength for his attack on me.

"How many men have you?" He glanced at Ricia, looked puzzled as he had each time he noticed her, then fixed his eyes on me. "I hope COMSPAC is patrolling the entire perimeter of the continent. I didn't have time to say much to Addison, but I think he understood. . . ." He faded off as I shook my head.

"Sorry, COMSPAC couldn't patrol Catalina Island today. There's no task force here. Just me—and. . . ." I caught Ricia's eye. "This is Ricia. She led me here."

He straightened himself, made a move to get to his feet. Ricia knelt quickly beside him. His face looked worn and old; his beard was iron gray, shot with white.

"We will help you," she said softly. "We will take you with us to a place where you will be safe."

"Am I. . . . am I dreaming this?" He touched Ricia's hand. "No, I see I'm not. You're as real as. . . . life." He ducked his head in a caricature of a stately bow. "I am Rome Hayle, my dear."

"Admiral Hayle!" I looked at the gaunt face in vain for a likeness to the dapper officer I had met once in Guam. "Are you the only one. . . . left?"

He nodded. "But"—he looked from me to Ricia—"who are you? How did you find me? How is it up above now?"

"Hold it, Admiral," I said. "I'll tell you the whole story—as much as I know of it."

" . . . . Ricia's bet paid off," I finished. "I woke up inside, damaged but alive. That was a couple of weeks ago."

"But in Heaven's name, why did you come *here*? You knew this damnable place is infested with them."

"For information. We don't know anything—nothing we can prove."

"You'll never get out alive. You should have gone back with what you had. Now there are three of us in the trap."

"Why didn't they kill you?"

"They tried hard enough. But I found a hidey-hole—up there." He pointed to the ceiling. "There's a narrow crawl space above; I can enter it through the wardrobe ceilings—a trapdoor arrangement. Access space for heating ducts."

"What happened to your men?"

"Most of them were cut down at their posts before we knew we were under attack."

"They hit you from inside?"

"They came up from below, intercepted us at about the seventieth floor, down from the top of the tower. About a dozen of us survived their first attack. They came at us in absolute silence, firing. I shot one; managed to find cover. Got the remnant of my boys together and tried to pull back, but they pressed us from both sides.

"Four of us got clear, to the upper levels. They picked Hieneman and Drake and Ludcrow off over the next week. I fooled them. Rigged Ludcrow's body up, propped in a doorway. When they fired, he fell. They thought they'd gotten me. They went away, and I haven't seen them since—up here."

"Up here?" Ricia queried him.

"I've been down a few times. The first month I was quite active scouting them out, spying. Then I began to get a little weak. Lack of sunshine, and the damned cold, I suppose. Always shivering. Plenty of food, though. . . ." His attention seemed to wander from his disjointed story, and he brought it back with an effort.

"They're not human, you know," he said, and I could hear the strain in his voice. I said nothing, waited.

"They call themselves. . . . Womboids. They prey on us. They need men to live—I don't know how, but they need them. The way ticks need cattle."

"What else did you learn about them, Admiral?" I had the feeling he was close to some unseen edge, and that the wrong word would send him over.

"They don't care whether they live or die," Hayle said hoarsely. "As long as something they call their Primary is safe. All they want is food and a place to breed. That last is very important to them. The ones that haven't bred are in a sort of special, protected category, as well as I could gather. They're. . . . tested. . . . in some way. Those that don't pass are killed as casually as you'd swat a fly."

"How did you learn all this?"

"I listened. There's a big room where they gather to eat." He described it. Ricia nodded. "The feasting hall; there is food stored there—enough for the whole city for a year or more. It was gathered there when the Long Winter began."

"They bring captives here, I think. They spoke of the need for women. Not the way a man would speak of women—don't misunderstand me. The way a butcher would speak of a new supply of beef!"

"They don't *eat* human flesh?"

"It's not that either. I hate to think of it, but I believe they use them in some unnatural way to breed more of their own obscene kind."

"When you say they're not human, Admiral, you're speaking—"

"I'm speaking fact, man! They're no more human than a scorpion! Yes, they look human—they may even walk around in human flesh, but the spirit that moves them is as alien as a boa constrictor."

"He is right," Ricia said, and shuddered as with a chill. "I felt it, too."

"I agree they're a clammy lot, but to jump from that to Aliens Among Us is quite a leap. The fact is, we don't know enough about them." I looked at Ricia. "Is there a back way into this Feast Hall? Something they might not know about?"

"There are service routes leading to the kitchens. It is possible that they have not discovered them."

"You'll need a gun. I guess we can borrow one from the Admiral."

"Wait a minute," Hayle barked. "You're not going to try an attack on them? There must be hundreds of them!"

"Nothing so dramatic. I want information, proof that these Womboids exist—that they're a threat."

"Don't be a damned fool! You have to get clear, now, before they discover you! I'll write a letter for COMSPAC; they'll send a force in here big enough to take this place lock, stock, and barrel! We can't let one of them escape, now that we've found their nest."

"Sorry, I'm not leaving until I've got something concrete. Tell COMSPAC they're a threat, you say. What kind of threat? Maybe they're a harmless secret society."

"Harmless! They killed my men!"

"Your men intruded on them, Admiral. I guess you could say the same of me. They don't seem to go out looking for trouble."

"Are you siding with these devils!" Hayle glared at me with red eyes.

"I'm trying to point out the futility of arousing any official interest in them without something more than a strange feeling to go on. *You* know this is something big; *I* know it. I can feel the threat in the air as thick as the smog over Naples. But we need proof."

"My letter—"

"They'll file it along with the UFO reports. I'm going down. Ricia, you stay here with the Admiral. If I'm not back in twenty-four hours—"

"Mal, do not speak foolishly. I am with you."

"You two are going down there, beard these vipers in their den? When you could get away clean, now?"

"You'll be all right here for another day, Admiral. Then we'll leave together."

Hayle stared at me. Then he got to his feet, painfully. "I've been without light, without the sound of a human voice for three months," he said heavily. "I'll not be without them again, as long as I can crawl."

I thought about it. "All right, Admiral," I said. "Buckle on a gun and let's get moving."

The route that Ricia showed us was a narrow, sharply spiraling ramp, almost lost at the far end of the corridor. We followed it down past arched openings at each floor, emerged into an echoing vault as big as the nave of a middlesized cathedral. Heavy equipment was ranged in dark rows along the center of the room. It looked like an abandoned factory.

"This is the upper kitchen," Ricia whispered. "Here the carcasses of Holgotha were prepared, and the hearts cut from the Riffa tree, and the great fishes. . . ." She stared, caught in a dream of barbaric banquets served long ago.

"They're not here," Hayle was sniffing the air. "I could smell them if they were. We haven't descended far enough."

"There is another kitchen below," Ricia said. "But they have been here—and they are near. The library senses their warmth."

"What's this 'library'?" Hayle asked sharply. I explained the miniature pickup and relay system. Hayle grunted. "Handy," he said. "Some day I'll want to know a great deal more about you, young lady, and about the people who built this fantastic pile."

Back on the ramp, we moved stealthily, pausing to listen every few yards. The walls were warmer here; I could sense it through my gloves. I sniffed, caught the taint of fresh decay. Beside me, Ricia put out a hand, touched my arm.

"Just ahead," she breathed.

"Give me the light."

She handed it to me. "Be careful." I nodded, waved her back. Hayle started forward.

"Stay here," I mouthed. He glared at me. I made a peremptory motion and turned away. He was a good officer; he took the order in silence.

Six feet farther, half around the next turn of the ramp, an arch opened on the right. The warmth and odor were stronger here. I poked my head out, looked into a long room much like the one above. If there was anyone in it, they were standing very still.

"I'm going in," I whispered. "If the coast is clear, you follow." I did not wait for the arguments; I started down the aisle between the giant cauldrons.

It was a hundred-yard walk to the small, square door in the opposite wall. I moved along, heel and toe, with my gun in my hand and my ears out on stalks. It was as silent as a deaf-mute's tomb.

At the door, I flattened myself against the wall and listened. There may have been a few faint sounds from beyond it—or maybe it was just imagination frisking in the dark. The door was a double one, hinged at both sides. I touched the nearest panel; it swung in, letting in light and a whiff of foul air like an opened coffin.

Tables were ranged in rows across a wide room with tall

shuttered windows. Twenty or thirty men sat at the tables, dwarfed by the scale of the high, vaulted ceiling. At that moment, one of them looked my way.

I froze, holding the door as it was, half an inch open; the movement of closing it would catch his eye more surely than the displacement. He stared across for a long moment. Then he turned back; I thought he spoke to someone across the table, but I was not sure. He was at least fifty yards from me, and the light was a dim flicker from a crude flambeau on a stand in the space between tables. No one moved from his seat. I decided the man had not seen me.

Another man entered the room, went to a serving counter, scooped up food, took a seat alone at a table. Another man rose, went out the way the other had entered. Minutes ticked past, while nothing happened, I let the door close gently, turned to cross back to the ramp where Ricia and Hayle waited, and a yellow light bloomed, a heat-lightning flash; sound racketed and roared from the walls. I dropped, rolled behind a leg-mounted rectangle of cold iron with an odor of grease and mold as a second shot thundered, and a third. There were sounds of scuffling feet, of fists hitting flesh, the clatter of a dropped gun. Hayle snarled something that was cut off in the middle by a blow. Then silence.

Chapter Fifteen

I waited while five minutes crawled across the darkness. Feet scraped and voices muttered across the big room; lights swept the aisles, I pulled my feet in just in time. Someone came toward me; I held the gun ready, flattened myself half under a massive cooker. He passed me by two yards away, looking in the other direction. The voices and footsteps moved away to the far end of the room. Lights bobbed there. Some instinct said that for the moment the coast was clear. I crawled out, easy-footed it along, behind the big, dark ovens. Voices muttered in the distance; the door into the dining room opened, let in a wedge of dirty light, shut again. Feet came and went. They had not given up yet; maybe they had instincts, too, that told them they had not quite finished the job.

✦   ✦   ✦

The archway beyond which I had left Ricia and Hayle was thirty feet away, and it meant crossing open ground. I got within ten feet of it before I realized a man was standing silently with his back to me, just inside the opening. I froze against the wall and waited, unable to go forward, unwilling to go back. Then he turned and disappeared. I followed, made the archway, saw him standing six feet away, looking past two bodies on the floor. In the first instant, I thought they were both dead; then I saw the glint of Hayle's eye, a tiny movement from Ricia. They were trussed in wire like giant, half-wound armatures. I slid around the edge of the wall, and Ricia saw me. The guard did not; his ears were tuned to some fancied sound from the ramp above. I could have taken him then, easily enough; then he stepped off, went up the ramp and out of sight.

I went to Ricia's side, knelt by her.

"He had a signaler. Do not let him see you! Go quickly!"

I was checking over the wires that bound her. There were hundreds of turns around her, cutting cruelly into her arms, her thighs, her ankles.

"No time for me, Mal! Listen! They spoke; they wait now for the instructions of their Primary. They do not know about you; they think that the old man and I are alone."

"I'll get these wires off."

"No! Find the one they call the Primary; he is their weakness! They spoke of the Chamber of the Dragon. I know the apartment they mean."

"The wires—"

"No time!" She cut me off. "There is a way out. Above the central bank of ovens there is a flue big enough for a man, I think. When you reach the kitchen above, go along the corridor to the far side, all the way to the end. There you will find a door decorated by carvings. He is there."

Someone was coming. I touched Ricia's face. "I'll be back," I said, then faded back against the wall, slipped through the archway and ran for cover.

It took me half an hour to work my way across to the big central unit. There was a wide hood above it. I climbed up, thrust my head and shoulders in; soot drifted down, and I resisted the impulse to sneeze. Metal handholds were set in the masonry. I used them, started up.

✦   ✦   ✦

The kitchen above was laid out like the lower one, except that the units were bigger, designed to accommodate gargantuan haunches of meat. There were tables the size of badminton courts, pots big enough to render missionaries in platoons. I moved past them, through the door at the far end, along a dim-lit corridor at the end of which men came and went. The doorways gave me concealment. I advanced as a lone skirmisher, five yards at a time. The door Ricia had told me about was plain enough—a high double panel with a carved lizard with two heads spitting fire at a bare-legged man with a spear.

The traffic thinned. A single man emerged from the door, went away along the cross corridor. For the moment, the coast was clear. I did not pause to weigh odds; I dashed, made it to the door and through into dimness and stale-smelling warmth. A man jumped up as I came in, gaped at me for a moment—just long enough for me to swing on him, knock him back against the wall. I caught him, hit him again. He fought back, clawing at me with untrimmed fingernails, until I got my thumbs in behind the big tendons of his neck. I felt his larynx break, kept choking until he flopped a final flop and went limp. I lowered him, checked for a pulse, caught the last feeble flutter. Killing him bothered me no more than swatting a moth. He was one less live enemy at my back.

There was a heavy hanging across a doorway in the left wall. I flipped it aside, stepped through into an evil-smelling room hung with decayed splendor and almost filled by a vast bed on which a bloated caricature of a man sprawled, staring at me with bulging eyes.

I showed him the gun, moved across and put myself to the left of the entry. I had a weird sensation that I was reliving another confrontation. I could almost feel the pressure of the water beyond the walls. But this time it was ice, and the walls were old, old, reeking of time and forgotten things.

"Are you the same one?" My voice came out hoarse. He did not answer. I jammed the gun cruelly against one bloated foot and the giant leg twitched away. He wheezed, grunted. Thick fluid oozed from his slack mouth.

"You can talk." I aimed the gun at his head. "Who are you? What do you want from us?"

"I want. . . . only peace, and silence." His voice was a high, thin sigh. "Why do you hurt me?"

"Don't pull that on me; I know about you, remember? Or maybe he was your brother. There's not much keeping you alive, Fat Stuff, just my curiosity. Give me answers or it goes off now."

"I am the Primary," he squeaked. "Nothing must injure me."

I raked the gun sight down his gross thigh, as big around as a turbine shaft; it left a red weal across the doughy flesh. He gave a high squeal and quivered.

"Why did you kidnap me? What did you want with the girl?"

"Women are needed," he piped. "More women. Bring many women, I will pay you well."

I could feel sweat popping out on my face. A sense of unreality made the giant slug on the bed seem like some gross fantasy, a dream of greed and evil. I jabbed it again. "Talk, damn you!" I felt my voice rise, but it was not important; only the answers were important now. "Who are you? Why do you kill without warning? How did you get here?" What are you?"

There was a quick sound behind me. I whirled, dropped as a wire-fine beam of vivid light crackled across above my head, and then my gun bucked and roared in my hand and a man leaned in the doorway, clutched at the hanging with one hand, crumpled slowly, the heat gun still lanced across. Behind me, the fat one screamed—an infinitely high, pure note of agony that ululated on and on, wailed down the scale to a choking rattle and died away like a moan of utter bereavement.

The man in the doorway fell, and his gun bounced clear. Smoke was rising from the bedding. A foul odor choked me. I staggered to my feet, saw the gaping, char-and-crimson wound that curved erratically down across the quivering bulk of the creature on the bed, laying open the vast paunch like a split melon.

As I watched, something stirred in the depths of the wound. A glistening black shape wriggled there, thrusting. A blind tendril like the head of a great soft worm poked clear, a sheen of black-ish red. I jerked the gun up, fired again and again, saw the writhing shape spatter, twist away, jerking and whipping with an unclean vitality as foot after foot of its hideous length emerged from the ripped abdomen. I was not aware of slamming another clip into the gun, but later I noticed the empty magazine on the floor where I had thrown it.

I pumped every round into the slug shape, and still it coiled out, yearning across the filth-spattered floor toward me and I backed until the wall stopped me, then dragged a heavy chest from the wall, toppled it on the frightful thing. Pinned, it whipped and beat its slimy coils against the floor. And on the bed, the fat man, like a great burst balloon, sagged, an empty bag.

Time seemed to stand still. I was in the outer room, still hearing the restless slap of the slug against the floor. A man stood near the door. I raised the gun, clicked it emptily at him. He made no move. His mouth hung slack; his eyes looked past me vacantly. I ran past him, knocked him aside. Out in the corridor, more men stood. As I watched, one staggered, fell against the wall. The others ignored him. None of them seemed to notice me. I pushed through them, found myself face to face with the man with the shriveled skin, the one I thought I had drowned.

"Who are you?" I hissed. I caught his coat, a rumpled brown suit, and shook him. His gaze turned on me from some remote distance.

"He is dead," he said.

"Who was he? What does it mean? What was that—thing?"

"Now the long dream dies," he said. Then the intelligence went out of his eyes. His mouth opened slackly. I shoved him away, ran on. No one tried to stop me.

Ricia and the Admiral lay where I had left them. Their guard was gone—wandered away, they said. The wires had made ugly marks on Ricia's skin, but she was able to walk. Hayle staggered at first, but after the first hundred yards he found his feet again.

We passed Womboids, a few standing, or moving aimlessly along in the dark, but most of them lying like firing squad victims. I turned one or two over; they were dead, without a mark on them.

"It's as though they'd forgotten how to breathe," Hayle said.

"Maybe they did," I said. "I think that somehow they drew their strength from the. . . . thing on the bed."

We tramped through the building, explored great halls and lavish apartments and vaulted corridors, and Ricia talked of the fetes and galas that she had known in the once-magnificent halls. We found the exit by accident; it was a sloping tunnel that led upward from wide double windows behind a terrace far up on the side of the tower. Half an hour later we stood on the ice crust under a dawn sky like spilled paint. Far away the sled was visible as a dark speck against the purple-and-red-dyed sky.

"We'll go to the house first for supplies," I said. "Then to the coast. Ricia's boat will be there. In ten days we'll be home. After that—I don't know."

"Omaha," the Admiral said. "CINCNAVOP is there, and they'll be operating, you can depend on it. I don't know how much sea power the Navy can still command, but it will be enough."

"If they believe us," I said.

"They'll believe me," Hayle declared. "I'll see to that."

We made the crossing in fifteen days; the weather was good— barring the eternal black-clouded skies and occasional falls of volcanic ash. We rested, ate and talked, and Ricia spent hours studying a one-volume encyclopedia we found aboard.

"I can understand why they thought they had to kill my party," Hayle said. We were sitting on the tiny afterdeck, smoking and watching another violent sunset. "We'd stumbled onto their hide-out—their Hidden Place, as they called it. But why the persecution of Ricia? She was no threat to them."

"I have a theory," I said, "that they recognized her for what she was—a member of the ancient race. Naturally, they'd want to question her."

"But that implied they knew. . . ."

"Certainly; the Primary spoke her language."

"I think," Ricia said hesitantly, "that he was. . . . of my people. Beneath the swollen body I thought I saw the likeness."

"You mean he—as an individual—was God knows how many thousands of years old?" Hayle snorted. "That's preposterous!"

"No older than Ricia." I smiled at her youthful face.

"That's different. She was in a low-energy comatose state. The Navy's been experimenting with similar techniques for years."

"They're not human, remember, Admiral—your own statement, I believe. They *used* humans. The slug thing that I killed—I think *that* was the Primary—not the swollen thing that served as host."

"Why did the others. . . . run down, when he died?" Hayle's voice was hoarse, as one speaking of the horribly dead.

"In some way, they were all linked to him. They existed to serve him."

"And what did *he* live for?"

"For the same reason we do—the instinct to survive. In our case, the race is made up of millions, billions of individuals. In his—

I think he was the race: a single, immortal individual, supported like a queen bee by his Womboids."

"What for? They lived in secret; I think they must have inhabited that tower for ages—literally. They had no luxuries, not even comfort. They just lived, parasites on the human race. Perhaps we never would have discovered them, if the changes in the planet hadn't brought their Hidden Place to light. And if Ricia hadn't come on the scene, perhaps not even then."

"It seems they've been with us a long time," I mused. "I wonder where they came from, how they established their role in the first place."

"Perhaps they're invaders from some other world." Hayle half smiled. "Perhaps the flying saucers landed a million years ago. But, then, perhaps they've always been here, a product of the same slime that we came up from. Perhaps they learned to use us as hosts long before we were men."

"Strange—all that history to come to an end, because one creature died."

Hayle narrowed his eyes. With his beard trimmed and his cheeks beginning to fill out, he was looking like a tough old Navy officer again.

"They tried to keep him alive; they spent themselves like flies to protect him. Strange creatures—at once so deadly, and so inept. With all the technical wealth of the frozen city to draw on, one would think they'd have been more effective in surviving."

"I think they had no intelligence of their own," I said. "They used the brains of the human bodies they infested, just as they used their limbs. And remember, Admiral, they weren't human; their needs and drives weren't ours. They wanted nothing but a safe, dark nest for their Primary."

"Still, they ventured out; you saw them in Georgia, in Miami, in the Mediterranean. And the villa you found there—I suspect they had inhabited it for quite some time."

"Ricia's people knew them," I pointed out. "I suppose that house was built on shore, and somehow sealed before it sank."

"Those oldsters had an astounding technology." Hayle wagged his head. "Not like ours, but in some ways, surpassing ours—as witness the marvelous little communications devices Ricia has shown me. How could such knowledge have been lost so utterly?"

"That was a long time ago, Admiral. The ice came down, and

ground everything to rubble before it. Weather and age and warfare and looting could account for the rest."

"And, do you not see," Ricia asked, "when human cities fell, the under-men alone, living long in their secret places, remembered the ancient wisdom. It would have made them kings among savage men. And they would have destroyed every reminder of man's former greatness."

"I wonder. . . ." Hayle puffed on his pipe. "What we know of the habits of ancient rulers seems to fit the pattern: impassive, long-lived, ruthless, worshipped as gods—and always the immense harem—and their treatment of women as inferiors, useful only for breeding. Perhaps it's from them that we derived our concept of sex as something secret and evil, surrounded with ancient taboos."

"A civilization that could build a city like Ricia's would have to leave *some* trace," I protested. "At least some legend, some tradition of knowledge."

Hayle was frowning. "There *are* anomalies," he said softly. "The ancient Arabs used storage batteries to plate their jewelry; the Greeks had an astronomical computer; even the bushmen and their boomerangs."

"There is another thing," Ricia said. "The minerals that your people have regarded as precious—the metals and stones. I think this is a racial memory of a lost technology. Silver is a conductor of electricity, better than copper. Diamond is a cutting tool; the ruby is necessary to the laser."

"And the fiber-reinforced metals," I suggested. "Sapphire 'whiskers' in a silver matrix, for example, and uranium."

"And gold, too," Hayle nodded. "Our satellites are plated with the stuff."

"Their value could not be explained by rarity alone," Ricia said.

"Hell, diamonds wouldn't be worth a dollar a pound if the supply weren't controlled by the producing governments," I pointed out. "And the same is true of most of the stones. Even gold is artificially supported. It was common enough among the South American Indians that they made ordinary drinking cups and ornaments from it."

"All this is theory," Hayle said. "When we've restored some degree of order to this catastrophe-wracked planet, then we'll investigate our cold-storage city. Perhaps then we'll learn the answers."

"Perhaps—and perhaps we'll never know. In a way, it's too bad the Primary is dead and his Womboids with him. There might have been a way to make him talk."

"We're well rid of the monster, and all his spawn," Hayle said harshly. "We will have our problems, God knows." He looked at the ruined sky. "But that's one curse we can live without."

Two days later we sighted the Louisiana coast. We made landfall west of a little town called Iowa, commandeered an abandoned car after digging it out of a mud bank. A few hours later we were on the outskirts of Omaha. Hayle took over, skirted the ruins of the city proper, took a winding route among black ash cones standing on the plain like chimneys, pulled up to a fence, much mended but still standing, surrounding a bare hundred-acre tract with a blockhouse and some sheds at its center. A squad of armed Marines watched us climb out of the car and come up to the gate. Hayle gave the password; the Marine sergeant used his talkie; then an officer came out of the blockhouse and looked us over. There was more confab; then they opened the gate, formed up a box around us, marched us across to the building.

Hayle looked impatient, but kept calm. I was still wearing my .45, so it must have been just routine. In the blockhouse they frisked us, looked the gun over, let me keep it. There were happy smiles and salutes all around when a fat Commodore arrived via elevator from somewhere below, greeted Hayle warmly, ushered us all into the car. He was bubbling with questions, but Hayle gave him the old Academy smile and said he would save it for the official briefing.

We stepped out into a wide, immaculate, gray-walled room packed with electronic gear. The Commodore took us across to an office with rugs, pictures, a big desk, pushed a buzzer on the desk, offered drinks. There was a tap, and three men came into the room, all portly, gray-haired desk sailors with adequate braid on their cuffs.

"Gentlemen," the Commodore was saying.

Ricia touched my arm. "Malcome!" she whispered in my ear. "The library says—"

Someone was holding out a hand to be shaken. I took it, nodded replies to introductions.

"Mal!" Ricia said urgently. "That one—in the center—he is one of. . . . them!"

I jerked as though a needle had hit me, remembering the dead

Primary. Apparently the Womboids came in varieties. Perhaps through some kind of selective propagation, they developed some who could live independently. The Commodore was talking:

" . . . . after so many months. I'm sure, gentlemen, that we shall all be most interested in what Admiral Hayle can tell us of what he encountered in Antarctica."

I was watching the officer in the center of the three, an Oriental-looking fellow with dead-black eyes. He had stepped back half a pace. His hand went to a side pocket, he palmed something, raised his arm unobtrusively.

I jerked the .45 from its holster, shot him in the chest, heard his gun bark, shot again as he slammed back, put a third slug into his head before they landed on me. I tried to yell; Hayle was staring, saying something. Then the door burst open and Marines spilled in. I caught a glimpse of knuckles, and my interest in the proceedings faded in a shower of lights.

The courtroom was a converted office, but no less ominous for that. Armed Marines lined the walls; grim-faced officers in tieless whites or dungarees sat behind the long table. Admiral Hayle sat at one side, two Marines with drawn guns behind his chair. I was still dizzy; my head buzzed like a burned relay. It had not taken them long to get a court together.

The Commodore was at the center of the judge's table, reading out the charges. It seemed that I had wantonly committed mayhem on the person of one General Yin, a military observer from a friendly nation. There seemed to be other, vaguer charges as well, having to do with breach of security, sabotage, false representations, kidnapping, and treason. It did not interest me much. My head hurt too badly. I put a hand up to feel it, got a sharp crack across the arm from someone standing behind me.

I looked around. Ricia was not in sight.

"Where is she?" I came half out of my seat and was slammed down hard. The Commodore said something in a harsh voice; the other members of the board looked at me with impassive faces.

"Get up," a voice said behind me; a hard hand helped me, urgently. The Commodore glared. I looked across at Hayle. He was watching me, his face set in anger.

" . . . . brutal murder," the Commodore was saying. "Have you anything to say to this court before sentence is passed?"

Hayle was on his feet. "The man is in no condition to conduct his own defense. I'm warning you, Commodore, this kangaroo court—"

"You'll be seated or I'll have you removed from the courtroom!" The Commodore's face was blustery red. "I don't know your role in this murder plot, Admiral, but I can promise you we've no patience with traitors here."

"I've told you enough to make it plain that there's more to this than appears at first glance," Hayle stormed. "This man deserves a hearing!"

"He'll have his hearing! Be seated, sir!"

Hayle locked eyes with the Commodore, then sat.

"Where's Ricia, Admiral?" I called before a hand cuffed me.

"Shut up, you!" the man behind me barked.

"The woman is being cared for," the Commodore snapped.

"What happened to her?" I yelled.

"She was injured."

"Injured how? How badly?"

"Silence! If you have anything to say that bears on the issue here, speak up now!"

"I shot him because he wasn't human," I said. My voice sounded loud and hollow in my ears. Babble broke out. The Commodore gaveled it down.

"How did you learn that he was not human?" one of the board members asked. His eyes bored into me.

"I. . . . can't tell you." Somehow, it seemed important to keep Ricia's library a secret.

"How did you know of the city under the ice?" another demanded.

"I was taken there—by them."

"By whom? Who do you mean by 'them'?"

"The Womboids. They—"

"How did you learn of the secret place under the water?" a third queried coldly.

I opened my mouth to answer, paused, trying to remember. I had not mentioned the sunken villa to anyone here, other than the Admiral. My eye went to him. He frowned, shot a look at me, shook his head. I looked back at the solemn faces of the board, and suddenly I knew.

The Commodore was human. The rest were Womboids.

The questioning went on for an hour; I gave half answers, vague answers. I was stalling, hoping for something, I didn't know what. My head ached; it was hot in the room. Hayle had objected again and been forcibly silenced.

The Womboids fired questions at me in a merciless cross fire. It was apparent that they were probing to discover how much I knew about them, and how I had learned it, rather than investigating the circumstances of the shooting. Even the Commodore was looking puzzled. He pounded the table, called for silence.

"This investigation is wandering far afield," he snapped. "This court has no interest in these fantasies. The man is either out of his head or seeking to create that impression. The question is simply: are there extenuating circumstances which might justify or mitigate the crime he committed. The answer is clear: No!" He looked across at me under beetled brows.

"The accused will stand."

I got up.

"This court finds you guilty as charged," he said flatly. "The sentence is death by firing squad—to be carried out immediately."

The door burst open. Three young officers—two Navy men and one Marine—strode into the room, each with a machine pistol across his chest. I swung around to face them, felt my teeth clamp, bracing for the shock. They brought their guns up, leveled them. The utter stillness was shattered by the racketing burst of fire that lanced from their muzzles. I staggered, saw the bright surface of the judge's table explode in splinters, saw the blank faces behind it open in unheard cries as they tumbled down and away in a rising dust cloud of broken plaster.

The silence rang with echoes. The Commodore was still sitting, his face as gray as the wall. Some of the Marines groped for holstered guns, raised their hands as the machine pistols swung to cover them.

"Everybody stand fast," the Marine captain said. "We've been the victims of a plot, but it wasn't the prisoner who was plotting. Admiral Hayle, will you assume command, sir?"

Hayle stood. "With pleasure, Captain."

Ricia was propped up in a clean white bed, looking a little pale, but bright-eyed and smiling.

"It is nothing, Malcome. The bullet from the little gun struck me in the side, but they have tended me well."

"It could have killed you. Damn me for not listening—I could have shot him before he got the gun up."

"It does not matter, Malcome. We are alive—and safe. The secret of the Womboids is known now; they have no more power to hurt us."

"There's no telling how many cells of them there are. We finished one off in Gonwondo; I think most of the Mediterranean group were killed. Now this bunch. They seem to be able to communicate in some way, so they'll be on the alert."

"We'll get them," Hayle said. "Don't worry about that angle, Irish."

"How did you do it, Ricia?" I took her hand; it was warm and firm. "Nothing I said got through; even the Admiral couldn't get a hearing."

Ricia smiled. "I convinced the good surgeon that he must make a special examination of the dead colonel." The smile faded. "He found—anomalies. The library told me that the judges were of the enemy. The rest you know."

"Astonishing thing, that." Colonel Barker, the army surgeon who had removed the bullet from Ricia's ribs, had come in time to hear her remark. "His heart seemed perfectly normal, until I probed for the bullet." His face twisted at the memory. "I found a bloody great worm in it—alive, mind you. Damned thing seemed to have roots, of a sort. Ran all through the body. Microscopic, of course. Never have noticed 'em, but for the young lady."

"You're full of surprises, Ricia," Hayle said. "How did you get him to listen to you—and you telling him his business at that? What kind of special powers of the ancients did you use on him?"

"No special power of the ancients, Admiral Hayle. Only the power that all women have." She looked at me and smiled a dazzling feminine smile.

"A woman can always have her desire—if her desire is great."

I looked into her dark eyes and agreed.

THE WALLS

Harry Trimble looked pleased when he stepped into the apartment. The lift door had hardly clacked shut behind him on the peering commuter faces in the car before he had slipped his arm behind Flora's back, bumped his face against her cheek and chuckled, "Well, what would you say to a little surprise? Something you've waited a long time for?"

Flora looked up from the dial-a-ration panel. "A surprise, Harry?"

"I know how you feel about the apartment, Flora. Well, from now on, you won't be seeing so much of it—"

"Harry!"

He winced at her clutch on his arm. Her face was pale under the day-glare strip. "We're not—moving to the country . . . ?"

Harry pried his arm free. "The country? What the devil are you talking about?" He was frowning now, the pleased look gone. "You should use the lamps more," he said. "You look sick." He glanced around the apartment, the four perfectly flat rectangular walls, the glassy surface of the variglow ceiling, the floor with its pattern of sink-away panels. His eye fell on the four-foot square of the TV screen.

"I'm having that thing taken out tomorrow," he said. The pleased look was coming back. He cocked an eye at Flora. "And I'm having a Full-wall installed!"

Flora glanced at the blank screen. "A Full-wall, Harry?"

"Yep!" Harry smacked a fist into a palm, taking a turn up and down the room. "We'll be the first in our cell block to have a Full-wall!"

"Why—that will be nice, Harry. . . ."

"Nice?" Harry punched the screen control, then deployed the two chairs with tray racks ready to receive the evening meal.

Behind him, figures jiggled on the screen. "It's a darn sight more than nice," he said, raising his voice over the shrill and thump of the music. "It's expensive, for one thing. Who else do you know that can afford—"

"But—"

"But nothing! Imagine it, Flora! It'll be like having a. . . . a balcony seat, looking out on other people's lives."

"But we have so little space now; won't it take up—"

"Of course not! How do you manage to stay so ignorant of technical progress? It's only an eighth of an inch thick. Think of it: that thick"—Harry indicated an eighth of an inch with his fingers—"and better color and detail than you've ever seen. It's all done with what they call an edge-excitation effect."

"Harry, the old screen is good enough. Couldn't we use the money for a trip—"

"How do you know if it's good enough? You never have it on. I have to turn it on myself when I get home."

Flora brought the trays and they ate silently, watching the screen. After dinner, Flora disposed of the trays, retracted the table and chairs, and extended the beds. They lay in the dark, not talking.

"It's a whole new system," Harry said suddenly. "The Full-wall people have their own programming scheme; they plan your whole day, wake you up at the right time with some lively music, give you breakfast menus to dial, then follow up with a good sitcom to get you into the day; then there's nap music, with subliminal hypnotics if you have trouble sleeping; then—"

"Harry—can I turn it off if I want to?"

"Turn it off?" Harry sounded puzzled. "The idea is to leave it on. That's why I'm having it installed for you, you know—so you can use it!"

"But sometimes I like to just think—"

"Think! Brood, you mean." He heaved a sigh. "Look, Flora, I know the place isn't fancy. Sure, you get a little tired of being here all the time; but there are plenty of people worse off—and now, with Full-wall, you'll get a feeling of more space—"

"Harry"—Flora spoke rapidly—"I wish we could go away. I mean leave the city, and get a little place where we can be alone, even if it means working hard, and where I can have a garden and maybe keep chickens and you could chop firewood—"

"Good God!" Harry roared, cutting her off. Then: "These fantasies of yours," he said quietly. "You have to learn to live in the real world, Flora. Live in the woods? Wet leaves, wet bark, bugs, mould; talk about depressing. . . ."

There was a long silence.

"I know; you're right, Harry," Flora said. "I'll enjoy the Full-wall. It was very sweet of you to think of getting it for me."

"Sure," Harry said. "It'll be better. You'll see. . . ."

The Full-wall was different, Flora agreed as soon as the service men had made the last adjustments and flipped it on. There was vivid color, fine detail, and a remarkable sense of depth. The shows were about the same—fast-paced, bursting with variety and energy. It was exciting at first, having full-sized people talking, eating, fighting, taking baths, making love, right in the room with you. If you sat across the room and half-closed your eyes, you could almost imagine you were watching real people. Of course, real people wouldn't carry on like that. But then, it was hard to say what real people might do. Flora had always thought Doll Starr wore padded brassieres, but when she stripped on Full-wall—there wasn't any fakery about it.

Harry was pleased, too, when he arrived home to find the wall on. He and Flora would dial dinner with one eye on the screen, then slip into bed and view until the Bull-Doze pills they'd started taking took effect. Perhaps things *were* better, Flora thought hopefully. More like they used to be.

But after a month or two, the Full-wall began to pall. The same faces, the same pratfalls, the same happy quiz masters, the puzzled prize-winners, the delinquent youths and fumbling dads, the bosoms—all the same.

On the sixty-third day, Flora switched the Full-wall off. The light and sound died, leaving a faint, dwindling glow. She eyed the glassy wall uneasily, as one might view the coffin of an acquaintance.

It was quiet in the apartment. Flora fussed with the dial-a-ration, averting her eyes from the dead screen. She turned to deploy the solitaire table and started violently. The screen, the residual glow having faded now, was a perfect mirror. She went close to it, touched the hard surface with a finger. It was almost invisible. She studied her reflected face; the large dark eyes with shadows under them, the cheekline, a trifle too hollow to be really chic, the hair drawn back in an uninspired bun. Behind her, the doubled room, unadorned now that all the furnishings were retracted into the floor except for the pictures on the wall: photographs of the children away at school, a sunny scene of green pastureland, a painting of rolling waves at sea.

She stepped back, considering the effect.

The floor and walls seemed to continue without interruption, except for a hardly noticeable line. It was as though the apartment were twice as large. If only it weren't so empty. . . .

Flora deployed the table and chairs, dialed a lunch, and sat, eating, watching her double. No wonder Harry seemed indifferent lately, she thought, noting the rounded shoulders, the insignificant bust, the slack posture. She would have to do something in the way of self-improvement.

Half an hour of the silent companionship of her image was enough. Flora snapped the screen back on, watched almost with relief as a grinning cowboy in velvet chaps made strumming motions while an intricately-fingered guitar melody blared from the soundtrack.

Thereafter, she turned the screen off every day, at first only for an hour, later for longer and longer periods. Once, she found herself chatting gaily to her reflection, and hastily fell silent. It wasn't as though she were becoming neurotic, she assured herself; it was just the feeling of roominess that made her like the mirror screen. And she was always careful to have it on when Harry arrived home.

It was about six months after the Full-wall had been installed that Harry emerged one day from the lift smiling in a way that reminded Flora of that earlier evening. He dropped his briefcase into his floor locker, looked around the apartment, humming to himself.

"What is it, Harry?" Flora asked.

Harry glanced at her. "It's not a log cabin in the woods," he said. "But maybe you'll like it anyway. . . ."

"What. . . . is it, dear. . . ."

"Don't sound so dubious." He broke into a broad smile. "I'm getting you another Full-wall."

Flora looked puzzled. "But this one is working perfectly, Harry."

"Of course it is," he snapped. "I mean you're getting another wall; you'll have two. What about that? Two Full-walls—and nobody else in the cell-block has one yet. The only question is—" he rubbed his hands together, striding up and down the room, eyeing the walls—"which wall is it to be? You can have it adjacent, or opposite. I went over the whole thing with the Full-wall people today. By God, they're doing a magnificent job of programming. You see, the two walls will be synchronized. You're getting the same show on both—you're seeing it from two angles, just as though you were right there in the middle of it. Their whole program has been built on that principle."

"Harry, I'm not sure I want another wall—"

"Oh, nonsense. What is this, some kind of self-denial urge? Why not have the best—if you can afford it. And by God, I can afford it. I'm hitting my stride—"

"Harry, could I go with you some day—tomorrow? I'd like to see where you work, meet your friends—"

"Flora, are you out of your mind? You've seen the commuter car; you know how crowded it is. And what would you do when you got there? Just stand around all day, blocking the aisle? Why don't you appreciate the luxury of having your own place, a little privacy, and now two Full-walls—"

"Then could I go somewhere else? I could take a later car. I want to get out in the open air, Harry. I. . . . haven't seen the sky for. . . . years, it seems."

"But. . . ." Harry groped for words, staring at Flora. "Why would you want to go up on the roof?"

"Not the roof; I want to get out of the city—just for a little while. I'll be back home in time to dial your dinner . . ."

"Do you mean to tell me you want to spend all that money to wedge yourself in a verticar and then transfer to a crosstown and travel maybe seventy miles, packed in like a sardine, standing up all the way, just so you can get out and stand in a wasteland and look back at the walls? And then get back in another car—if you're lucky—and come back again?"

"No—I don't know—I just want to get out, Harry. The roof. Could I go to the roof?"

Harry came over to pat Flora awkwardly on the arm. "Now, take it easy, Flora. You're a little tired and stale; I know. I get the same way sometimes. But don't get the idea that you're missing anything by not having to get into that rat-race. Heaven knows *I* wish I could stay home. And this new wall is going to make things different. You'll see. . . ."

The new Full-wall was installed adjacent to the first, with a joint so beautifully fitted that only the finest line marked the junction. As soon as she was alone with it, Flora switched it off. Now two reflections stared back at her from behind what appeared to be two intersecting planes of clear glass. She waved an arm. The two slave figures aped her. She walked toward the mirrored corner. They advanced. She stepped back; they retreated.

She went to the far corner of the room and studied the effect. It wasn't as nice as before. Instead of a simple room, neatly bounded on all four sides by solid walls, she seemed now to occupy a stage set off by windows through which other, similar stages were visible, endlessly repeated. The old feeling of intimate companionship with her reflected self was gone; the two mirror-women were strangers, silently watching her. Defiantly, she stuck out her tongue. The two reflections grimaced menacingly. With a small cry, Flora ran to the switch, turned the screens on.

They were seldom off after that. Sometimes, when the hammering of hooves became too wearing, or the shouting of comics too strident, she would blank them out, and sit, back to the mirror walls, sipping a cup of hot coflet, and waiting—but they were always on when Harry arrived, sometimes glum, sometimes brisk and satisfied. He would settle himself in his chair, waiting patiently enough for dinner, watching the screens.

"They're all right," he would declare, nodding. "Look at that, Flora. Look at the way that fellow whipped right across there. By golly, you've got to hand it to the Full-wall people."

"Harry—where do they make the shows? The ones that show the beautiful scenery, and trees and rolling hills, and mountains?"

Harry was chewing. "Don't know," he said. "On location, I suppose."

"Then there really are places like that? I mean, they aren't just making it up?"

Harry stared at her, mouth full and half open. He grunted and resumed chewing. He swallowed. "I suppose that's another of your cracks."

"I don't understand, Harry," Flora said. He took another bite, glanced sideways at her puzzled expression.

"Of course they aren't making it up. How the devil could they make up a mountain?"

"I'd like to see those places."

"Here we go again," Harry said. "I was hoping I could enjoy a nice meal and then view awhile, but I guess you're not going to allow that."

"Of course, Harry. I just said—"

"I know what you said. Well, look at them then." He waved his hand at the screen. "There it is; the whole world. You can sit right here and view it all—"

"But I want to do more than just view it. I want to live it. I want to be in those places, and feel leaves under my feet, and have rain fall on my face—"

Harry frowned incredulously. "You mean you want to be an actress?"

"No, of course not—"

"I don't know what you want. You have a home, two Full-walls, and this isn't all. I'm working toward something, Flora. . . ."

Flora sighed. "Yes, Harry. I'm very lucky."

"Darn right." Harry nodded emphatically, eyes on the screens. "Dial me another coflet, will you?"

The third Full-wall came as a surprise. Flora had taken the 1100 car to the roboclinic on the 478th level for her annual checkup. When she returned home—there it was. She hardly noticed the chorus of gasps cut off abruptly as the door shut in the faces of the other wives in the car. Flora stood, impressed in spite of herself by the fantastic panorama filling her apartment. Directly before her, the studio audience gaped up from massed seats. A fat man in the front row reached inside a red plain shirt to scratch. Flora could see the perspiration on his forehead. Farther back, a couple nuzzled, eyes on the stage. *Who were they*, Flora wondered; *How did they manage to get out of their apartments and offices and sit in a real theatre. . . .*

To the left, an owlish youth blinked from a brightly lit cage. And on the right, the MC caressed the mike, chattering.

Flora deployed her chair, sank down, looking first this way, then that. There was so much going on—and she in the middle of it. She watched for half an hour, then retracted the chair, deployed the bed. She was tired from the trip. A little nap. . . .

She stopped with the first zipper. The MC was staring directly at her, leering. The owlish youth blinked at her. The fat man scratched himself, staring up at her from the front row. She couldn't undress in front of all of them. . . .

She glanced around, located the switch near the door. With the click, the scene died around her. The glowing walls seemed to press close, fading slowly. Flora turned to the one remaining opaque wall, undressed slowly, her eyes on the familiar pictures. The children— she hadn't seen them since the last semiannual vacation week. The cost of travel was so high, and the crowding. . . .

She turned to the bed—and the three mirror-bright walls confronted her. She stared at the pale figure before her, stark against the wall patched with its faded mementos. She took a step; on either side, an endless rank of gaunt nude figures stepped in unison. She whirled, fixed her eyes gratefully on the familiar wall, the thin crevice outlining the door, the picture of the sea. . . .

She closed her eyes, groped her way to the bed. Once covered by the sheet, she opened her eyes. The beds stood in a row, all identical, each with its huddled figure, like an infinite charity ward, she thought—or like a morgue where all the world lay dead. . . .

Harry munched his yeast chop, his head moving from side to side as he followed the action across the three walls.

"It's marvelous, Flora. Marvelous. But it can be better yet," he added mysteriously.

"Harry—couldn't we move to a bigger place—and maybe do away with two of the walls. I—"

"Flora, you know better than that. I'm lucky to have gotten this apartment when I did; there's nothing—absolutely nothing available." He chuckled. "In a way, the situation is good job insurance. You know, I couldn't be fired, even if the company wanted to: They couldn't get a replacement. A man can't very well take a job if he hasn't a place to live in the city—and I can sit on this place as long as I like; we might get tired of issue rations, but by God we could hold on; so—not that anybody's in danger of getting fired."

"We could move out of the city, Harry. When I was a girl—"

"Oh, not again!" Harry groaned. "I thought that was all threshed out, long ago." He fixed a pained look on Flora. "Try to understand, Flora. The population of the world has doubled since you were a girl. Do you realize what that means? There are more people alive now than had been born in all previous human history up to fifty years ago. That farm you remember visiting as a kid—it's all paved now, and there are tall buildings there. The highways you remember, full of private autos, all driving across open country; they're all gone. There aren't any highways, or any open country except the TV settings and a few estates like the President's acre and a half—not that any sun hits it, with all those buildings around it—and maybe some essential dry-land farms for stuff they can't synthesize or get from the sea."

"There has to be some place we could go. It wasn't meant that people should spend their lives like this—away from the sun, the sea. . . ."

A shadow crossed Harry's face. "I can remember things, too, Flora," he said softly. "We spent a week at the beach once, when I was a small boy. I remember getting up at dawn with the sky all pink and purple, and going down to the water's edge. There were little creatures in the sand—little wild things. I could see tiny fish darting along in a wave crest, just before it broke. I could feel the sand with my toes. The gulls sailed around overhead, and there was even a tree—

"But it's gone now. There isn't any beach, anywhere. That's all over. . . ."

He broke off. "Never mind. That was then. This is now. They've paved the beach, and built processing plants on it, and they've paved the farms and the parks and the gardens—but they've given us Full-wall to make up for it. And—"

There was a buzz from the door. Harry got to his feet.

"They're here, Flora. Wait'll you see. . . ."

Something seemed to tighten around Flora's throat as the man emerged from the lift, gingerly handling the great roll of wall screen.

"Harry. . . ."

"Four walls," Harry said triumphantly. "I told you I was working toward something, remember? Well, this is it. By God, the Harry Trimbles have shown 'em!"

"Harry—I can't—not four walls. . . ."

"I know you're a little overwhelmed—but you deserve it, Flora—"

"Harry, I don't WANT four walls! I can't stand it! It will be all around me—"

Harry stepped to her side, gripped her wrist fiercely. "Shut up!" he hissed. "Do you want the workmen to think you're out of your mind?" He grinned at the men. "How about a coflet, boys?"

"You kiddin'?" one inquired. The other went silently about the work of rolling out the panel, attaching contact strips. Another reached for the sea-scene—

"No!" Flora threw herself against the wall, as though to cover the pictures with her body. "You can't take my pictures! Harry, don't let them."

"Look, sister, I don't want your crummy pictures."

"Flora, get hold of yourself! Here, I'll help you put the pictures in your floor locker."

"Bunch of nuts," one of the men muttered.

"Here, keep a civil tongue in your head," Harry started.

The man who had spoken stepped up to him. He was taller than Harry and solidly built. "Any more crap outa you and I'll break you in half. You and the old bag shut up and keep outa my way. I gotta job to do."

Harry sat beside Flora, his face white with fury. "You and your vaporings," he hissed. "So I have to endure this. I have a good mind to. . . ." he trailed off.

The men finished and left with all four walls blaring.

"Harry," Flora's voice shook. "How will you get out? They've put it right across the door; they've sealed us in. . . ."

"Don't be a bigger idiot than you have to." Harry's voice was ugly over the thunder from the screens. He went to the newly covered wall, groped, found the tiny pin-switch. At a touch, the panel slid aside as always, revealing the blank face of the lift shaft safety door. A moment later it too slid aside and Harry forced his way into the car. Flora caught a glimpse of his flushed angry face as the door closed.

Around her, the walls roared. A saloon fight was in full swing. She ducked as a chair sailed toward her, whirled to see it smash down a man behind her. Shots rang out. Men ran this way and that. The noise was deafening. That man, Flora thought; the vicious one; he had set it too loud purposely.

The scene shifted. Horses galloped across the room; dust clouds rose, nearly choking her in the verisimilitude of the illusion. It was as though she crouched under a small square canopy of ceiling in the middle of the immense plain.

Now there were cattle, wild-eyed, with tossing horns, bellowing, thundering in an unbroken sea across the screens, charging at Flora out of the wall, pouring past her on left and right. She screamed, shut her eyes, and ran blindly to the wall, groping for the switch.

The uproar subsided. Flora gasped in relief, her head humming. She felt faint, dizzy; she had to lie down— Everything was going black around her; the glowing walls swirled, fading. Flora sank to the floor.

Later—perhaps a few minutes, maybe hours—she had no way of knowing—Flora sat up. She looked out across an infinite vista of tile floor, which swept away to the distant horizon in all directions as far as the eye could see; and over all that vast plain, hollow-eyed women crouched at intervals of fifteen feet, in endless numbers, waiting.

Flora stared into the eyes of the nearest reflection. It stared back, a stranger. She moved her head quickly, to try to catch a glimpse of the next woman—but no matter how fast she moved, the nearer woman anticipated her, interposing her face between Flora and all the others. Flora turned; a cold-eyed woman guarded this rank, too.

"Please," Flora heard herself pleading. "Please, please—"

She bit her lip, eyes shut. She had to get hold of herself. These were only mirrors—she knew that. Only mirrors. The other women—they were mere reflections. Even the hostile ones who hid the others—they were herself, mirrored in the walls.

She opened her eyes. She knew there were joints in the glassy wall, all she had to do was find them, and the illusion of the endless plain would collapse. There—that thin black line, like a wire stretched from floor to ceiling—that was a corner of the room. She was not lost in an infinitude of weeping women on a vast plain; she was right there, in her own apartment—alone. She turned, finding the other corners. They were all there, all visible; she knew what they were. . . .

But why did they continue to look like wires, setting apart the squares of floor, each with its silent, grieving occupant. . . . ?

She closed her eyes, again fighting down the panic. She would tell Harry. As soon as he came home—it was only a few hours— she would explain it to him.

"I'm sick, Harry. You have to send me away to some place where I'll lie in a real bed, with sheets and blankets, beside an open window, looking out across the fields and forests. Someone—someone kind—will bring me a tray, with a bowl of soup—real soup, made from real chickens and with real bread and even a glass of milk, and a napkin, made of real cloth. . . ."

She should find her bed, and deploy it, and rest there until Harry came, but she was so tired. It was better to wait here, just relaxing and not thinking about the immense floor and the other women who waited with her. . . .

She slept.

When she awoke, she sat up, confused. There had been a dream. . . .

But how strange. The walls of the cell block were transparent now; she could see all the other apartments, stretching away to every side. She nodded; it was as she thought. They were all as barren and featureless as her own—and Harry was wrong. They all had four Full-walls. And the other women—the other wives, shut up like her in these small, mean cells; they were all aging, and sick, and faded, starved for fresh air and sunshine. She nodded again, and the woman in the next apartment nodded in sympathy. All the women were nodding; they all agreed—poor things.

When Harry came, she would show him how it was. He would see that the Full-walls weren't enough. They all had them, and they were all unhappy. When Harry came—

It was time now. She knew it. After so many years, you didn't need a watch to tell when Harry was due. She had better get up, make herself presentable. She rose unsteadily to her feet. The other husbands were coming, too, Flora noted; all the wives were getting ready. They moved about, opening their floor lockers, patting at their hair, slipping into another dress. Flora went to the dial-a-ration and all around, in all the apartments, the wives deployed the tables and dialed the dinners. She tried to see what the woman next door was dialing, but it was too far. She laughed at the way her neighbor craned to see what SHE was preparing. The other woman laughed, too. She was a good sport.

"Kelpies," Flora called cheerily. "And mockspam, and coflet. . . ."

Dinner was ready now. Flora turned to the door-wall and waited. Harry would be so pleased at not having to wait. Then, after dinner she'd explain about her illness—

Was it the right wall she was waiting before? The line around the door was so fine you couldn't really see it. She laughed at how funny it would be if Harry came in and found her standing, staring at the wrong wall.

She turned, and saw a movement on her left—in the next apartment. Flora watched as the door opened. A man stepped in. The next-door woman went forward to meet him—

To meet Harry! It was Harry! Flora whirled. Her four walls stood blank and glassy, while all around her, the other wives greeted Harry, seated him at their tables, and offered him coflet. . . .

"Harry!" she screamed, throwing herself at the wall. It threw her back. She ran to the next wall, hammering, screaming. Harry! Harry!"

In all the other apartments, Harry chewed, nodded, smiled. The other wives poured, fussed over Harry, nibbled daintily. And none of them—not one of them—paid the slightest attention to her. . . .

She stood in the center of the room, not screaming now, only sobbing silently. In the four glass walls that enclosed her, she stood alone. There was no point in calling any longer.

No matter how she screamed, how she beat against the walls, or how she called for Harry—she knew that no one would ever hear.

COCOON

Sid Throndyke overrode his respirator to heave a deep sigh.

"Wow!" he said, flipping to his wife's personal channel. "A tough day on the Office channel."

The contact screens attached to his eyeballs stayed blank: Cluster was out. Impatiently, Sid toed the console, checking the channels: Light, Medium and Deep Sitcom; auto-hypno; Light and Deep Narco; four, six, and eighty-party Social; and finally, muttering to himself, Psychan. Cluster's identity symbol appeared on his screens.

"There you are," he grieved. "Psychan again. After a hard day, the least a man expects is to find his wife tuned to his channel—"

"Oh, Sid; there's this wonderful analyst. A new model. It's doing so much for me, really wonderful. . . ."

"I know," Sid grumped. "That orgasm-association technique. That's all I hear. I'd think you'd want to keep in touch with the Sitcoms, so you know what's going on; but I suppose you've been tied into Psychan all day—while I burned my skull out on Office."

"Now, Sid; didn't I program your dinner and everything?"

"Um." Mollified, Sid groped with his tongue for the dinner lever, eased the limp plastic tube into his mouth. He sucked a mouthful of the soft paste—

"Cluster! You know I hate Vege-pap. Looks like you could at least dial a nice Prote-sim or Sucromash. . . ."

"Sid, you ought to tune to Psychan. It would do you a world of good. . . ." Her sub-vocalized voice trailed off in the earphones. Sid snorted, dialed a double Prote-sim *and* a Sucromash, fuming at the delay. He gulped his dinner, not even noticing the rich gluey consistency; then, in a somewhat better mood, flipped to the Light Sitcom.

It was good enough stuff, he conceded; the husband was a congenital psychopathic inferior who maintained his family in luxury by a series of fantastic accidents. You had to chuckle when his suicide attempt failed at the last moment, after he'd lost all that blood. The look on his face when they dragged him back. . . .

But somehow it wasn't enough. Sid dialed the medium; it wasn't much better. The deep, maybe.

Sid viewed for a few minutes with growing impatience. Sure, you had to hand it to the Sitcom people; there was a lot of meat in the deep sitcom. It was pretty subtle stuff, the way the wife got the money the husband had been saving and spent it for a vacation trip for her Chihuahua; had a real social content, too deep for most folks. But like the rest of the sitcoms, it was historical. Sure, using old-time settings gave a lot of scope for action. But how about something more pertinent to the contemporary situation? Nowadays, even though people led the kind of rich, full lives that Vital Programming supplied, there was still a certain lack. Maybe it was just a sort of atavistic need for gross muscular exertion. He'd viewed a discussion of the idea a few nights earlier on the usual Wednesday night four-party hookup with the boys. Still, in his case, he had plenty of muscle tone. He'd spent plenty on a micro-spasm attachment for use with the narco channel. . . .

That was a thought. Sid didn't usually like narco; too synthetic, as he'd explained to the boys. They hadn't liked the remark, he remembered. Probably they were all narco fans. But what the hell, a man had a right to a few maverick notions.

Sid tuned to the Narco channel. It was a traditional sex fantasy, in which the familiar colorless hero repeatedly fended off the advances of coitus-seeking girls. It was beautifully staged, with plenty of action, but like the sitcoms, laid in one of those never-never historical settings. Sid flipped past with a sub-vocal grunt. It wasn't much better than Cluster's orgasm-association treatments.

The stylized identity-symbol of the Pubinf announcer flashed on Sid's screens, vibrating in resonance with the impersonal voice of the Official announcer:

" .... cause for concern. CentProg states that control will have been re-established within the hour. Some discomfort may result from vibration in sectors north of Civic Center, but normalcy will be restored shortly. Now, a word on the food situation."

A hearty, gelatinous voice took over: "Say, folks, have you considered switching to Vege-pap? Vege-pap now comes in a variety of rich flavors, all, of course, equally nourishing, every big swallow loaded with the kind of molecule that keeps those metabolisms rocking along at the pace of today's more-fun-than-ever sitcoms— and today's stimulating narco and social channels, too!

"Starting with First Feeding tomorrow, you'll have that opportunity you've wanted to try Vege-pap. Old-fashioned foods, like Prote-sim and Sucromash, will continue to be available of course, where exceptional situations warrant. Now—"

"What's that!" Sid sub-vocalized. He toed the replay key, listened again. Then he dug a toe viciously against the tuning key, flipping to the Psychan monitor.

"Cluster!" he barked at his wife's identity pattern. "Have you heard about this nonsense? Some damn fool on Pubinf is blathering about Vege-pap for everybody! By God, this is a free country. I'd like to see anyone try—"

"Sid," Cluster's voice came faintly, imploring. "P-P-Please, S-S-Sid. . . ."

"Damn it, Cluster. . . . !" Sid stopped talking, coughed, gulped. His throat was burning. In his excitement he'd been vocalizing. The realization steadied him. He'd have to calm down. He'd been behaving like an animal. . . .

"Cluster, darling. Kindly interrupt your treatment. I have to talk to you. Now. It's important." Confound it, if she didn't switch to his channel now—

"Yes, Sid." Cluster's voice had a ragged undertone. Sid half-suspected she was vocalizing then too. . . .

"I was listening to Pubinf," he said, aware of a sense of dignity in the telling. No narco-addict he, but a mature-minded auditor of a serious channel like Pubinf. "They're raving about cutting off Prote-sim. Never heard of such nonsense. Have you heard anything about this?"

"No, Sid. You should know I never—"

"I know! But I thought maybe you'd heard something. . . ."

"Sid, I've been under treatment all day—except the time I spent programming your dinner."

"You can get Prote-sim in exceptional situations, they said! I wonder what that's supposed to mean? Why, I've been a Prote-sim man for years. . . ."

"Maybe it will do you good, Sid. Something different. . . ."

"Different? What in the world do I want with something different? I have a comfortable routine, well-balanced, creative. I'm not interested in having any government fat-head telling me what to eat."

"But Vege-sim might be good; build you up or something."

"Build me up? What are you talking about? I view sports regularly; and aren't you forgetting my Micro-spasm accessory? Hah! I'm a very physically-minded man, when it comes to that."

"I know you are, Sid. I didn't mean. . . . I only meant, maybe a little variety. . . ."

Sid was silent, thinking. Variety. Hmmmm. Might be something in that. Maybe he *was* in a rut, a little.

"Cluster," he said suddenly. "You know, it's a funny thing; I've kind of gotten out of touch. Oh, I don't mean with important affairs. Heck, I hardly ever tune in Narco, or auto-hypno, for that matter. But I mean, after all, it's been quite a while now I guess, since we gave up well, you know, physical contact."

"Sid! If you're going to be awful, I'm switching right back to my Psychan—"

"I don't mean to be getting personal, Cluster. I was just thinking. . . . By golly, how long has it been since that first contract with CentProg?"

"Why. . . . I haven't any idea. That was so long ago. I can't see what difference it makes. Heavens, Sid, life today is so rich and full—"

"Don't get me wrong. I'm not talking about wanting to change, or anything idiotic. Just wondering. You know."

"Poor Sid. If you could spend more time with wonderful channels like Psychan, and not have to bother with that boring old Office. . . ."

Sid chuckled sub-vocally. "A man needs the feeling of achievement he gets from doing a job, Cluster. I wouldn't be happy, just relaxing with Sitcom all the time. And after all, Indexing is an important job. If we fellows in the game all quit, where'd CentProg be? Eh?"

"I hadn't thought of it like that, Sid. I guess it is pretty important."

"Darn right, kid. They haven't built the computer yet that can handle Indexing—or Value Judgment, or Criticism—. It'll be a while yet before the machine replaces man." Sid chuckled again. Cluster was such a kid in a lot of ways.

Still, it had been a long time. Funny, how you didn't think much about time, under Vital Programming. After all, your program was so full, you didn't have time to moon over the past. You popped out of Dream-stim, had a fast breakfast (Vege-pap; hah! He'd see about that!), then over to Office channel. That kept a fellow on his toes, right up till quitting time. Then dinner with Cluster, and right into the evening's round of Sitcoms, Socials, Narcos—whatever you wanted.

But how long had it been? A long time, no doubt. Measured in, say, years, the way folks used to be in the habit of thinking.

Years and year. Yes, by golly. Years and years.

Quite suddenly, Sid was uneasy. How long had it been? He had been about twenty-eight—the term came awkwardly to mind— twenty-eight when he and Cluster first met. Then there was that first anniversary—a wild time that had been with friends over for TV. And then Vital Programming had come along. He and Cluster had been among the first to sign up.

God, what a long time it had been. TV. Imagine sitting. The thought of being propped up against coarse chairs, out in the open, made Sid wince. And other people around—faces right out in the open and everything. Staring at a little screen no more than five feet square. How in the world had people stood it? Still, it was all in what you were used to. People were adaptable. They had had to be to survive in those primitive conditions. You had to give the old-timers credit. He and Cluster were a pretty lucky couple to have lived in the era when Vital Programming was developed. They could see the contrast right in their own lives. The younger folks, now—

"Sid," Cluster broke in plaintively. "May I finish my treatment now?"

Sid dialed off, annoyed. Cluster wasn't interested in his problems. She was so wrapped up in Psychan these days, she couldn't even discuss the sitcoms intelligently. Well, Sid Throndyke wasn't a man to be pushed around. He nudged the 'fone switch, gave a number. An operator answered.

"I want the Pubinf office."

There was a moment's silence. "That number is unavailable," the recorded voice said.

"Unavailable, hell! I want to talk to them down there! What's all this about cutting off Prote-sim?"

"That information is not available."

"Look," Sid said, calming himself with an effort. "I want to talk to someone at Pubinf—"

"The line is available now."

An unfamiliar identity pattern appeared on Sid's screens.

"I want to find out about this food business," Sid began—

"A temporary measure," a harassed voice said. "Due to the emergency."

"What emergency?" Sid stared at the pattern belligerently. As he watched, it wavered, almost imperceptibly. A moment later, he felt a distinct tremor through the form-hugging plastic cocoon.

"What. . . . !" he gasped, "what was that?!"

"There's no cause for alarm," the Pubinf voice said. "You'll be kept fully informed through regular—"

A second shock rumbled. Sid gasped. "What the devil's going on. . . . ?"

The Pubinf pattern was gone. Sid blinked at the blank screens, then switched to his monitor channel. He had to talk to someone. Cluster would be furious at another interruption, but—

"Sid!" Cluster's voice rasped in Sid's hemispherical canals. She was vocalizing now for sure, he thought wildly.

"They broke right in!" Cluster cried. "Just as I was ready to climax—"

"Who?" Sid demanded. "What's going on here? What are you raving about?"

"Not an identity pattern, either," Cluster wailed. "Sid, it was a—a—face."

"What?" Sid blinked. He hadn't heard Cluster use obscenity before. This must be serious.

"Calm yourself," he said. "Now tell me exactly what happened."

"I told you: a—face. It was horrible, Sid. On the Psychan channel. And he was shouting—"

"Shouting what?"

"I don't know. Something about 'Get out.' Oh, Sid, I've never been so humiliated. . . ."

"Listen, Cluster," Sid said. "You tune in to a nice narco now, and get some rest. I'll deal with this."

"A face," Cluster sobbed. "A great, nasty *hairy* face—"

"That's enough!" Sid snapped. He cut Cluster's identity pattern with an impatient gouge of his toe. Sometimes it seemed like women enjoyed obscenity. . . .

Now what? He was far from giving up on the Vege-pap issue, and now this: a respectable married woman insulted right in her own cocoon. Things were going to hell. But he'd soon see about that. With a decisive twist of the ankle, Sid flipped to the Police channel.

"I want to report an outrage."

The police identity pattern blanked abruptly. Then a face appeared.

Sid sucked in a breath out of phase with his respirator. *This* wasn't the police channel. The face stared at him, mouth working: a pale face, with whiskers sprouting from hollow cheeks, lips sunken over toothless gums. Then the audio came in, in midsentence:

" . . . . to warn you. You've got to listen, you fools! You'll all die here! It's already at the north edge of the city. The big barrier wall's holding, but—"

The screen blanked; the bland police pattern reappeared.

"The foregoing interruption was the result of circumstances beyond the control of CentProg," a taped voice said smoothly. "Normal service will now be resumed."

"Police!" Sid yelled. He was vocalizing now, and be damned to it! There was just so much a decent citizen would stand for—

The screen flickered again. The police pattern disappeared. Sid held his breath—

A face appeared. This was a different one, Sid was sure. It was hairier than the other one, but not as hollow-cheeked. He watched in dumb shock as the mouth opened—

"Listen," a hoarse voice said. "Everybody, listen. We're blanketing all the channels this time—I hope. This is our last try. There's only a few of us. It wasn't easy getting into here—and there's no time left. We've got to move fast."

The voice stopped as the man on the screen breathed hoarsely, swallowed. Then he went on:

"It's the ice; it's moving down on us, fast, a god-awful big glacier. The walls can't stand much longer. It'll either wipe the city off the map or bury it. Either way, anybody that stays is done for.

"Listen; it won't be easy, but you've got to try. Don't try to go down. You can't get out below because of the drifts. Go up, onto the roofs. It's your only chance—you must go up."

The image on Sid's contact screens trembled violently, then blanked. Moments later, Sid felt a tremor—worse, this time. His cocoon seemed to pull at him. For a moment he was aware of the drag of a hundred tiny contacts grafted to the skin, a hundred tiny conductors penetrating to nerve conduits—

An almost suffocating wave of claustrophobia swept over him. The universe seemed to be crushing in on him, immobile, helpless, a grub buried in an immense anthill—

The shock passed. Slowly, Sid regained a grip on himself. His respirator was cycling erratically, attempting to match to his ragged breathing impulses. His chest ached from the strain. He groped with a toe, keyed in Cluster's identity pattern.

"Cluster! Did you feel it? Everything was rocking. . . ."

There was no reply. Sid called again. No answer. Was she ignoring him, or—

Maybe she was hurt, alone and helpless—

Sid fought for calm. No need for panic. Dial CentProg, report the malfunction. He felt with trembling toes, and punched the keys. . . .

CentProg's channel was dark, lifeless. Sid stared, unbelieving. It wasn't possible. He switched wildly to the light sitcom—

Everything normal here. The husband fell down the stairs, smashing his new camera. . . .

But this was no time to get involved. Sid flipped through the medium and deep Sitcoms: all normal. Maybe he could get through to the police now—

Mel Goldfarb's pattern blinked on the personal call code. Sid tuned him in.

"Mel! What's it all about? My God, that earthquake—"

"I don't like it, Sid. I felt it, over here in South Sector. The. . . . uh. . . . face. . . . said the North Sector. You're over that side. What did you—"

"My God, I thought the roof was going to fall in, Mel. It was terrible! Look, I'm trying to get through to the police. Keep in touch, hey?"

"Wait, Sid; I'm worried—"

Sid cut the switch, flipped to the police channel. If that depraved son of a bitch showed his face again—

The police pattern appeared. Sid paused to gather his thoughts. First things first. . . .

"That earthquake," he said. "What's happening? And the maniac who's been exposing his face. My wife—"

"The foregoing interruption was the result of circumstances beyond the control of CentProg. Normal service will now be resumed."

"What are you talking about? *Nothing* is beyond the control of CentProg—"

"The foregoing interruption was the result of circumstances beyond the control of CentProg. Normal service will now be resumed."

"That's enough of your damned nonsense! What about this crazy guy showing his bare face? How do I know that he won't—"

"The foregoing interruption was the result of circumstances beyond the control of CentProg. Normal service will now be resumed."

Sid stared, aghast. A taped voice! A brush-off! He was supposed to settle for that? Well, by God, he had a contract. . . .

Mel's code flashed again. Sid tuned him in. "Mel, this is a damned outrage. I called the police channel and do you know what I got? A canned announcement—"

"Sid," Mel cut in. "Do you suppose it meant anything? I mean the. . . . uh. . . . guy with the. . . . uh. . . . face. All that about getting out, and the glacier wiping out the city."

"What?" Sid stared at Mel's pattern, trying to make sense of what he was saying. "Glacier?" he said. "Wipe out what?"

"You saw him, didn't you? The crazy bird, cut in on all channels. He said the ice was going to wipe out the city. . . ."

Sid thought back. The damned obscene face. He hadn't really listened to what it was raving about. But it was something about getting out. . . .

"Tell me that again, Mel."

Mel repeated the bare-faced man's warning. "Do you suppose

there's anything in it? I mean, the shocks, and everything. And you can't get the police channel. And I tried to tune in to Pubinf just now and I got a canned voice, just like you did. . . ."

"It's crazy, Mel. It can't. . . ."

"I don't know. I've tried to reach a couple of the fellows; I can't get through. . . ."

"Mel," Sid asked suddenly. "How long has it been? I mean, how long since CentProg has been handling things?"

"What? My God, Sid, what a question. I don't know."

"A long time, eh, Mel? A lot could have happened outside."

"My contract—"

"But how do we know? I was talking to Cluster just now; we couldn't remember. I mean, how can you gauge a thing like that? We have our routine, and everything goes along, and nobody thinks about anything like. . . . outside. Then all of a sudden—"

"I'm trying Pubinf again," Mel said. "I don't like this—"

Mel was gone. Sid tried to think. Pubinf was handing out canned brush-offs, just like Police Channel. CentProg. . . . maybe it was okay now. . . .

CentProg was still dark. Sid was staring at the blank screens when a new shock sent heavy vibrations through his cocoon. Sid gasped, tried to keep cool. It would pass; it wasn't anything, it couldn't be. . . .

The vibrations built, heavy, hard shocks that drove the air from Sid's lungs, yanked painfully at arms, legs, neck, and his groin. . . .

It was a long time before the nausea passed. Sid lay, drawing breath painfully, fighting down the vertigo. The pain—it was a help, in a way. It helped to clear his head. Something was wrong, badly wrong. He had to think now, do the right thing. It wouldn't do to panic. If only there wouldn't be another earthquake. . . .

Something wet splattered against Sid's half-open mouth. He recoiled, automatically spitting the mucky stuff, snorting—

It was Vege-pap, gushing down from the feeding tube. Sid averted his face, felt the cool semi-liquid pattering against the cocoon, spreading over it, sloshing down the sides. Something was broken. . . .

Sid groped for the cut-off with his tongue, gagging at the viscous mess pouring over his face. Of course, it hadn't actually touched his skin, except for his lips; the cocoon protected him.

But he could feel the thick weight of it, awash in the fluid that supported the plastic cocoon. He could sense it quite clearly, flowing under him, forcing him up in the chamber as the hydrostatic balance was upset. With a shock of pain, Sid felt a set of neuro contacts along his spinal cord come taut. He gritted his teeth, felt searing agony as the contacts ripped loose.

Half of the world went dark and cold. Sid was only dimly aware of the pressure against his face and chest as he pressed against the cell roof. All sensation was gone from his legs now, from his left arm, his back. His left contact screen was blank, unseeing. Groaning with the effort, Sid strained to reach out with a toe, key the emergency signal—

Hopeless. Without the boosters he could never make it. His legs were dead, paralyzed. He was helpless.

He tried to scream, choked, fought silently in the swaddling cocoon, no longer a euphorically caressing second skin but a dead, clammy weight, blinding him. He twisted, feeling unused muscles cramp at the effort, touched the lever that controlled the face-plate. He'd had a reputation as an open-air fiend once—but that had been—he didn't know how long. The lever was stiff. Sid lunged against it again. It gave. There was a sudden lessening of pressure as the burden of Vege-pap slopped out through the opening. Sid sank away from the ceiling of the tiny cubicle, felt his cocoon ground on the bottom.

For a long time Sid lay, dazed by pain and shock, not even thinking, waiting for the agony to subside. . . .

Then the itching began. It penetrated Sid's daze, set him twitching in a frenzy of discomfort. The tearing loose of the dorsal contacts had opened dozens of tiny rents in the cocoon; a sticky mixture of the supporting water bath and Vege-pap seeped in, irritating the tender skin. Sid writhed, struggled to scratch—and discovered that, miraculously, the left arm responded now. The motor nerves which had been stunned by the electroneural trickle-flow through the contacts were recovering control. Feebly, Sid's groping hand reached his inflamed hip—and scrabbled against the smooth sheath of plastic.

He had to get out. The cocoon was a confining nightmare, a dead husk that had to be shed. The face-plate was open. Sid felt upward, found the edge, tugged—

Slippery as an eel, he slithered from the cocoon, hung for an instant as the remaining contacts came taut, then slammed to the floor a foot below. Sid didn't feel the pain of the fall; as the contacts ripped free, he fainted.

When Sid recovered consciousness, his first thought was that the narco channel was getting a little *too* graphic. He groped for a tuning switch—

Then he remembered. The earthquake, Mel, the canned announcement—

And he had opened his face-plate and fought to get out—and here he was. He blinked dully, then moved his left hand. It took a long time, but he managed to peel the contact screens from his eyes. He looked around. He was lying on the floor in a rectangular tunnel. A dim light came from a glowing green spot along the corridor. Sid remembered seeing it before, a long time ago. . . . the day he and Cluster had entered their cocoons.

Now that he was detached from the stimuli of the cocoon, it seemed to Sid, he was able to think a little more clearly. It had hurt to be torn free from the security of the cocoon, but it wasn't so bad now. A sort of numbness had set in. But he couldn't lie here and rest; he had to do something, fast. First, there was Cluster. She hadn't answered. Her cocoon was situated right next to his—

Sid tried to move; his leg twitched; his arm fumbled over the floor. It was smooth and wet, gummy with the Vege-pap that was still spilling down from the open face-plate. The smell of the stuff was sickening. Irrationally, Sid had a sudden mouth-watering hunger for Prote-sim.

Sid fixed his eyes on the green light, trying to remember. He and Cluster had been wheeled along the corridor, laughing and talking gaily. Somehow, out here, things took on a different perspective. That had been—God! *Years ago.* How long? Maybe— twenty years? Longer. Fifty, maybe. Maybe longer. How could you know? For a while they had tuned to Pubinf, followed the news, kept up with friends on the outside. But more and more of their friends had signed contracts with CentProg. The news sort of dried up. You lost interest.

But what mattered now wasn't how long, it was what he was going to do. Of course, an attendant would be along soon in any case to check up, but meanwhile, Cluster might be in trouble—

✧ ✧ ✧

The tremor was bad this time. Sid felt the floor rock, felt the hard paving under him ripple like the surface of a pond. Somewhere, a rumbling sound rolled, and somewhere something heavy fell. The green light flickered, then burned steadily again.

A shape moved in the gloom of the corridor; there was the wet slap of footsteps. Sid sub-vocalized a calm "Hi, fellows." The silence rang in his ears. My God, of course they couldn't hear him. He tried again, consciously vocalizing, a tremendous shout—

A feeble croak, and a fit of coughing. When he recovered his breath, a bare and hairy face, greenish white, was bending over him.

" . . . . this poor devil," the man was saying in a thin choked voice.

Another face appeared over the first face's shoulder. Sid recognized them both. They were the two that had been breaking into decent channels, with their wild talk about a glacier. . . .

"Listen, fellow," one of the bare-faced men said. Sid stared with fascinated disgust at the clammy pale skin, the sprouting hairs, the loose toothless mouth, the darting pink tongue. God, people were horrible to look at!

" . . . . be along after a while. Didn't mean to stir up anybody in your shape. You been in too long, fellow. You can't make it."

"I'm. . . . good. . . . shape. . . ." Sid whispered indignantly.

"We can't do anything for you. You'll have to wait till the maintenance unit comes along. I'm pretty sure you'll be okay. The ice's piled itself up in a wall now, and split around the city walls. I think they'll hold. Course, the ice will cover the city, but that won't matter. CentProg will still handle everything. Plenty of energy from the pile and the solar cells, and the recycling will handle the food okay. . . ."

" . . . . Cluster. . . ." Sid gasped. The bare-faced man leaned closer. Sid explained about his wife. The man checked nearby face-plates. He came back and knelt by Sid. "Rest easy, fellow," he said. "They all look all right. Your wife's okay. Now, we're going to have to go on. But you'll be okay. Plenty of Vege-pap around, I see. Just eat a little now and then. The Maintenance machine will be along and get you tucked back in."

"Where. . . . ?" Sid managed.

"Us? We're heading south. Matt here knows where we can get clothes and supplies, maybe even a flier. We never were too set on this Vital Programming. We've only been in maybe a few years and we always did a lot of auto-gym work, keeping in shape. Didn't like the idea of wasting away. . . . Matt's the one found out about the ice. He came for me. . . ."

Sid was aware of the other man talking. It was hard to hear him. A sudden thought struck Sid. " . . . . how long. . . . ?" he asked.

It took three tries, but the bare-faced man got the idea at last.

"I'll take a look, fellow," he said. He went to Sid's open face-plate, peered at it, called the other man over. Then he came back, his feet spattering in the puddled Vege-pap.

"Your record says. . . . 2043," he said. He looked at Sid with wide eyes. They were red and irritated, Sid saw. It made his own eyes itch.

"If that's right, you been here since the beginning. My God, that's over. . . . two hundred years. . . ."

The second bare-faced man, Matt, was pulling the other away. He was saying something, but Sid wasn't listening. Two hundred years. It seemed impossible. But after all, why not? In a controlled environment, with no wear and tear, no disease, you could live as long as CentProg kept everything running. But two hundred years. . . .

Sid looked around. The two men were gone. He tried to remember just what had happened, but it was too hard. The ice, they had said, wouldn't crush the city. But it would flow around it, encase it in ice, and the snow would fall, and cover it, and the city would lie under the ice.

Ages might pass. In the cells, the cocoons would keep everyone snug and happy. There would be the traditional sitcoms, and Narco, and Psychan. . . .

And up above, the ice.

Sid remembered the awful moments in the cocoon, when the shock waves had rocked him; the black wave of fear that had closed in; the paralyzing claustrophobia.

The ice would build up and build up. Ice, two miles thick. . . .

Why hadn't they waited? Sid groped, pushed himself up, rolled over. He was stronger already. Why hadn't they waited? He'd used the micro-spasm unit regularly—every so often. He had good muscle tone. It was just that he was a little stiff. He scrabbled at the floor, moved his body a few inches. Nothing to it. He remembered the reason for the green light; it was the elevator. They had brought him and Cluster down in it. All he had to do was get to it, and—

What about Cluster? He could try to bring her along. It would be lonely to be without her. But she wouldn't want to leave. She'd been here—two hundred years. Sid almost chuckled. Cluster wouldn't like the idea of being as old as that. . . .

No, he'd go alone. He couldn't stay, of course. It would never be the same again for him. He pulled himself along, an inch, another. He rested, sucked up some Vege-pap from where it spread near his mouth. . . .

He went on. It was a long way to the green light, but if you took it an inch at a time, an inch at a time. . . .

He reached the door. There hadn't been any more shocks. Along the corridor, the glass face-plates stood closed, peaceful, orderly. The mess on the floor was the only thing. But the maintenance units would be along. The bare-faced man had said so.

You opened the door to the elevator by breaking a beam of light; Sid remembered that. He raised his arm; it was getting strong, all right. It was hardly any effort to lift it right up—

The door opened with a whoosh of air. Sid worked his way inside. Halfway in, the door tried to close on him; his weight must have triggered the door-closing mechanism. But it touched him and flew open again. It was working fine, Sid thought.

He pulled his legs in, then rested. He would have to get up to the switch, somehow, and that was going to be tricky. Still, he had gotten this far okay. Just a little farther, and he'd catch up with the bare-faced men, and they'd set out together.

It took Sid an hour of hard work, but he managed to reach, first, the low stool, then the chrome-plated control button. With a lurch the car started up. Sid fell back to the floor and fought back wave on wave of vertigo. It was hectic, being outside. But he wouldn't go back now; not even to see Cluster's familiar identity pattern again. Never again. He had to get out.

The elevator came to a stop. The door slid open—and a blast of sub-arctic air struck Sid like a blow from a giant hammer. His naked body—mere flaccid skin over atrophied bones—curled like a grub in the flames. For a long moment all sensation was washed away in the shock of the cold. Then there was pain; pain that went on and on. . . .

✧ ✧ ✧

And then the pain went, and it was almost like being back again, back in the cocoon, warm and comfortable, secure and protected and safe. But not quite the same. A thought stirred in Sid's mind. He pushed at the fog of cotton-wool, fought to grasp the thought that bobbed on the surface of the blissful warmth.

He opened his eyes. Out across the white expanse of roof-tops, beyond the last rim of the snow, the glittering jagged shape of the ice-face reared up, crystal-blue, gigantic; and in the high arched blue-black sky, a star burned with a brilliant fire.

This was what he wanted to tell Cluster, Sid thought. This, about the deep sky, and the star, so far away—and yet a man could see it.

But it was too late now to tell Cluster, too late to tell anyone. The bare-faced men were gone. Sid was alone; alone now under the sky.

Long ago, Sid thought, on the shore of some warm and muddy sea, some yearning sea-thing had crawled out to blink at the open sky, gulp a few breaths of burning oxygen, and die.

But not in vain. The urge to climb out was the thing. That was the force that was bigger than all the laws of nature, greater than all the distant suns blazing in their meaningless lonely splendor.

The other ones, the ones below, the secure and comfortable ones in their snug cocoons under the snow, they had lost the great urge. The thing that made a man.

But he, Sid Throndyke—he had made it.

Sid lay with his eyes on the star and the silent snow drifted over him to form a still, small mound; and then the mound was buried, and then the city.

And only the ice and the star remained.

FOUNDER'S DAY

I

The girl said, "No." She shook her head, turned her ice-chip blue eyes back to the programming console that almost filled her work cubicle. "Have some sense, Gus."

"We could live with my family for a while—"

"You're already one over legal. And if you think I'd crowd in with that whole bunch—"

"Only until I get my next step-increase!"

Her fingers were already flickering over the keys. "See *my* side, Gus. Mel Fundy's offered me a five-year contract—with an option."

"Contract!"

"It's better than no marriage at all!"

"Marriage! That's just a lousy business proposition!"

"Not so lousy. I'm accepting. It'll mean a class B flat for just the two of us—and class B rations."

"You—and that dried-up. . . ." Gus pictured her with Fundy's crab-claws touching her.

"Better get back to your slot, Gus," she dismissed him. "You've still got a job to hold down."

He turned away. A small, balding man with a large face and a curved back was coming along the two-foot aisle, darting sharp looks into the cubicles. His eyes turned hot when he saw Gus.

"You're docked half a unit, Addison! If I find you out of your position again, there'll be charges!"

"It won't happen again," Gus muttered. "Ever."

The shift-end buzzer went at 8 A.M. Gus pushed along the exit lane into car 98, stood packed in with the other workers while it rocketed along the horizontal track, halting every twelve seconds to discharge passengers, then shot upward three-quarters of a mile to his flat-level. In the two-foot wide corridor, a banner poster showed a Colonization Service Officer looking stern, and the slogan: FILL YOUR BLOCK QUOTA! Gus keyed the door and stepped into the familiar odor of Home: a heavy, dirt-sweet smell of human sweat and excrement and sex that seemed to settle over him like an oily patina.

"Augustus." From the food-prep ledge at the far end of the living aisle his mother's collapsed, sagging face caressed him like a damp hand. "I have a surprise for you! Mock giblets and a custard!"

"I'm not hungry."

"Evening, Son." His father's head poked from the study cubicle. "Since you don't care for your custard, mind if I have it? Stomach's been a little feisty lately." As if to prove it he belched, grimaced.

Three feet from Gus's face, the curtains of the dressing alcove twitched. Through a gap, a pale, oversized buttock showed. It moved sensuously, and Gus saw the curve of a full breast, the soft, pink nipple peering like a blind eye past the edge of the curtain. Desire washed up through him like sewage in a plugged manhole. He turned his eyes away and saw a narrow, rabbity face glaring at him in feeble ferocity from the washing nook.

"What are you staring at, you young—"

"Tell her to keep the curtains shut, Uncle Fred," Gus grated.

"You young degenerate! Your own aunt!"

"Gus didn't do anything," an uncertain voice said behind him. "She's done the same thing to me."

Gus turned to his brother, a spindle-armed, ribby-chested lad with a bad complexion. "Thanks, Len. But they can think what they like. I'm leaving. I just came to say good-by."

Lenny's mouth opened. "You're. . . . going?"

Gus didn't look at Lenny's face. He knew the expression he would see there: admiration, love, dismay. And there was nothing he could give in return.

The silence was broken by a squeak from Mother. "Augustus." She spoke quickly, in a false-bright voice, as though nothing had been said. "I've been thinking, this evening you and your father might go to see Mr. Geyer about a recommendation for class C testing—"

Father cleared his throat. "Now, Ada, you know we've been all over that—"

"There may have been a change—"

"There's never a change," Gus cut her off harshly. "I'll never get a better job, never get a flat of my own, never get married. There just isn't *room.*"

Father frowned, the corners of his mouth drawing down in an unwittingly comic expression. "Now, see here, Son," he started.

"Never mind," Gus said. "I'll be out of here in a minute, and leave the whole thing to you—custard and all."

"Oh, God!" Gus saw his mother's face crumple into a red-blotched mask of grief, a repellent expression of weak, smothering, useless mother love.

"Say something to him, George," she whimpered. "He's going— out *there!*"

"You mean. . . ." Father elaborated a frown. "You mean the colonies?"

"Sure, that's what he means," Lenny burst out. "Gus, you're going to Alpha!"

"Catch *me* volunteering for anything," Uncle Fred shook his head. "Stories I've heard. . . ."

"Augustus, I've been thinking," Mother began babbling. "We'll leave the whole flat to you, this lovely apartment, and we'll go into Barracks, just visit you here on Sundays, just come and bring you a nice casserole or soup, you know how fond you are of my lichen soup, and—"

"I've got to go," Gus backed a step.

"After all we've done for you!" Mother keened suddenly. "All the years we've scraped and saved, so we could give you the best of everything. . . ."

"Now, Son, better think it over," Father mumbled. "Remember, there's no turning back if you volunteer. You'll never see your home again—or your mother. . . ." His voice trailed off. Even to his ears the prospect sounded attractive.

"Good luck, Gus," Lenny caught his hand. "I'll. . . . see you."

"Sure, Lenny."

"He's going!" Mother wailed. "Stop him, George!"

Gus looked back at the faces staring at him, tried and failed to summon a twinge of regret at leaving them.

"It isn't fair," Mother moaned. Gus pressed the button and the door slid back.

"Say, if that custard isn't cold," Father was saying as the panel closed behind Gus.

2

Recruitment Center Number Sixty-one was a white-lit acre of noise and animal warmth and tension and people packed elbow to elbow under the low ceiling with its signs reading CLASS ONE-SPECIAL and TEST UNITS D-G and PRE-PROCESSING (DEFERRED STATUS) and its painted arrows cryptic in red and green and black. After an hour's waiting, Gus's head was ringing dizzily.

His turn came. A woman in a tan uniform thrust a plastic tag at him, looking past his left ear.

"Station twenty-five on your left," she intoned. "Move along. . . ."

"I'd like to ask some questions," Gus started. The woman flicked her eyes at him; her voice was drowned in the chopping of other voices as the press from behind thrust Gus forward. A thick-shouldered man with reddish hair put his face near Gus's.

"Some mob," he shouted. "Geeze, it's a regular evacuation, like."

"Yeah," Gus said. "I've heard Alpha was next best to Hell, but it seems to be popular."

"Hah!" the redhead leaned closer. "You know the world population as of Sunday night stat cut-off? Twenty-nine billion plus— and the repro factor says she'll double in twelve hundred and four days. And you know why?" he warmed to his subject. "No politician's going to vote to cut down the vote supply—"

"You—over here." A hand grabbed Gus and thrust him toward a table behind which sat a pale man with thin, wispy hair. He pushed two small punched cards across.

"Sign these."

"First I'd like to ask a few questions," Gus started.

"Sign or get out. Snap it up, Mac."

❖   ❖   ❖

"I want to know what I'm getting into. What's it like, out on Alpha Three? What kind of contract do I—"

A hand closed on Gus's arm. A man in Ground Corps uniform loomed beside him.

"Trouble, fella?"

"I walked in here voluntarily." Gus threw the hand off. "All I want—"

"We process twenty thousand a day through here, fella. You can see we got no time for special attention. You've seen the broadcasts; you know about New Earth—"

"What assurance have I got—"

"No assurance at all, fella. None at all. Take it or leave it."

"You're holding up the line," the thin-haired man barked. "You want to sign, or you want to go back home. . . . ?"

Gus picked up the stylus and signed.

An hour later, aboard a converted cargo-carrier, Gus sat cold and airsick on a canvas strip seat between the red-headed man, whose name he had learned was Hogan, and a fattish fellow who complained continuously in a tremulous tone:

" . . . . give a man time to think. Big step, going out to the colonies at my time of life. Leaving a good job. . . ."

"They washed a lot of 'em out on the physical," Hogan said. "Figures. Tough out on Alpha; why haul freight that can't make it, hah? Costs plenty to lift a man four light years."

"I thought they took anybody," Gus said. "I never heard of anyone who volunteered coming back home."

"I heard they send 'em to labor camps." Hogan spoke confidentially from the corner of his mouth. "Can't afford to send malcontents back to the hive."

"Maybe," Gus said. "All I know is, I passed and I'm going—and I don't want to come back, ever."

"Yeah," Hogan nodded. "We made it. To hell with them other guys."

" . . . . no time to think it over, consider the matter in depth," the fat man said. "It's not what I'd call fair, not fair at all. . . ."

They debarked on a flat, dusty-tan plain that stretched away to a distant rampart of smoke-blue mountains. Gus resisted an impulse to clutch the railing as he descended the ramp; the open sky made him dizzy. The air was thin, after the pressurized city and the transport's canned air. Gus felt lightheaded. He hadn't eaten all day. He looked at his watch, was astonished to see that it had been less than five hours since he had left the flat.

Uniformed cadremen called orders up and down the line. The irregular ranks of recruits started off, following a dun-colored lead car. After half an hour, Gus's legs ached from the unaccustomed exercise. His breath was like fire in his throat. The car moved steadily ahead, laying a trail of dust across the empty desert.

"Where the hell we going?" Hogan's voice wheezed beside him. "There's nothing here but this damned desert."

"Must be Mojave Spaceport."

"They're trying to kill us," Hogan complained. "What do you say we fall out, catch some rest?"

Gus thought about dropping back, throwing himself down, resting. He pictured a cadreman coming over, ordering him back.

Back home.

He kept going.

They marched on through the afternoon, with one brief break during which paper trays of gray mush were handed out. Marching, they watched the sun go down like a pour of molten metal. Under the stars, they marched. It was after midnight when a string of lights appeared in the distance. Gus slogged on, no longer conscious of the pain in his feet and legs. When the halt was called on a broad sweep of flood-lit blacktop, he was herded along with the others into a barracks that smelled of new plastic and disinfectants. He fell on the narrow bunk pointed out to him, sank down into a deeper sleep than he had ever known—

—and awoke in the pre-dawn chill to the shouts of the noncoms. After a breakfast of brown mush, the recruits were lined up before the barracks and a cadre officer mounted a low platform to address them.

"You men have a lot of questions to ask," he said. His amplified voice echoed across the pavement. "You want to know what you're getting into, what kind of handout of jobs or farm land or gold mines you'll get on New Earth." He waited ten seconds while a murmur built up.

"I'll tell you," he said. The murmur stilled.

"You'll get just one thing on Alpha Three, an even chance." The officer stepped down and walked away. The murmur rose to an angry mutter. A noncom took the platform and barked, "That's enough, you Covvs! When the major said an even chance, that meant nobody gets special privileges! Nobody! Maybe some of you were big shots once; forget all that. From now on, it's what you can *do* that counts. Only half of you are going to Alpha. We'll find out which half today. Now. . . ." He dictated orders. Gus found himself in a group of twenty men tramping out across the pavement toward a tall, open-work structure. A tall, black-haired man marched beside him.

"These boys don't give away much," he said. "A man'd think they had something to hide."

"No talking in ranks!" a wide-faced cadreman with gaps between his teeth barked. "You'll find out all you need to know soon enough, and you won't like it." He leered and moved on. There was no more talking.

At the tower, the men were herded into a large open-sided lift that lurched as it rumbled upward. Gus watched the desert floor sink away, spreading out below like a dirty blanket. He shied as the gate whooshed open beside him at the top.

"Out, you Covvs!" the burly noncome shouted. Nobody moved.

"You," the cadreman's eyes fixed on Gus. "Let's go. You look like a big, tough boy. All it takes is a little guts."

Gus looked out at the railless platform, the four-foot catwalk extending across to a wider platform twenty feet distant. He felt his feet freeze to the car floor.

The noncom shook his head, brushed past Gus, walked halfway across the catwalk, turned and folded his arms.

"Alpha's that way," he jerked his head to indicate the far end of the walk.

Gus took a breath and walked quickly across. Others followed. Three stayed behind, refusing the walk. The noncom gestured.

"Take 'em back!" The car door closed on them. The cadreman faced his charges.

"This scares you," he said. "Sure, it's something new; you never had to do anything like that before. Well, out on Alpha everything'll be new. You Covvs'll have to adapt or die."

"What if somebody fell?" the black-bearded man asked.

"He'd be dead," the noncom said flatly. "That's real rock down there. If you're going to die, it's better to do it here than after the government's wasted the cost of shipping you four lights into space."

After the tower, there was a climb up a tortuous construction of bars and angles, a maze on edge that led to dead ends and impasses that forced the climber to descend, find a new route, while his hands ached and his legs trembled with fatigue. Then there was a water hazard: Locked in a large cage suspended over a muddy pond, Gus listened to instructions, held his breath as the cage submerged, rose, dripping, submerged again. . . . and again. When the torture ended he was half drowned. Two unconscious men were carried away. Then there was an obstacle course, with warning signs posted. Several men ignored the signs—or forgot— or lost their balance. They were carried away. Gus stared at one blood-spattered face, unbelieving.

"They can't do this!" Hogan said. "By God, these birds have gone out of their minds! They. . . ." He fell silent as the gap-toothed noncom strolled past.

There was a half-hour break while the colonists ate another mush ration; then the day went on. There was a run across a rock-strewn ground where a misstep meant a broken ankle, or worse; a passage through a twisted, eighteen-inch duct where panic could mean entrapment, upside down; a ride in a centrifuge that left Gus dizzy, shaking, soggy with cold sweat. None of the trials were particularly strenuous—or even dangerous, if the subject kept his head and followed instructions. But steadily the roster of men dwindled. By nightfall, only Gus and eight others were left of the twenty who had started together. Hogan and the black-haired man—Franz—were among them.

"Haven't you caught on to what's going on here yet?" Hogan whispered hoarsely to Gus as the survivors tramped back toward the barracks area. "I heard about this kind of place. They brought us out here to do away with us. The whole deal—free trip to a new planet, the whole colonization program—it's a phony, a cover-up for killing off everybody who's not satisfied with things."

"You're nuts," Franz said.

"Yeah? You've heard the talk about euthanasia. . . ."

"A little gas in the hive would be easier," Gus said.

"That pond! If I wouldn't of seen it, I'd of called the man a liar told me about it!"

"Sure, it's a screwy setup," Franz conceded. "But this is a crash program. They had to improvise. . . ."

A murmuring sound had grown unnoticed in the distance. Now, as it swelled, Gus thought of distant thunder, and his imagination pictured cool wind, a cloudburst after the misery of the day's heat.

"Look!" Men were pointing. A flickering white star at zenith grew visibly brighter, and the sound grew with it. The rumble rolled across the plain, and the light brightened into a glittering play of fire at the end of a trail of luminosity.

"Stand fast!" the noncoms shouted as the ranks broke. A jet plane thundered across from the east, shot upward, dwindling toward the descending ship, which grew, waxing like a moon, as a hot wind sprang up, blowing outward from the landing point ten miles distant. A glint of high sunlight showed on the flank of the great vessel. It sank gently on its pillar of fire, dropped again into darkness, a moving tower of lights, sliding down to settle in its bed of roiling, fiery cloud. Slowly, the bellow of the titanic engines died, the glare faded. Echoes washed back and forth across the plain.

"Starship!" the words ran through the ranks. Gus felt his heart begin to thud in his chest. Starship!

There was no sleep that night. "You'll get plenty from now on," the cadreman told the recruits, as they formed up into double lines leading to a white-painted building that gleamed pale in the polyarcs. It seemed to Gus that the plain was filled with men, shuffling toward the lighted doorways. Hours passed before he reached the building. He blinked in the greenish glare of the long, antiseptically bare room. Teams of surgically masked men and women worked over rows of tables.

"Strip and get on the board," a voice chanted. Technicians closed in around Gus. He backed, gripped by a sudden panic.

"Wait—"

Hands caught him. He fought, but cursing men forced him back. Hyposprays jetted icy cold against his arms. Questions clamored in his brain but before he could form them into words he felt himself sinking down into the fleecy softness of sleep. . . .

3

Someone was talking urgently. The voice had been going on for a long time, he knew, but now it began to penetrate:

" . . . . you understand? Come on, Covv, wake up!"

Gus tried to speak, said "Awwrrr. . . ."

"Come on, on your feet!"

Gus forced his eyes open. It was a different face that bent over him, not one of the technicians. A half-familiar face, except for the half-inch beard and hollow cheeks.

"Sergeant. . . . Berg. . . ." Gus got out.

"That's right, Covv, come on, let's move, there's work to be done."

"Wha' went wrong. . . ."

"Hah? What didn't go wrong? Hull damage, mutiny—but that's not for you to worry about, Covv. We're ten hours out; you've had your sleep—"

"Ten hours. . . . from Earth?"

"Hah? From Alpha Three, Covv! Eighteen hundred and fourteen days out of Terra."

Gus rocked as though he had been struck. Almost. . . . five years.

"We're almost there," he said. Berg was urging him to his feet.

"That's right. And you've been tapped for ship's complement—you and a few other Covvs—to help out during approach. Coolie labor. Follow me."

Staggering a little, Gus trailed the noncom along a tight gray corridor, green-lit by a glare-strip running along the low ceiling. Passing an open door, he caught a glimpse of a wrecked wall, sheet plastic partitioning bulging out of line, broken pipes and tangled wires, a scatter of debris.

"What happened?" he asked.

"Never mind," Berg growled. "You're just a dumb Covv. Stay that way."

They rode a lift up, walked along another corridor, came into the Christmas tree brilliance of the bridge. Silent, harried-looking men in rumpled tan peered worriedly into screens and instrument faces. Officers muttered together; technicians chanted into vocoders. A young-looking officer with short blond hair gestured to Berg.

"This is the last of 'em, sir," the noncom said.

"I'll use him as a messenger. No communications with sections aft of Station Twenty-eight now. The tub's coming apart."

"Stand by here," Berg told Gus, and went away.

"Lieutenant, take over on six," a guttural voice called. The blond lieutenant moved to a gimbaled seat before a screen that showed a vivid crescent against velvet black. A moon was visible at the edge of the screen, a tiny blob of greenish-white. No stars showed; the sensitivity of the screen had dimmed in response to the blaze of the nearby sun.

Gus moved back against the wall. For the next hour he stood there, forgotten, watching the image of the planet grow on the screens as the weary officer worked over the maze of controls that swept in a twenty-foot horseshoe around the compartment.

" . . . . we're not going to try it—not while I'm on the bridge." The words caught Gus's attention. A lean, hawk-faced officer tossed papers onto the floor. "We'll have to divert!"

"You're refusing to carry out my instructions?" The squat, white-haired man who Gus knew was the captain raised his voice. "You press me too far, Leone—"

"I'll put her down for you on Planet Four," the first officer shouted him down. "That's the best I can do!"

The captain cursed the tall man. Other voices joined in the dispute. In the end the captain bellowed his capitulation:

"Planet Four, then, Leone! And there'll be charges filed, I guarantee you that!"

"File and be damned!"

The argument went on. Pressed back against the wall, Gus watched as the crescent swelled, grew to fill the screen, became a curve of dusty-lighted horizon, then a hazy plain dotted with the tiny white flecks of clouds. Faint, eerie whistlings started up, climbed the scale; buffeting started. The men on the bridge had forgotten their differences now. Crisp commands and curt acknowledgements were the only words spoken.

Under Gus, the deck bucked and hammered. He went down, held onto a stanchion as the shaking grew, the scream of air became a frantic tornado—

Then, quite suddenly, the motion smoothed out as a new thunder vibrated through the deck: the roar of the engines waking to life.

Minutes crawled past while the Niagara-rumble went on and on. Then a shock slammed the deck, sent Gus sprawling. Half-dazed, he got to his feet, saw the officers swinging from their places, whooping, slapping each other's backs. The captain bustled past, leaving the bridge. The big General Display screen showed a stretch of dull gray-green hills under a watery sky.

"What the devil are you doing here?" a voice cracked at Gus like a whip. It was First Officer Leone. "Get off the bridge, you bloody Covv!"

"Sir," Sergeant Berg said, coming up, "Captain's orders—"

"Damn the captain! Damn the lot of you." He waved an arm to include everyone on the bridge. "Reservists! The bunch of you wouldn't make a wart on a regular officer's rump!"

Gus made his way alone back down to the level where he had been brought out of Coldsleep. A cadreman greeted him with a curse.

"Where the hell have you been, Covv? You're on the defrost detail. Get aft and report to Hensley in the meat room—and don't get lost!"

"I wasn't lost," Gus said, returning the noncom's glare. "But I think a fellow named Leone was."

"Ahhh. . . ." the noncom gave him terse directions. He followed them to a narrow, high-aisled chamber, bright-lit, frosty. A bowlegged NCO waddled up to him, pointed to a rack of heavy parkas, assigned him to a crew. Gus watched as they undogged a thick, foot-and-a-half square door, drew out a slab on which the frost-covered body of a man lay under a thin plastic membrane.

"Automatics are out," the foreman explained. "We got to unload these Covvs by hand—what's left of 'em."

"What do you mean?"

"We took a four-ton rock through the hull, about fifty hours ago. Lost a bunch of officers and some crew—and before Leone got around to checking, we lost a lot of Covvs. Splinter right through the master panel." The man lifted the plastic, which peeled away from the waxy flesh with a crinkling sound. "Spoiled, you might say—like this one."

Gus looked at the drawn, hollow face, the glint of yellowish teeth behind the gray lips. The plastic dropped back and the crew moved on to the next door.

In the next five hours, Gus saw twenty-one more corpses. One hundred and forty-one presumably intact colonists were rolled into the revival room. Gus caught glimpses of the gagging, shivering men as they responded to the efforts of the Med crews.

"It ain't easy to die and come to life again," the bandy-legged corporal conceded, watching as a man retched and bucked against the hold-down straps.

The work went on. The horror had gone out of it now; it was simply monotonous, hard, bone-chilling work. He had learned to spot the symptoms of tragedy early: a bulge of frost around a door invariably meant a dead man inside. The trickle of life processes of a living Coldsleep subject generated sufficient heat to prevent frosting inside the capsule.

There was the tell-tale trace on the next door. Gus opened it, tugged to break the ice seal, slid the tray out. There was a heavy layer of ice over the plastic. Gus leaned close, his attention caught by something in the face under the ice. He stripped the sheet back from the body, felt an icy shock that locked his breath in his throat.

The face was that of his younger brother, Lenny.

"Tough," the corporal said, flicking an eye curiously at Gus. "According to the tag, he was in the draft next to yours; must have come into Mojave the day after you. We was five weeks loading. . . ."

Gus thought of the screening trials, the torture of the dunking cage, the walk across emptiness on the narrow catwalk. And Lenny, trying to follow him, going through all of it, and dying like this.

"You said by the time Leone got around to checking, some of the colonists were dead," Gus said in a ragged tone. "What did you mean?"

"Forget it, Covv. Let's get back to work. We got the live ones to think about." The corporal put a hand on the small pistol strapped to his hip. "We're not out of the woods yet—any of us."

The ship had been on the ground twenty-seven hours when Gus' turn came to walk down the landing ramp and out under the chill sky of a new world. A light, misty rain was falling. There was a sour smell of burned vegetation and over it a hint of green, growing things, alien but fresh, not unpleasant.

The charred ground was a churn of black mud trampled by the

thousands of men who had debarked ahead of him. They were lined up in irregular ranks, row after row, that stretched out of sight over a rise of ground. Gus's group was formed up and marched off toward the far end of the bivouac area.

"This don't look like much to me," Hogan said. His red hair looked wilder than ever. Like the other colonists, he had acquired an inch of beard while in Coldsleep.

"This isn't where we were supposed to land," Gus told him. "We're on the wrong planet."

"Hah? How do you know?"

Gus told him what he had heard during his stay on the bridge.

"Cripes!" Hogan waved a hand at the treeless, rolling tundra. "The wrong planet! That means there ain't no colony here, no housing, no nothing!"

"As the man said," Franz put in, "we're on our own. We can carve our own town out of this—"

"Yeah? With no trees, no lumber, no running water—"

"Sure, there's running water. It's running down my neck right now."

"We been had!" Hogan burst out. "This ain't the deal I signed on for!"

"You signed like the rest of us, no questions asked."

"Yeah, but—"

"Don't say it," Franz said. "You'll break my heart."

"No shelter," Hogan said an hour later. "I heard the best food all went to the colonists. Where is it?"

"Wait until the ship's unloaded," Franz said.

"Nothing's come off that tub yet but us Covvs." Hogan rubbed his hands together for warmth, looking toward the grim tower of the ship. The damage done to the hull by the meteorite was clearly visible as a pockmark near the upper end.

"They're probably still busy doing emergency repairs," Franz said.

"Don't look like a little hole like that could of done all that damage," Hogan said.

"That ship's nearly as complicated as a human body," a man standing by said. "Poking a hole in it's like shooting a hole in you."

"Hey—look there!" Hogan pointed. A new group of parka-clad colonists was filing over the brow of the hill.

"Women!" Franz whispered.

"Females, by God!" Hogan burst out.

"It figures," someone said. "You can't make a colony without women!"

"Boys, they kept that one up their sleeve!"

The men watched as squad after squad of female colonists toiled up the hill, forming up beyond the men. Then they turned at the sound of car engines. A carryall towing a small trailer came along the line, stopped near Gus. A cadreman jumped down, pulled back the tarp covering the trailer, hauled out a heavy bundle.

"All right, you Covvs," he shouted as the car pulled away. "You're going to dig in. File up here and draw shovels!"

"Shovels? Is he kidding?" Hogan looked around at the others.

"Dig for what?" someone called.

"Shelter," the corporal barked. "Unless you want to sleep out in the open."

"What about our pre-fabs?"

"Yeah—and our rations!"

"There's power equipment aboard the ship! If there's digging to be done, by God, let's use it!"

The corporal unlimbered his foot-long club. "I told you Covvs," he started, and his voice was drowned by the clamor as the men closed in on him.

"We want food!"

"To hell with digging!"

"When you going to hand out the women?"

"I. . . . I'll go see." The noncom backed away, then turned, went off quickly down-slope. Voices were being raised all across the hill now. Gus saw other cadremen withdrawing, one with blood on his face and minus his cap. The uproar grew. A carryall raced up from the ship, took cadremen aboard. Clubs swung at colonists who gave chase.

"After 'em!" Hogan yelled. Gus grabbed his arm. "Stop, you damned fool! This is a mistake!"

"It's time we started getting a fair deal around here! We've not convicts, by God!"

"The power's all theirs," Gus said. "This won't help us!"

"We outnumber them a hundred to one," Hogan crowed. "Look at 'em run! I guess the digging party's off!" He shook off Gus's grip, looked toward the women. "Boys, let's pay a call. Them little ladies look lonesome—"

Gus shoved the redhead back. "Start that, and we're done for! Can't you see the spot we're in?"

"What spot?" Hogan began to bluster. "We showed 'em they can't push us around!"

"They're loading up, going back aboard." Gus pointed. Heads turned to watch the last of the cars wheeling up the ramp.

"They're scared of us—"

"We jumped them, forced their hand—"

"Yeah?" Hogan frowned ferociously. "So they ran from us."

"You damned fool," Gus said wearily. "Suppose they don't come back out?"

"They can't do this to us," Hogan whined for the fortieth time. The suns—both of them—had set hours before. The rain had turned to sleet that froze on the springy turf and on the men's clothing.

"It must be five below," Franz said. "You think they'll leave us out here to freeze, Gus?"

"I don't know."

"They're in there, eating our rations, sleeping in soft beds," Hogan growled. "The dirty blood-suckers!"

"Can't much blame 'em," Franz said. "With boneheads like you roughing 'em up. You expect 'em to come out and let you finish the job?"

"They can't get away with it!"

"They can get away with anything they want to," Gus said. "Nobody back on Earth knows what's going on out here. It takes ten years to ask a question and get an answer. And in ten years the population will have tripled. They'll have other things to think about than us. We're expendable."

A ripple of talk was passing through the ranks of men squatting on the exposed hillside under the relentless sleet. Dark figures were advancing from the direction of the women's area.

"It's the girls," Hogan said. "They want company."

"Leave them alone, Hogan," Gus said. "Let's see what they want."

The leader of the women's delegation was a strong-looking blonde in her late twenties, muffled in an oversized parka. She planted herself in front of the men. They closed in, gaping.

"Who's in charge over here?" she demanded.

"Nobody, baby," Hogan started. "It's every man for himself. . . ." He reached out with a meaty paw. The girl brushed it aside. "Pass that for now, Porky," she said briskly. "We've got important things to talk about, like not freezing to death. What are you fellows doing about it?"

"Not a damn thing, honey. What can we do?" Hogan jerked a thumb toward the lights of the ship. "Those lousy crots have cut us off—"

"I saw what happened; you damned fools started a riot. I don't blame them for pulling out. But what are you going to do about it *now*? You going to let your women freeze?"

"*Our* women?"

"Whose women you think we are, Porky? There's even one for you—if you can keep her alive."

"We've got a few shovels," Gus said. "We can dig in. This sod ought to be good enough to make huts of."

"Dig holes for over nine thousand people, with a couple dozen shovels?" Hogan jeered. "Are you nuts—"

A crackle like near-by lightning sounded. "Attention-on," a vast voice boomed across the bivouac. "This is Captain Harris-is. . . ." Floodlights sprang into life at the base of the ship.

"You people are guilty of mutiny-any," the great voice rolled. "I'd be justified in whatever measures I chose to take at this point-oint. Including leaving you to suffer the consequences of your own actions-shuns." There was a pause to allow the thought to sink in.

"However, as it happens, I have repairs to undertake-ache. I'm shorthanded-dead. Time is important-ant-ant."

"Tough," Hogan growled.

"I want twenty volunteers to aid in the work of preparing my ship for space-ace. In return, I'll see to it that certain supplies are made available to you people-lull."

A mutter went up from the men. "The son of a bitch is holding us up for our own rations!" Hogan yelled.

"At the first sign of disorder, I'll clear a one-mile radius around the ship," the captain's voice boomed out. "I'm offering you mutineers the one chance you'll get-et! I suggest you think it over carefully! I want you to select twenty strong workers and send them forward-herd!"

"Let's rush the crots when they open the ports," Hogan shouted over the surf-noise of the crowd. "We can take the ship and rip those crots limb from limb! There's enough supplies aboard to last us for years! We can live in the ship until a rescue ship gets here!"

Faces were turning toward Hogan. Greedy eyes glistened in half-frozen faces.

"Let's go get 'em!" Hogan yelled. "Let's—"

Gus stepped after him, caught him by the shoulder, spun him around, and hit him square in the mouth with all his strength. Hogan went back and down and lay still.

"I'm volunteering for the work crew," Gus called, and started forward. A path opened to let him through.

Franz walked at Gus's side, leading the little troop of volunteers down the slope to the ship. The big floods bathed them in bluish light. Gus could feel the muscles of his stomach tighten, imagining guns aimed from the open ports. Or maybe it would be a touch of the main drive. . . .

No guns fired. No flame blossomed beyond the gigantic landing jacks rising from the mud. A squad of crewmen met them, searched them for weapons, detailed them off, marched them away. Gus and the blond woman were escorted to the Power Section, handed over to a bald, grim-faced engineering officer.

"Only two? And one of them a woman? Damn the captain's arrogance! I told the—" He shut himself up, barked at a greasy-handed corporal who gave the newcomers a ration of mush and set them to work disassembling a fire-blackened mechanism.

"What's the rush?" the girl asked the NCO. "Why work all night? We're all tired—you too. How long since you've slept?"

"Too bloody long. But it's captain's orders."

"What's he doing for the colonists? Has he sent out the food and shelter he promised?"

"How do I know?" the man muttered. "Just stick to the job and can the chatter."

Half an hour later, with the corporal and the engineer busy cursing over a frozen valve at the far end of the room, the girl whispered to Gus, "I think we're being double-crossed."

"Maybe."

"What'll we do?"

"Keep working."

Another hour passed. Abruptly, the engineer threw down the

calibrator with which he had been working, stamped out through the outer door.

"Try keeping the corporal occupied for a few minutes," Gus hissed at the girl. She nodded, rose, and went over to the corporal.

"I feel a little dizzy, sugar," she said, and folded against him. Gus went quickly to the door and out into the green-lit corridor.

He emerged in the darkened anteroom outside the bridge.

" . . . . nine hours at the outside!" a harsh voice was saying. "We lift before then, or we don't lift!"

"I don't trust your calculations, Leone."

"I showed you the fatigue profiles; check them for yourself— but do it fast! The structure is deflecting at the rate of two centimeters per hour. We'll have major strains in three hours, and buckling in eight—"

"I'll need six hours, minimum, to unload cargo, after the priority one work is out of the way—"

"Forget unloading, Captain. Your first job is to get your ship back, intact!"

"And you with it, eh, Leone?"

"The other officers feel as I do."

"After you've brow-beaten them! What about the colonists? Their equipment, their rations—"

"We can't spare the food," Leone said crisply. "You know what the damage inventory showed. We'll be lucky if we make it ourselves. The Covvs will manage—they'll have to. That's what they're here for, remember?"

"They were slated for an established colony on Three—"

"They can survive on Four. It's chilly, but no worse than plenty of areas of Terra."

"You're a cold-blooded devil, Leone."

"It's what you've got to do. . . ."

Gus stepped back, departed as silently as he had come.

The engineer whirled with an oath as Gus appeared. Gus stepped directly to him, and without warning hit him hard in the stomach, hit him again on the jaw as he doubled over. The corporal yelled and jumped, tugging at his gun. He went down hard as the girl threw herself at his legs. Gus knocked him cold with a blow on the head.

"Let's get out of here!" Gus helped the girl up; her nose was bleeding. He led her into the corridor, headed back toward the loading deck. They had gone fifty yards when a crew of armed men burst from a crossway and cut them off. It took three of them to hold the blond girl. Gus saw a club swinging toward his head; then the world burst into a shower of fireworks.

4

Bright light glared in Gus's face. He was lying on his back on the floor, his hands locked behind him. Across the small room, a tall man in a tan uniform sat at a desk. Gus sat up painfully; at the sound, the man turned. It was the first officer, Leone. He gave Gus a sardonic look. His eyes were red, his chin unshaven.

"I could have had you shot," he said. "But I wanted to learn a few things first. Speak freely and I may be able to do something for you. Now: who was in on the scheme with you? Are those"—he tilted his head to indicate the planet outside—"poor grubbers planning some sort of attack?"

"I'm on my own," Gus said.

"Come on, man, speak up! You're already deep enough: striking an officer, desertion—"

"I'm not in your army," Gus cut him off. "I want to see the captain, if you haven't eaten him for breakfast."

Leone laughed. "To claim your rights, I suppose."

"Something like that."

"There are no rights," Leone said flatly. "Only necessities."

"Like food and shelter. Those people out there came here expecting a decent chance. You plan to abandon them here—with nothing."

"Ah, so that was what was behind your little dash for freedom." Leone nodded as if pleased. "You need to adjust your thinking, Covv—"

"My name's Addison. Calling us Covvs won't take us off your conscience."

"Wrong on two counts. I have no conscience. As for names, they imply family ties, a place in a social structure. You have none—except what you might have made for yourself, out there." Leone shook his head. "No, Covv it is. It's the role you were born for—you and millions like you." He poured himself a drink from a bottle on the desk, tossed it back with a practiced flip of the wrist.

"There was a time when I wondered at the purpose of it all—man's slow climb up to the present mad carnival of spawning that's turned a planet into nothing more than a surface on which nameless, faceless nonentities breed endlessly, in a doomed effort to convert the entire mass of the world into human flesh. It seemed so pointless. But now I understand." Leone smiled crookedly. He was very drunk.

"Ah, you're wondering, but too proud to ask! Proud! Yes, every little unremembered mote of humanity has his share of that fatuous delusion of self-importance! Funny; very funny!" Leone leaned toward Gus, waving the glass in his hand. "Don't you know your function, Covv?" He grinned expectantly. Gus looked at him silently.

"You're a statistic!" Leone poured again, raised the glass in a mock toast. "Nature brings forth millions, that one may survive. And you're one out of the millions."

"Now that you have it all figured out," Gus said, "what are you going to do about us? Those people will freeze out there."

"Perhaps," Leone said carelessly. "Perhaps not. The toughest will survive—if they can. Survive to breed. And in time, devour this world, and jump on to a new star. Meanwhile, it hardly matters what happens to a statistic."

"They were promised an even chance."

"Promises, promises. Death in the end is the only promise, my boy. As for those ciphers out there in the cold—think of them as fish eggs, if that will help you. Spawned by the million so that one or two can live to spawn in turn. Life goes on—as long as you've got plenty of fish eggs."

"They're not fish eggs. They're men, and they deserve simple justice—"

"You call justice simple?" Leone leaned forward, almost rolled from his chair before he caught himself. "The most sophisticated concept with which the mind of man deludes itself—and that's the only place it exists: in men's minds. What does the Universe know about justice, Covv? Suns burn, planets whirl, chemicals react. The fox devours the bunny rabbit with a clear conscience—just the way Alpha Four will devour those poor clots out there." He waved an arm. "And that's as it should be. Nature's way. Survive—

or don't survive. It's natural—like an earthquake. It'll kill you without the least ill-will in the world."

"You're not an earthquake," Gus said. "It's you that's holding back the food those men need."

"Don't come whining to me for your lousy justice!" Leone shouted, swaying in his chair. "We were having a well-earned drink in the wardroom when the rock hit. Killed half the officers of this damned tub—killed my friend, my best friend, damn you! After five years, cruise almost over. . . . and all for the sake of a load of caviar. . . ."

Leone gulped the rest of his drink, threw the glass across the room. "Don't chatter to me about what's fair," he muttered. "It's what's real that counts." He put his head down on his arms and snored.

It took Gus five minutes to reach the desk, grope in the drawers until he found the electrokey which unlocked the cuffs on his wrists. There was a crew-type coverall in the closet. Gus donned it, added a small handgun from a wall chest. In the passageway, all was silent. Most of the crew were busy, Gus knew. He made his way down to the lower levels, finally encountered a familiar corridor leading to the Power Section. He passed two men on the way; they hardly glanced at him.

The red-painted door to the Power Control Room stood ajar. Gus slipped past it, closed it silently, dogged it down. The engineering officer yelped when Gus poked the gun into his back.

"Quiet," Gus cautioned. He prodded the man along to a parts locker, motioned him inside.

"What do you hope to gain by this, you madman?" The man's red face blazed almost purple. "You're asking to be shot down—"

"So are you. No noise." Gus shut the door and locked it. He went on to the room that housed the control servos. Three technicians worked over a disassembled chassis. They whirled when Gus snapped an order at them. Their hands went up slowly. Gus herded two of them into a parts locker. The third backed away, trembling and sweating, as Gus pressed the gun to his chest.

"Show me how this setup works," Gus ordered.

The technician began a confused lecture on the theory of cyclic fusion-fission reactors.

"Skip all that," Gus told him. "Tell me about these controls."

The technician explained. Gus listened, asked questions. After fifteen minutes he indicated a red plastic panel cover.

"That's the damper control unit?"

"That's right."

"Open it up."

"Now, just a minute, fellow," the man said quickly. "You don't know what you're getting into—"

"Do as I said."

"You tamper with that, you can throw the whole core out of balance!"

Gus rammed the gun hard into the man's chest.

"OK, OK." He set to work with fingers that shook.

Gus studied the maze of exposed circuitry. "What happens if you cut those conduits?" he pointed. The technician backed away, shaking his head. "Wait a minute, fellow—"

Gus cuffed the side of his head hard enough to send the man sprawling.

"The whole revert circuit will be thrown on the line! You'll get a feed into the interlock system, and—"

"Put it in English!"

"She'd climb past crit and blow! She'd blow the side of the planet out!"

"What if you just cut that one?" Gus indicated another lead.

The technician shook his head. "Nearly as bad," his voice broke. "She'd run away and the core would begin to heat. She'd run red in an hour, and slag down in three. The gamma count—"

"Any way to stop it, once it starts?"

"Not once you let her climb past critical! You red-line her, and we're all finished!"

"Cut that lead," Gus commanded.

"You're out of your mind—" The man launched himself at Gus; he hit him with the gun, sent him reeling. There was a heavy pair of bolt-cutters on the nearby bench. Gus used them to snap through the pencil-thick lead. At once, a bell sounded stridently. Gus tossed the cutters aside, dragged the groaning man to a tool locker; then he went to the wall phone, punched a code from the list beside it.

"Captain, this is one of the fish eggs," he said. "I think we'd better have a talk about a choice you're going to have to make."

5

Gus stood with Captain Harris on a hillside a mile from the ship, watching with the others as the spot of dull red grew on the side of the gleaming tower that was the stricken starship. A sigh went up from the men as a long ripple appeared across the flawless curve of the great hull.

"Broke her back," the captain said tonelessly.

"She'll cool down enough by spring for us to go aboard and salvage whatever might be of use to the colony. Meanwhile, what we took off her before she got too hot ought to last us."

Harris gave Gus an ice-blue glare that reminded him of a girl left behind on faraway Terra. The memory seemed as remote as the planet.

"Yes—you should be able to survive until then—"

"*We* ought to survive," Gus corrected. "We're all in this together, now."

"When the story of your treachery gets out—"

"It's to your advantage not to let it," Gus interrupted the threat. "Better stick to the story we agreed on, about my lucky hunch and your heroic action, saving as much as you did."

"My officers would tear me apart if they knew I'd come to terms with a mutinous, sabotaging scoundrel!"

"The colonists would rip all of you apart if they knew you'd planned to maroon them."

"I'm still wondering if you'd have made good your threat to blow her apart."

"Either way, you'd have lost. This way, you have a certain amount of goodwill going for you with the colonists. They think you chose to lose the ship rather than abandon them."

"If there'd been any other way. . . ."

A tall figure staggered across toward the two men.

"Cap'n. . . ." Leone blurted. "I tol' you. . . . tol' you she'd buckle."

"Yes, you told me, Leone. Go sleep it off."

"Last cruise," Leone muttered, watching the ship as the proud nose visibly leaned as the weakened structure yielded to the massive pressure of gravity. "My retirement, flat of my own, wife. . . . all gone, now. Stuck here, on this. . . . this cold desert!"

"We'll march south," Gus said. "Maybe we'll find better country."

"I'm not sure we should leave this area," Harris said. "If we're to have any chance of rescue—"

"We're pollen on the wind," Gus said. "Nobody will ever miss us. It's up to us, now; what we do for ourselves. Nobody else cares."

"My authority—"

"Doesn't mean a thing," Gus cut him off. "We're all Covvs together, swimming in the same waters."

"Shark-infested waters!"

Gus nodded. "We won't all make it; but some of us will."

Harris seemed to shudder. "How can you be sure?"

"We have a chance," Gus said. "That's all any man can ask for."

PLACEMENT TEST

I

Reading the paper in his hand, Mart Maldon felt his mouth go dry. Across the desk, Dean Wormwell's eyes, blurry behind thick contact lenses, strayed to his fingerwatch.

"Quota'd out?" Maldon's voice emerged as a squeak. "Three days before graduation?"

"Umm, yes, Mr. Maldon. Pity, but there you are. . . ." Wormwell's jowls twitched upward briefly. "No reflection on you, of course. . . ."

Maldon found his voice. "They can't do this to me—I stand number two in my class—"

Wormwell held up a pudgy palm. "Personal considerations are not involved, Mr. Maldon. Student load is based on quarterly allocated funding; funds were cut. Analogy Theory was one of the courses receiving a quota reduction—"

"An Theory. . . .? But I'm a Microtronics major; that's an elective—an optional one-hour course—"

The Dean rose, stood with his fingertips on the desk. "The details are there, in the notification letter—"

"What about the detail that I waited four years for enrollment, and I've worked like a malamute for five more—"

"Mr. Maldon!" Wormwell's eyes bulged. "We work within a system! You don't expect *personal* exceptions to be made, I trust?"

213

"But, Dean—there's a howling need for qualified Microtronic Engineers—"

"That will do, Mr. Maldon. Turn in your student tag to the Registrar and you'll receive an appointment for Placement Testing."

"All right." Maldon's chair banged as he stood up. "I can still pass Testing and get Placed; I know as much Micro as any graduate—"

"Ah—I believe you're forgetting the limitation on non-academically qualified testees in Technical Specialty Testing. I suggest you accept a Phase Two Placement for the present. . . ."

"Phase Two—But that's for unskilled labor!"

"You need work, Mr. Maldon. A city of a hundred million can't support idlers. And dormitory life is far from pleasant for an untagged man." The Dean waited, glancing pointedly at the door. Maldon silently gathered up his letter and left.

2

It was hot in the test cubicle. Maldon shifted on the thinly-padded bench, looking over the test form:

1) In the following list of words, which word is repeated most often: dog, cat, cow, cat, pig. . . .

2) Would you like to ask persons entering a building to show you their pass?

3) Would you like to check forms to see if the names have been entered in the correct space?

"Testing materials are on the desk," a wall-speaker said. "Use the stylus to mark the answers you think are correct. Mark only one answer to each question. You will have one hour in which to complete the test. You may start now. . . ."

Back in the Hall twenty minutes later, Maldon took a seat on a bench against the wall beside a heavy-faced man who sat with one hand clutching the other as though holding a captured mouse. Opposite him, a nervous youth in issue coveralls shook a cigarette from a crumpled plastic pack lettered GRANYAUCK WELFARE—ONE DAILY RATION, puffed it alight, exhaled an acrid whiff of combustion retardant.

"That's a real smoke," he said in a high, rapid voice, rolling the thin, grayish cylinder between his fingers. "Half an inch of doctored tobacco and an inch and a half of filter." He grinned sourly and dropped the cigarette on the floor between his feet.

The heavy-faced man moved his head half an inch.

"That's safety first, Mac. Guys like you throw 'em around, they burn down and go out by theirself."

"Sure—if they'd make 'em half an inch shorter you could throw 'em away without lighting 'em at all."

Across the room a small man with jug ears moved along, glancing at the yellow or pink cards in the hands of the waiting men and women. He stopped, plucked a card from the hand of a narrow-faced boy with an open mouth showing crowded yellow teeth.

"You've already *passed*," the little man said irritably. "You don't come back here anymore. Take the card and go to the place that's written on it. Here. . . ." he pointed.

"Sixteen years I'm foreman of number nine gang-lathe at Philly Maintenance," the man sitting beside Mart said suddenly. He unfolded his hands, held out the right one. The tips of all four fingers were missing to the first knuckles. He put the hand away.

"When I get out of the Medicare, they classify me J-4 and send me here. And you know what?" He looked at Mart. "I can't pass the tests. . . ."

"Maldon, Mart," an amplified voice said. "Report to the Monitor's desk. . . ."

He walked across to the corner where the small man sat now, deftly sorting cards. He looked up, pinched a pink card from the stack, jabbed it at Maldon. Words jumped out at him: NOT QUALIFIED.

Mart tossed the card back on the desk. "You must be mixed up," he said. "A ten-year-old kid could pass that test—"

"Maybe so," the monitor said sharply. "But *you* didn't. Next testing on Wednesday, eight A.M.—"

"Hold on a minute," Mart said. "I've had five years of Microtronics—"

The monitor was nodding. "Sure, sure. Come back Wednesday."

"You don't get the idea—"

"You're the one that doesn't get the idea, fellow." He studied Maldon for a moment. "Look," he said, in a more reasonable tone. "What you want, you want to go in for Adjustment."

"Thanks for the tip," Maldon said. "I'm not quite ready to have my brains scrambled."

"Ha! A smart-alec!" The monitor pointed to his chest. "Do I look like my brains were scrambled?"

Maldon looked him over as though in doubt.

"You've been Adjusted, huh? What's it like?"

"Adjustment? There's nothing to it. You have a problem finding work, it helps you, that's all. I've seen fellows like you before. You'll never pass Phase Two testing until you do it."

"To Hell with Phase Two testing! I've registered for Tech Testing. I'll just wait."

The monitor nodded, prodding at his teeth with a pencil. "Yeah, you could wait. I remember one guy waited nine years; then he got his Adjustment and we placed him in a week."

"Nine years?" Maldon shook his head. "Who makes up these rules?"

"Who makes 'em up? Nobody! They're in the book."

Maldon leaned on the desk. "Then who writes the book? Where do I find them?"

"You mean the Chief?" the small man rolled his eyes toward the ceiling. "On the next level up. But don't waste your time, friend. You can't get in there. They don't have time to argue with everybody who comes in here. It's the system—"

"Yeah," Maldon said, turning away. "So I hear."

3

Maldon rode the elevator up one floor, stepped off in a blank-walled foyer, adorned by a stone urn filled with sand, a potted yucca, framed unit citations and a polished slab door lettered PLACEMENT BOARD—AUTHORIZED PERSONNEL ONLY. He tried it, found it solidly locked.

It was very quiet. Somewhere, air pumps hummed. Maldon stood by the door and waited. After ten minutes, the elevator door hissed open, disgorged a slow-moving man in blue GS coveralls with a yellow identity tag. He held the tag to a two-inch rectangle of glass beside the door. There was a click. The door slid back. Maldon moved quickly, crowding through behind the workman.

"Hey, what gives," the man said.

"It's all right, I'm a coordinator," Maldon said quickly.

"Oh." The man looked Maldon over. "Hey," he said. "Where's your I.D.?"

"It's a new experimental system. It's tattooed on my left foot."

"Hah!" the man said. "They always got to try out new stuff." He went on along the deep-carpeted corridor. Maldon followed slowly, reading signs over doors. He turned in under one that read CRITERIA SECTION. A girl with features compressed by fat looked up, her lower jaw working busily. She reached, pressed a button on the desk top.

"Hi," Maldon said, using a large smile. "I'd like to see the chief of the section."

The girl chewed, looking at him.

"I won't take up much of his time. . . ."

"You sure won't, Buster," the girl said. The hall door opened. A uniformed man looked in. The girl waved a thumb at Maldon.

"He comes busting in," she said. "No tag, yet."

The guard jerked his head toward the corridor. "Let's go. . . ."

"Look, I've got to see the chief—"

The cop took his arm, helped him to the door. "You birds give me a swifty. Why don't you go to Placement like the sign says?"

"Look, they tell me I've got to have some kind of electronic lobotomy to make me dumb enough to be a receptionist or a watchman—"

"Let's watch them cracks," the guard said. He shoved Maldon out into the waiting room. "Out! And don't pull any more fasties until you got a tag, see?"

4

Sitting at a shiny imitation-oak table in the Public Library, Mart turned the pages of a booklet titled *Adjustment Fits the Man to the Job.*

". . . . neuroses arising from job tension," he read at random. "Thus, the Adjusted worker enjoys the deep-down satisfaction which comes from Doing a Job, free from conflict-inducing nonproductive impulses and the distractions of feckless speculative intellectual activity. . . ."

Mart rose and went to the librarian's console.

"I want something a little more objective," he said in a hoarse library whisper. "This is nothing but propaganda."

The librarian paused in her button-punching to peer at the booklet. "That's put out by the Placement people themselves," she said sharply. She was a jawless woman with a green tag against a ribby chest and thin, black-dyed hair. "It contains all the information anyone needs."

"Not quite; it doesn't tell who grades Placement tests and decides who gets their brain poached."

"Well!" the woman's button chin drew in. "I'm sure I never heard Adjustment referred to in *those terms* before!"

"Do you have any technical information on it—or anything on Placement policy in general?"

"Certainly not for indiscriminate use by—" she searched for a word, "—browsers!"

"Look, I've got a right to know what goes on in my own town, I hope," Mart said, forgetting to whisper. "What is it, a conspiracy. . . . ?"

"You're paranoiac!" The librarian's lean fingers snatched the pamphlet from Maldon's hand. "You come stamping in here— without even a tag—a great healthy creature like you—" her voice cut like a sheet-metal file. Heads turned.

"All I want is information—"

"—living in luxury on MY tax money! You ought to be—"

5

It was an hour later. In a ninth-floor corridor of the GRAN-YAUCK TIMES-HERALD building, Mart leaned against a wall, mentally rehearsing speeches. A stout man emerged from a door lettered EDITOR IN CHIEF. Mart stepped forward to intercept him.

"Pardon me, sir. I have to see you. . . ."

Sharp blue eyes under wild-growing brows darted at Maldon "Yes? What is it?"

"I have a story for you. It's about the Placement procedure."

"Whoa, buddy. Who are you?"

"My name's Maldon. I'm an Applied Tech graduate—almost—but I can't get placed in Microtronics. I don't have a tag—and the only way to get one is to get a job—but first I have to let the government operate on my brains—"

"Hmmmp!" The man looked Maldon up and down, started on.

"Listen!" Maldon caught at the portly man's arm. "They're making idiots out of intelligent people so they can do work you could train a chimp to do, and if you ask any questions—"

"All right, Mac. . . ." A voice behind Maldon growled. A large hand took him by the shoulder, propelled him toward the walkaway entrance, urged him through the door. He straightened his coat, looked back. A heavy-set man with a pink card in a plastic cover clipped to his collar dusted his hands, looking satisfied.

"Don't come around lots," he called cheerfully as the door slammed.

6

"Hi, Glamis," Mart said to the small, neat woman behind the small, neat desk. She smiled nervously, straightened the mathematically precise stack of papers before her.

"Mart, it's lovely to see you again, of course. . . ." her eyes went to the blank place where his tag should have been. "But you really should have gone to your assigned SocAd Advisor—"

"I couldn't get an appointment until January." He pulled a chair around to the desk and sat down. "I've left school. I went in for Phase Two Placement testing this morning. I flunked."

"Oh. . . . I'm so sorry, Mart." She arranged a small smile on her face. "But you can go back on Wednesday—"

"Uh-huh. And then on Friday, and then the following Monday—"

"Why, Mart, I'm sure you'll do better next time," the girl said brightly. She flipped through the pages of a calendar pad. "Wednesday's testing is for. . . . ah. . . . Vehicle Positioning Specialists, Instrumentation Inspectors, Sanitary Facility Supervisors—"

"Uh-huh. Toilet Attendants," Mart said. "Meter Readers—"

"There are others," Glamis went on hastily. "Traffic flow coordinators—"

"Pushing stop-light buttons on the turnpike. But it doesn't matter what the job titles are. I can't pass the tests."

"Why, Mart. . . . Whatever do you mean?"

"I mean that to get the kind of jobs that are open you have to be a nice, steady moron. And if you don't happen to qualify as such, they're prepared to make you into one."

"Mart, you're exaggerating! The treatment merely slows the synaptic response time slightly—and its effects can be reversed at any time. People of exceptional qualities are needed to handle the type work—"

"How can I fake the test results, Glamis? I need a job—unless I want to get used to Welfare coveralls and two T rations a day."

"Mart! I'm shocked that you'd suggest such a thing! Not that it would work. You can't fool the Board that easily—"

"Then fix it so I go in for Tech testing; you know I can pass."

She shook her head. "Heavens, Mart, Tech Testing is all done at Central Personnel in City Tower—Level Fifty. Nobody goes up there, without at least a blue tag—" She frowned sympathetically. "You should simply have your adjustment, and—"

Maldon looked surprised. "You really expect me to go down there and have them cut my I.Q. down to 80 so I can get a job shoveling garbage?"

"Really, Mart; you can't expect society to adjust to *you*. You have to adjust to *it*."

"Look, I can punch commuters' tickets just as well as if I were stupid. I could—"

Glamis shook her head. "No, you couldn't, Mart. The Board knows what it's doing." She lowered her voice. "I'll be perfectly frank with you. These jobs *must* be filled. But they can't afford to put perceptive, active minds on rote tasks. There'd only be trouble. They need people who'll be contented and happy punching tickets."

Mart sat pulling at his lower lip. "All right, Glamis. Maybe I will go in for Adjustment. . . ."

"Oh, wonderful, Mart." She smiled. "I'm *sure* you'll be happier—"

"But first, I want to know more about it. I want to be sure they aren't going to make a permanent idiot out of me."

She tsked, handed over a small folder from a pile on the corner of the desk.

"This will tell you—"

He shook his head. "I saw that. It's just a throwaway for the public. I want to know how the thing works; circuit diagrams, technical specs."

"Why, Mart, I don't have anything of that sort—and even if I did—"

"You can get 'em. I'll wait."

"Mart, I *do* want to help you. . . . but. . . . what. . . . ?"

"I'm not going in for Adjustment until I know something about it," he said flatly. "I want to put my mind at ease that they're not going to burn out my cortex."

Glamis nibbled her upper lip. "Perhaps I *could* get something from Central Files." She stood. "Wait here; I won't be long."

She was back in five minutes carrying a thick book with a cover of heavy manila stock on which were the words, *GSM 8765-89. Operation and Maintenance, EET Mark II.* Underneath, in smaller print, was a notice:

This Field Manual for Use of Authorized Personnel Only.

"Thanks, Glamis." Mart rifled the pages, glimpsed fine print and intricate diagrams. "I'll bring it back tomorrow." He headed for the door.

"Oh, you can't take it out of the office! You're not even *supposed* to *look* at it!"

"You'll get it back." He winked and closed the door on her worried voice.

7

The cubicle reminded Mart of the one at the Placement center, three days earlier, except that it contained a high, narrow cot in place of a desk and chair. A damp-looking attendant in a white coat flipped a wall switch, twiddled a dial.

"Strip to your waist, place your clothing and shoes in the basket, remove all metal objects from your pockets, no watches or other jewelry must be worn," he recited in a rapid monotone. "When you are ready, lie down on your back—" he slapped the cot—"hands at your sides, breathe deeply, do not touch any of the equipment. I will return in approximately five minutes. Do not leave the stall." He whisked the curtain aside and was gone.

Mart slipped a flat plastic tool kit from his pocket, opened it out, picked the largest screwdriver, and went to work on the metal panel cover set against the wall. He lifted it off and looked in at a maze of junction blocks, vari-colored wires, bright screw-heads, fuses, tiny condensers.

He pulled a scrap of paper from his pocket, compared it to the circuits before him. The large black lead, here. . . . He put a finger on it. And the matching red one, leading up from the 30 MFD condenser. . . .

With a twist, he freed the two connectors, reversed them, tightened them back in place. Working quickly, he snipped wires, fitted jumpers in place, added a massive resistor from his pocket. There; with luck, the check instruments would give the proper readings now—but the current designed to lightly scorch his synapses would flow harmlessly round and round within the apparatus. He clapped the cover back in place, screwed it down, and had just pulled off his shirt when the attendant thrust his head inside the curtains.

"Let's go, let's get those clothes off and get on the cot," he said, and disappeared.

Maldon emptied his pockets, pulled off his shoes, stretched out on the cot. A minute or two ticked past. There was an odor of alcohol in the air. The curtain jumped aside. The round-faced attendant took his left arm, swiped a cold tuft of cotton across it, held a hypo-spray an inch from the skin, and depressed the plunger. Mart felt a momentary sting.

"You've been given a harmless soporific," the attendant said tonelessly. "Just relax, don't attempt to change the position of the headset or chest contacts after I have placed them in position, are you beginning to feel drowsy. . . . ?"

Mart nodded. A tingling had begun in his fingertips; his head seemed to be inflating slowly. There was a touch of something cold across his wrists, then his ankles, pressure against his chest. . . .

"Do not be alarmed, the restraint is for your own protection, relax and breathe deeply, it will hasten the effects of the soporific. . . ." The voice echoed, fading and swelling. For a moment, the panicky thought came to Mart that perhaps he had made a mistake, that the modified apparatus would send a lethal charge through his brain. . . . Then that thought was gone with all the others, lost in a swirling as of a soft green mist.

8

He was sitting on the side of the cot, and the attendant was offering him a small plastic cup. He took it, tasted the sweet liquid, handed it back.

"You should drink this," the attendant said. "It's very good for you."

Mart ignored him. He was still alive; and the attendant appeared to have noticed nothing unusual. So far, so good. He glanced at his hand. *One, two, three, four, five. . . .* He could still count. *My name is Mart Maldon, age twenty-eight, place of residence, Welfare Dorm 69, Wing Two, nineteenth floor, room 1906. . . .*

His memory seemed to be OK. *Twenty-seven times eighteen is. . . . four hundred and eighty-six. . . .*

He could still do simple arithmetic.

"Come on, fellow, drink the nice cup, then put your clothes on."

He shook his head, reached for his shirt, then remembered to move slowly, uncertainly, like a moron ought to. He fumbled clumsily with his shirt. . . .

The attendant muttered, put the cup down, snatched the shirt, helped Mart into it, buttoned it for him.

"Put your stuff in your pockets, come on, that's a good fellow. . . ."

He allowed himself to be led along the corridor, smiling vaguely at people hurrying past. In the processing room, a starched woman back of a small desk stamped papers, took his hand and impressed his thumbprint on them, slid them across the desk.

"Sign your name here. . . ." she pointed. Maldon stood gaping at the paper.

"Write your name here!" She tapped the paper impatiently. Maldon reached up and wiped his nose with a forefinger, letting his mouth hang open.

The woman looked past him. "A Nine-oh-one," she snapped. "Take him back—"

Maldon grabbed the pen and wrote his name in large, scrawling letters. The woman snapped the form apart, thrust one sheet at him.

"Uh, I was thinking," he explained, folding the paper clumsily.

"Next!" the woman snapped, waving him on. He nodded submissively and shuffled slowly to the door.

9

The Placement monitor looked at the form Maldon had given him. He looked up, smiling. "Well, so you finally wised up. Good boy. And today you got a nice score. We're going to be able to place you. You like bridges, hah?"

Maldon hesitated, then nodded.

"Sure you like bridges. Out in the open air. You're going to be an important man. When the cars come up, you lean out and see that they put the money in the box. You get to wear a uniform...." The small man rambled on, filling out forms. Maldon stood by, looking at nothing.

"Here you go. Now, you go where it says right here, see? Just get on the cross-town shuttle, right outside on this level, the one with the big number nine. You know what a nine is, OK?"

Maldon blinked, nodded. The clerk frowned. "Sometimes I think them guys overdo a good thing. But you'll get to feeling better in a few days; you'll sharpen up, like me. Now, you go on over there, and they'll give you your I.D. and your uniform and put you to work. OK?"

"Uh, thanks...." Maldon crossed the wide room, pushed through the turnstile, emerged into the late-afternoon sunlight on the fourth-level walkaway. The glare panel by the shuttle entrance read NEXT—9. He thrust his papers into his pocket and ran for it.

10

Maldon left his Dormitory promptly at eight the next morning, dressed in his threadbare Student-issue suit, carrying the heavy duffel bag of Port Authority uniforms which had been issued to him the day before. His new yellow tag was pinned prominently to his lapel.

He took a cargo car to street level, caught an uptown car, dropped off in the run-down neighborhood of second-hand stores centered around Fifth Avenue and Forty-fifth Street. He picked a shabby establishment barricaded behind racks of dowdy garments, stepped into a long, dim-lit room smelling of naphtha and moldy wool. Behind a counter, a short man with a circlet of fuzz above his ears and a vest hanging open over a tight-belted paunch looked him over. Mart hoisted the bag up, opened it, dumped the clothing out onto the counter. The paunchy man followed the action with his eyes.

"What'll you give me for this stuff?" Mart said.

The man behind the counter prodded the dark blue tunic, put a finger under the light blue trousers, rubbed the cloth. He leaned across the counter, glanced toward the door, squinted at Mart's badge. His eyes flicked to Mart's face, back to the clothing. He spread his hands.

"Five credits."

"For all of it? It's worth a hundred anyway."

The man glanced sharply at Maldon's face, back at his tag, frowning.

"Don't let the tag throw you," Maldon said. "It's stolen—just like the rest of the stuff."

"Hey." The paunchy man thrust his lips out. "What kinda talk is that? I run a respectable joint. What are you, some kinda cop?"

"I haven't got any time to waste," Maldon said. "There's nobody listening. Let's get down to business. You can strip off the braid and buttons and—"

"Ten credits, my top offer," the man said in a low voice. "I gotta stay alive, ain't I? Any bum can get outfitted free at the Welfare; who's buying my stuff?"

"I don't know. Make it twenty."

"Fifteen; it's robbery."

"Throw in a set of Maintenance coveralls, and it's a deal."

"I ain't got the real article, but close. . . ."

Ten minutes later, Mart left the store wearing a grease-stained coverall with the cuffs turned up, the yellow tag clipped to the breast pocket.

II

The girl at the bleached-driftwood desk placed austerely at the exact center of the quarter-acre of fog-gray rug stared at Maldon distastefully.

"I know of no trouble with the equipment—" she started in a lofty tone.

"Look, sister, I'm in the plumbing line; you run your dictyper." Maldon swung a greasy toolbox around by the leather strap as though he were about to lower it to the rug. "They tell me the Exec gym, Level 9, City Tower, that's where I go. Now, you want to tell me where the steam room is, or do I go back and file a beef with the Union. . . . ?"

"Next time come up the service shaft, Clyde!" she jabbed at a button; a panel whooshed aside across the room. "Men to the right, women to the left, co-ed straight ahead. Take your choice."

He went along the tiled corridor, passed steam-frosted doors. The passage turned right, angled left again. Mart pushed through a door, looked around at chromium and red plastic benches, horses, parallel bars, racks of graduated weights. A fat man in white shorts lay on the floor, half-heartedly pedaling his feet in the air. Mart crossed the room, tried another door.

Warm, sun-colored light streamed through an obscure-glass ceiling. Tropical plants in tubs nodded wide leaves over a mat of grass-green carpet edging a turquoise-tiled pool with chrome railings. Two brown-skinned men in brief trunks and sun-glasses sprawled on inflated rafts. There was a door to the right lettered EXECUTIVE DRESSING ROOM—MEMBERS ONLY. Mart went to it, stepped inside.

Tall, ivory-colored lockers lined two walls, with a wide padded bench between them. Beyond, bright shower heads winked in a darkened shower room. Maldon put the toolbox on the bench, opened it, took out a twelve-inch prybar.

By levering at the top of the tall locker, he was able to bulge it out sufficiently to see the long metal strip on the back of the door which secured it. He went back to the toolbox, picked out a slim pair of pincers; with them he gripped the locking strip, levered up; the door opened with a sudden clang. The locker was empty.

He tried the next; it contained a handsome pale tan suit which would have fitted him nicely at the age of twelve. He went to the next locker. . . .

Four lockers later, a door popped open on a dark maroon suit of expensive-looking polyon, a pair of plain scarlet shoes, a crisp pink shirt. Mart checked quickly. There was a wallet stuffed with ten-credit notes, a club membership card, and a blue I.D. with a gold alligator clip. Mart left the money on the shelf, rolled the clothing and stuffed it into the toolbox, made for the door. It swung open and the smaller of the two sun bathers pushed past him with a sharp glance. Mart walked quickly around the end of the pool, stepped into the corridor. At the far end of it, the girl from the desk stood talking emphatically to a surprised-looking man. Their eyes turned toward Mart. He pushed through the first door on the left into a room with a row of white-sheeted tables, standing lamps with wide reflectors, an array of belted and rollered equipment. A vast bulk of a man with hairy forearms and a bald head, wearing a tight white leotard and white sneakers folded a newspaper and looked up from his bench, wobbling a toothpick in the corner of his mouth. There was a pink tag on his chest.

"Uh. . . . showers?" Mart inquired. The fat man nodded toward a door behind him. Mart stepped to it, found himself in a long room studded with shower-heads and control knobs. There was no other door out. He turned back, bumped into the fat man in the doorway.

"So somebody finally decided to do something about the leak," he said around the toothpick. "Three months since I phoned it in. You guys take your time, hah?"

"I've got to go back for my tools," Mart said, starting past him. The fat man blocked him without moving. "So what's in the box?"

"Ah, they're the wrong tools. . . ." He tried to sidle past. The big man took the toothpick from his mouth, frowned at it.

"You got a pipe wrench, ain't you? You got crescents, a screwdriver. What else you need to fix a lousy leak?"

"Well, I need my sprog-depressor," Mart said, "and my detrafficator rings, and possibly a marpilizer or two. . . ."

"How come you ain't got—what you said—in there." The fat man eyed the toolbox. "Ain't that standard equipment?"

"Yes, indeed—but I only have a right-hand one, and—"

"Let's have a look—" A fat hand reached for the tool-kit. Mart backed.

"—but I might be able to make it work," he finished. He glanced around the room. "Which one was it?"

"That third needle-battery on the right. You can see the drip. I'm tryna read, it drives me nuts."

Mart put the toolbox down. "If you don't mind, it makes me nervous to work in front of an audience. . . ."

The fat man grunted and withdrew. Mart opened the box, took out a wrench, began loosening a wide hex-sided locking ring. Water began to dribble, then spurt. Mart went to the door, flung it open.

"Hey, you didn't tell me the water wasn't turned off. . . ."

"Huh?"

"You'll have to turn off the master valve; hurry up, before the place is flooded!"

The fat man jumped up, headed for the door.

"Stand by it, wait five minutes, then turn it back on!" Mart called after him. The door banged. Mart hauled the toolbox out into the massage room, quickly stripped off the grimy coverall. His eye fell on a rack of neatly-packaged underwear, socks, toothbrushes, combs. He helped himself to a set, removed the last of the Welfare issue clothing—

A shout sounded outside the door, running feet. The door burst open. It was the big man from the executive locker room.

"Where's Charlie? Some rascal's stolen my clothing. . . . !"

Mart grabbed up a towel, dropped it over his head and rubbed vigorously, humming loudly, his back to the newcomer.

"The workman—there's his toolbox!"

Mart whirled, pulled the towel free, snatched the box from the hand of the invader, with a hearty shove sent him reeling into the shower room. He slammed the door, turned the key and dropped it down a drain. The shouts from inside were barely audible. He wrapped the towel around himself and dashed into the hall. There were people, some in white, others in towels or street clothes, all talking at once.

"Down there!" Mart shouted, pointing vaguely. "Don't let him get away!" He plunged through the press, along the hall. Doors opened and shut.

"Hey, what's he doing with a toolbox?" someone shouted. Mart whirled, dived through a door, found himself in a dense, hot fog.

A woman with pink skin beaded with perspiration and a towel wrapped turban-fashion around her head stared at him.

"What are you doing in here? Co-ed is the next room along."

Mart gulped and dived past her, slammed through a plain door, found himself in a small room stacked with cartons. There was another door in the opposite wall. He went through it, emerged in a dusty hall. Three doors down, he found an empty storeroom.

Five minutes later he emerged, dressed in a handsome maroon suit. He strode briskly along to a door marked EXIT, came out into a carpeted foyer with a rank of open elevator doors. He stepped into one. The yellow-tagged attendant whooshed the door shut.

"Tag, sir?" Maldon showed the blue I.D. The operator nodded. "Down, sir?"

"No," Mart said. "Up."

12

He stepped out into the cool silence of Level Fifty.

"Which way to the Class One Testing Rooms?" he asked briskly.

The operator pointed. The door-lined corridor seemed to stretch endlessly.

"Going to try for the Big One, eh, sir?" the operator said. "Boy, you couldn't hire me to take on them kind of jobs. Me, I wouldn't want the responsibility." The closing door cut off the view of his wagging head.

Maldon set off, trying to look purposeful. Somewhere on this level were the Central Personnel Files, according to Glamis. It shouldn't be too hard to find them. After that. . . . well, he could play it by ear.

A menu-board directory at a cross-corridor a hundred yards from his starting-point indicated PERSONNEL ANALYSIS to the right. Mart followed the passage, passed open doors through which he caught glimpses of soft colors, air-conditioner grills, potted plants, and immaculate young women with precise hair styles sitting before immense keyboards or behind bare desks. Chaste lettering on doors read PROGRAMMING; REQUIREMENTS; DATA EXTRAPOLATION—PHASE III. . . .

Ahead, Maldon heard a clattering, rising in volume as he

approached a wide double door. He peered through glass, saw a long room crowded with massive metal cases ranked in rows, floor to ceiling. Men in tan dust smocks moved in the aisles, referring to papers in their hands, jotting notes, punching keys set in the consoles spaced at intervals on the giant cabinets. At a desk near the door, a man with a wide, sad mouth and a worried expression looked up, caught sight of Mart. It was no time to hesitate. He pushed through the door.

"Morning," he said genially over the busy sound of the data machines. "I'm looking for Central Personnel. I wonder if I'm in the right place?"

The sad man opened his mouth, then closed it. He had a green tag attached to the collar of his open-necked shirt.

"You from Special Actions?" he said doubtfully.

"Aptical foddering," Maldon said pleasantly. "I'd never been over here in Personnel Analysis, so I said, what the heck, I'll just run over myself." He was holding a relaxed smile in place, modeled after the one Dean Wormwell had customarily worn when condescending to students.

"Well, sir, this is Data Processing; what you probably want is Files. . . ."

Mart considered quickly. "Just what is the scope of the work you do here?"

The clerk got to his feet. "We maintain the Master Personnel Cards up-to-date," he started, then paused. "Uh, could I just see that I.D., sir?"

Maldon let the smile cool a degree or two, flashed the blue card; the clerk craned as Mart tucked the tag away.

"Now," Mart went on briskly, "suppose you just start at the beginning and give me a rundown." He glanced at a wall-clock. "Make it a fast briefing. I'm a little pressed for time."

The clerk hitched at his belt, looked around. "Well, sir, let's start over here. . . ."

Ten minutes later, they stood before a high, glass-fronted housing inside which row on row of tape reels nestled on shiny rods; bright-colored plastic fittings of complex shape jammed the space over, under and behind each row.

" . . . it's all completely cybernetic-governed, of course," the clerk was saying. "We process an average of four hundred and nineteen thousand personnel actions per day, with an average relay-delay of not over four microseconds."

"What's the source of your input?" Mart inquired in the tone of one dutifully asking the routine questions.

"All the Directorates feed their data in to us—"

"Placement Testing?" Mart asked idly.

"Oh, sure, that's our biggest single data input."

"Including Class Five and Seven categories, for example?"

The clerk nodded. "Eight through Two. Your Tech categories are handled separately, over in Banks Y and Z. There. . . ." He pointed to a pair of red-painted cabinets.

"I see. That's where the new graduates from the Technical Institutions are listed, eh?"

"Right, sir. They're scheduled out from there to Testing alphabetically, and then ranked by score for Grading, Classification, and Placement."

Mart nodded and moved along the aisle. There were two-inch high letters stenciled on the frames of the data cases. He stopped before a large letter B.

"Let's look at a typical record," Mart suggested. The clerk stepped to the console, pressed a button. A foot-square screen glowed. Print popped into focus on it: BAJUL, FELIX B. 654-8734-099-B1.

Below the heading was an intricate pattern of dots.

"May I?" Mart reached for the button, pushed it. There was a click and the name changed: BAKARSKI, HYMAN A.

He looked at the meaningless code under the name.

"I take it each dot has a significance?"

"In the first row, you have the physical profile; that's the first nine spaces. Then psych, that's the next twenty-one. Then. . . ." He lectured on. Mart nodded.

" . . . educational profile, right here. . . ."

"Now," Mart cut in. "Suppose there were an error—say in the median scores attained by an individual. How would you correct that?"

The clerk frowned pulling down the corners of his mouth into well-worn grooves.

"I don't mean on your part, of course," Mart said hastily. "But I imagine that the data processing equipment occasionally drops a decimal, eh?" He smiled understandingly.

"Well, we do get maybe one or two a year—but there's no harm done. On the next run-through, the card's automatically kicked out."

"So you don't. . . . ah. . . . make corrections?"

"Well, only when a Change Entry comes through."

The clerk twirled knobs; the card moved aside, up; a single dot swelled on the screen, resolved into a pattern of dots.

"Say it was on this item; I'd just wipe that code, and overprint the change. Only takes a second, and—"

"Suppose, for example, you wanted this record corrected to show graduation from a Tech Institute?"

"Well, that would be this symbol here; eighth row, fourth entry. The code for technical specialty would be in the 900 series. You punch it in here." He indicated rows of colored buttons. "Then the file's automatically transferred to the V bank."

"Well, this has been a fascinating tour," Mart said. "I'll make it a point to enter a commendation in the files."

The sad-faced man smiled wanly. "Well, I try to do my job. . . ."

"Now, if you don't mind, I'll just stroll around and watch for a few minutes before I rush along to my conference."

"Well, nobody's supposed to be back here in the stacks except—"

"That's quite all right. I'd prefer to look it over alone." He turned his back on the clerk and strolled off. A glance back at the end of the stack showed the clerk settling into his chair, shaking his head.

Mart moved quickly past the ends of the stacks, turned in at the third row, followed the letters through O, N, stopped before M. He punched a button, read the name that flashed on the screen: MAJONOVITCH.

He tapped at the key; names flashed briefly: MAKISS. . . . MALACHI. . . . MALDON, SALLY. . . . MALDON, MART—

He looked up. A technician was standing at the end of the stack, looking at him. He nodded.

"Quite an apparatus you have here . . ."

The technician said nothing. He wore a pink tag and his mouth was open half an inch. Mart looked away, up at the ceiling, down at the floor, back at the technician. He was still standing, looking. Abruptly his mouth closed with a decisive snap; he started to turn toward the clerk's desk—

Mart reached for the control knobs, quickly dialed for the eighth row, entry four; the single dot shifted into position, enlarged. The technician, distracted by the sudden move, turned, came hurrying along the aisle.

"Hey, nobody's supposed to mess with the—"

"Now, my man," Mart said in a firm tone. "Answer each question in as few words as possible. You will be graded on promptness and accuracy of response. What is the number of digits in the Technical Specialty series—the 900 group?"

Taken aback, the technician raised his eyebrows, said, "Three—but—"

"And what is the specific code for Microtronics Engineer—cum laude?"

There was a sudden racket from the door. Voices were raised in hurried inquiry. The clerk's voice replied. The technician stood undecided, scratching his head. Mart jabbed at the colored buttons: 901. . . . 922. . . . 936. . . . He coded a dozen three-digit Specialties into his record at random.

From the corner of his eye he saw a light blink on one of the red-painted panels; his record was being automatically transferred to the Technically Qualified files. He poked the button which whirled his card from the screen and turned, stepped off toward the far end of the room. The technician came after him.

"Hey there, what card was that you were messing with. . . . ?"

"No harm done," Mart reassured him. "Just correcting an error. You'll have to excuse me now; I've just remembered a pressing engagement. . . ."

"I better check; what card was it?"

"Oh—just one picked at random."

"But. . . . we got a hundred million cards in here. . . ."

"Correct!" Maldon said. "So far you're batting a thousand. Now, we have time for just one more question: is there another door out of here?"

"Mister, you better wait a minute till I see the super—"

Mart spotted two unmarked doors, side by side. "Don't bother; what would you tell him? That there was, just possibly, a teentsy weentsy flaw in one of your hundred million cards? I'm sure that would upset him." He pulled the nearest door open. The technician's mouth worked frantically.

"Hey, that's—" he started.

"Don't call us—we'll call you!" Mart stepped past the door; it swung to behind him. Just before it closed, he saw that he was standing in a four foot by six foot closet. He whirled, grabbed for the door; there was no knob on the inside. It shut with a decisive click!

He was alone in pitch darkness.

Maldon felt hastily over the surfaces of the walls, found them bare and featureless. He jumped, failed to touch the ceiling. Outside he heard the technician's voice, shouting. At any moment he would open the door and that would be that. . . .

Mart went to his knees, explored the floor. It was smooth. Then his elbow cracked against metal—

He reached, found a grill just above floor level, two feet wide and a foot high. A steady flow of cool air came from it. There were screw-heads at each corner. Outside, the shouts continued. There were answering shouts.

Mart felt over his pockets, brought out a coin, removed the screws. The grill fell forward into his hands. He laid it aside, started in head-first, encountered a sharp turn just beyond the wall. He wriggled over on his side, pushed hard, negotiated the turn by pulling with his hands pressed against the sides of the metal duct. There was light ahead, cross-hatched by a grid. He reached it, peered into a noisy room where great panels loomed, their faces a solid maze of dials and indicator lights. He tried the grill. It seemed solid. The duct made a right-angle turn here. Maldon worked his way around the bend, found that the duct widened six inches. When his feet were in position, he swung a kick at the grill. The limited space made it awkward; he kicked again and again; the grill gave, one more kick and it clattered into the room beyond. Mart struggled out through the opening.

The room was brightly lit, deserted. There were large printed notices here and there on the wall warning of danger. Mart turned, re-entered the duct, made his way back to the closet. The voices were still audible outside the door. He reached through the opening, found the grill, propped it in position as the door flew open. He froze, waiting. There was a moment of silence.

"But," the technician's voice said, "I tell you the guy walked into the utility closet here like he was boarding a rocket for Paris! I didn't let the door out of my sight, that's why I was standing back at the back and yelling, like you was chewing me out for. . . ."

"You must have made an error; it must have been the other door there. . . ."

The door closed. Mart let out a breath. Now perhaps he'd have a few minutes' respite in which to figure a route off Level Fifty.

13

He prowled the lanes between the vast cybernetic machines, turned a corner, almost collided with a young woman with red-blonde hair, dark eyes, and a pouting red mouth which opened in a surprised O.

"You shouldn't be in here," she said, motioning over her shoulder with a pencil. "All examinees must remain in the examination room until the entire battery of tests have been completed."

"I. . . . ah. . . ."

"I know," the girl said, less severely. "Four hours at a stretch. It's awful. But you'd better go back in now before somebody sees you."

He nodded, smiled, and moved toward the door she had indicated. He looked back. She was studying the instrument dials, not watching him. He went past the door and tried the next. It opened and he stepped into a small, tidy office. A large-eyed woman with tightly dressed brown hair looked up from a desk adorned by a single rosebud in a slim vase and a sign reading PLACEMENT OFFICER. Her eyes went to a wall-clock.

"You're too late for today's testing, I'm afraid," she said. "You'll have to return on Wednesday; that's afternoon testing. Mondays we test in the morning." She smiled sympathetically. "Quite a few make that mistake."

"Oh," Mart said. "Ah. . . . couldn't I start late?"

The woman was shaking her head. "Oh, it wouldn't be possible. The first results are already coming in. . . ." She nodded toward a miniature version of the giant machines in the next room. A humming and clicking sounded briefly from it. She tapped a key on her desk. There was a sharp buzz from the small machine. He gazed at the apparatus. Again it clicked and hummed. Again she tapped, eliciting another buzz.

Mart stood, considering. His only problem now was to leave the building without attracting attention. His record had been altered to show his completion of a Technical Specialty; twelve of them, in fact. It might have been better if he had settled for one. Someone might notice—

"I see you're admiring the Profiler," the woman said. "It's a very compact model, isn't it? Are you a Cyberneticist, by any chance?"

Maldon started. "No. . . ."

"What name is that? I'll check your file over to see that everything's in order for Wednesday's testing."

Mart took a deep breath. This was no time to panic. . . ."Maldon," he said. "Mart Maldon."

The woman swung an elaborate telephone-dial-like instrument out from a recess, dialed a long code, then sat back. Ten seconds passed. With a click, a small panel on the desktop glowed. The woman leaned forward, reading. She looked up.

"Why, Mr. Maldon! You have a remarkable record! I don't believe I've ever encountered a testee with such a wide—and varied—background!"

"Oh," Mart said, with a weak smile. "It was nothing. . . ."

"Eidetics, Cellular Psychology, Autonomics. . . ."

"I hate narrow specialization," Mart said.

" . . . . Cybernetics Engineering—why, Mr. Maldon, you were teasing me!"

"Well. . . ." Maldon edged toward the door.

"My, we'll certainly be looking forward to seeing your test results, Mr. Maldon! And Oh! Do let me show you the new Profiler you were admiring." She hopped up, came round the desk. "It's such a time saver—and of course, saves a vast number of operations within the master banks. Now when the individual testee depresses his COMPLETED key, his test pattern in binary form is transferred directly to this unit for recognition. It's capable of making over a thousand yes-no comparisons per second profiling the results in decimal terms and recoding them into the master record, without the necessity for activating a single major sequence within the master—and, of course, every activation costs the taxpayer seventy-nine credits!"

"Very impressive," Mart said. If he could interrupt the flow of information long enough to ask a few innocent-sounding directions. . . .

A discreet buzzer sounded. The woman depressed a key on the desk communicator.

"Miss Frinkles, could you step in a moment? There's a report of a madman loose in the building. . . ."

"Good Heavens!" She looked at Mart as she slipped through the door. "Please, do excuse me a moment. . . ."

Mart waited half a minute, started to follow; a thought struck him. He looked at the Profiler. All test results were processed through this little device; what if. . . .

A quick inspection indicated that the apparatus was a close relative of the desktop units used at Applied Tech in the ill-fated Analogy Theory class. The input, in the form of a binary series established by the testee's answers to his quiz, was compared with the master pattern for the specialty indicated by the first three digits of the signal. The results were translated into a profile, ready for transmittal to the Master Files.

This was almost too simple. . . .

Mart pressed a lever at the back of the housing, lifted it off. Miss Frinkles had been right about this being a new model; most of the circuitry was miniaturized and built up into replaceable subassemblies. What he needed was a set of tools. . . .

He tried Miss Frinkles' desk, turned up a nail file and two bobby pins. It wouldn't be necessary to fake an input; all that was needed was to key the coder section to show the final result. He crouched, peered in the side of the unit. There, to the left was the tiny bank of contacts which would open or close to indicate the score in a nine-digit profile. There were nine rows of nine contacts, squeezed into an area of one half-inch square. It was going to be a ticklish operation. . . .

Mart straightened a hairpin, reached in, delicately touched the row of minute relays; the top row of contacts snapped closed, and a red light went on at the side of the machine. Mart tossed the wire aside, and quickly referred to his record, still in focus on Miss Frinkles' desktop viewer, then tickled tumblers to show his five letter, four digit personal identity code. Then he pressed a cancel key, to blank the deskscreen, and dropped the cover back in place on the Profiler. He was sitting in a low chair, leafing through a late issue of *Popular Statistics* when Miss Frinkles returned.

"It seems a maintenance man ran berserk down on Nine Level," she said breathlessly. "He killed three people, then set fire to—"

"Well, I must be running along," Mart said, rising. "A very nice little machine you have there. Tell me, are there any manual controls?"

"Oh, yes, didn't you notice them? Each test result must be validated by me before it's released to the Master Files. Suppose someone cheated, or finished late; it wouldn't do to let a disqualified score past."

"Oh, no indeed. And to transfer the data to the Master File, you just press this?" Mart said, leaning across and depressing the key he had seen Miss Frinkles use earlier. There was a sharp buzz from the Profiler. The red light went out.

"Oh, you mustn't—" Miss Frinkles exclaimed. "Not that it would matter in this case, of course," she added apologetically, "but—"

The door opened and the red-head stepped into the room. "Oh," she said, looking at Mart. "There you are. I looked for you in the Testing room—"

Miss Frinkles looked up with a surprised expression. "But I was under the impression—" She smiled. "Oh, Mr. Maldon, you *are* a tease! You'd already completed your testing, and you let me think you came in late. . . . !"

Mart smiled modestly.

"Oh, Barbara, we must look at his score. He has a fantastic academic record. At least ten Specialized degrees, and magna cum laude in every one. . . ."

The screen glowed. Miss Frinkles adjusted a knob, scanned past the first frame to a second. She stared.

"Mr. Maldon! I knew you'd do well, but a *perfect* score!"

The hall door banged wide. "Miss Frinkles—" a tall man stared at Mart, looked him up and down. He backed a step. "Who're you? Where did you get that suit—"

"MISTER Cludd!" Miss Frinkles said in an icy tone. "Kindly refrain from bursting into my office unannounced—and kindly show a trifle more civility to my guest, who happens to be a very remarkable young man who has just completed one of the finest test profiles it has been my pleasure to see during my service with Placement!"

"Eh? Are you sure? I mean—that suit. . . . and the shoes. . . ."

"I like a conservative outfit," Mart said desperately.

"You mean he's been here all morning. . . . ?" Mr. Cludd looked suddenly uncomfortable.

"Of course!"

"He was in my exam group, Mr. Cludd," the red-haired girl put in. "I'll vouch for that. Why?"

"Well. . . . it just happens the maniac they're looking for is dressed in a similar suit, and. . . . well, I guess I lost my head. I was just coming in to tell you he'd been seen on this floor. He made a getaway through a service entrance leading to the helipad on the roof, and. . . ." he ran down.

"Thank you, Mr. Cludd," Miss Frinkles said icily. Cludd mumbled and withdrew. Miss Frinkles turned to Mart.

"I'm so thrilled, Mr. Maldon. . . ."

"Golly, yes," Barbara said.

"It isn't every day I have the opportunity to Place an applicant of your qualifications. Naturally, you'll have the widest possible choice. I'll give you the current prospectus, and next week—"

"Couldn't you place me right now, Miss Frinkles?"

"You mean—today?"

"Immediately." Mart looked at the redhead. "I like it here. What openings have you got in your department?"

Miss Frinkles gasped, flushed, smiled, then turned and played with the buttons on her console, watching the small screen. "Wonderful," she breathed. "The opening is still unfilled. I was afraid one of the other units might have filled it in the past hour." She poked at more keys. A white card in a narrow platinum holder with a jeweled alligator clip popped from a slot. She rose and handed it to Mart reverently.

"Your new I.D., sir. And I know you're going to make a wonderful chief!"

14

Mart sat behind the three-yard-long desk of polished rosewood, surveying the tennis-court-sized expanse of ankle-deep carpet which stretched across to a wide door of deep-polished mahogany, then

swiveled to gaze out through wide windows of insulated, polar-
ized, tinted glass at the towers of Granyauck, looming up in a deep
blue sky. He turned back, opened the silver box that rested
between a jade penholder and an ebony paperweight on the otherwise unadorned desk, lifted out a Chanel dope-stick, sniffed it
appreciatively. He adjusted his feet comfortably on the desktop,
pressed a tiny silver button set in the arm of the chair. A moment
later the door opened with the faintest of sounds.

"Barbara—" Mart began.

"There you are," a deep voice said.

Mart's feet came off the desk with a crash. The large man
approaching him across the rug had a familiar look about him. . . .

"That was a dirty trick, locking me in the shower. We hadn't
figured on that one. Slowed us up something awful." He swung
a chair around and sat down.

"But," Mart said. "But. . . . but. . . ."

"Three days, nine hours, and fourteen minutes," the newcomer
said, eyeing a finger watch. "I must say you made the most of it.
Never figured on you bollixing the examination records, too; most
of 'em stop with the faked Academic Record, and figure to take
their chances on the exam."

"Most of 'em?" Mart repeated weakly.

"Sure. You didn't think you were the only one selected to go
before the Special Placement Board, did you?"

"Selected? Special. . . ." Mart's voice trailed off.

"Well, surely you're beginning to understand now, Maldon," the
man from whom Mart had stolen the suit said. "We picked you
as a potential Top Executive over three years ago. We've followed
your record closely ever since. You were on every one of the Board
Members' nomination lists—"

"But—but I was quota'd out—"

"Oh, we could have let you graduate, go through testing, pick
up a green tag and a spot on a promotion list, plug away for twenty
years, make Exec rank—but we can't waste the time. We need talent,
Mart. And we need it now!"

Mart took a deep breath and slammed the desk. "Why in the
name of ten thousand devils didn't you just TELL me!"

The visitor shook his head. "Nope; we need good men, Mart—
need 'em bad. We need to find the superior individuals; we can't
afford to waste time bolstering up the folklore that the will of the

people constitutes wisdom. This is a city of a hundred million people—and it's growing at a rate that will double that in a decade. We have problems, Mart. Vast, urgent problems. We need men that can solve 'em. We can test you in academic knowledge, cook up psychological profiles—but we have to KNOW. We have to find out how you react in a real-life situation; what you do to help yourself when you're dumped on the walkaway, broke and hopeless. If you go in and have your brain burned, scratch one. If you meekly register to wait out a Class Two test opening—well, good luck to you. If you walk in and take what you want. . . ." he looked around the office, " . . . . then welcome to the Club."

WORLDMASTER

I

In the boat bay four Deck Police held guns on me while two more shook me down. When they finished, they formed up a box around me.

"All right, this way, sir," the Warrant said. He was a dandified overweight lad with pale hard little eyes like unripe olives. Four power guns snapped around to hold on me, rib-high. I stumbled a little and the nearest gun jumped. The boys were a hair more nervous than they looked. As for myself, I was long past the nervous stage; it took all I had left just to stay on my feet with nothing left over to wonder about the curious reception given to a surviving captain paying his courtesy call on his admiral after a twenty-eight-hour action in which two fleets had been wiped out.

Here aboard the flagship everything was as smooth and silent as a hotel for dying millionaires. We went along a wide corridor lit like the big window at Cartier's and carpeted in a pale blue as soft as a summer breeze, took the high-speed lift up the command deck. There were more DPs here, spit-and-polished in blue-black class A's with white gloves, mirror-bright boots, and chromalloy dress armor. The guns they aimed at me were fancy

Honor Guard models with ebony stocks and bright-plated barrels; but they would fire real slugs if occasion demanded. The Warrant came up beside me, smelling a little sweeter than ordinary after-shave. "Perhaps you'd like to step along to the head and tidy up a bit before going in," he told me. "I have a clean uniform ready for you and—"

"This one's okay," I said. "Oh, it's got a few cuts and tears and a couple of scorched spots no bigger than the doily under a demitasse, but it came by them honorably, as the saying goes. Maybe I need a shave, but no worse than I did yesterday. I've been a little busy, mister—" I cut it off before it got entirely out of hand. "Let's take a chance and go in. The admiral may be curious about what happened to his fleet."

The Warrant's mouth tightened up as though he had a string threaded through his lip.

"I'm afraid I'll have to insist—" he started. I brushed past him. One of the ratings beside the door leading into the admiral's quarters jabbed his gun at me as I came toward him.

"Go ahead, son, fire it," I said. "You've got it set on full automatic; in this confined space you'll fry all of us blacker than a newlywed's toast."

The annunciator above the door crackled, "Purdy, take those weapons away from those men before there's an accident!" a voice barked. "I'll see Captain Maclamore immediately. Mac, stop scaring my men to death."

The door slid back. I went through into a wide room flooded with artificial sunlight as cheerful as paper flowers and smelling of expensive cigar smoke. From a big easy chair under the windorama with a view of a field of ripe wheat nodding under a light breeze, Admiral Banastre Tarleton gave me the old Academy smile, looking hard and efficient and younger than four stars had any right to. Behind him Commodore Sean Braze glowered, his hands behind his back, big shoulders bulging under his tailor-made tunic, a pistol strapped to his hip as inconspicuously as a rattlesnake at a picnic. A captain with a small crinkled face and quick eyes looked at me from a chair off to the right. I threw a sloppy salute and the braid dangling from my torn cuff flopped against my sleeve. "Sit down, Mac." Tarleton nodded toward a chair placed to half face him. I didn't move. He frowned a little but let it pass.

"I'm glad to see you here," he said. "How are you feeling?"

"I don't know how I'm feeling, Admiral," I said. "I don't think I want to know."

"You fought your command like half the devils in Hell, Mac. I'm writing you up for the Cross."

I didn't say anything. I felt dizzy. I was wondering if it was too late to take the offer of a chair.

"Sit down before you fall down, Captain," the man on the right said. Little bright lights were sleeting down all around me. They faded and I was still standing. I didn't know what I was proving.

"Anybody get out with you?" Braze was asking me. He was a man who couldn't ask to have the salt passed without making it sound like a sneer.

"Sure," I said. "My Gunnery Officer, Max Arena—the upper half of him, anyway. Why?"

"I saw it on the big command screen," Tarleton said. "A lucky break, Mac. A salvage crew couldn't have sliced that nav dome away cleaner with cutting torches."

"Yeah," I said.

"Here—" the monkey faced captain started. Tarleton flicked a hand at him and he faded off.

"Something bothering you, Mac?" Tarleton was giving me the wise, patient look he'd learned from watching old Bing Crosby films.

"Why should anything be bothering me?" I heard myself asking. "I've just had my ship shot out from under me, and my crew wiped out, and seen what was formerly the UN Battle Fleet blasted into radioactive vapor while the flagship that mounted sixteen percent of our total firepower pulled back half a million miles and watched without firing a shot. You've probably got all kinds of reasons for that, Admiral. Reasons that would be way over my head. Some of them might even be good. I wouldn't know."

"Watch your tongue, Maclamore!" Braze said. "You're talking to a superior officer!"

"That's enough, Sean," Tarleton said sharply. He was giving me a harder, less contrived look now. "Sure, you've had a rough time, Mac. I'm sorry about that; if there'd been any other way. . . ." He made a short, choppy gesture with his hand. Then he lifted his chin, got the firm-lipped look back in place. "But the Bloc didn't fare any better. They're blasted out of space—permanently. It was an even trade."

Maybe my eyelids flickered; maybe I gave him a look that nailed his heart to his backbone; and maybe I was just a little man with a big headache, trying not to show it.

"An even trade," he repeated. He seemed to like the sound of it. "I watched the action very closely, Mac," he went on. "If the tide had started to turn to favor the Bloc, I'd have hit them with everything I had." He worked his mouth as though he were trying a new set of teeth for size; but it was an idea he was testing the fit of.

"And if the tide had started running our way, I'd have come in, helped finish them off. As it was. . . . an even match. The board's clean." He looked at me with something dangerous sparkling back behind his eyes. "Except for my flagship," he added softly.

The wrinklefaced captain was leaning forward; his hands were opening and closing. Braze took his hands out from behind himself and fingered the pistol bolt. I just waited.

"You see what that means, don't you, Mac?" Tarleton ran his fingers through his still-blond, still-curly hair, wiped his hand down the back of his neck the way he used to do in the locker room at the half, when he was cooking up the strategy that was going to flatten the opposition. "For the past ten years, both sides have poured ninety-five percent of their military budgets into their space arms, while planet-based forces fought themselves into an undeclared truce. Both sides together couldn't put a hundred thousand armed and equipped men in the field today—and if they did—"

He leaned back, took a deep breath; I couldn't blame him for that; he was breathing the heady air of power.

"I have the only effective fighting apparatus on or off the planet, Mac." He held out his hand, palm up, like a kid showing me his shiny new quarter. "I hold the balance of power, right here."

"Why tell *him* this, Banny?" the brown-faced captain said quickly.

"Button your lip, Captain," Tarleton snapped. "Keep it buttoned." He heaved himself out of his chair, shot a hard look at me, took a turn up and down the room, stopped in front of me.

"I need good men, Mac," he said. He was staring at me, his jaw muscles knotted and relaxed. I looked past him at Braze, over at the other man. "Uh-huh," I said. "That you do."

Braze took a step in my direction. His carefully lamp-tanned face was as dark as an Indian's. Tarleton's face twitched in a humorless smile.

"How long has it been?" he asked. "Sixty years? Sixty-five? Two giant powers, sitting across the world from each other, snarling and trading slaps. Sixty years of petty wars, petty truces—of people dying—for nothing—of wasted time, wasted talent, wasted resources—while the whole damned universe is waiting to be taken!"

He turned on his heel, stamped another couple of laps, pulled up in front of me again.

"I decided to put an end to it. I made up my mind—hell, over a year ago. My strategy since that time has been directed toward this moment. I planned it, I maneuvered it." He closed his hand as though he was crushing a bug. "And I brought it off!"

He looked at me, happy, wanting to hear me say something; I didn't say it. He went back to his chair, sat down, picked up the long blackish cigar from the ashtray at his elbow, drew on it, put it down again, blew the smoke out suddenly.

"There comes a time," he said flatly, "when a man has to act on what he knows to be right. When he can no longer afford the luxury of a set of mottos as a substitute for intelligence. Sure, I swore to uphold the Constitution; it's easy to die for a flag, a principle, an oath—but that won't save humankind from its own stupidity. Maybe someday the descendants of the people whose necks I'm saving in spite of themselves will thank me. Or maybe they won't. Maybe I'll go down in the book as the villain—a new and better Benedict Arnold. I still say to hell with it. If all it takes to break the cycle is the sacrifice of one man's personal—shall I say honor?—then that's a small price. I'm prepared to pay it."

I heard him talking but it all seemed to be coming from a long way off, remote, unreal. It didn't reach me. I nodded toward the one he'd told to shut up.

"As the man said, why tell me?" I asked him, just to be saying something.

"I want you with me, Mac," he said.

I looked at him.

"I wanted you in it from the beginning, but. . . ." He frowned again. I was making him do a lot of frowning tonight. "Maybe you can guess why I didn't speak to you earlier. It wasn't easy sending you out with the others. I'm glad you came through. Damned glad. Maybe it's. . . . some kind of sign." His lips twitched in what I guess he thought was a smile.

"It wasn't easy—but you managed it." I wasn't sure whether I said it or just thought it. The roaring in my head was loud now; a hot black was closing in from the sides. I pushed it back. For some reason I didn't want to fall down right now; not here, not in front of Braze and the little man with the darting eyes.

"We used to be friends, Mac," Tarleton was saying. "There was a time. . . ." He got up again. It seemed he couldn't stay in one place. "Hell, it's simple enough; I'm asking for your help," he finished.

"Yeah, we were friends, Banny," I said. For an instant there was that strange hollow feeling, the heart-stopping glimpse back down the yellowed and forgotten years to the old Academy walls and the leaves that were on the cinder track as you walked across, heavy-shouldered in the practice gear, the cleats making you feel tall and tough, and the faces of girls, and the smell of night air, and the fast car bucking under you and Banny, passing a flask back, and then again, across the field while the crowd roared, his arm back, the ball tumbling down the blue sky and the solid smack and then away and running—

"But you found other friends," I was saying, with no more than an instant's pause. "They took you down another path, I guess. Somewhere along there we lost it. I guess today we buried it."

"That's right, we've taken our separate ways," he said. "But we can still find common land. I didn't make the Navy, Mac—but after I picked it as a way of life, I learned to live with it—to beat it at its game. You didn't. You bucked it. Sure, you made your points— but they don't pay off for those. What do you expect, a medal for stubbornness? Hell, if it hadn't been for me keeping an eye on you, you'd have been—" He stopped. "Suffice it to say I got you your command," he ground out.

I nodded. "I didn't know," I said. "It was a wonderful thing while I had it. I'm grateful to you. And then you took it away. It was a tough way to lose my ship, Banny. In a way I'd almost rather not have had it—but not quite."

He planted himself again, tried to catch my eye. Somehow I seemed to be looking past him.

"I make no apologies," he snapped. "I did what I had to do. Now there's more to be done. I'm going down tonight to make my report to Congress. There are Cabinet members to see, the President to be dealt with. It won't be easy. It's not won yet. A wrong word in the wrong place and I could still fumble this. I'm being frank with you, Mac. I need a good man I can trust." He reached out and clapped me on my upper arm—a caricature of the old gesture, as self-consciously counterfeit as a whore's passion. I shook the hand off.

"Don't be a fool," he said in a low voice, close to me. "What do you think your alternative is?"

"I don't know, Admiral," I said. "But you'll think of something."

Braze came over. "I don't like this, Banny," he said. "You've said too damned much to him." He gave me a look like a hired gun marking down a target for later on. The other fellow was up now, not wanting to be left out. He flicked his eyes at me, then at the gun at Braze's belt.

"This fellow's no good for us," he said in a rapid, breathless voice, like a girl about to make a daring suggestion. "You'll have to. . . . dispose of him."

Tarleton swung around and looked at him.

"Have you ever killed a man, Walters?" he asked in a tight voice. Walters' tongue popped out, touched his lips. His eyes went to the gun again, darted away.

"No, but—"

"I have," Tarleton said. He walked across to the windorama, punched the control; the scene shifted to heavy seas breaking across a reef under a rock-gray sky.

"Last chance, Mac," he said in a mock-hearty voice. "The thing happens; it's far too late to stop it now. Will you be in it—or out?" He turned to face me, his clean-cut American Boy features set in a recruiting-poster smile.

"Count me out," I said. "I wouldn't be good at running the world." I looked at the other two. "Beside which, I wouldn't like the company."

Braze lifted a lip to show me a square-looking canine. Walters half-closed his eyes and snorted softly through his nose.

"What about it, Banny?" Braze said. "Walters is right. You can't dump Maclamore back with the other internees."

Tarleton turned on him. "You're telling me what I can and can't do, Braze?"

"I'm making a recommendation," the Commodore came back. "My neck is in this with yours now—"

"Another word of mutiny out of you, mister, and I'll give orders that will have your precious neck stretched before the big hand gets to the twelve. Want to try me?" His voice was like something cut into a plate-glass window. He went to his chair and pushed a button set in the arm.

"Purdy, send those four morons of yours in here—and try not to shoot yourself through the foot in the process." He went over and watched the waves some more. The door opened with a sigh and the goon squad appeared with the Warrant out front, fussing over them like a headwaiter figuring the tip on ten pounds of room-service caviar.

"Find quarters for Captain Maclamore on U deck," Tarleton said in a flat voice.

The Warrant bustled forward, all business now. "All right, move along there—" he started. Tarleton whirled on him.

"And keep a civil tongue in your head, damn you! You're talking to a Naval officer!"

Purdy swallowed hard. I turned and walked out past the ready gun muzzles. I didn't bother with the salute this time. The time for saluting was all over.

2

The medic finished with me and left, and I lay back, listening to the small ship-noises that murmured through the walls. It had been about an hour now since the last faint shocks that meant contact with one of the chunks of debris that was all that was left of forty-two fighting ships—twenty-two UN, the rest Bloc. At least Tarleton had gone through the motions of picking up what few survivors there might have been from the slaughter—perhaps a few hundred dazed and bloody men, the accidental leftovers of the power plays of Grand Strategy.

I had come through in better shape than most of them, I guessed. With the exception of a few minor cuts and bruises and a mild concussion, aggravated by twenty-eight hours without food or sleep, I was in as good shape as I had been before the fight. My arms and legs still worked; my heart was pumping away as usual; my lungs were doing their job. The brain was still numb, true, but it was working—working for its life.

Tarleton may or may not have meant it when he turned down

Braze's suggestion—but he had told me far too much for any man to hear who was arrayed on the opposite side of the fence from the Commodore. I didn't need to break out of my cell to look for trouble: it would come to me. Braze was a man who always took the simple direct course. It had won him a commodore's star; he'd stay with the technique. He'd make his move at the last minute before the ground party boarded the boats for the trip down, to minimize the chance of word getting to Tarleton; he'd have an account of an attempted escape ready for later, if Tarleton got curious—an unlikely eventuality. The Admiral would have his hands full digesting his conquests, with no time left over for pondering the fates of obscure former acquaintances.

They'd be going down tonight, Tarleton had said. He'd have a good-sized shore party with him; all of his top advisors—or whatever ratfaced little men like Walters called themselves—and a nice showing of armed sailors, tricked out in dress blues and sidearms, as a gentle reminder of the planet-wrecking power orbiting ten thousand miles out.

The flagship carried a complement of two thousand eleven men, all long since screened for reliability, no doubt. If I knew Banny Tarleton, he'd have half of them along on his triumphal march. That would call for twenty heavy scout boats. He'd use bays one through ten on the upper boat deck for reasons of ease of loading and orbital dynamics. . . .

I was building an elaborate structure of fancy on a feeble foundation of guesses, but I had to carry the extrapolation as far as I could. I wouldn't get a second chance to make my try; maybe not even the first one—and my quota of mistakes was already used up.

I got up and took a couple of turns up and down the room. I still felt lightheaded, but the meal and the bath and the dressings and the shots and the pills had helped a lot. The plain set of ducks Purdy had provided were comfortable enough, but I missed the contents of a couple of small special pockets that had been built into my own clothes—the ones that had been taken away and burned. The hardware was gone—but with a little luck I might be able to improvise suitable substitutes.

A quick inspection of the room turned up an empty closet, a chest with four empty drawers, a wall mirror, a molded polyfoam chair that weighed two pounds soaking wet, a framed tridograph of the Kennedy monument complete with shrapnel scars, and the built-in bunk to which the medics had lowered me, groaning, ten minutes earlier. Not much there from which to assemble a blaster—

I felt the tremor then—the teacup-rattling nudge of a scout boat kicking free. Quite suddenly my mouth had that dry feeling. Boat number two pushed off, then a third. Tarleton wasn't wasting any time. At least there wouldn't be any long tedious wait to see whether my guesses had been right. The time for action was here. I set my heart rate up two notches and metered a trickle of adrenalin into my system, then went over to the door, flattened myself against the wall to the left of it, and waited.

Seven boats were away now. A couple of minutes ticked past like ice ages. Then there was a soft stealthy noise outside the door. With my ear against the wall, I could imagine I heard voices. I set myself—

The door slid smoothly back and a man came through it fast— a big thick-shouldered DP with pinkish hair on an acneed neck, a use-worn Mark XX gripped in a freckled fist the size of a catcher's mitt. I half-turned to the left, drove my right into his side just behind the holster hard enough to jar the monogram off the hanky in my hip pocket—not fancy, but effective. He made an ugly noise and went down clawing at himself like a cat, and I was over him, diving for the gun that skidded to the wall and bounced back into my hand, and I was rolling, bringing it up, seeing the lightning-flicker and feeling the hard tight snarl of the weapon in my hand as I slashed it across the open doorway. The man there fell into the room, hit like a horse falling in harness, and the air was full of the nauseating stench of burned flesh and abdominal wounds.

I got up, stepped to the redhead, kicked him hard above the cheekbone; he gave up the attempt to loop the loop on the rug. At the door I gave a quick glance both ways: nobody in sight. There was another gentle shock. Number eight? Or had I missed one. . . . ?

It was a hot two minutes' work to get the unbloodied uniform off its owner. It wasn't a good fit, but I buckled everything up tight, strapped on the gun in a way that I hoped would conceal the fold I'd taken in the waist band, tried the boots: too big. I didn't like touching the other fellow, but I had to. My feet complained a little, but they went in, shrinking from the warmth of the dead man's shoes. The redhead was still breathing; I thought seriously about putting a burst into his head, then settled for strapping his ankles and wrists and wadding a shirt sleeve in his mouth. It cost me an extra minute and a half. So much for the price of a human life.

Out in the corridor things were still quiet: Braze's work again. He wouldn't have wanted witnesses. I locked the door and headed for the boat.

Four more boats were away by the time I reached the steel double doors that sealed U deck off from the main transverse. I pushed against them, swore, kicked the panel. It gave off a dull clang. I kicked it again, then yanked out the power gun, set it for a needle beam, heard sounds on the other side, slammed the weapon back into its holster in time to see the door jump back and a square-jawed DP plant himself flatfooted in the opening, gun out and aimed.

"Thanks, brother—" I started past him. He backed, but kept me covered. A confused scowl was getting ready to settle onto his face.

"Hold your water, paisan—"

"Knock it off," I rapped. "Jeezus—can't you see I'm missing formation? My boat—"

"What you doing on U deck?"

"Look—I had a sidekick, see? I wanted to see the guy. Okay, satisfied? You want me shot for desertion?"

"Go on," he waved the gun at me, looking disgusted. "But you'll never make it."

"Thanks, buddy—" I struck off at a dead run. . . .

I had lost count, not sure whether it was eighteen or nineteen— or maybe twenty, too late. . . .

I rounded the last corner, came into the low-ceilinged boat deck, felt a throb of some kind of emotion—fear or relief or a mixture— at the sight of thirty or forty blue-uniformed men formed up in a ragged column, filing toward the black rectangle of Number Two loading port. I dropped back to a walk, came up to the column, moved along with them. One man looked over his shoulder at me with a blank expression; the rest ignored me. A middle-aged Warrant with a long leathery face saw me, snarled silently, came back.

"You're Gronski, huh? Nice to see you in formation, Gronski. You see me after breakaway; you and me got to have a little talk about things—okay, Gronski?"

I looked sullen; it wasn't hard. It's a lot like looking scared. "Okay, Chief," I muttered.

"By God, that's 'Aye, aye, Mr. Funderburk' to you, swabbie!"

"Aye, aye, Mr. Funderburk," I growled out. He spun with a squeak of shoe leather and walked away. The man in front of me turned and looked me up and down.

"You ain't Gronski," he said.

"What else is new?" I snarled. "So I'm helping out a pal—okay?"

"You and Funnybutt are gonna get along," he predicted and showed me his back again. I kept my eyes on it until it was safely tucked away in the gloom of the troop hold. Wedged in between two silent men on the narrow shock seat, I held my breath, waiting for the yell that would mean somebody hadn't been fooled. I wondered what lucky accident had made Gronski late, what other lucky accident had assigned him to a detail with a Warrant who didn't know his face. . . .

But calculating the odds on what was already accomplished was just sorting over dry bones. The odds ahead were what counted. They didn't look good, but they were all I had. I'd take them—and play the angles as they fell like Rubinstein cutting the original soundtrack of the "Flight of the Bumblebee."

3

We berthed at Arlington Memorial just after midnight, and as soon as he had the platoon formed up on the ramp Funderburk called me over. I answered the summons with a certain reluctance; I had closed and locked the door to the room where Braze's gunboys were awaiting discovery, but there was no way of knowing how long it would be before someone went around to check. The trip down had taken about two hours and a half. Of course, even if the room had been opened, it didn't necessarily mean that anyone would have found it necessary to advise the Admiral—

Or did it?

"Gronski, I got a little job for you," Funderburk barked. "A couple of the brass up front had a little trouble with the turbulence on the way in: looks like they kind of come unfed. It don't look good all over the officers' head. Maybe you could kind of see about it."

"Sure. I mean, aye, aye, Mr. Funderburk. Do I get a mop or just wipe it up with my sleeve?"

"Oh, a wise one, huh? Swell, Gronski. You and me are gonna see a lot of each other. You want a mop, you scout around and find one. Take all the time you want. But I kind of advise you to be all finished in twenty minutes because that's how long I'm giving the detail for chow. I don't guess you'll miss the flapjacks, unless you got a tougher appetite than most."

"I'll finish in ten. Save me a stool at the bar."

Funderburk nodded. "Yeah, I can see you and me are gonna click good, Gronski. See you on the gig list." He turned and walked away—just like that. I didn't wait around to see if he'd change his mind. I walked, resisting the impulse to run, to the utility shack behind the flight kitchen, went through it and out the side door and around to the front, crossed a patch of grass and pushed into a steamy odor of GI coffee and floor wax. A door across the room was lettered MEN. Inside, I forced the door to the broom closet, took out a pair of coveralls and a push broom.

Back out in the predawn gloom ten minutes later with my hair carefully rumpled and a layer of mud disguising the shine on my boots that showed under the too-short cuffs, I moved off briskly; in half a block I found a blue-painted custodial cart lettered UNSA. It started up with a ragged hum; I wheeled it away from the curb and headed for the lights of the main gate.

The boy on the guard post was no more than eighteen, a snubnosed farm lad, still getting a kick out of the sidearm and the badge and the white-painted helmet liner. I pulled up to him, gave him a sheepish grin, waved toward a cluster of glare signs half a block away, wan in the misty night. I picked a name from a bilious pink announcement looming above the others: "Just slipping down to Maggie's for a pack of bolts, Lootenant," I told him. "Boy, a man really gets to hankering for a smoke—"

"You guys give me a swiftie," the kid said. "Where do you get them big ideas? You think the government buys them scooters for you birds to joy-ride on? Climb down offa there and try stretching your legs one time."

"You're too sharp for me, Lootenant," I admitted. He watched, arms folded, while I wheeled the cart over to the side, parked it beside the guard shack. I gave him a wave that expressed the emotions of a game loser bowing to superior guile, and ankled off toward the bright lights. At the corner I looked back: he was still looking military, savoring the satisfaction of rules enforced. I hoped he wouldn't remember the base pass he hadn't asked to see until I was hull-down over the horizon.

By the light of a polyarc over a narrow alley behind a row of vice parlors, I sorted through my worldly goods; the odds and ends that a trusted killer named Gronski had had in his pockets when he set out on his final assignment. It wasn't much: a keyring, a white plastic comb clogged with grime, a wallet with a curled UNSA ID bearing an unflattering view of what had never been a pretty face, some outdated credit cards from the less expensive bean-and-sex joints around Charleston, South Carolina, six Cs in cash, and a pair of half-hearted pornographic snaps of a tired-looking girl with ribs. I pocketed the money, went along the alley to a public disposal chute, and put the loot down into the odor of hot iron and fruit rinds.

Clothes were my first problem. When Tarleton got the word that I was gone, a cordon would move out through the town as fast as a late-model Turbocad riot car could roll. It would be nice if I could be over the bridge and into DC proper before then. Nobody got into the megalopolis nowadays without a full scope and NAC. A set of baggy overalls might be good enough to get me past a recruit pulling the graveyard shift on a class-two passenger depot; I'd have to do a lot better to satisfy the gray-suit boys on the front door to the capitol.

Tarleton would figure me to make a run for the hills; for the West Coast, maybe, or the anonymity of the Paved State that had once been called the Land of Flowers. He'd assume that for the moment my objective would be limited to survival; he wouldn't expect me to walk deeper into his net; not now; not until I had lain up for a while to lick my wounds and lay my plans. . . .

Or so my second-guessing bump told me. Maybe it was as transparent as a bride's nightie that I'd head for important ears to pour my story into. Maybe the gunnies were just around the next corner, waiting to cut me down. Maybe I was already a dead man, just looking for a place to stretch out.

And maybe I'd better stop being so goddamned smart and get on with the job at hand, before I got myself picked up for loitering and did ninety standing on my ear in the vag tank.

✧   ✧   ✧

Halfway down the wrong side of a street that had been classy about the time the sailmakers in Boston began to decry the collapse of civilization, a dim-lit window hung with two-tone burlap sports jackets and cardboard shoes caught my eye. There was a dust-dimmed glare strip along the top, lending the display all the gaiety of a funeral in the rain. It wasn't the smartest haberdashery in town, but it wouldn't be the best wired, either. I went to the end of the street, took a left, found an alley mouth, came back up behind my target. Aside from kicking a couple of rusted cans and clipping a shin on a post and swearing loud enough to wake up the old maid at the end of the block, I came in as slick as a traveling salesman making a late housecall. The lock wasn't much: a mail-order electro job set in perished plastic. I put a hip against it and pushed; the door frame damn near fell in with me.

It took five minutes to look over the stock and select a plain black suit suitable for the county to bury a pauper in. I added a gray shirt that looked as though it would hold its shape as long as nobody washed it, a tie with a picture of a Balinese maiden, a pair of ventilated shoes with steel taps on the heels that would be all that was left after the first rain. The cash register tallied three Cs and some change. I wrote out an IOU, signed it, and tucked it in under the wire spring. That meant that half an hour after the store opened Tarleton would have a description of my new elegance—but by then it wouldn't matter. I'd either be across the bridge or dead.

Three streets farther up the gentle slope above the river I found what I needed: a blackened brick front holding up two squares of age-tarnished plastex and a door that had once been painted red. The left window bore the legend IRV'S HOUSE OF TATTOO ARTISTRY and the right balanced the composition with a picture of a mermaid seated on an anchor holding a drowned sailor. I walked past once, saw the glimmer of a light in a side window visible along a two-foot airspace that ran back on the right. There seemed to be no activity in the drinking establishment next door; I slid into the alley, walked over bottles, cans, things that squashed, other things that crunched. If there were any dead bodies, I didn't notice them.

At the rear there was a small court walled by taller buildings on either side, a high fence with a gate letting onto a wider alley. The light from the side window showed up a few blades of green spring grass poking up among cinders. Two concrete steps led up to a back door. I stood on the bottom one and knocked, two short, one long, two short. Nothing happened.

A bird let off a string of notes somewhere, stopped suddenly as though he had just discovered he was in the wrong place. It's an uncomfortable feeling; I know it well.

I rapped again, same code, only louder. Still nothing. I stepped back down, found a pebble, threw it at a closed shutter up above, then went back and put an ear against the door. Sounds came, faint and ill-tempered. I heard the bolt rattle; the door opened half an inch. There was heavy breathing.

"It's a hot rasper," I said quickly. "Marple up on the avtake before the fuzz gondle."

"Ha? Wha—?" a clogged voice started, broke off to cough. I leaned on the door. "I got to see Irv," I snapped. "Transik apple ready, tonight for sure." The door yielded. I stepped into an odor of last month's broccoli, last week's booze, and a lifetime of rancid bacon fat and overdue laundry. A fat citizen in a gray bathrobe with a torn sleeve thumbed uncombed gray hair back from a red eye set in gray fat. The fingernail was gray too. So was his neck. Maybe he liked gray.

"You run the skin gallery?" I asked him.

"What's the grift, Jack?" He pulled the knot tight on the robe, shot a look out the door, pushed it shut. I watched his right hand.

"I need a job done," I told him. "They sent me to you."

He grunted, looking me over. The hand lingered on the belt.

"You mentioned a name," he said.

"Maybe you'll do," I said. The hand moved then, slipped inside the robe, was halfway out again with a Browning before I clamped down on his wrist. He shifted, slammed his left at my stomach; I half-turned, took it on the hip, jerked the hand out, bent it back, and caught the gun as he dropped it. He didn't make a sound.

"No need for the iron," I told him. "I want papers—fast. Let's step along to your workshop. Time is of the essence."

"What kinda gag—?"

I hit him on the side of the head with the gun hard enough to stagger him. "No time for talking it up. Action. Now." I motioned toward the curtain that hung in the kitchen entry.

"You got me wrong, mister." He was rubbing his face; his hard palm made a scratchy sound going over the stubble. "I run a legitimate little art tattoo parlor here—"

I took a step toward him, rammed the gun at his belly. "Ever heard of a desperate man, Irv? That's me. Maybe every tattoo joint on the planet isn't in the hot-paper line, but I'm guessing this one is—and I get what I want or you die trying. Better hope you can do it."

He worked his mouth, then turned and pushed through the curtains. I followed.

It took Irv an hour to produce a new ID, a set of travel orders, a Geneva card, and a special pass to the Visitors' Gallery at the House. Once he got into the swing of it, he was a true artist, as intent on perfection as Cellini buffing a pinhead blemish off a twenty-foot bronze.

"The orders are okay," he told me as he handed them over, "the G-card, too. Hell, it's pra'tically genuine. The pass—maybe. But don't try to fool nobody but maybe some broad in a bar with that ID. Them Security boys will have that number checked out—"

"That's okay. The stuff looks good. How much do I owe you?"

He lifted his shoulders. "Hundred Cs," he said.

"Add fifty for getting you up," I said. "And another fifty for the crack on the head. I'll mail it to you as soon as I hear from home."

"The crack on the head's for free," he said. "How's about leaving the Browning. You don't get them with Cracker Jacks any more."

I nodded. "Let's go down." He went ahead of me down the stairs, back through the kitchen, opened the door. I took the magazine out of the gun, tossed it out into the yard, handed him the Browning. He took it and thrust it away, out of sight.

"The guy who worked on your hands was good," he said softly. "Navy?"

I nodded. He ran a hand through the gray hair.

"I worked with a lot of Navy guys in my time," he said. The red eyes were as sharp as scalpels. "You done time on a lot of quarterdecks, would be my guess. You don't need to sweat me. I don't know no cops."

"Give me three hours," I said. "Then yell your head off. Maybe you could use the Brownie points at headquarters."

"Yeah," he said. I went out and the door closed on his still-gray face.

4

It was a brisk ten-minute walk to Monticello Boulevard. I made it without attracting any attention other than a close look by a pair of prowl-car cops who would never know how close they came to a bonus and promotion, and a business offer from a moonlighting Washington secretary holding a lonely vigil at the Tube entry. A wheelcab cruising the outer lane answered my wave, pulled off on the loading strip.

"You licensed for DC?" I asked him.

"Whattaya, blind?" He pointed to a three-inch gold sticker on his canopy. I got in and he gunned off toward the lights of the bridge.

"You know Eisenhower Drive?" I asked him.

"Does a mouse know cheese?" he came back, fast and snappy.

"Number Nine Eighty-five," I said.

"Senator I. Albert Pulster," he said. I saw his eyes in the mirror, watching me. "You know Pulster?"

"My brother-in-law," I said.

"Yeah?" He sounded impressed—like a car salesman getting the lowdown on a ten-year-old trade-in. "Pulster's a big noise in this town these days," he said. "Three years to election and you can't open a pictonews without you get a mug shot of the guy. He's parlayed that committee into a clear shot at the White House."

The control booth was a blaze of garish light across the wet pavement ahead. The white-uniformed CIA man was leaning out, letting me catch the dazzle of the brass on his collar. The cab pulled up and the panel slid down, letting in the cool river air. I handed over the ID and the orders directing me to report to Fort McNair a day earlier. He looked them over, turned, shoved the card into the scope that transmitted the finger-print image to the CBI master file, read off the name that popped onto the four-inch screen. It would be mine—the only risk at this point was that Tarleton had already put a flag out on it. . . .

He hadn't. The guard held out a plain plastic rectangle.

"Right thumb, please," he said in a bored voice. I gave it to him; he pressed it on the sensitive plate, shoved it into the same slot, got the same result. All right so far. If he stopped now, I was in; if he went one step farther and checked out the crystal pattern of the card itself. . . .

"Hey," the driver shot a look at me. "He says he's Pulster's brother-in-law."

"So?"

"I never heard of Pulster having no brother-in-law."

The CIA man gave him a heavy-lidded look. "Let's you leave us do our job, fella; you stick to watching those traffic signs." He handed me my phony papers, pushed the button to raise the barrier, waved us on across. My driver drove fast, shoulders hunched. He didn't talk any more all the way out to Eisenhower.

Number Nine Eighty-five was a big iron gate with twin baby spots mounted up high on an eight-foot fieldstone wall that looked solid enough to withstand a two day mortar bombardment. A graveled drive led back between hundred-year oaks to a lofty three-story façade gleaming a well-tended oyster-white in the faint starlight. There was a porte-cochère high enough to clear the footman on a four-horse carriage, wide enough for three Caddies abreast. There were more windows than I remembered on the west front at Versailles, a door reminiscent of the main entrance to Saint Peter's Basilica, wide steps that were probably scrubbed five times a day by English butlers using toothbrushes. Or maybe not: maybe the servant problem had even penetrated as far as the Pulster residence.

I thumbed a button set in a black iron plate, jumped when a feminine voice immediately said, "Yes, sir?"

"How do you know I'm not a madam?" I snapped back.

"You don't have the build for it, sweetheart," the voice said, sharp now. "You want to tell me what it's all about, or do I just call a couple sets of law to help get you straightened out?"

I squinted, spotted the eye up in the angle of the iron curlicue at the top of the gate.

"I want to see the Senator," I said. "Wake him up if you have to. It's important."

"Would there be a name?"

"Maclamore."

"Uh-huh. Army?"

"Navy. Captain Maclamore. Six-one, one-ninety stripped, brown hair, brown eyes, and a nasty disposition. Hop to it."

"Not even one little old star? Captains we usually take in batches of nine on alternate Wednesdays, and this being Thursday. . . . well, you see how it is."

"You're cute," I told the eye. "With a couple more like you I could start a finishing school for snake charmers. Now run along and tell Albert you're keeping his favorite relative waiting out in the hot sun."

"Like that, huh?" the voice said coolly. "You could have said so. What are you trying to do—lose me my job?"

"It's a thought," I admitted. There was no answer. I took a couple of steps, turned, took two back. The tension was building up now. My small cuts and burns were hurting like big ones; it was time for another load of those nice drugs Purdy's medic had fed me. Instead all I had was the withdrawal symptoms, a letdown of the past few hours' fever-bright energy into a high singing sensation back of the eyes and a tendency to start arguments with disembodied voices. . . .

There was a buzz and a click and the gate rolled back. I went through it, saw a small white-painted wagon rolling along the drive toward me on fat rubber wheels. It stopped and the voice was back.

"If you'll step aboard, sir. . . . ?"

I did and the robocart whisked me up to the steps, past them, along to a ramp that slanted up behind shrubbery to an open entry. I got off and went through it into a wide airy hall full of a melancholy yellow light from wide stained-glass panels above a gallery trimmed in white-painted wrought iron. A waxed and polished girl with a pert brown face, pouty purple lips, and a cast plastic hairdo came out of a carved door, waved toward a chair that looked like a Scottish king might have been crowned in it once.

"If you'll just be seated, Captain—"

"Still mad, huh? Where's his bedroom? I'll overlook it if his hair's not combed—"

"Please, Captain Maclamore." She did a bump and grind, showed me a fine set of big white teeth, came up close, and let me get a load of the hundred-C-an-ounce stuff she wore behind her ears.

"The Senator will be with you in just a moment. . . ." Her voice changed tone on the last words; she'd noticed the bruise on my jaw, the patch of singed hair, the small cuts beside my eye where an instrument face had blown out. I worked up a quick smile that probably looked like the preliminary to a death rattle.

"A little accident on the way over," I said. "But it's all right. I got the other fellow's number."

A bell jangled then—or maybe it purred; it just seemed to me like a jangle. The light was too bright, too sour; the tick of an antique spring-driven clock picked at me like a knifepoint. My cheap stiff clothes rasped on my skin—

Feet rattled on the stairway behind me. I turned, and Senator I. Albert Pulster, short, dapper, red-faced, his hair neatly combed, came across the floor, held out a hand worn smooth by shaking.

"Well, Mac—a long time. Not since Edna's funeral, I think. . . ."

I shook the hand. It felt hard and dry, but no harder or dryer than my own.

"I've got to talk to you, Albert," I said. "Fast and private."

He nodded as though he'd been expecting it. "Ah. . . . a personal matter. . . . ?"

"As personal as dying."

He indicated the door the girl had come out of. I followed him in.

Pulster's face looked hollow, as though all the juice had been sucked out of it by a big spider, leaving only a shell like crumpled tissue paper. All that in three minutes.

"Where is he now?" he asked in a voice as thin as his face.

"My guess would be that he's in a closed-door conference with some of his friends from the Hill. Naturally, he'll try to do it the easy way first. Why walk over Congress if he can bring them in with him?"

A little life was showing in Albert's eyes now, a little color was coming back into his cheeks. He leaned forward, clasped his hands together as though he was afraid they'd get away.

"And he doesn't know you're here?" His voice was quick now, emotionless, stripped for action.

"I'd guess he knows by now that I got off the ship. Beyond that—it depends on how good his intelligence apparatus is. He may have three squads with Mark Xs trampling across the lawn right now."

Albert's mouth twitched. "No, he doesn't," he said flatly. He fingered the edge of his desk, pulled out a big drawer, swung it up on spring-balanced slides, pivoted it to face me. It was a regulation battle-display console, the kind usually installed in a two-man interceptor: it showed four stretches of unoccupied lawn with fountains and flowers. Below it was a fire-control panel that would have done credit to a five-thousand-tonner.

"A man needs certain resources in these troubled times," Albert said. "I've never proposed to furnish a sitting target for the first Oswald who might rap at the gate."

I nodded. "That's why I joined the Navy: too dangerous down here." I pushed his toy back to him. "He's counting on putting this over fast and smooth: the public will wake up and it will be all over. The right publicity in the right places—now—will kill him."

Albert was shaking his head, looking shocked. "Publicity—no! Not a word, Mac. Good Lord, man—" He clamped his teeth and breathed through his nose, looking at me, through me; then he focused in, blinked a couple of times.

"Mac, there's no time to waste. What kind of force would it take to neutralize the flagship?" he snapped out. "Assuming the worst: That Tarleton heard of the move, was able to communicate with the vessel, that she was fully alerted."

"A couple of hundred megaton-seconds," I said. "With luck."

"I have no capital ships at my disposal," Albert thought aloud. "I do have over one hundred battle-ready medium recon units attached to National Guard organizations in the Seventeenth District." He looked at me hard. "What do you mean, Mac—'with luck'?"

"Tarleton stripped the ship to make his Roman Holiday. There'll be skeleton crews on all sections. I don't know who he left on the bridge: he brought all his top boys down with him—he'd have to, otherwise he might find himself looking down his own Hellbores. Assuming a fairly competent man, he'll be able to lay down about fifty-percent firepower—and as for maneuverability. . . ."

"We can saturate her," Albert said. "Run her gauntlet, grapple to her, force an entry, and sweep her clean! And then"—Albert stopped, let his expression slide back to the casual—"but we'll worry about that later. Our immediate need—"

But he'd already done the damage. "You said 'after,'" I told him. "Go on."

"Why, then, of course, I'd restore matters to normality as soon as possible." He gave me a sharp look, like a pawnbroker wondering if the customer knows the pearls are real. "I think you could anticipate an appointment to star rank—perhaps even—"

"Forget it, Albert," I said softly. "With fast action and the kind of luck that makes Sweepstakes winners, we might be able to get together enough firepower to hit her once—now—while he's off-balance, before he expects anything—and knock her out. You've got your hundred boats; if you can swing the North American Defense Complex into it, we just might blanket her defenses with one strike—"

"Mac, you're raving," Albert said flatly. "You don't seem to understand—"

"That ship's a juggernaut hanging over all of us. I think a call to Kajevnikoff might bring their South American Net into it too—"

"You're talking like a traitor!" Pulster got to his feet, his face back to its normal shade now.

"I'm taking that ship intact." He tried to get his voice under control. "Be sensible, man! I'm offering you command of the strike force. You needn't expose yourself unnecessarily, of course. In fact, I'd expect you to command from a safe distance, then move in after boarding by my troops—"

"You're wasting time, Pulster," I told him. "Start the ball rolling—now. One word—one hint to Tarleton, and he'll neutralize every resource on the planet before you can say 'dictator.'"

"What do you mean—dictator!"

"One's like another as far as I'm concerned. In fact, between you and Banny, I might even pick him. I came here to stop something, not barter it."

Albert's hand went to his console, stopped self-consciously. He was thinking so hard I could almost smell the wires burning. I took a step toward him, slid a hand inside my coat as though I had something hidden there.

"Get away from the desk, Senator," I said. He backed slowly—toward the window.

"Uh-uh. Over there." I indicated the discreet door to the sena-torial john.

"Look here, Mac: this is too big to toss away like an old coat. The man that controls that vessel, controls the planet! It's almost in our hands! You did the right thing, coming here—and I'll never forget it was you who—"

I stepped in, hit him hard under the ribs to double him over, brought a right up under his jaw hard enough to lift his toes off the floor. He went back and down like a shroud full of baseballs, lay on his back with one eye half open. I didn't check to see whether he was breathing; I hooked a finger in his collar, dragged him to the toilet door, half threw him inside, set the latch, closed it. I looked around the room. There was a mirror on one wall with a table with flowers under it. I went over to it and a hollow-eyed bum in a sleazy greenish-black suit and a wilted collar looked out at me as though I'd caught him in the act of murder.

"It's okay, pal," I said aloud, feeing my tongue thick in my mouth. "That was just a warmup, almost an accident, you might say. The rough part's just beginning."

Back out in the big sad empty hall I told the girl that the Senator had suffered a sudden pain in the stomach. "He's in the john," I said bluntly. "Hiding, if you ask me. Pain in the stomach, hah! A great thing when a fellow can't come to his own relations when he's had a little run of bad luck."

The look that she'd varnished up for VIP use melted away like witnesses at a traffic smash. I made it to the door without a guide—no little cart appeared to ride me out to the gate. I walked, wondering how long it would be before she went in—and whether she would know which button to push on the console to sweep the drive with fire.

But nothing happened: nobody yelled, no bells rang, no guns fired. I reached the gate and the big electrolock gave me a buzz like a Bronx cheer as I went through. I looked back at the eye: if it had been a mouth, it would have yawned. There's nothing like a little poverty to make a man invisible.

5

My last two Cs bought me a cab ride as far as Potomac Quay. I made the three blocks to the Wellington Arms on foot, trying not to hurry even when sirens came screaming across from

Pennsylvania Avenue and three Monojag cop cars raced overhead, heading the way I'd come. It was a fair guess that Miss Linoleum had overcome her maidenly modesty sufficiently to force the door not many minutes after I made it off the grounds.

I went up the broad pseudomarble steps, past a Swiss admiral with enough Austrian knots to equip a troop of dragoons, in through a twelve-foot-high glass door, crossed a stretch of polished black floor big enough for the New Year's Yacht Show. Under the muted glare strip that read INQUIRIES I found a small neat man with big dark eyes that flicked over me once and caught everything except the hole in my left sock.

"I have some information that has to be placed in the Vice President's hands at once," I told him. "What can you do for me?"

He reached without looking and slid a gold-mounted pad and stylus across to me, spun it around so that *Wellington Arms* was at the top, the pen poised ready to be written with.

"If you'd care to leave a message—"

I put my face closer to him. "I'm a little marked up; you noticed that. I got that way getting here. It's that kind of information. Take a chance and let me talk to his secretary."

He hesitated, then reached for a small voice-only communicator, gold to match the pad. I waited while he played with the buttons out of sight over the counter, murmured into the phone. Time passed. More discreet conversation. Then he nodded.

"Mr. Lastwell will be down in a moment," he said. "Or so he says," he added in a lower tone. "You've got time for a smoke. You may even have time for a chow-mein dinner."

"It's a corny line," I said, "but minutes could make a difference. Maybe seconds."

The clerk gave me another X-ray look; this time I figured he caught the hole in the sock. He leaned a little across the counter, squared up the pad. "Political?" he murmured.

"It's not show biz," I said mysteriously. "Or is it?"

That satisfied him. He went off to the other end of the counter and began making entries in a card file. Probably the names of people to be shot after the next election. I looked at the clock: slim gold hands pointed at gold dots representing half past one. There was a lot of gold around the Wellington Arms.

He came through the bleached-teak doors from the bar, a thin, tired-looking man, walking fast, frowning, shoulders a little rounded, eyes whisking over the room like mice. He saw me, checked his stride, looked me over as he came up.

"I'm Marvin Lastwell. You're the person. . . . ?"

"Maclamore. Is the Vice President here?"

"Eh? Yes, of course he's here. If he were elsewhere, I'd be with him, hmm? What was it you had, Mr., er, Maclamore?"

"Do we talk here?"

He looked around as though he were surprised to find himself in the lobby. "Hmm. There's a lounge just along—"

"This is private," I cut him off. "Let's go where it will stay that way."

He sucked his cheeks in. "Now, look here, Mr., er, Maclamore—"

"On the off chance this could be important, play along this once, Mr. Lastwell. I can't spill this in front of every pickup the local gossip ghouls have planted in this mausoleum."

"Hmm. Very well, Mr., er, Maclamore." He led the way off along a corridor carpeted in dove-gray pile deep enough to lose a golfball in. I followed, wondering why a mild-looking fellow like Marvin Lastwell thought it necessary to carry a Browning 2mm under his arm.

The penthouse at the Wellington was no more ornate than Buckingham Palace, and smaller, though not much. Lastwell showed me into a spacious, dim-lit library lined with the kind of leather-bound books lawyers keep around the office to impress the customers and maybe open once in a while on a rainy afternoon when trade is slow, just to see what they're missing. Lastwell went behind a big dark mahogany desk, sat down fussily, pushed a big silver ashtray with a cigar butt off to one side, flicked on a lamp that threw an eerie green reflection back up on his face, giving his worried features a look of Satanic ferocity. I wondered if he'd practiced it in front of a mirror.

"Now, Mr., er, Maclamore," he said, "what is it you wanted to tell me?"

I was still standing, looking at the cigar butt, probably left there by the last ward-heeler who'd dropped in to mend a fence. It looked as out of place on Lastwell's desk as a roulette wheel at a Methodist retreat. He saw me looking at it and started to reach for it, then changed his mind, scratched his nose instead. I could feel a sudden tension in him.

"Maybe I didn't make myself clear," I said. "It was the Vice President I wanted to see."

Lastwell curved the corners of his mouth into a smile like a meat-eating bird—or maybe it was just the light.

"No, Captain, you can hardly—" He caught himself, clamped his jaw shut. The abrupt silence hung between us like a shout.

"Like that, huh?" I said softly.

He sighed, his hand hardly seemed to move, but now the Browning was in it. He held the gun with that graceful negligence they only get when they know how to use them. He motioned with his head toward a chair.

"Just sit down," he said in an entirely new voice. "You'll have a few minutes' wait."

I moved toward the chair he'd indicated; the gun muzzle followed. It was too late at night to start thinking, but I made the attempt. The cigar was the skinny black brand that Tarleton smoked. I'd probably missed him by minutes. He hadn't been close behind me—he'd been a good jump ahead. He'd had time to give his pitch—whatever proposition he'd worked out—to the Veep. It had been a risky move, but it seemed the Veep had listened. He'd mentioned me; as for how much he'd said, the next few seconds would tell me that.

I reached the chair, but instead of sitting in it, I turned to face Lastwell. The gun twitched alertly, holding low on my chest. That could be design—or accident.

"Maybe your boss would like to hear my side," I said, just to keep him talking. "Maybe my angle's better."

"Shut up and sit in the chair," Lastwell said, in the tone of a tired teacher talking to the oldest pupil in the eighth grade.

"Sit in it yourself," I came back. "The graveyard's full of wise guys who didn't stick around to get the whole story. Did Tarleton tell you I was Weapons Officer aboard *Rapacious*? Hell, the whole tub's wired to blow at a signal from—"

"You were captain of *Sagacious*," Lastwell cut in. "Save your lies, Maclamore—"

"Not two years ago I wasn't, when she was fitted out—"

"Save it," he said. Lastwell let his voice rise a decibel and a half; the gun jerked up as he spoke, centered on my chest now. I gave him a discouraged look, leaned forward as though about to sit, and dived across the desk. The Browning bucked and shrieked and a cannon ball hit me in the chest and then my hands were on his neck, sinking into doughy flesh, and we were going down together, slamming the floor and the gun was bouncing clear and then I was on my knees, with Lastwell bent back under me, his mouth open, tongue out, eyes bulging like lanced boils.

"Talk it up," I ground out past my teeth. I gave him a quarter of a second to think it over, then gave him a thumb under the Adam's apple. A thin sound came from him, like a rivet scoring a brake drum.

"He. . . . here. . . . half-hour. . . ."

I gave him enough air to work with but not enough to encourage enterprise.

"Who's here now?"

"No—nobody. Sent. . . . them away."

"How many are in this?"

"Just. . . . the two of them. . . ."

"Plus you. Where are they?"

"They're. . . . gone to see. . . . others. Back soon. . . ."

"Tarleton coming back here?"

"No. . . . to his place." Lastwell gulped air, flopped his arms. "Please. . . . my back. . . ."

I smiled at him. "Get ready to die," I said.

"No! Please!" What color was left went out of his face like dirty water down a drain.

"Tell the rest," I snapped.

"He's. . . . expecting you. . . . there. . . . if I don't get you. . . . here. State Police. . . ."

"Say your prayers," I ordered. "When you wake up in the next world, remember how it felt to die a dirty death." I rammed my fingers in hard to the carotid arteries, watched his eyes turn up; he slumped and I let his head bump the carpet. He'd come around in half an hour with a sore throat and a set of memories that he could mull over at bedtime for a lot of sleepless nights.

I left him where he was, picked up the gun, tucked it away. There was a chewed place across my coat front where the needles had hit, a corresponding rip in the shirt. The chromalloy plate underneath that covered the artificial heart and lungs showed hardly a scratch to commemorate the event. Six inches higher or to the left, and he'd have found unshielded hide. It wasn't like Banny Tarleton to forget to mention a detail like that. Maybe he was slipping; maybe that was the break that had let me get this far. Maybe I could ride it a little farther, and maybe I was already out on the skim ice, too far from shore to walk back.

I'd tried to stop Tarleton with indirect methods; they hadn't worked. Now there was only one direction left: straight ahead, into the trap he had laid.

Now I'd have to kill him with my own hands.

6

I rummaged in Lastwell's closet, found a shapeless tan waterproof and a narrow-brimmed hat. The private elevator rode me down to the second floor. The silence in the corridor was all that you'd expect for a hundred Cs a day. I walked along to the rear of the building, found a locked door to a service stair. There was a nice manual knob on it; I gripped it hard, gave it a sharp twist. Metal broke and tinkled, and the door swung in. The luxury ended sharply at the threshold: there was a scarred chair, a dirty coffee cup, a magazine, cigarette butts on a concrete landing above a flight of narrow concrete steps. I went down, passed another landing, kept going. The stairs ended at a wooden door. I tried it, stepped through into the shadows and the hum of heavy equipment. A shoe scraped and a big-bellied man in a monogrammed coverall separated himself from the gray bulk of a compressor unit. He frowned, wiped a hand over a bald head, opened his mouth—

"Fire inspector," I told him briskly. "Goddamn place is a deathtrap. That your chair on the landing?"

He gobbled, almost swallowed his toothpick, spat it on the floor. "Yah, it's my chair—"

"Get it out of there. And police those butts while you're at it." I jerked my head toward the back of the big room. "Where's your fire exit?"

"Hah?"

"Don't stall," I barked. "Got it blocked, I'll bet. You birds are all alike: think fire regulations are something to wrap your lunch in."

He gave me a red-eyed look, hitched at his shoulder strap. "Back here." His Potsdam accent was thick enough to spread on pretzels like cream cheese. I followed him along to a red-painted metal-clad door set a foot above floor level.

"Red light's out," I noted, sharp as a mousetrap. There was a big barrel bolt on the door at chest height. I slid it back, jerked the door open. Dust and night air whirled in.

"Okay, get that landing clear, like I said." I hooked a thumb over my shoulder and stepped out into dead leaves. He grunted and went away. I eased my head above the ragged grass growing along the edge of the stairwell; a security light on the side of the building showed me a garbage-disposal unit, a white-painted curb, the squat shape of a late model Turbocad parked under a row of dark windows. I slid the Browning into my hand, went up, across to the car. It was a four-seater, dull back with a gold eagle on the door. I thumbed the latch; no surprise there: it was locked. I went down on my left side, eased under the curve of the hood. There were a lot of wires; I traced one, jerked it loose, tapped the frame; sparks jumped and a solid *snick!* sounded above. I crawled back out, pulled open the door, slid in behind the wheel. The switch resisted for a moment; then something snapped and it turned. The turbos started up with a whine like a waitress looking at a half-C tip. The Cad slid out along the drive, smooth as a porpoise in deep water. I nosed out into the bleak light of the polyarcs along the quay, took the inner lane, and headed at a meticulously legal speed for Georgetown.

A big fire a few years back had cleared away ten blocks of high-class slums and given the culture-minded administration of that day the perfect excuse to erect a village of colonial-style official mansions that were as authentic as the medals on a Vermouth bottle. Admiral Banastre Tarleton had the one at the end of the line, a solid-looking red-brick finish that disguised half an inch of flint steel, with lots of pretty white woodwork, a copper-sheathed roof made of bomb-proof polyon, and two neat little cupolas that housed some of the most sensitive detection gear ever sidetracked from a naval yard. I picked it out from two blocks away by the glare of lights from windows on all three floors.

There was an intersection nostalgically lit by gas flares on tall poles; I crossed it, slowed, moving along in the shadow of a row of seventy-foot elms with concrete cores and permanentized leaves. The moon was up now, shedding its fairy glow on the bricked street, the wide inorganic lawns, the stately fronts, creating a fragile illusion of the simple elegance of a past age—if you could ignore the lighted spires of the city looming up behind.

The last house on the right before Tarleton's place was a boxy planter's mansion with a row of stately columns and a balcony from which a queen could wave to the passing crowds. It was boarded up tight; not everybody was willing to give up the comfort of a modern apartment a mile up in the Washington sky for the dubious distinction of a Georgetown address. Half the houses here were empty, shuttered, awaiting a bid from a social-climbing freshman Congressman or a South American diplomat eager to get a lease signed before the government that sent him collapsed in a hail of gunfire.

There was a sudden movement among moon shadows on the drive opposite the Tarleton house: a heavy car appeared—armored, by the ponderous sway of its suspension as it trundled out to block the street. It was too late for me to think up any stunning moves that would leave the opposition breathless; I cut the wheel hard, swung into the artificial cinder drive that led up to the bright-lit front of the Tarleton mansion. Behind me, the interceptor gunned its turbos, closed in on my rear bumper. Men appeared in the wide doorway ahead; I caught glimpses of others spotted across the lawn that was pool-table green in the splash of light from the house. They ringed me in as I braked to a stop. I set the brake hard, flung the door open, stepped out, gave my coat belt a tug, picked out a middle-sized fellow with a face as sensitive as a zinc bartop.

"Those clowns in the armor better get on the ball," I told him. "I could have waltzed right past 'em. And those boys you've got out trampling the flowerbeds: tell 'em to hit the dirt and stay put; they're not in a tango contest—"

"Where do you fit the picture, mister?" His voice was a whisper; I saw the scar across his throat, ear to ear. He was a man who'd looked death in the eye from razor range. He was looking at the car now, not liking it much, but pushed a little off-balance by the eagle and the words OFFICE OF THE CENTRAL BUREAU OF INTELLIGENCE.

I started around the front of the car, headed for the stairs. "Hot stuff for the Admiral," I said. "He's inside, right?"

He didn't move. I stopped before I rammed him.

"Maybe I better see some paper, mister," he whispered. "Turn around and put the mitts on top of the car."

"Pull up your socks, rookie," I advised loudly. "You think I carry a card when I'm working?" I crowded him a little. "Come on, come on, what I got won't wait." He gave—about a quarter of an inch. "Any you boys know this mug?" he called in his faint croak. His face was close enough to mine to give me a good whiff of burnt licorice: he was on the pink stuff. That wouldn't make him any easier to take.

I saw heads shake; two or three voices denied the pleasure of my acquaintance.

I hunched my shoulders. "I'm going in," I announced. "I got my orders from topside—"

Someone came out through the open door, saw me, and stopped dead. For an instant I had trouble placing the horsey weatherbeaten face under the brimless cap. He opened his mouth, showing uneven brown teeth, and said "Hey!" It was Funderburk, the Warrant from the flagship. I took the first half of a deep breath, nodded toward him as casually as a pickpocket saying 'Good morning' to a plainclothes cop.

"Ask him," I said. "He knows me."

Funderburk came down the steps, three or four expressions chasing each other over his face.

"Yeah," he said. He nodded, as if vastly satisfied. "Yeah."

"You make this bird?" the scarred man whispered.

I tried to coax a little moisture into my dry mouth. My minor wounds throbbed, but no worse than an equal number of nerve cancers. I was hungry and tired, but Scott had probably felt at least as bad, writing the last page of his journal on the ice cap; my head throbbed a little, but one of those ancient Egyptians whose family doc had sawed his skull open with a stone knife would have laughed it off.

"Sure," Funderburk said from under a curled lip. "Gronski. Anchorman of the section. Two months ago they plant the slob in my outfit, and I guess I ain't hardly seen the guy three times since." He spat, offside, but just barely. "The Commodore's Number-One Boy. Better play it closer than a skin-diver's tights, Ajax. He's a privileged character, he is."

There was a mutter in which I caught the word "Braze." I poked Ajax with a finger.

"I'll mention you were doing a job," I said. "But don't work it to death." I brushed past him and past Funderburk, went up the steps and through the door. No power guns roared. No large dogs came bounding out to sample my leg. Nobody even hit me over the head with a blackjack. So far, so good.

One man was walking behind me, one on my right. I went across the wide Wedgwood-blue reception hall, past a gilt-framed mirror that showed me a glimpse of a pale unshaven face with eyes like char-wounds. He looked like Mussolini just before the crowd got him. The stairs were carpeted in wine red that somehow didn't clash with the walls; maybe it was the soft yellow light from a tinkly glass chandelier that hung on a long gold chain from somewhere high above. The banister was wide and cool and white under my hand. The footsteps of the two goons thumped on the treads behind me.

I passed a landing with a tall double-hung window with lacy curtains and dark drapes, a painting of a small boy in red velvet pants, a weathered-oak clock that didn't tick. Then I was coming up into a wide hall done in dusty green with big white-painted wood panel doors with bright brass knobs. A man sat in a chair at the end beside a curved-leg Sheraton table with a brass ashtray from which a curl of smoke went up under a green-shaded lamp. There was a power gun in his lap. He watched me come, his hands on the gun.

One of the doors was open; voices came from inside. I felt like a man striding briskly toward the gallows, but the thin bluff I was riding couldn't survive any doubts or hesitations at this point. I went on, turned in at the lighted door, and was in a big high-ceilinged room with a desk, heavy leather-covered chairs, book-cases, a bar in one corner. Three men standing there looked around at me. Two of them I'd never seen before, the third was a captain whose name I couldn't remember. He frowned at me, looked at the others.

"Where's the admiral?" the man behind me asked.

Nobody answered. The captain was still frowning at me. "I've seen you before," he said. "Who are you—?"

"Guy named Gronski," my escort said. "The Commodore's dog-robber."

"You have a message from Commodore Braze?" one of the other men asked sharply.

"I want to see the Admiral," I said, looking stubborn. "I've already told Ajax this is a red-hot item—"

"You can tell it again—" the third man snapped. "I'm Admiral Tarleton's aide—"

"And I'm bad news from back home," I snarled. "I'm not up here to jackass around with a front man—" I whirled on the captain. "Can't you people get the message? This is *hot!*"

The Captain's eyes went to the door in the wall behind me. "He's just stepped down the hall," he said uneasily. "He's—"

"Never mind that, Johnson," the aide snapped out. "I'll inform him—"

"We'll both inform him," the captain said. "I'm assigned here as exec—"

"Save the jurisdictional wrangles until later," the other man cut in. "If this is as important as this fellow seems to think—"

"It's worse," I barked. "I'm warning you bastards somebody's gonna suffer. . . ."

The aide and the captain slammed down their glasses and stamped out of the room, neck and neck. I poked a finger at the two who had escorted me. "All right, get back on post," I rapped out. "Believe me, when I tell the admiral. . . ." They faded away like shadows at sunset. The man at the bar had his mouth open. I walked across to him, looking confidential.

"There's one other little thing," I started as I came up to him— and chopped out with the side of my hand, caught him across the cheekbone. He almost leaped the bar. Glasses went flying, but thudded almost silently to the rug. I dragged him behind the bar, went across to the connecting door, gave the knob a hard twist. I almost broke my wrist.

Out in the hall the two who had gone out were nowhere in sight; the gun-handler still sat his chair beside the lamp. I gave him a hard look as though wondering whether he'd shaved that morning, strode along to the next door, reached for it—

"Hey!" He came out of his chair, gun forward. "Get away from that door!"

I turned toward him as he came up, jumped sideways, and kicked out. The burst caught me across the shin, slammed me back against the wall. My head hit hard and brilliant constellations shimmered all around. I clawed, swam up from abyssal deeps where light never penetrated, saw him stepping back, the gun still aimed. Someone yelled—a high tight string of words. Feet pounded. There was a harsh reek of burnt synthetics. I rolled over on my face, got my hands under me. I was staring at the big white door when it opened inward. Admiral Banastre Tarleton stood there, a Norge stunner in his hand. Without pausing to calculate the odds, I planted both feet against the wall behind me, launched myself at his knees. I heard the soft whisper of the Norge as I hit, and the crisper sound of something tearing in his leg, and then we were down together and the stunner hissed again and my left side was dead, but I rolled clear, scrabbled with one arm, saw a man in the doorway just as I caught the edge of the thick metal panel, hurled it shut with what was left of my strength. The dull *boom!* shut off the outside world as completely as the lid of a coffin.

I looked around. Tarleton was on his back, his head propped up at an awkward angle against the leg of a canopied four-poster bed. His face was as white as bleached bone, and the Norge was in his fist, aimed square at my face.

"I don't know how you got here, Mac," he said in a voice forced high by the agony of a broken knee. "I must have more traitors in my organization than I thought."

"Glad to see you still have your sense of humor, Banny," I said. I thought about trying for the Browning, but it was just a thought. The stunner held on me as steadily as a deck gun. There was a little sensation in the shoulder where it had caught me; a feeling as though a quarter of beef had been stitched on with a dull needle to replace the scorched arm. My legs were all right, with the exception of the burned plastic and scorched metal below my knee where the power gun had seared it.

"A traitor is a revolutionary who fails," Tarleton stated. "We won't fail."

"Now it's 'we,'" I noted. "A few hours ago it was all 'I.'"

"I'm not alone now, Mac. I've talked to people. Not a shot will be fired."

I nodded. "How does it feel, Banny? In a few hours you'll own the world. You and Napoleon. Take it apart and put it back together to suit yourself. More fun than jigsaw puzzles any day. And you'll have CBI men walking ten deep around you. No more broken legs from wild-eyed reformers who walk into your bedroom past what you call an organization." I was talking to hear myself, to keep my mind off what was coming, to defer for another few seconds the only end the scene could have.

"You moved fast, Mac. I thought"—the gun wavered, then steadied—"thought I had a few secrets."

"Tough, not being able to tip your hand. All that power—if you just don't give it away before the hook's set."

There was a muffled pounding, faint and far away. Tarleton jerked his head up. I could almost make out voices, shouting.

"Get over there," Tarleton ordered. "Open that door."

I shook my head. "Open it yourself, Banny. They're your friends."

He moved, and his cheekbones went almost green. The gun sagged and my hand was halfway to the needler before he caught it. There was greasy-looking sweat on his face. His voice was a croak. "Better do it, Mac. If I feel myself blacking out, I'll have to shoot you."

I didn't say anything. I was wondering why he hadn't shot already. He stared at me for five seconds, while I waited. . . .

Then he twisted, reached up and back, fumbled over the bedside table and suddenly sound was blasting into the room:

"—open! The fire's into the stairwell! Can you hear me, Admiral? We can't get the door open—"

"Benny!" Tarleton snapped as the shout cut off. "Blast the door down. I'm hurt. I can't get to it!" He flipped keys.

"I got him," the voice snapped. "Admiral, listen to me: you have to get it open from your side! There's nothing out here bigger than a Mark X—it'll never cut that chromalloy!"

"Get in here, Benny!" Tarleton's voice was a hoarse roar. "Don't give a damn how you do it, but get in here!"

There were many voices yelling together now.

"—out of here!"

"—too late. Let it go, Rudy!"

"—all roast together!"

"—son of a bitch is out of his mind!"

There was a loud crash, as though a heavy table had gone over, scuffling noises, a cracking roar. Banny flicked it off. His eyes were on mine. "Jacobs was always a little careless with a weapon," he said in a voice like dry leaves.

"A good man," I said. "Reflexes like a cat. Damn near got my kneecap."

"And morals to match. It was my fault; I should have warned

him about the house. Genuine antiques: wood, varnish, cloth. With the right draft there'll be nothing left but a red-hot shell in half an hour."

"You've been forgetting a lot of things, Banny. Like telling your boys where to aim to stop me. You wouldn't have liked the look on Lastwell's face when he put a burst into my chest."

"You must have wanted to get me pretty badly, Mac." He tossed the stunner aside. "It looks like you get your wish. Save yourself— if it's not too late."

He watched me get to my feet; my paralyzed shoulder felt as though my Siamese twin had just been sawed off, and I missed him. The dead hand bumped my side.

"Just the one way down?"

"Service stairs at the back."

There was a tiled bathroom visible through a half-open door. I flipped on the water in the big old-style bathtub, came back out, and hauled a wool blanket off the bed.

"Get going, damn you," Tarleton said in a blurred voice. "No. . . . time. . . ." His head went sideways and he hit the floor with a thud like a split log. That was good: it would be easier for him that way. He'd been keeping himself conscious on pure willpower; he wouldn't be needing that now.

The blanket wanted to float. I shoved it under, remembering the sound of the fire bellowing in the hall. I could almost hear it through the soundproofing now. Precious seconds were passing. . . .

Back in the bedroom Banny Tarleton lay on his side, his mouth open, eyes shut. He didn't look like a world-beater now; he looked like a fellow who had had a bad dream and fallen out of bed.

He was heavy. I pulled him onto the wet blanket, rolled him in it with a double fold over his head, hoisted him onto my shoulder—a neat trick with one good arm, when I couldn't tell the shoulder was there, except for the feeling of needles prickling along the edge of the paralyzed area. The door seemed a long way off. I reached it, put my working hand against it; it hissed. That didn't change anything: I thumbed the electrolock, heard the grumble inside the armored panel. The knob turned, and the door bucked back against me, driven by a solid wall of black-and-orange flame. I shielded my face as well as I could with one hand and a flap of the blanket and walked out into it.

❖   ❖   ❖

The sound was all around me like the thunder of a scarlet Niagara. Under my feet the floorboards were warped and buckled. Pain slashed at me like gale-driven sleet, like frozen knives raking at my face, my back, my thighs. . . .

A section of plaster fell in front of me with a dull boom, drove back the flames for an instant, and through the smoke I saw a once-white balustrade beside the stair, a smoking wraith of blackened iron now. Through a dervish-mad whirl of pale fire, I saw the chandelier, a snarl of black metal from which glass dripped like sun-bright water. The clock stood upright on the landing, burning proudly, like a martyred monk. Beside it, the boy in red pants curled, fumed, was gone in a leap of white fire. Charred steps crumbled under my foot and I staggered; the smell of burning wool was rank in my throat. I could see the varnished floor below, with fire running over it like burning brandy on a pudding, a black crescent moving out behind to consume the bright wood. Somewhere above there was a thunderous smash, and the air was filled with whirling fireflies. Something large and black fell past me, bounced along the floor ahead. I stepped over it, felt a ghostly touch of cool air, and suddenly the flames were gone from around me, and over the surf-roar of the fire I heard thin cries that seemed to come from a remote distance.

"Sweet Mother of Christ!" a high womanish voice wailed. "Look at the poor devil! He's burned as black as a tar mop!"

There was a smoke-blurred figure before me, and then others, and then the weight was gone from my back and I took another step but there seemed to be something wrong with my feet, and I was falling, falling, like a star burning its fiery path across a night sky. . . .

7

I was afloat in cool waters, listening to the distant rumble of thunder portending gentle rain. Then the rumble was a voice, coming from far away on some frosty white mountaintop sparkling in the blue sky. I was flying, soaring down from the icy heights—or was it the cool translucent depths from which I floated up toward light, warmth, pain. . . .

I opened my eyes, saw a vague cloudy shape hovering over me.

"How are you feeling, Mac?" Admiral Banastre Tarleton's voice asked.

"Like a barbecued steer," I said—but no sound came out. Or maybe I grunted.

"Don't try to talk," Tarleton said quickly. "You breathed a lot of smoke, got some fire in your lungs. You're lucky they were made in a factory."

I had the impression someone had come up, muttered to Tarleton. Then he was back.

"You're at Bethesda. They tell me you're out of danger. You were out for eighteen hours. Second-degree burns on the face, the left hand, the back of your thighs. The coat you were wearing helped. Some kind of expanded polymer job. Bioprosthetics are having a swell time clucking over how their work stood up to the fire. Both legs were melted back to bare metal, and the right elbow was fused. They'll have a new set ready for you in about two weeks, when the bandages come off. You won't even have scars."

I tried again, managed a croak. My throat felt like rawhide dried in the desert sun.

"You'll be wondering about how certain things have gone, Mac," Tarleton went on. "Funny thing, after the fire there seemed to be a certain temporary loss of momentum in the movement. I guess my little band of gentleman-adventurers used up all their drive running out on me when things got hot. My own perspective got a little warped: I had to keep reminding myself that in a society of maniacs, the sane man has a duty to rule. And those lads who got the hell out when the flames got knee-high: they did the sane thing. You can't fight that. It took a crazy man to walk through the fire for me."

It was a long speech. I had a long one of my own ready: I was going to tell him all about how it had been a mistake to rush me to the hospital, because as soon as I could walk, I'd have to come after him to finish what I'd started; that sick or well, sane or crazy, there were things loose in the world that were worse than man's animal ferocity, and one of them was the ferocity of the Righteous Intellect; and that the most benevolent of despotisms rotted in the end into the blind arrogance of tyranny. . . .

But all I managed was a whimper like a sick pup.

The frosty haze was closing in again. Tarleton's voice came from far away, as far as the stars: "I have an appointment with the Vice President now, Mac. I'll have to explain some things to him. Maybe he'll understand, maybe not. Maybe things have gone too far. Whichever way it goes, I'd like to leave one thought with you: Theories are beautiful things—simple and precise as cut glass— as long as they're only theories. When you find in your hand the power to make them come true. . . . suddenly, it's not so simple. . . ."

Then he was gone, and the snow was drifting over me, silent and deep.

It was hours later, I don't know how many. I was half awake, reasonably clearheaded, wondering if Tarleton had really been there, or if I had dreamed the whole passage. There was a tri-D screen by the bed, playing the kind of soft music that's guaranteed not to intrude on the bridge-table conversation. It stopped abruptly in mid-moan and a voice harsh with excitement broke in:

"We interrupt this program to bring you the following bulletin: The Vice President has been assassinated and the Secretaries of Defense and State and the Attorney General as well as a number of lesser officials cut down in a burst of gunfire that shattered a secret meeting of the National Defense Council at two-nineteen P.M. Eastern Standard Time today—less than ten minutes ago. An unofficial statement by a newsman who was first on the scene indicates that a heavy-caliber machine pistol smuggled into the Capitol by Admiral Banastre Tarleton was the massacre weapon. Tarleton, still heavily bandaged from yesterday's fire and with a cast on his leg, is reported to have died in the answering fire from a Secret Service man who broke down a door to gain entry to the room. A spokesman for the CBI stated that Admiral Tarleton, a national hero since his destruction of Bloc naval forces in a deep-space battle two days ago, apparently broke under the double tragedy of the loss of the majority of his forces in the fighting, followed by the disastrous fire which swept his Georgetown home—"

The sound cut off then. I got an eyelid up, made out the hovering figure of a man in pale-green hospital togs. He fumbled at my left arm, made soothing noises, and things got vague again. . . .

Voices picked at me. I came back from soft cool shadowland, saw faces floating like pink moons above me. I recognized one of them: Nulty, Under-Secretary of Defense.

" . . . . ranking surviving officer," he was saying. "As senior line captain since the terrible losses in Monday's engagement. . . . assured you'll be fit for duty in three weeks. . . . temporary rank of vice admiral. . . . grave crisis. . . ." His voice faded in and out. Other voices seemed to come and go. Time passed. Then I was awake, feeling the artificial clearheadedness of drug-induced alertness. Nulty was sitting beside the bed.

" . . . . hope you've understood what we've been saying, Maclamore," he said. "It's of vital importance that the flagship be fully operational as soon as possible. I've posted Captain Selkirk to her as acting CO until you could assume command. We don't know what the Bloc may be doing at this moment, but it's vital that our defensive posture not be permitted to deteriorate, in spite of the terrible tragedies that have struck us."

"Why me?" I managed.

"All but a handful of staff officers of flag rank were lost in the fight," he said in a voice that quivered with tension and fatigue. "The President agreed; you're Academy-trained, with vast operational experience—"

"What about Braze?"

"He. . . . was one of those lost in the assassination."

"So now *Rapacious* is my baby. . . . ?"

"I'm hoping you'll be able to board her within a day or two. I've ordered special medical facilities installed, and the surgeon general has agreed you can complete your convalescence there. I have reports for you to read, Maclamore. The Bloc is aware of the confusion here. They'll be wasting no time. . . ." His face was close to me, worried.

"What will you do, Admiral?" he demanded. "You'll be commanding the entire surviving armed force of the UN. What will you do. . . . ?"

A man in green came then and whispered, and Nulty went away. The lights went off. It was late; the shadows of evening were long on the walls.

I lay in the darkness and pondered my reply.

The Day Before Forever

Prologue

Somewhere a bell was ringing. The Old Man reached out in the darkness, fumbled across rumpled silks for the heavy velvet pull cord. He tugged it twice, imperiously.

"Sir!" a voice responded instantly.

"Get him!"

The Old Man lay back among the scattered cushions.

He's alive, he thought. *Somewhere in the city, he's alive again. . . .*

I

It was a narrow street, without curbs or sidewalks, jammed between flat gray walls that ran in a straight line as far as I could see. Misty light filtered down from above on a heavy ornamental ironwork gate set in the wall across the way. There were no people in sight, no parked cars, no doorways, no windows. Just the wall and the gate and the street, and a rumble through my shoes like heavy machinery grinding up boulders in the distance.

I took a step away from the wall and the pain hit me. The top of my skull felt like the place John Henry had picked to drive his last spike. Cold rain was trickling down my face and a cut on my lip was leaking salty blood that mixed with the rain. I looked at the palms of my hands; they were crisscrossed with shallow cuts, and there was rust and grime in the cuts. That started me trying to remember when I'd had my last tetanus shot, but thinking just made my head hurt worse.

A few feet to the left an alley mouth cut back into the wall behind me; I had a feeling something unpleasant might come out of it any minute now, and a little curiosity stirred as to what might be at the other end, but it was just a passing thought. I needed a dark hole to crawl into and hide before I could take a lot of interest in unimportant matters like where I was and what I was running from. I got a good grip on my head and pushed away from the wall. The pavement rocked like a Channel steamer in a three-quarter gale, but it stayed under me. I made the thirty feet across the street and put a shoulder against the wall to steady it and waited for the little whirly lights to go away. My pulse was hammering a little, but no worse than you'd expect after the kind of weekend that could put a man out on a strange pavement talking to himself. The chills were fading out now, and I was starting to sweat. My coat felt tight under the arms, and the collar was rubbing the back of my neck. I looked at my sleeve. It was stiff, shiny cloth; no class, no style. Somebody else's coat. I breathed through my teeth a few times to blow some of the fog out of my brain, but it didn't seem to help. It must have been one hell of a party, but it was all gone now, like easy money.

I checked my pockets; except for some loose threads and a pinch of lint I was as clean as a Salvation Army lassie catching the last bus back from the track.

The placard attached to the gate caught my eyes. Weathered block letters spelled out:

PARK CLOSED AT SUNDOWN
BY ORDER OF COMMISSION
ENTER AT RISK OF LIFE

I looked through the gate. If it was a park, there might be a nice patch of grass to lie down on. The line about risk of life might have called for some looking into, but next to a nap, what was a little gamble like that? I pushed on the iron curlicues and the gate swung in.

White marble steps led down, flanked by big urns full of black fronds. At the bottom, a wide flagstone walk led away between clipped borders and flowering shrubs. The dark green smell of night-blooming flowers was strong here; I heard the soft play of water in a fountain that caught reflections from lights strung in the hedges. Away in the distance beyond the park other lights crossed the sky in rows like high bridges. The light breeze made lonesome noises in the branches over me. It was a nice place, but something in the air kept me from wanting to curl up on the grass and compose a sonnet about it.

The walkway I was on was of patterned brick, bordered by little white flowers that led away into the shadows of trees. I followed it, listening for sneaky footsteps behind me. As far as I could tell, there weren't any; but the exposed feeling up my back didn't go away.

There was something on the grass, under the trees ahead. Something pale, with a shape that I couldn't quite make out. At first I thought it was an old pair of pants; then it looked like a naked man lying with his upper half in shadow. I kept on trying to make it look that way until I was ten feet from it; at that range, I quit kidding myself. It was a man, all right; but his upper half wasn't in shadow. It wasn't there at all. He'd been cut in two just below the ribs.

I circled around him, maybe with a vague idea of finding the rest of him. Up closer, I could see he'd been bisected by hand, not neatly, but in a businesslike way, as if the cutter had a lot of carcasses to get out tonight and couldn't waste too much time on fancy cleaverwork. There wasn't much blood around; he'd been drained before being cut up. I was just getting ready to roll him over in case he was lying on a clue, when something made a little sound no louder than a grain of corn popping.

I moved off across turf like black Wilton, stepped in under an odor of juniper, and stared at a lot of shadowy shapes that might have been twenty-man gangs for all I knew, and waited for something that seemed to be about to happen. A minute went by that way.

With no more sound than a shadow makes moving on a wall, a man stepped into view fifteen feet from me. He put his head up and sniffed the air like a hound. When he turned his head his eyes caught the light with a dull shine. He stood with one shoulder high, the other twisted under the load of a hump like a crouched monkey. His face was pockmarked, and there were scars across his shaved skull. A lumpy strip of keloid ran from under his left ear down under the collar of a thick sweater. Heavy thigh muscles showed through tight pants with a camouflage pattern of diagonal gray lozenges. There was a heavy wooden handle in his belt with a blade that was honed to a thin finger of steel like a butcher's trimming knife. He swung slowly; when he was facing my way, he stopped. I stood still and tried to think like a plant. He squinted into the shadows, and then grinned, not a pretty grin.

"Come out nice, sweetie." He had a husky bass growl that went with the scar on his throat. "Keep the hands in sight."

I didn't move. He made a quick motion with his left hand; there was a soft sound and a second man came out of the bushes on his left, hefting a working length of iron pipe. This one was older, wider, with thick arms and bowed legs and a stubbly beard shot with gray. He had little sow's eyes that flicked past me and back.

The hunchback touched his filed blade with a finger and said, "All alone in the park, hey? That ain't smart, palsy."

"Chill the buzz," the one with the beard said through his left nostril. "Slice it and haul, that's the rax."

He reached inside his shirt, brought something out gripped in his fist; I got a whiff of a volatile polyester.

The hunchback moved closer.

"You got anybody'll buy you for live meat?" he talked with a lot of mouth movement that showed me a thick pink tongue and broken teeth. Off to my left, somebody was generating a fair amount of noise making yardage around to my rear. I ignored that, ignored the question.

"Better open up." The hunchback slid the knife out and held it on his palm. I took a step out from under the tree then.

"Don't scare me to death," I told him. "I've got friends on the force."

"Talks like a Cruster," the bearded one whined. "Caw, Rutch, take the mothering weed down and let's fade."

"Try me, baby," I threw a line at him, just to keep him interested. "I eat your kind for breakfast."

Behind me, a stick cracked. Rutch tossed the knife on his palm, then stepped in and feinted short. I didn't move. That meant I was slow. Beaver hefted his pipe and took a bite out of the inside of his cheek. Rutch was watching my hands. He didn't see any guns, so he moved in that last foot and gave the high sign.

Behind me, the Indian fighter took a noisy step and wrapped arms around me and leaned back. That put him where I wanted him. I used my right shoe to rake down his shin and tramped hard on his arch. The grip slipped an inch, which gave me room to snap-kick the hunchback below the knee. The bone went with a crunch like a dropped plate. I gripped hands with myself and gave the lad behind me a couple of elbows in the short ribs; he *oofed* and let go and Rutch fell past me in time for me to meet Beaver coming in with his club swung up overhead like the royal executioner getting set to lop off a head. I caught his arm between my crossed wrists, shifted grips, and broke his elbow. He hit on his face and squealed and the club bounced off my back.

The one who had done the back door work was on his hands and knees, coming up. He looked like a half-breed Chinaman, with a wide, shiny face and lots of unhealthy-looking fat along the jaw line. I sent him back with a knee to the chin and stood over him, breathing hard; my wind wasn't what it should have been. I was glad none of them looked like getting up.

The Chinaman and the beard were out cold, but the one called Rutch was humping on the grass like a baby mouse in a bonfire. I went over to him and flipped him on his back.

"Your boys are soft, and too slow for the work," I told him. I nodded at what was on the grass. "Yours?"

He spat in the direction of my left knee and missed.

"Nice town," I said. "What's the name of it?"

His mouth worked. The stubble on his head was orange-red, and up close I could see the pale freckles across the knob of gristle he used for a nose. A tough redhead, in spite of the crooked back. I put a foot on his hand and leaned on it.

"Tell it, Red. What's the racket?"

He made a move and I leaned a little harder.

"Deathers. . . . in the park. . . . tonight. . . . !" He said it in quick gasps, like a drowning man dictating a will between waves.

"More detail, Red. I catch on slow."

"Blackies. . . ." There was a little foam at the corners of his mouth and he was grunting softly, like a hound dreaming of rabbits. I didn't blame him for that. A broken knee is pretty hard to bottle

up. Then his eyes rolled up. I started to turn away, half heard the
sound and swung back, saw the shine on the blade in his hand
an instant before the blow low on my back and the hot-poker pain
of the knife going in.

The shock effect on the human nervous system of a stab wound
varies a lot with different subjects. Sometimes the victim falls out
flat on his face before he's lost the first ounce of blood. Other times
he'll walk home, go to bed, and quietly bleed to death, unaware
that he's even been hit. With me it was somewhere in between. I
felt the blade hit bone and deflect upward, and all the while my
right hand was coming around edge-on in a flat arc that connected
with Red's superior maxillary just below the nose, a messy spot.
He fell back hard and didn't move, and I stood over him, trying
to get hold of my side with both hands. A heavy pulse was gushing
down over my hip like a spillway. I took three steps, felt my knees
going, sat down hard on the ground, still trying to hold the wound
closed. I was clear-headed, but the strength had gone out of me.
I sat there listening to my pulse hammer in my ears and thinking
about trying it again just as soon as it quieted down.

*Come on, Dravek, on your feet. Back home you're supposed to be
a tough guy. . . .*

I made what I thought was a move to get up and went over
sideways, slowly, like an old tree falling. I lay there with a mouthful
of sod, listening to the wind sighing in the trees, a soft gobbling
sound from Rutch or one of his boys—and another sound, like
stealthy feet creeping up through the underbrush. Or maybe it was
just the bats flapping their wings in the attic. My eyes were wide
open and I could see the fat Chinaman's feet, and beyond him a
lot of black shadows. One of the shadows moved, and a man was
standing there, looking at me.

He was small, lean, spidery, dressed in tight black. He came
across toward me, through a sort of luminous mist that had sprung
up suddenly. I thought of a couple of things I wanted to say, but
somebody had cut the strings operating my talk-box. I watched
him skirt the Chinaman, come over, and stop a couple of feet from
me. It was very dark now; I could barely make out the shape of
his boots against the black. I heard a sound that seemed to be a
nice easy laugh, like a guy who's just heard a mildly funny joke,
and a voice from a long way off seemed to say, "Neat, very neat. . . ."

Things got hazy then. I felt hands moving over me; the pain in my side was like a line of fading red fire.

"Lie still," somebody said in a whispery voice. "I have to stop the bleeding."

I started to say that Red had put the point in an inch too high, that all he'd sliced was fat and gristle, but it came out as a grunt.

"I gave you a shot of fun juice," the same voice said. It was a breathy tenor, as soft as a fog at sea. "It was all I had."

The hands did some more things that hurt, but it was a remoter pain now. A nice warm feeling was spreading up my side. I lay still and breathed.

"There," the voice said. "Do you suppose you could stand?"

I grunted on purpose this time and rolled over on my face. I got my knees under me and rested on all fours, watching the trees sail past like the view from a merry-go-round.

"We'd better hurry," the little man said. "They're close."

I said, "Yeah," and got my feet under me and climbed to my feet like a weekend Alpinist doing the last few yards to the top of Annapurna. We looked at each other across a stretch of smooth-mowed grass unmarred by anything except three and a half corpses. He was a slender-built, dainty-moving man with the sharp, complicated features of a Bourbon king, a sleek, narrow head with bugged-out eyes set on the corner of it, deft hands in black kid gloves. The tight pants were tucked into short boots, and he wore a ducky little vest with ruffles along the top edge over a black turtleneck.

"Who were they?" I asked, just to break the silence. My voice came out in a croak.

He glanced down at the nearest of them, who happened to be the Chinaman; the fat face had that vacant, collapsed look you see on photos of bodies found on a battlefield. The little man lifted a lip and showed me a row of sharp teeth that were too white to be real.

"Scum," he said delicately. "Baiters; cold-meat men. Their kind are the lowest of the low." He laughed. "Whereas I am the highest of the low." I could hardly hear him for the zinging in my head. My legs felt like something snipped out of cardboard. I rubbed the back of my head, but it didn't help. I still felt like a guy who's stepped into what he thought was the men's room and wound up in the third act of *Aïda*.

"You a cop?" I said.

"A. . . . ?"

"Cop. Dick. The law."

He said "ah" and lifted his chin. A light came and went behind his eyes. "No, I am not a, ah, cop. But we'll talk later. You've lost a considerable amount of blood, but I think you can manage the walk. It's just to the edge of the park." His voice was coming through with a lot of static, like a transatlantic broadcast.

"I was just passing through on my way to the Greyhound station," I got the words out past a tongue like a sock full of sand. "Just point me that way and I'll drift out of your life."

He shook his head. "That's hardly safe, while the native wildlife is abroad. Just. . . . along. . . . my place. . . . car. . . ." He was tuning in and out now; the static was getting worse on the short-wave band. I thought about lying down, but then my feet were working. He was towing me along and I gave up and followed, trying not to bump my head on my knees. I remember going under dark shrubbery, pushing through a hedge like a barbed-wire entanglement over what felt like dead men's bones but were probably just tree roots. Then I was getting helped into the seat of a small shiny car that looked like something hand-tooled for the King of Siam. It did a U-turn on a Kennedy dime and took off straight up. I knew then I was dreaming, so I leaned back into a seat upholstered with clouds and let it all slide.

2

Voices woke me. For a while I tried to ignore them, but something in the tone of the conversation made me prick up my ears.

One of the voices belonged to the little man from the park, a couple of lifetimes ago. He sounded as though he had a nice glow working; or maybe he was just excited. The female voice was husky and low—lower than his—with an edge to it like a sawed board. It was saying:

" . . . . you're a fool to take a risk like this, Jess!"

"Minka, my dear, they have no way of knowing—"

"How do you know what they have? This is Death Control you're playing with now, not some tee-cee meat-legger!"

I felt as dopey as a shanghaied deckhand, but I got an eyelid up, was looking at a high ceiling with ornate fretwork in gold and white. The walls under it were white, with little dabs of bright-colored tile here and there. There were a couple of chairs like pastel-toned eggshells perched on slim shiny rods, and a low table with a silver bowl half the size of a washtub, full of oversized bananas and pears, and grapes as big as golf balls. The floor was white, and there were silky-looking rugs spread on it.

I was lying on a neat little white bunk like a night nurse's cot, set up in a corner. My shirt was gone, and there was a layer of rubbery clear plastic over the six-inch slash in my side. I turned my head, not without a certain effort, and was looking past a row of columns along the far side of the room at blue sky that showed between them. Beyond the columns a terrace spread out, catching yellow sunlight. The little man was there, dressed in a pale pink suit with lace at the wrists. He was sitting in a violet chair worrying a fingernail.

The woman sitting with him was like something painted up to stand in front of a cigar store. Her hair was a varnished swirl of indigo, like a breaking wave, and there were faint orange spirals drawn on her cheeks, with the ends trailing down under her chin. Her outfit seemed to consist of a lot of colored ribbons, carelessly draped. All of this didn't disguise the fact that the bone structure was good enough to send a fashion photographer grabbing for his baby spots.

"You don't know who—or what—he might be," she was saying. "I thought your Secret Society had rules about picking up strangers."

"This is different! They were tracking him! They wanted him alive! Don't you see it?" The small man was waving both arms now. "If they *want* him—*I* want him!"

"Why do they want him?" she came back fast.

"I've admitted I don't know—yet. But you may be sure I'll find out. And then. . . ."

"Then it's going to fall in on you, Jess! They don't bother with the rats in the dump—until one of them comes out and tries to steal the food off their plates."

Jess brought his hands up and made a clawing motion, as if he were shredding a curtain.

"Don't be a blind grub of a stupid Preke! After all these years, this is an opportunity—the first in my time—"

"I *am* a Preke." The woman's face was stiff as a plaster cast, and under the lacquer job, about the same color. "That's all I ever was—ever will be. And you're—what you are. Face it, Jess, make the best—"

"Accept this? From them?" Jess jumped up and raked at his chest as if he were trying to tear off a sign somebody had hung on him. "I could hold the universe in my hands!" He showed her his cupped palms. "But they—these upstarts who aren't fit to carry out my grandfather's garbage—they say 'no!'"

"You're not your grandfather, Jess."

"You'd preach to me, you bedizened Preke trollop!" He leaned across toward the woman and shook the backs of his hands at her. She lifted a corner of her mouth at him.

"I've liked you for what you are, Jess; the other never meant anything to me."

"You're a lying, scheming Preke slut!" Jess was screeching like a dry bearing now. "After all I've done to raise you from your filthy dirtside beginnings, when I need your help—"

"Be quiet, Jess. You'll wake him."

"Bah! I've shot him full of enough lethenol to paralyze a platoon of Blackies. . . ." But he got up. I closed my eyes, listened to them come in and cross the floor to me. Neither of them said anything for half a minute.

"Caw, he's big enough," the woman said.

Jess tittered. "I had to strap two lift units to him to get him here."

"Was he badly hurt?"

"Just a nasty cut. I've given him two liters of blood, full spec with nutes."

"Why would they want anyone—alive?"

"He must know something," Jess sounded awed. "Something important."

"What could he know, that ETORP needs?"

"That's what I have to discover."

"You're a fool, Jess."

"Will you help me—or do you really intend to desert me, now that I need you?" Jess hissed the last words like a stepped-on snake.

"If it's what you want—of course I'll do what I can," the girl's voice was dull.

"Good girl. I knew you would. . . ." Their feet went away.

Something clicked and the room became very still. I opened my eyes again. I was alone.

For a while I lay there where I was and looked at the fancy ceiling and waited for the memories to come flooding back; but nothing happened. I was still just Steve Dravek, former tough guy, once reputed to be a pretty savvy character but now not even sure what day it was or what continent I was on. Jess had sounded American, and so did the girl, but that didn't prove anything. The park could have been anywhere, and the street. . . . Well, in retrospect the street was a lot like something out of a dream fraught with obscure psychological significance. I wouldn't count the street.

Okay, Dravek; so where does that leave us?

In unfamiliar surroundings, broke, and nursing a knife wound— not a totally unique situation. I've come to in some pretty strange places in my time: from flophouses and fifty-cent dormitories where you could hear the crickets running footraces in the woodwork, to hundred-dollar-a-night suites with mink bath mats, where little lost ladies tapped discreetly at unexpected hours, trailing ninety-dollar-a-dram smells. A few times, I've started a day in a vacant lot with my pockets inside out; and now and then I've even awakened in a chintzy little bedroom with lots of hard morning sun shining in on the installment-plan furniture, showing up cracks in the wallpaper and flaws in complexions; and once I woke up in the hold of a Panamanian-registry banana scow sailing out of Mobile under a former Nazi destroyer skipper. He lived on mush for six weeks after I kicked in the door to his cabin and laid the schnapps bottle he was breakfasting from alongside his jaw. I was only seventeen at the time, but already pretty husky.

Yeah, I knew what it was like to wake up a little confused, throbbing a little here and there, with a mouth like an abandoned mouse nest and nothing but a set of raw knuckles and a fresh tattoo to help me reconstruct preceding events. But this time I didn't remember the celebration, or the cause for the celebration. What I did remember was an office paneled in dark, waxy wood, and a mean-looking old geezer with crew-cut white hair, nodding and saying, "Sure, Steve, if that's the way you want it."

Frazier. The name came slowly, like something remembered from a long time ago.

But what the hell—Frazier was my drinking buddy, a lean, wiry kid with bushy black hair and enough reach to spot most light-heavies ten pounds and a horseshoe. . . .

But he was the old man, too. . . . I shook my head to get rid of the double exposure, and did some deep breathing. *Try again, Dravek.*

This time I got a big room like a blimp hangar, full of pipes and noise and sharp, sour smells. Lots of smoke in the air—or mist—and more mist rising from tanks like oversized oxygen bottles.

No help there. Once more.

This time I got a woman's face: high cheekbones, big dark eyes, red-brown hair that came down to slim shoulders, the willowy figure of a thoroughbred. . . . but no name; no identity.

Come on, Dravek! You can do better than that: Address, phone number, occupation, last seen on the night of. . . .

Back to that. I turned my head and was looking across the room at a flat black case, lying on the table by the door. It looked like a case with something in it.

Sitting up was hard work, but no harder than carrying a safe up a fire escape. The side gave signals, and I felt a warm, wet-diaper feeling against my ribs that meant something had ripped a little, but I got my feet on the floor and pushed. Nothing happened except for a little sweat popping out where my hackles would have been if I'd had any hackles. The next try was better; I was as heavy as a lead-lined casket, but I made it across to the table. Coach called another time out then while I sat on the floor and pushed back a low fog that wanted to roll in over the scene. When my head cleared I went to work on the case.

It was rectangular, about two inches thick, six inches by eight, made of a soft, leathery material. My finger touched something and the top snicked back. I poked around in the kind of junk women have carted in handbags since Nefertiti's day. There was a long, curved comb, metal tubes of paint, a little box that rattled, some plastic shapes like charms for a charm bracelet, a folded paper that looked like a photostat of a magazine article. I opened it; except for the shorthand spelling, it read like a news item, written in the gushy tones of a fashion hack, all about the new Raped Look and the exciting corpse-colors that were taking the Crust by storm. There was nothing in that for me.

I started to toss it back and the line of print at the top caught my eye. It wasn't much, just a date: Sarday, Ma 33, 2103.

For a minute, the floor under my feet, the whole room, the city around me, seemed to turn to a thin gas, something my suppressed id had thought up during one of those long, hard nights just before the fever breaks.

"Twenty-one-oh-three," I said. "Ha—that's a good one." I dropped the paper on the floor and looked around at the room. It looked solid enough. There was a cool breeze moving in off the terrace now, and out beyond the columns I could see a couple of friendly-looking clouds. They had a nice familiar look that helped a lot just then.

"That makes next week my birthday," I said, but it didn't come out sounding cute. "My hundred and sixty-second. . . ."

There wasn't much more I could do with that. I put the stuff back in the handbag and ate a couple of grapes to restore my strength and started checking the room.

There were three sealed openings in the wall that were probably doors, but poking and prodding didn't open them. I went out on the terrace and looked out across empty space at a couple of fanciful-looking towers poking up through a cloud layer maybe five hundred feet below. The drop from the balustrade was vertical. That didn't tell me much about where I was, except that it was a place I'd never heard of. I went back inside, prowled the wall near the bed where the tile patterns looked a little different, found a hairline crack, and leaned on it. Something clicked and a closet door popped open. I found a plain dark pullover to replace the shirt I'd been wearing. A drawer under the closet contained a supply of the kind of frilly items the little man called Jess would want next to his skin. I poked around under them, touched something cool and smooth. It looked like the offspring of an automatic and a mixmaster. I thought about taking it, but I wasn't sure which end the medicine came out of.

Another few minutes of scratching at the wall used up the rest of my energy, but netted me no more trophies. I ate one of the bananas and stretched out on the bed to wait. I listened to the wind flirting around the columns and tried to stay awake; but after a while I dropped off into a restless dream about a big room full of noise and excited faces, and a smaller room with smoke curling out past an open door, and a big tank, painted green. There was a man in a white uniform with blood on his face, and a woman, crying, and I was saying, "That's an order, damn your guts!" And then they were all backing away and I picked up the bundle in my arms and went in through the smoky door and heard behind me the sound of the woman, crying.

3

The sunny blue sky had turned to scarlet and purple before my host came back, humming a little tune between his teeth. The woman was with him. She left after a minute, and I played possum while he thumbed back my eyelid; then he went across to the wall and got busy poking buttons on a console that swung out on command. He took something out of a slot, held it up to the light and frowned at it, came back over to me and took hold of my arm. That was my signal to take hold of his neck. He squawked and flapped his arms and the thing in his hand hit the floor. I got my feet under me and stood up; he went for a pocket with one hand and I shifted grips and took him up against the wall. His eyes goggled at me.

"What have you got that's good for a lethenol hangover, Jess?" I leaned on him and let him get a swallow of air in past my thumb.

"Let me go. . . ." It was a thin squeak like a rubber rat.

"How long have I been here?"

"Thirty hours—but—"

"Who are you, Jess? What's your racket?"

"Are you. . . . out of your mind? I saw you were in difficulty—"

"Why'd you butt in? It strikes me that park's rough territory for a little fellow like you."

He kicked and made choking sounds and I slacked off a little to let some of the purple drain out of his face.

He twisted his mouth into a grin like a wounded fox. "One has one's little hobbies," he got out, and tried to bite me. I pounded his head on the wall a few times. They both sounded solid. All this effort started my head humming again. "You're tough, Jess," I told him. "I'm tougher."

He tried with a finger for the eye, and I knocked him down and held him on the floor with a knee in his back and slapped his pockets. I found a couple of scented tissues and some plastic tokens. He said a few things, none of them helpful.

"You're making me curious, Jess," I tried to talk without panting. "It must be important dope you're hanging on to."

"If you'll take your thumb out of my throat so that we can talk together like civilized men, I'll tell you what I can. Otherwise, you may kill me and be damned to you!" He said it in a new voice, nothing like the whine he'd been using.

I let him sit up. "Let's start with who *they* are," I said. "The ones that wanted me alive."

"Blackies. Commission men." He spat the words.

"Make it plainer."

"Death Control, damn you! How plain does it have to be?"

"How do you know it's me they want?"

"I heard them talking. In the park."

"So you snatched me out from under their noses. What made me worth taking the chance?"

He tried out a couple of expressions, settled on a sad smile like a mortician suggesting a more appropriate tribute to a departed loved one.

"Really, you have a suspicious nature. I overheard nothing further than that they had seen you enter the park." He gave me a quick look. "By the way, how did *you* happen to be there?"

"I wandered in off the street. Maybe I was a little drunk."

He gave me a catty smile. He was getting his wind back fast. "I saw your work. Very clever—except for the carelessness just at the last."

"Yeah. Red fooled me."

"You would have bled to death."

I nodded. "Thanks for sticking me back together. That's one I owe you."

"How are you feeling now?" He cocked his head as if the answer was worth a lot of money and he didn't want to miss any overtones.

"Like it happened to two other guys. By the way, you wouldn't have a drink around the place?"

He looked at my hand holding his ruffled shirt. "May I?"

I stepped back and he got up and went past me to the alcove with the buttons, and punched a couple. He said "ah" and came back with a right-looking glass.

"Better get two."

He followed instructions. I traded glasses, watched him drink half of his, then tried mine. It tasted like perfumed apple juice, but I drank it anyway. Maybe it helped. My head seemed to clear a little. Jess dabbed the blood off his chin with a tissue. He got out a flat case and extracted a thin cigarette no thicker than a matchstick, fitted it into a pair of little silver tongs, took a sip from it like a hummingbird sampling the first nectar of spring. He was looking relaxed now, as if we were old school chums having a cozy chat.

"You're a stranger here in the city," he said, making it casual. "Where do you come from?"

"Well, Jess, I have a little problem there. I don't exactly remember how I got to your town. I was hoping you might tell me."

He looked solemn and alert, like a sympathetic judge just before he hits you with the book. "I?"

"Our gentlemanly arrangement isn't going to work out unless you play, too, Jess."

"Really, you're asking the impossible," he said. "What would I know of you—a perfect stranger?"

I banged my glass on the table and leaned over and put my face an inch from his. "Try a guess," I said.

He looked me in the eye. "Very well," he said. "My guess is that you're an ice case, illegally out of low-O."

"What's that mean?"

"If I'm right," he said, "for the past hundred years or more, your body has been in an ETORP cryothesis vault—frozen solid at absolute zero."

Half an hour later, with a couple more innocent-tasting drinks under my belt, I was still asking questions and getting answers that made me ask more questions.

" . . . . most of the low-O's were placed in a cold stasis by relatives: persons who were ill, with a then-incurable ailment—or injured in an accident. Their hope was that in time a cure would be found, and they'd be awakened. Of course, they never were. The dead stay dead. ETORP owns them now."

"I was never sick a day in my life. Outside of that, it sounds like a good story."

Jess shook his head. "The difficulty is that there hasn't been an authorized thaw for over fifty years, to my knowledge. And if you'd been revived under official sanction, you'd have awakened in an

ETORP 'doc ward, with a cephalotaper clamped to your skull, pumping you full of a canned ETORP briefing, not wandering the streets in an amnesiac condition."

"Maybe a relative did the job."

"Relatives—of a corpse who's been on ice for a century? Not even your own great-great-grandchildren would know anything of you—and if they did—would they give up their own visas for you?" Jess wagged his head. "And in any event, laws have been passed. We can't have the dead waking up, they tell us; there's no room for them, with a world population of twenty billion. And they cite the legal complications, hold up the specter of old diseases released. They make a good case, but the real reason is. . . ." he looked at me, watching for my reaction. "Spare parts," he said crisply.

"Go on."

"Consider it!" He leaned toward me, slitted his eyes. "Perfectly good arms and legs and kidneys, going to waste—and outside— people needing them, dying for want of them! They're ready to pay ETORP's price, perform any service in return for life and health!"

"What's this ETORP?"

"Eternity, Incorporated."

"Sounds like a cemetery."

"A. . . . ?"

"Where you bury the dead ones."

"The Blackies would gather you in for a trick like that." He sounded a little indignant. "The minerals are valuable, even if the hulk is useless."

"You were telling me about ETORP."

"ETORP controls the most precious commodity of all: life. It issues birth permits and life visas, performs transplants and cosmetic surgery, supplies rejuve and longevity treatments and drugs. Technically, it's a private corporation, operating under the Public Constitution. In fact, it rules our society with an iron hand."

"What about the government?"

"Pah! A withered organ, dangling anachronistically from the body politic. What power is there that compares with life? Money? Military force? What are they to a dying man?"

"Nice business. How did ETORP get the monopoly?"

"The company began simply enough, with patented drugs and techniques, invented in their own laboratories and closely controlled. Then they developed the frozen organ banks; then whole-body cryothesia. After the development of the cancer cures and the perfection of *ex-utero* cultures, there was a last-ditch legal fight with a group calling themselves the Free Life Party. They charged the company with murder and abortion, sacrilege, desecration of the dead, all manner of crimes. They lost, of course. The bait ETORP had to dangle over judges' heads was irresistible. After that, ETORP's power burgeoned at geometric rates. It bought and sold legislators like poker chips. It became a tyrant that ruled with a whip in one hand and a sweet in the other! And all the while, its vaults were filling with freeze cases, waiting for a resurrection that would never come."

"So Uncle Elmer never woke up after all. . . ."

"So sad," Jess said. "All those trusting souls, saying goodbye, kissing their children and wives and going off to the hospital, leaving pitiful little notes to be opened on anniversaries, going under the anesthetic babbling of the parties they'd stage when they came back. . . . and now—a century later—sawed apart to be sold from open stock to the lucky ones with negotiable skills, or handed out as door prizes to faithful company hacks. And bodies! Whole bodies, an almost unlimited supply, something that had never been plentiful. That was where the power was, Steve—that was what made ETORP! What was a billion dollars to a ninety-year-old mummy in a wheelchair? He'd pay it all for a twenty-year-old body—possibly keeping a million or two in reserve for a new stake."

"Maybe I'm slow. What good would a dead body do him?"

"Dead?" Jess' eyebrows went up. "It's the *living* body that's valuable, Steve. A young hulk, cured of its once-fatal ailments, will fetch its weight in graymarket chits." I was still frowning at him, and he added, "For brain transfer, you understand."

"Do I?"

He looked surprised. "There are always wealthy Crusters and Dooses with lapsed visas. For a price, it's easy enough to arrange new papers—but those are worthless to a man with a dying body. And prime hulks are in short supply. Dirties won't do, of course; riddled with defects."

"You're talking about scooping out a man's brains and putting somebody else's in?"

"Even in your day the surgical transplant of limbs and organs was practiced. The brain is simply another organ."

"OK; so I'm wanted by the law for illegally rising from the dead. Where does that leave us? Who thawed me? And why?"

Jess thought about it for three puffs of his dope stick. "Steve—how old were you—*are* you?"

I felt the question over in my mind. I had the feeling the answer was on the tip of my tongue, but I couldn't quite pin it down. "About fifty," I said. "Middle-aged."

Jess got up and went across to a table, came back with a hand mirror and an ivory handle.

"Look at yourself."

I took the mirror. It was a good glass, nine inches square. It showed me a face that was mine, all right; but the hairline was an inch lower on the forehead than it should have been, and the lines I'd collected in a lot of years were gone like the shine on five-dollar shoes. I looked like a new recruit for the freshman grid squad, turned down for underage.

4

"Tell me about yourself, Steve," Jess said. "Anything at all. Start at the beginning—your earliest memories."

"I remember the early days all right. My childhood, if you can call it that." I rubbed the side of my face and tried to think about it, but the ideas that should have been ready to jump into my mind felt rusty and old, as if I hadn't thought about them, hadn't used the words, for a long, long time.

"I was kicked up in a tough part of Philly, went to sea, joined the Army when the Chinese busted loose in Burma. After the war I went to school, got enough education to start in as a white-collar man with a grocery chain. Five years later, I owned the company. . . ." I listened to myself talking, remembering it all in a vague, academic sort of way, as if it was something I saw in the movies.

"Go on."

"The office; the plant. A big car with two telephones. . . ." Shadowy memories were taking shape; but there was something dark there I didn't like.

"What else?" Jess whispered.

"I remember my days at sea better." This was a safer subject; I was talking to myself now, looking into the past. "That was real: The stinks and the rust on the deck and the mold growing on my shore shoes, and coastlines in the morning like white reefs coming out of the mist, and the noise and the lights in port at night, and the waterfront joints and the lousy booze and the guy that used to play sad tunes on the fantail after the hatches were down."

"It sounds quite romantic."

"Like a case of the yaws. But it had a certain something; something to do with being young and tough, sleep anywhere, eat anything, fight anybody. . . ."

"Tell me about your business associates. Perhaps one of them. . . ." he let it trail off. I thought about it, tried to sort out the conflicting impressions. A young fellow with black hair; an old bird with a neck like a turkey. . . .

"My best pal was a fellow I served with in China and Nepal. He saved my life once; plugged the hole in my wrist where a Chink .25 mm went through." I remembered it all: The two-mile walk back to the forward aid station, handling the gun left-handed while the woods buzzed with scatter-shell fragments; the surgeons clucking like hens and then settling down to three hours of needlework that would have won prizes at the county fair, while Frazier poured slugs for both of us and kept my cigar lit. They'd done a nice job of putting nerves and blood vessels back together, but the carpal joint was never the same, and there was an inch-wide scar that was the reason I'd taken to wearing my Rolex Oyster on my left wrist. . . . I had a sudden idea, one that had been ducking around the edge of my consciousness, flapping its arms for attention ever since I woke up in the rain.

I flipped my cuff back and looked at the wrist. The skin was unflawed. The scar was gone.

"What is it?" Jess was watching my face. I turned the cuff back down.

"Nothing. Just another little slip in my grip on reality. What would you say to another shot of what we just had?"

He watched me while I poured out a nice jolt. I took it back without bothering to roll it on my tongue.

"This freezing process," I said. "Does it remove scars?"

"Why, no—"

"Does it make you look younger?"

"Nothing of that sort, Steve—"

"Then scratch your theory."

"What do you mean?"

"If I was one of your freeze cases, I'd remember a brick wall running at me, or a sickbed and a flock of medicine bottles and some old goat shaking his whiskers and saying, 'Ice this boy until I figure out what to do next.'"

Jess pushed his lips in and out. "It's quite possible that the trauma associated with the shock—"

"It wasn't an accident; no scars, remember? And if I had a fatal ailment—who cured it?"

He looked a little nervous. "Perhaps you weren't cured."

"Relax, cancer's not catching."

"Steve—this is no joking matter! We have to find out who you are, what you know that makes you a threat to ETORP!"

"I'm no threat. I'm just a mixed-up guy who wants to get unmixed and back to minding my own business."

"They're afraid of you! Nothing else could explain a class Y search for you—and therein lies a weapon to be used against them!"

"If you're talking revolution, count me out."

"Count you out—on the quest for the greatest prize the world has ever known?"

"What are you dancing around the edge of, Jess?"

His eyes went to slits with a glint back of them like Midas thinking about Fort Knox.

"Immortality."

"Sure. Throw in flying carpets while you're at it."

"It's no myth, Steve! They have it! It's there, don't you understand? We don't have to die! We could live forever! But will they share it with us? No, they let us toil and die like grubs in an ant heap!"

"You toil, Jess? Don't tickle me; my side still hurts."

"Longevity treatments, rejuve!" Jess spat out the words like a dirty taste. "A sop for the tech class they need to keep their corrupt machine functioning. Limb and organ graft and regeneration—and the ultimate iniquity, brain transfer, and the attendant black market in bodies that makes it unsafe for an unarmed man to walk abroad at night. And all in order to keep up the value of their stock-in-trade!"

"Times haven't changed much," I said. "In my day it was Zionist plots and pills you could drop in the gas tank to convert water to gasoline."

"You think I'm raving? Consider it, Steve! Medical research long ago synthesized protoplasm, created life in the laboratory, cured cancer—and in the process, inevitably discovered the secret of the aging process. It's a disease, like any other—and they've cured it. Nature doesn't care, you see; her intent was only to preserve the individual past the breeding age. Fifteen years to sexual maturity, another fifteen years of vigorous life to see the next generation on the way—then—decay. Just as we've begun to learn to live, we begin to die! No wonder the race lives in anarchy and turmoil, each generation repeating the mistakes of the one before. The world is run by children, while our mature minds, seasoned by life, go down to death. And they could stop it!"

"How could they keep a thing like that a secret—if they had it?"

"By limiting its use to a favored few—in whose interest it would be, of course, to preserve the deception."

"Uh-huh—but somebody would notice after a while if old Mr. Gotrocks never showed up in the obit column."

"Who? Who keeps records of such things? It's not as it was in your day, Steve; we have no public figures as you knew them; we live in a rigidly stratified society; Dooses know little of the activities of Crusters; Threevees never venture down to Forkwaters; and no graded citizen ever sets foot dirtside, among the visaless Preke rabble."

"That's all guesswork, Jess. Why get excited about it—"

"There are those of us who feel that man wasn't meant to die in his prime, Steve! It's not his destiny! Life eternal is almost in our grasp—life in which to see the stars and the planets and the riches thereof—"

"Seventy years are long enough. I won't waste 'em chasing a pot of gold at the end of a cardboard rainbow."

"Seventy years?" Jess popped his eyes at me. "I'm seventy-nine now!" his voice broke. "I expect to live to a hundred and fifteen, even without the blessing of ETORP. But there's more, Steve—so much more—and that's where you can help!"

"Sorry—I've got other plans."

"Plans? You, a nobody without even an identity?"

Just then, as if it had been waiting for the signal, a cool chime cut through the still of the evening.

Jess came out of his chair like a cocky featherweight answering the bell for Round 2. All his teeth were showing in a grin that had no humor in it. The tone sounded again, twice, three times.

"Minka?" Jess asked the air.

The chime stopped and somebody pounded on the door.

"Just like old times," I said. "That sounds like copper to me, Jess."

"How could they. . . . ?" he started and then closed his mouth. He gave me a narrow-eyed look.

"You can trust me now," he said, "or not, just as you please. Neither of us wants you found here. There's one way out for us."

"What have you got in mind?"

"Out there." He pointed to the terrace. "I'll give them something to think about. What you do is up to you." He didn't wait to catch my reaction, just started across toward the door. That left me a couple of seconds to think it over. I looked around, saw three blank walls and the columns leading to the terrace. I went out, stood in the shadows.

Jess opened the door—and was backing into the room, holding his hands out from his sides. A man was pushing him and another was behind, looking as happy as his kind of face could. They were lean, slim-hipped lads, buckled into black uniforms with silver cord down the pants seams and more silver worked into their stiff stand-up collars. They wore holsters strapped down low, in working position, and their eyes had that screw-you-Jack look that spelled cop or professional soldier as far as you could hear a pair of heels click.

"Say all the right things," one of them said in a filed-steel voice, "and you could live to cash in your chits."

"What's all this?" Jess sounded a little breathless. "My visa is in order—"

The cop backhanded him down onto the floor.

"Topside wants you bad," the cop nodded. "I guess this is the first clean spring from the Palace in sixty years. Now, let's have it all: How you handled the outer ring, how you took the main vault, who did the thaw job—the works."

Jess was sitting up, looking tearful. "You're making a mistake—"

The Blackie hit him. Jess curled up on the rug and made noises like a lonely pup.

"Start now and save muscle all around," the Blackie said. "Who was your first contact?"

Jess looked up at him. "He was a big fellow, about seven-three, with chin whiskers and a glass eye," he said in a nasty tone. "I didn't get the name."

"Funny man." The Blackie swung his foot and caught Jess in the shoulder as he rolled away. The other cop kicked him back.

"Where's the other one at?"

They fanned out and looked at the bare walls. One of them blew air out over his lower lip and looked at his partner.

"I thought you had this pile staked off."

"Maybe the mothering crot's got an outlaw shaft."

"He couldn't have used it. Power block, remember?"

"We should have called this in, Supe."

I backed a quiet step; a light breeze moved palm fans in a pot beside me. They weren't big enough to help much. The boys inside didn't look any smarter than their kind usually do, but after a while it was going to occur to them to take a peek out on the back porch.

"He couldn't have gone out—" one of the cops said, and stopped. I could almost hear his brains working: If there were two guys in a locked room and only one in sight, how many are still hiding under the rug?

I thought about stepping out and trying the honest citizen route, but those guns the boys packed looked big and impatient. And even if I didn't buy Jess' program a hundred percent, there were a couple of things about this pair that put me on the other side.

"I don't like it, Supe," the number two cop was saying. "We shouldn't of played wise with a Y priority."

"There's twenty-year chits in it for the ones that take him solo. . . ." The voices were keeping up the patter, coming my way. I blinked sweat out of my eyes and waited. What I needed was a break, one lousy little break. It was too much to ask for, too much to expect from a frail-looking little fellow who had already absorbed more punches than a Golden Gloves runner-up losing the big one. But something about the little I'd seen of Jess made me set myself and get ready. . . .

When it came, it was a bleat like a docked sheep. "I'll tell you! Why should I lose my visa for that mothering weed?"

The feet held up and then went back and I eased over to the right and faded an eye past the edge of the open door. Jess was on his feet. What was holding him there was the boss Blackie. He was standing with his back to me. He had his legs planted well apart and was holding a handful of Jess' pretty green shirt in his left fist and bending him backward over the table. There was a lot of blood on the little man's face, and one eye was swollen almost shut. The other cop was leaning against the wall to the right. If he had moved his eyes an eighth of an inch he'd have been looking straight at me. I stayed where I was and waited.

"We got all night," the cop said. "Tell it now or tell it in an hour, we don't care. We like our work."

Jess mumbled something, but I wasn't paying much attention to the conversation. What I was watching was Jess' right hand. It was feeling over the table, out of sight of the other cop. The fingers worked carefully, deliberately, as though they had all the time in the world. They teased the drawer open, came out with the tip of a thin blade between them. The fingers worked the knife around until they could touch the narrow black-taped grip, closed over it. Jess' arm came up slowly, carefully, poised for a moment with the needletip just touching the black cloth stretched over the ribs of the man bending over him. Then with a smooth thrust, he put it in.

The Blackie jerked once, as if he had touched something hot. He pivoted slowly, still holding Jess.

"What are you doing?" his partner took a step toward him. The cop's hand went to his side, caressed the knife hilt that was tight against the black cloth. Then his knees went, and he hit the floor hard. The other Blackie came forward a step, raked at the gun at his hip, and I was into the room and behind him. He was slow turning and I hit him in the neck, twice, and he dropped the gun and jackknifed to the floor and lay twisted, the way they do when the spine is shattered.

I kicked the gun across the room and Jess staggered away from the table, breathing with a lot of noise. I looked at the door.

"They came alone," Jess gasped it out. He wiped blood off his mouth. "They were keeping this play to themselves. Nice for us, Steve. No one knows where they were." He made a face and I saw he was grinning.

"You're a great actor," I said. "What do you do for an encore?"

"We make a good team," he said. "A pity to break it up."

I went to the bar and poured myself a stiff one and swallowed it.

"Let's put this pair in the back closet," I said. "Then get a map of New York City, circa 1970. I think I may have an idea."

The map on the tabletop screen showed the eastern half of the state plus a chunk of Pennsylvania and Jersey. The highway grid looked a lot denser than it should have, but otherwise it was pretty normal.

"Higher mag," I said, and he focused down until the city filled the screen. I asked him to center it on Long Island, the Jamaica section, and he worked the knobs and got a blowup that showed every street and major building. I pointed to a spot. "That's it: my old plant."

"And you imagine that would be intact today? The building probably doesn't exist—"

"The spot I'm looking for wasn't exactly in a building, Jess. It was under one—a place that was built to last. I made some arrangements for that."

"You think you might have left some clue there?"

"It's a place to look."

He poked a lever. A red dot popped up at the top of the screen, and he used two knobs to guide it down to mark the plant. Then he blanked the screen and a new map came onto it. It looked like one of those webs built by a drunk spider. There were cryptic symbols all over it like Chinese alphabet soup. Jess looked up at me. There was a strange look in his eye.

"Interesting spot you've picked," he said. "This is a cartogram of modern Granyauck, overlying the site of the town you used to know. As you'll notice, the former islands have been joined to the mainland by various hydraulic works. The section you call Long Island, here. . . ." he pointed to a green blob that covered a piece of the screen—"is an ETORP preserve. The specific point in which you expressed an interest happens to coincide almost precisely with the most closely guarded premises in the North American Sector."

"What is it?"

"The Cryothesis Center," he said. "Vulgarly known as the Ice Palace." He smiled. "I think we've made a connection, Steve."

✧ ✧ ✧

Jess was pacing the floor. "It poses an interesting problem, Steve. I won't say it can't be done—I pride myself on my ability to enter presumably closed precincts—but the question remains—is it worth the risk involved?"

"If you want to back out, I'll go in alone."

"I'd like nothing better than to back out." He looked at me and I thought he looked a little pale around the jaw. "But as you said, it's our only lead. Therefore, the question is: How best to beard ETORP in his stronghold?"

He went back to his fancy desk and punched more keys, spent the next hour muttering at technical diagrams that were over my head like the Goodyear blimp.

"The Hudson outfall appears the likeliest spot," he said. "That means going dirtside, but it can't be helped."

"When do we start?"

"As soon as your wound has knit. And it will be as well for you to stay out of sight for a few days. After a century, that shouldn't matter much."

I conceded the point.

We ate then, and afterward sat out on the terrace and listened to music, some of it old enough to sound familiar. Then he showed me to a room papered with black roses and I stretched out in a shaft of moonlight and after a while slid down into a dream about a small pale face behind a pane of frosted glass and the vague shadows of forgotten sorrows as remote as a pharaoh's last wish.

5

We waited three days to make our move; my side was still tender, but Jess' medicine had healed it to a thin scar.

He fitted me out with a set of shiny black long johns that turned out to be lightweight scuba gear and led the way by back routes down into the depths of the city to a high blank wall with lights far up on it and that grim look that prisons and military installations have.

"This is the outer perimeter wall of the reserve," Jess said. I looked up at the top, fifty feet up in deep shadow.

"How do we get over it?"

"We don't, of course. We circumvent it. Come along."

I trailed him to the end of the alley, and we were facing a chest-high wall with lots of dark, cold air beyond it. I looked over it, saw black water swirling twenty feet below.

"A pleasant evening for a swim," Jess said. He pulled off his jacket and produced a slim-barreled gun from somewhere and made clicking sounds with it, checking the action. I stripped down to my frogman suit and turned up the heat control a notch higher. Jess looked me over to be sure I hadn't left my seat flap hanging down, and vaulted up on the coping of the wall, agile as a squirrel.

"Stay clear of the rungs when you dive," he said. "And be sure to keep your comset open. Its range is only about a hundred feet, under water." He gave me a casual wave, like a movie star dismissing a fan, and tilted over the edge. I hopped up on the wall, swung both legs over, and kicked off without looking, feet-first.

It seemed like a long fall before I hit water as hard as a sidewalk and felt myself tumbling in a strong current that sucked the heat out of me like a blotter. I straightened myself out facing upstream and looked for Jess. It was like swimming in an inkwell. I found my heat control and thumbed it up, then tried my water jets.

"Use more power," Jess' voice tinned very faintly in my left ear. "You're drifting off."

I found the controls and used them and Jess guided me his way. When I was three feet from him, I saw the faint phosphorescent outline of his suit. He was hanging onto a mossy pipe projecting from the retaining wall.

"We have a brisk little swim ahead of us," he told me. "The duct I was hoping to use is blocked, but there should be another, a hundred and forty meters upstream."

It was a half-hour battle. Once I angled out a little too far and the tide took me and rolled me half a dozen times before I got my keel under me again. After a while the wall beside me changed from mossy concrete to rusted metal.

"Steer for the lights," Jess transmitted. A minute or two later, I saw a greenish arc glowing off to my right that turned out to be the open mouth of a six-foot conduit. There were some symbols painted on it in luminous pink and a mechanism bolted to the side. Jess was perched on the housing, tinkering. I heard him say "ah" and the louvers that blocked the mouth pivoted and I could see light coming from inside the duct. Water was boiling out of it like a millrace. He headed in, using the hand rungs, and I followed. The miniature pump strapped to my back hummed and the straps sawed under my arms. We passed up a pair of side branches and the duct narrowed. There was a glow-strip along the side here, with more symbols. Jess checked each one we came to, after a while held up and said, "There should be a hatch here."

I flattened myself against the curved wall and held on and watched while he checked over the section ahead. Then his head and shoulders disappeared. I came up beside him and his legs went up inside a vertical shaft a yard in diameter. There were rungs there. I hauled myself up after him and after ten feet, the shaft angled and we were coming out of water into open air.

"I suppose this is a maintenance lock," Jess said. It was a square room, twenty feet on a side, with motor-operated valves all over one wall and color-coded piping on the other ones. I could hear pumps throbbing somewhere. The ceiling shed a glow like phosphorescent mold on Jess' face. In the tight black suit, he looked like a detail from Hieronymus Bosch.

I was looking at a panel set between banked valves.

"Try this," I said.

Jess looked at me, said nothing. He unclipped a tool kit from his belt and went to work. Five minutes later he grinned at me and turned something slowly and the look of strain tightened. Beyond the wall, something made a solid snick.

"That's it," he said.

I went past him and pushed on the panel and a section of wall slid back and I was looking into a silent corridor with a row of green ceiling lights that stretched away into distance.

"So much for the impregnability of ETORP," Jess said. "We're inside the Ice Palace. There are a thousand Blackies patrolling a few feet overhead, but we seem to have this level to ourselves. Now what?"

I didn't answer him right away. I was looking at the corridor, and feeling little icy fingers running up my backbone.

"Did you ever walk into a strange place and have the feeling you'd been there before?" I spoke carefully, so as not to shatter a fragile thought.

"It's called the *déjà vu*," Jess said, watching me.

"There's something down there," I said. "Something I won't like."

"What is it, Steve?" Jess' voice was like a freezing man breathing on the dying spark of his last match.

"I don't know," I said. I looked along the hall, but it was just a hall now. I pointed toward the far end.

"Come on, Jess," I said. "I don't know whether it's a hunch or a nightmare, but I think what we want's that way."

"There's dust here," Jess said. "This section's not in use, hasn't been for a long time."

The corridor ran for a couple of hundred feet and ended in a right-angle turn with a cubbyhole full of shelves. There was nothing on them but dust. Under the shelves there was a row of hooks designed for coats, but no coats were hanging on them. Jess stamped on the floor, looked at the ceiling.

"There must be a route leading from here," he said. "This appears to be a dressing room, where special protective clothing was donned."

I was looking at the hooks. Something about them bothered me. I counted them. Twelve. I got a grip on the third from the right and pulled down. It felt pretty solid. I pushed up hard, and it clicked and folded back. Jess was watching me with his mouth open. I fingered the next one, then took hold of the fifth in line, flipped it up. I could feel a little sweat on my forehead under the mask. I reached for the hanger between the other two and lifted it and something made a crunching sound and the wall on the right jumped open half an inch.

"How did you know, Steve?"

"I don't know," I said, and pushed the door open and went through into a place I'd seen somewhere, a long time ago, in a dream of another life.

It was a wide room with walls that were cracked and water-stained, with green mold growing in little tufts along the cracks. There were cracks across the floor, too, and some curled chips of perished plastic were all that was left of the composition tiles. I saw this by the light of a small hand flash that Jess played over the floor and held on a door across the room.

I went across to it and turned the old-fashioned doorknob and went into a small office drifted half an inch deep in dust and scraps of paper as brown as autumn leaves. There was a collapsed jumble of leather scraps and rusted springs in one corner that had been a big chair. Across from it was a teakwood desk. There was a small bowl on the desk with a little dust at the bottom, and a shred of something that might have been a flower stem, once.

"Daisies," I said. "White daisies."

"Steve, do you know this place?" Jess whispered.

"It's my old plant," I said. "This was my office."

I went to the desk, opened the drawer, and took out a bottle. A scrap of label read EMY ARTIN.

"What else do you remember, Steve?"

I was looking at a picture frame hanging on the wall. The glass was dirty but intact, but there was nothing behind it but a little ash. I lifted it down and uncovered a steel plate with a round knob, set in the wall. It was a safe, and the door was ajar.

"Someone's been here before you," Jess' voice grated.

I reached far back in the safe and felt over the upper surface, found a pinhole. "I need a wire," I said. Jess checked a pouch at his belt and produced one. I poked it up in the hole and it snicked and the back of the safe tilted forward into my hand. There was a drawer behind it. I pulled it out. Except for a few flakes of dry black paint, it was empty.

"What did you expect to find here?" Jess asked me.

"I don't know." I blew into the empty steel box and the paint chips danced and whirled up into my face. I started to toss it aside and found myself looking at the bottom of the drawer. The paint there was dry, peeling.

"What is it?" Jess was watching my face.

"There was no paint on the inside," I said. "It's black carballoy. . . ." I picked at the paint with a fingernail, and more of it flaked away and I was looking at words etched in the hard metal:

IN THE SEALED WING

6

 . . . . Frazier was looking at me with the kind of look you give a dog that's been run over. Gatley was standing behind him and Smith and Jacobs and a couple of men from the maintenance shop.

"Follow your orders, damn you!" I was yelling, and the blood was thudding in my temples like nine-pound sledges. "I told you to wall it off, and by God I meant I wanted it walled off! I never want sunlight to shine in there again!"

"We all know how you feel, Steve," Frazier was saying. "But there's no use—"

Hobart pushed up beside him and his fat face came open and said, "Look here, Dravek, we have fifty thousand dollars invested in this project—"

I swung on him and somebody tried for my arms from behind and I broke his leg and then they were all backed against the wall in a bunch but Frazier, who was always the only one with the guts to face me. There was blood on his mouth. A mechanic named Brownie was on the floor, groaning.

"He's gone crazy!" Hobart was yelling, and Frazier was looking me in the eye and saying, "All right, Steve, if that's what you want. . . ."

"Do you know what it means?" It seemed like a long time had passed, but Jess was still standing beside me with the light in his hand and I was holding the box. I tossed it on the floor and the clatter was muffled in the dust.

"Yeah," I said. "I know." I went back out into the outer room. The egg-crate ceiling was a dark tapestry of sooty spider webs and the walls that had been a soft tan were blackish-green, but I knew the way now. On the far side, a door was set in an alcove beside a rusty pipe pushing up from the rotted casing of a water cooler. It squeaked and opened and Jess' light showed us another room, full of dust and age and piles of shapeless debris where chairs and tables had been.

"Waiting room," I said. "Receptionist's desk over there." I went past the jumble of rusted-out metal and along a hall where dust came up in clouds, through a pair of doors that fell off their hinges when I kicked them and down steps to a pair of rusted steel doors that were standing open.

I looked at the doors, feeling the kind of feeling that Petrie must have had when he read the inscription over King Tut's tomb. My pulse was slamming, slow and heavy, a funeral march. I didn't want to see what was on the other side. I took a deep breath and Jess came down beside me and put the light inside. It made long shadows in a wide, high room, with piping and fallen scaffolding along one wall and a half-completed framework of steel plating looming up in the background like a wrecked tanker. There was lots of dust here, too, and a faint rotten smell in the air.

Jess' light fingered the wall ahead, flicked up along the side of the big tank, showed up piping and condensers and power transformers rafter-mounted up under the black ceiling.

"What was it all for?" Jess asked. "What sort of work did you do here?"

"We were a food packaging and processing outfit. The big tank was part of a new process we developed."

"Why wasn't it completed?"

"I don't remember."

Jess played the light around some more, and held it on the floor. Footprints in the dust led toward the far wall. They skirted a coil of heavy cable with cracked insulation, went on into shadows. My face felt clammy and the palms of my hands were numb. There was something waiting for me up ahead and the fear of it was like cold lead in my stomach. I stepped off, following the trail, and Jess came behind, lighting the way.

On the other side of the big unfinished tank there was a deep bay with a railed gallery. I went up the companionway, along past open-sided cubicles with stainless steel tubs, still bright under the dust. The stink was stronger here. The footprints turned in at the last bay. I ducked under the low hood, and stopped that way, bent over, looking through a framed opening that had been made by tearing out a wall. The light made complicated shadows across a room full of machinery. Cables and tubes and pipes led from the apparatus to a ten-foot tank like an iron lung. A hatch at one end of the tank was standing open. I could see something inside; something that took hold of my guts like a giant bird's claw and squeezed. I reached and swung the door back and the thing inside glided out on a white porcelain slab and I was looking down at a man's face, dry and brown as carved wood, with shaggy, dry hair, sandy brown, and a glint of teeth showing at the edge of the withered lips.

The body was nothing but purplish-brown leather stretched over bones. There were a couple of dozen tiny wounds visible on the skin.

"This is a life-support tank," Jess said. "It's been sabotaged. See the broken wires?"

"This is just a kid," I said. "Not more than sixteen years old. The hair's long, but there's no sign of a beard."

"He appears to have desiccated perfectly in the sterile atmosphere."

"The guy that sent us here didn't do it just to show us this," I said. "There's got to be more. Give me a hand."

I took hold of the right arm; it felt as hard and dry as last year's corn husks, and about as heavy. There was nothing under the cadaver except a blackish stain on the porcelain.

Jess played the light inside the tank, showed up a tangle of conduits and wires. The body was on its back, one leg drawn up a little, the arms at the sides, the fists closed. One fist looked a little different than the other. I bent over and looked.

"He's got something in his hand," I said. I broke off one of the fingers getting it out. It was a metal tube three inches long, half an inch in diameter. There was a screw cap at one end. I twisted it off and pulled out tightly rolled papers.

I unrolled them and a couple of faded newspaper clippings slid out into my hand. I smoothed the top one out and read it:

Police today continued their investigation into the mystery surrounding the discovery of an unidentified body in a midtown hotel late yesterday. Although the apparent cause of death was suicide from a small-caliber gas gun, a small wound in the roof of the mouth indicated possible foul play. The victim, apparently in his late thirties, was dressed in the uniform of a major in the UN Constabulary. UN Headquarters has so far declined to comment. (IP)

The next one was a bigger spread, two long columns in small, crabbed type that had a familiar look to it. The headline read: MAN GUNNED IN DAYLIGHT MURDER. The story under it told me that just before press time a gray Monojag had pulled up to the Waldorf and a man in the back seat had poked a 6mm Bren gun out the window and fired a full clip into a man in a brown overcoat coming out the revolving door. An employee of the hotel had been slightly injured in the knee by a ricochet. Examination of the body failed to produce any indication of the identity of the murdered man. The Monojag had driven off and made good its escape. Police were following up several clues and expected to make an arrest at any moment.

I handed the clip to Jess and another one dropped. I picked it up and was looking at a picture of myself.

It wasn't a bad likeness, except that it showed a little more hair than seemed just right, and there was a small scar high on the right cheekbone that didn't look familiar. And there was something wrong with the expression. But the part that hit my nervous system like a fire hose full of ice water was the caption:

BODY IGNORED BY PASSENGERS

The lines below read:

Civil Peace Under-Commissioner Arkwright announced today that record search has so far failed to identify the visaless body discovered late yesterday in Mid-city Tube Central.

The corpse, which had been ignored for several hours by Tube patrons who assumed the man was sleeping, is thought to be that of a criminal sought by Peace authorities for violation of the Life Act. See story page 115.

"What is it?" I said. "A gag, or a fake, or a little slip in the editorial department?"

Jess was reading the clip. He didn't answer. I looked at the picture some more. It was me, all right; and something about it bothered me. . . .

"This is no fake," I said. "The guy in the picture was dead when they took it, all right."

Jess glanced at the photo. "Why do you say that?"

"You prop the body up, get the eyelids open, and set the lights to give you a little reflection off the eyeball, tuck the tongue back inside and run a comb through the hair. It looks OK—unless you know what to look for. The Chinese used to use the trick to keep the Red Cross happy about the prisoners."

"Horrible. Still, since he was dead when they found him, I suppose it's understandable."

"Maybe I'm a little slow. Back where I come from, a fellow doesn't often get a look at his own obituary."

Jess gave me his pained look. "You talk as if you imagined that was a picture of yourself."

"Imagine, hell! I know a picture of me when I see it."

"The coincidence in appearance *is* rather striking—"

"Ha!"

"The clips could refer to relatives of yours. Perhaps it's a vendetta—a rather fantastic vendetta, I confess—"

"It's a swell theory," I cut him off. "Except that I don't know anything about a feud, and I never had a twin."

"You had a grandfather."

"Make that a little plainer."

"Take another look at the date on the clip," he said. "It's over sixty years old."

My face felt like something chipped out of ice, but I pushed it into a grin.

"That clears that up. I'm not a fresh corpse on a slab down at the city morgue; I'm a nice settled cadaver who's been pushing up daisies the bigger half of a century."

Jess nodded as if that meant something. Maybe it did. I was still hanging in the air feeling for the floor with my toes. There was another paper back of the clips. Jess put the light on it while I unrolled it. It was covered with typing. I smoothed it out on the side of the tank and read it:

Number Three gave me most of it. The major almost had it, but he slipped somewhere and they took him. He had the best chance of any of us. Less time had gone by and the organization he was up against wasn't as solid yet, and his taping was better. He spent ten years getting ready, but they nailed him. Three had a tough time, but he picked up his cues and carried it a little farther, and from what he found out gave me the tip that brought me here. But none of it would have happened except for Frazier. He was the only man that could have handled the Plan. He knew what he was doing when he picked him for the job.

What I'm going to try may not work, and if it doesn't, I'll wind up like the major and this poor kid here who never even had a name. But it's what I have to do. Maybe I'm wasting my time writing long chatty letters to a guy that doesn't exist, never will exist. But I'm banking on it that I'm not the last. OK, you read the note Number Three left, and came here, just like I did. The box was empty when I found it, too, but his tip to try the sealed wing was there. The paint I put back over it won't last more than ten years, and that ought to be long enough—unless *he* finds you first. But that's where he outfoxed himself.

Maybe the old devil knew himself better than he thought he did. The story about making the setup torture proof was a little far-fetched. He couldn't afford to let himself know. Maybe he even saw this coming some day. But if he did, why—[word scratched out].

To hell with that. Let's keep this short. I've got plenty of time, my trail's covered and cold, maybe he thinks I'm dead. I tried hard enough to make him think so. Five years I've laid doggo now. But now it's time to move. Can't stall forever. Because I found it.

It's a place you know—but maybe you don't. The systems are getting old. There are gaps in my briefing. Number Three said there might be. He had it all, right up to the beginning of the Plan. I remember the trial, and the start of the project, but it all seems a little academic, like a story you've heard too many times. Or it did. Now that I've seen what I have, it eats at me. I haven't had eighty years to forget, like he has. But now I'm ready to make my try. Maybe he'll be ready for me, and I'll wash up on a beach a thousand miles from there. But I've got to try it now, before I get any rustier. Maybe I've already waited too long, but I had to wait, give myself every break there was—because if I fail, there may not be a Number Five.

Funny how I can't stick to the point. I guess I want to talk to somebody; but there's nobody a man can trust. ETORP's stranglehold is getting tighter every day. Now they have private

cops with little black lapel badges crawling every street in
the city, and there's a lot of talk about some kind of legal-
ized euthanasia, with ETORP running it on a contract deal.
Some organization. Maybe I ought to feel proud; maybe I do,
in a way. But I'll break it, or get killed. I hope I make it. I've
got to make it. It may be the last chance. Just on the off
chance something goes wrong, I'm leaving this for you. If
anybody else finds this it's got to be him, and what good is
a code with him? You'll know what to do with it. And if you
don't, you've forgotten too much—or never got it—

It's too complicated for me. Things moved fast after my
day. We would have called it magic, and maybe it is. Black
magic. Bad magic. But part of it's a fairy tale. I make a lousy
prince, but I have to try.

Funny, when you read this, you'll know I didn't make it;
but here it is: MUSKY LAKE. Third, fifth, fourth. 247.

Cute, huh?

Now it's up to you. I'm going to put this in a place that
will remind you what he's turned into, what he did to this
poor kid, and left him here for us to find. I'll give it to him
to pass to you.

Good luck.

1

"It's in Wisconsin, a few miles out of a little place called Oatavie,"
I said. "A lake, about half a mile across, in a high valley with pine
woods backing up the slopes all around. The name on the map
was Otter Lake, but I always thought of it as Musky Lake. That's
where I caught my first one."

Jess looked blank.

"A fish, a big one; a fighter. I took him on a ten-pound fly line.
It's a thing you don't forget."

"That area is heavily wooded, a desolation," Jess said. "Why
would he send you there?"

"I guess that's what we have to find out," I said, and stopped,
listening for a sound off to the left, back in what had been a
freight-loading bay—or maybe I just smelled something wrong.

I grabbed Jess' shoulder and just had time to say "Douse the light" before there was a smash of sound and a blue-white glare lit up the room like an operating theater and men in black were coming through double doors that were swung back wide from the old freight platform. We froze, watching them fan out along both walls.

The spot we stood in was still in deep shadow that narrowed in on us as a big dolly-mounted light came through the doors. I ducked, felt over the floor, came up with a ragged piece of steel plate the size of my hand. There was a nice zone of shadow cast by a column that widened out in the direction of the gallery. I threw the piece of plate high and hard, right down the strip of shadow. It made a hell of a clatter when it hit. The light swung off-side and we ducked out and ran for it.

Jess took the lead. He reached the brick wall and went flat against it and had his gun out, firing. I took the door in a running dive, and something boomed in the room behind me, and Jess came through and fell against me and we went down together. Blood was pumping from a wound in his back I couldn't have covered with my hand. I hooked his arm and he was on his feet; his legs were like broken straws, but his knife was in his hand.

"Leave me. . . ." he sucked in air and it bubbled. " . . . . by the door. . . . I'll greet. . . . the first one. . . . through. . . ."

I slung him over my shoulder and ran. It was a fifty-foot straightaway; I made it to the far end and got the door to the receptionist's room open and a gun roared behind me and slugs kicked chunks out of the frame. The only light was a faint glow like moonlight from the ceiling strips. I crossed the room in three jumps and my foot hit something under the dust layer and I went down with Jess on top of me. I grabbed for him and my hand slipped on blood that covered his left side. Big feet were pounding close. I grabbed Jess by the belt and pitched him into the office behind me, dived after him. Maybe my feet cleared the door before the Blackie slammed into the room.

For a second or two there was a silence like the one just after you pull the grenade pin. Then a heavy gun racketed outside the door, one of those high-speed jobs that sprays out slugs like a fire hose. The back of the door over me blew off in a hail of plastic splinters. I hugged the floor and heard him come across and I set myself and the door banged and he was through, bringing the gun around, and I grabbed his ankle; he arced backward and fell across Jess, kicking like a bass hooked in the eye. I caught his gun before it hit the floor and swung to see Jess' grin fade and his face set; and the knife in his hand fell in the dust, with Blackie blood on the blade.

I backed through the outer office trying to look two ways at once, and heard a soft sound and got the gun around in time and blew the face off a Blackie coming in from the hall. I got in the doorway, and put another burst out through it and went flat and somebody chewed up the door frame above my head. I could see the door Jess and I had come in by, half an hour before, standing an inch ajar, ten feet along the hall. Maybe they hadn't seen it yet in the bad light. If I was going to use it, it had to be now, before the place got crowded again. I came up and out and swung the gun and got off part of a burst before the Blackie who had been waiting for me blew the gun out of my hands. The impact of the slugs knocked me back against the wall. I saw blood on my sleeve, and I could tell I'd been hit in the body, but there was no pain, just a numbness spreading from the left side of my belly. I wedged myself against the door frame and watched him come across to me. He swung the gun over his shoulder by the strap and reached for me and I slid a hand in under the wrist and grabbed him and brought him in close and turned him and locked my forearm across his throat and broke up everything in there. I threw him away from me and waded across to the open panel and through it and got it closed behind me. For a few minutes, I leaned against the wall trying to talk myself out of lying down on the floor and having a nice long rest. I watched the blood flowing down the leg of the black scuba suit through a blackish haze full of little lights. There was some muffled noise racketing near me, but it didn't seem to concern me any more. . . .

. . . . I was lying down after all, and there was a lot of pounding going on, about six inches from my head. I felt like I ought to be on my feet, going somewhere, and I got up on all fours and discovered an anvil was chained to my left side. I fumbled with the place where the hook was in for a couple of minutes and then decided it was too much trouble. I moved and the anvil dragged and the hook cut into me and I was on my face again, resting.

OK, Dravek; show your stuff. Jess looked pretty good back there. Full of surprises, Jess was. Blackies will find that cute door pretty soon. Must be a nice trail leading to it. Shame to make it too easy for the mothering worms. Jess used to say that. Some Jess. Knew what he was getting into. A swimmer, Jess was. Better to go that way than here. In the dust. Helpful, at that. Caked up on my belly, along the arm. Not losing as much blood now. Blood Jess gave me. Nice place he had, good bed to lie in. Like to be there now. . . .

I had four legs and four arms—or was it six of each? Tricky, figuring which ones to use when. Used to wonder if a horse didn't ever get mixed up, kick himself in the ankle. Four arms, and two legs, or maybe three. Wires all crossed, hard to make 'em work right. Missed then, hurt my face. *My God, but the pain is there now, Steve-boy. Help keep you awake, your mind on your business. Left, right, use the leg, drag the other one, keep going. . . .*

8

I could hear the big generator pulling hard, and the sparks fountained out, and Frazier was yelling, but I couldn't hear what he was saying. I was watching the two-inch strip of cherry red weld stitching another plate into what was going to be a million-dollar setup. Million, hell, a hundred million, over the next ten years! Nobody could match Frazier when it came to tech management; he had a nose for that kind of talent that could comb a potential genius out of a crowd of downy-cheeked grads quicker than I could spot a shaved ace in a set of bicycles. The new process was going to turn the food-processing racket on its ear, and Draco, Inc. would be sole proprietor. . . .

Frazier was there, hauling at my arm and pointing across the room. The outer door was open, a white glare against the dark, and I could see them silhouetted in it for a second before it closed behind them, her tall and slim, and the little one beside her. They were coming down into the big room and I waved and started that way and something up above shifted and sparks hissed and somebody yelled and the garish flicker of the big welding torch cut out. Frazier waved his arms and went over that way, fast. Somebody was yelling: " . . . . it's hot! Get that plate clear, Brownie! Nulty, shut her down! All the way down!"

I got over to where a section of plate had dropped and sliced into

*the big cables ten feet from the side of the welder. There was a lot
of smoke and a stench like burned cork. I got a couple of choice
phrases ready for the framer who'd let it happen, and something made
me turn and she was there, right in the thick of the smoke, holding
something up in her hand, and I yelled and started toward her and
saw her turn toward the sound of my voice and. . . .*

I was on the floor with my face against cold stone and I could
still feel the scream that had ripped the inside out of my throat,
and the churn of the generator was a deep throbbing coming
through the floor and I got my head up and was looking at the
open mouth of a manhole. There was a black toolcase lying beside
it. It was Jess'. He'd left it there, after he'd used it to unlock the
outer door. I was in the maintenance room above the big duct,
and the rumbling noise was the pumps down below. I didn't
remember how I'd gotten there.

I made a move to sit up and a big hook I'd forgotten about
came down and ripped into my belly. I curled over it and rode
the current of fire for a while; then I got a hand on the edge of
the manhole and pulled. The fire was still burning, but I knew
how to put it out. Down below the water was cold and black, deep
enough to drown all the pain of living.

My face was over the opening; I could see a black glint down
below. *One more pull, Dravek; you can do it*. One arm wasn't
helping much, but who needs two arms? I used the good knee and
felt my chest go over the edge and I was sliding down and then
falling into soft black that closed over me. . . .

The shock brought me out of it. For a while—maybe a few
seconds, maybe longer—I rolled with the turbulence. Then I
slammed something hard and the pain went clear through me from
the top of my head to the end of my toes; and all of a sudden
I knew I was in a duct, being carried along by the high-pressure
stream, with my head banging the walls at regular intervals. I felt
the duct widen, and I remembered the louvers ahead and got a
hand on the water jets and pointed myself upstream and gave them
a blast. I slammed the louvers hard, hung up there for a second
or two—then slid between them and was out in the deep river,
rolling end over end.

The cold was cutting through the suit, and I groped a little
and thumbed the heat control up some, but not too much,

because a little low-temperature anesthesia was a good idea for right then.

While I was doing all this, the river was taking me along to wherever it was going, which even in this day of improved methods for propagating human misery was probably the sea. I've been a sailor, but I never liked the idea of Davy Jones's locker. I got my head pointed upstream again and used my jets and steered for the right side of the channel. It wasn't easy to maneuver, because one leg seemed to be dead from the hip down, and the left arm had something wrong with it. The fire in my belly didn't seem important right then. I figured I'd get to think about it plenty, later, if there was a later.

I used the jets and edged forward and in less than a minute found an iron rung and held on. I had one good leg, and about an arm and a half; the fingers on the left one didn't seem to want to close like they should. I got an overhead grip and pulled up and got a toe on a rung and made another foot. This went on for a long time. Two or three times I forgot what I was doing and started to slide back, but each time an instinct that used to keep monkeys from falling out of trees made my hand grab and hold on.

The time came when I reached and there wasn't any rung, or any wall, and that seemed like a dirty shame and I went on feeling the air for about as long as it takes to light a slow fire under a missionary and watch it burn down. After a while I got a grip with a fingernail and hauled the legs up over the edge, which was no harder than swinging a piano in my teeth, and fell a couple of feet. That put me where I'd been trying to get: on my back in an empty street, with four slugs in me and cops looking for me, waiting to finish the job.

I crawled over to the nearest wall and lay against it and tried to check myself over. The trouble with the arm seemed to be due to a hole I could stick the end of my little finger in, just below the elbow. The leg was a little more complicated. The hip was broken up, but there was no wound on the outside; the suit was intact there. That meant the slug had gone in through the belly and hit the pelvic bone from the inside.

That brought me to the big one. I got my hand inside the suit just far enough to feel what I knew was there, and passed out cold.

When I came out of that one, I was lying on my side kissing

cold pavement and watching someone ducking along in the shadows cast by a light on a tall pole far up the street. I thought about reaching for the little gadget Jess had told me was a reliable short-range killer, but nothing happened. I was part of the stone; just an eye peering back from that last thin edge, watching the show.

The oncoming figure went into a shadow that was too black to see through and came out, closer, and skittered across the street to my side and came along to me and stopped and looked both ways before she looked down. It was Minka, the girl with the blue hair. I started to open my mouth to give her my usual cheery greeting, and her face swelled up and spread until it blanked out the light and I gave it all up and let the darkness take me.

9

Voices were talking.

" . . . . say this cull's a Blackie-twister! That makes him fast freight!"

"Don't be hasty. It's a prime hulk. This is no Dirtie. He'll fetch top price from a Forkwaters stiff-hack, once he's patched a little—"

"The insides are messed up bad, Darklord. It wouldn't be worth the expense to rebuild—"

"I said *patch*, Acey! Caveat empty, as the old saying goes. If he's moved quickly, who's to know?"

"I say slice him. The heart alone—"

"Have you no sense of the fitness of things? Look at that skin! As white and smooth as a star-lady's rump." A meaty chuckle. "And I speak from first hand. . . ." The chuckle went out of the voice and a hard note came in. "But where's his cullmark, eh? Mmmmm? He must have his tattoo; he must have. He must. He. . . ."

"Too much talk! Talk makes trouble. Cut 'em pretty and they'll fetch enough. Don't get greedy, that's the secret. Don't get greedy and don't listen to talk. He's no trimmed Cruster on a drop. There's something chancy about this weed. I say slice him, slice him fine!"

"Seems a pity, with wholemeat units bringing what they do; but perhaps you're right. Very well, Acey; limb and gut, I think, and of course, epidermal—but cut it nicely, no telltales—"

Then I heard a new voice, one I'd heard before, somewhere.

" .... that filthy little slicer touch him!"

"My dear, you do Acey a disservice! He's the finest technician in the business, ETORP-trained, mind you! If it hadn't been for a trifling indiscretion in certain informal arrangements...."

"Where's Jess?"

"Who knows? We found only this one—what they left of him."

"Did he talk?"

"My dear, he was fully occupied with surviving."

"I want him fixed! You know I can pay!"

"Ah, but will you pay in negotiable coin?"

"Just fix him!"

"Ah, Minky-pet, grudging affection is cold comfort to a tender-hearted man like myself, hardly worth the bartering for...." Heavy breathing. "Well, Minky-love. And after you've been so precious formal with good Uncle Abdullah...."

"Do something for him! Can't you see he's bleeding to death?"

"Patience, love. This hulk is in pitiable condition. It requires expensive internals. The liver is a ruin; two of those nasty little darts have shredded it into sausage! Now where am I to find a sound liver on such notice? Such organs don't grow on trees—"

"Lucky for you they grow on men. You've got plenty of those."

"You'd have me slice one of my own, for the benefit of this stranger?"

"No. For the benefit of your own greasy flesh!"

"Hmmm. Frankly, and most directly put. As it happens, I have a fine fresh liver on hand, just gutted out, a trifle large for the trade, but this big fellow shouldn't mind that."

"Give him whatever he needs. Just fix him, I don't care how you do it!"

There was more talk after that, but I wasn't paying much attention—the pain was rising around me like pouring day at a brass foundry. I heard some small, whimpery sounds, figured out they were coming from me, tried to cut them out, gave up, and groaned out loud. Somebody was hauling at my arm, somebody was sawing off my leg. It didn't seem to matter much. I was off somewhere in the rosy distance now, floating on a nice soft cloud with just a few needles in it that poked me when I tried to move. Somebody came along with a skinning knife then, and cut me into slices and stretched them out in the sun to dry, and somebody else collected the slices and sewed them back together, swearing all the while. It didn't interest me a lot; but after a while the voices got louder, more insistent, and I opened my mouth to tell them to go away and then there was a thick smell like all the hospital corridors I ever smelled dumped in my face at once and the cloud faded into a thin mist that closed over me and shut out the light and the sound and I spun back down into nothingness.

10

I woke up propped in a bed, blinking across at a room lit like the seduction scene from *Don Giovanni*. There was a lot of flowery gauze curtain, pale yellow velvet drapes pulled back from floor-to-ceiling glass, a tangerine rug, a couple of small paintings that were swirls of pink and orange and burnt umber, a few sticks of furniture that looked as if they would disappear if you pushed the right button.

Minka was sitting in one of the chairs. She looked better minus the orange paint and the blue hair and the ribbons. There was a filmy toga-like wrap around her now, that showed off her figure better than a shower bath. Her hair was a soft brown, and her mouth looked soft and young without the paint. I opened my mouth to say hello and a grunt came out. She looked up.

"How is it?" Her voice was soft, like somebody who's been there herself.

"A little confused," I said. "But resting comfortably." It came out in a weak chirp, like a baby bird. I had to lie back and rest up after the effort.

She was standing by the bed. "Jess?" she said.

"Dead."

"I guess I knew; but they said you couldn't have come that far alone, with all those spinners in you."

I had a sudden thought and moved a hand down, not without a certain effort, and felt a leg where a leg ought to be.

"You're all right now," she said. "That little man with the rat's eyes is a wizard."

"I seem to remember something about needing some replacement parts."

"He grafted a liver, and some nerve tissue, and the femoral artery was in bad shape. It was luck he had stock on hand. There was a man, a giant, who'd been killed just a few hours before."

I let that one hang in the air. She went away then, and I had another nice nap. I woke up hungry, and she fed me soup. I ate it and watched her face. She was a girl with lots on her mind.

When the soup was gone, she made a lot out of fluffing pillows and getting the light just right. Then she lit up a dope stick and said, "Why did you do it?"

"There was some information I wanted. I had an idea I might find it there."

"And did you?"

"I'm not sure."

"Jess thought you knew something that was very important for— certain people."

"He was wrong about that."

"Who are you? Where did you come from?" She sounded as if she hated to ask the question and didn't want to know the answer.

"This is going to sound a little screwy," I said. "But I'm not sure about that either."

"You mean—amnesia?"

"Maybe that's what you'd call it. I know my name, and I can tie my own shoes. Outside of that. . . ."

"Jess said he found you in the park. He said a cutter squad attacked you and you. . . . killed them with your bare hands."

"That's where it starts. Before that it's a little mixed up. I thought I had a few clues, but I seem to be two other guys."

"You're a strange man. You have a strange way of talking—and not only the accent. You joke about death and suffering."

"I was hoping maybe you could tell me something useful on those subjects."

"What do you mean?"

"About some of the funny angles of all this. About why Jess thought I was important enough to bring home for a souvenir, and why the cops are after me."

"I know what he told me," she said. "That's all. About the rest— I don't know anything."

"You must have a few ideas. You paid the fat man's price."

She looked at me and a shudder took her and shook her like a dog shakes a rat.

"I'm sorry," I said. "We're a cagey pair, sparring around and trying to sneak a look at the other fellow's hand. Why don't we try it showdown?"

"I've told you all I can." She looked past me. Her face was tight.

"Sure," I said. "In that case maybe I'd better catch another few winks. We wouldn't want all that fine craftsmanship to go to waste."

II

I did a lot of sleeping during the next few days. It might have been something the girl put in my soup—or maybe it was just Mother Nature, stitching me back together. There were a lot of things I didn't care for in the Twenty-second Century, but their medicine was as far ahead of the old familiar GP as a 747 was a dog cart. Minka stayed close, doing nurse's chores with a lot of efficiency and as little conversation as possible. Quite a few days slipped by, while I lay on my back and watched the clouds out beyond a balcony like Jess' and didn't think about a lot of things. Then one evening I had a sudden urge to get out of bed and sample some fresh air.

I got a leg over the side of the bed and that worked OK so I stood up and started across toward the columns. I was halfway there when Minka came into the room.

"What are you doing?" She was right there, with an arm around me, propping me up. "Are you trying to kill yourself?"

Her hand was against my bare back; it was smooth and soft and warm. The arm that went with it was nice, too. I put an arm around her, pulled her to me.

"Are you out of your mind. . . . ?" she whispered. But she didn't pull away. Up close like this I could smell the faint perfume of her hair. My hands were on the slimness of her waist, and I moved them down over the curve of hips that were the way hips ought to be. The tissue paper thing she was wearing got in my way and I threw it into the corner. Then her arms were around my neck, and her body was against mine, and her skin was like the finest silk ever spun, and her lips were as soft as a whisper in the dark.

"Steve," she said in my ear. "Oh, Steve. . . ."

12

"You're a strange, savage man," Minka said. She was lying on her side on the bed looking at me, and the moonlight from the terrace reflected in her eyes and made pale highlights in her hair. "I've never known a man like you, Steve."

"You don't know me now," I said. "I don't know myself."

"I brought you here because I wanted to learn things from you. But I don't care about that, now."

"I've got to go, Minka. You know that."

"Stay here, Steve. You'll be safe here. Out there they'll kill you."

"Out there is where the answers are."

"Jess wanted answers—and they killed him. Why not forget all that—"

"There are places I've got to go, things that want me to do them."

"Things that are more important than what we might have together?" In the pale light her body glowed like ivory.

"You're all the woman a man could want," I said. "But this is something I have to do."

"Why? Do you think you can change the world, like Jess did? You can't, Steve. No one man can. We've made this world what it is. It's the way we wanted it: safe, comfortable, plenty of food for all, plenty of leisure, a long life—for those who don't rock the boat. You've been dirtside; you've seen how they live there. Do you want to go back to that?"

"I'm no world-saver, Minka. But I don't like unfinished business."

"They've lost your trail; they'll never find you! I can get you a new tag, a cullmark—everything—"

I shook my head.

"Why are you doing this? What could you possibly learn that would be worth risking your life for?"

"It's something I have to do for a friend. He's counting on me."

She laughed, not a pretty laugh. "And you wouldn't be the one to let a friend down, would you, Steve?"

13

I left the next afternoon, briefed to the ears, armed with a neat little watch-pocket blaster, and feeling better than anybody had a right to, two weeks after having new insides installed. I rode an elevator that dropped so fast my stomach was ready to climb out and have a look by the time the door opened and palmed me out onto a pavement halfway between a street and a corridor. A cold light like a winter afternoon was filtering down from a high glass roof. There were lots of people, pushing along on important business; the grim looks on their faces were normal, but the clothes they wore were like something from Westercon II. A tired-looking fellow in bulbous, color-slashed bloomers pushed past me using his elbow like an experienced commuter. A fellow in baggy-kneed tights and floppy sleeves jostled a woman in pink ruffs out of his way; she passed it on to a young kid in a tight coverall with dummy laces at the wrists and shins. Nobody looked at me. I felt like I was back home.

I moved off along the walk, mingled with men in capes and three-cornered hats, women in all-over ruffles and stand-up lace collars and some stripped to the waist and painted like barber poles, and a few of both sexes wrapped in old bed-sheets. They looked like survivors of a three-day fancy-dress ball.

There were signs plastered over the walls in screaming pink and electroshock blue and agony yellow. I picked one that read DRINK in purple script and turned in at what seemed to be an open doorway, but something banged me on the nose like a glass wall, and something else went *bzapp!* and I was back out on the pavement. To hell with it. I didn't need a drink anyway.

Up ahead, there was a big TV screen ten feet square sticking out over the walk, with words and pictures flickering across it. Letters across the top said "THRVEE MALL WEST-OFCL." I watched it for a minute while quick flashes of strange faces and factory smokestacks and desert landscapes and explosions came and went over subtitles in condensed headline prose.

A little farther along I came to what Minka had told me to look for: A wide frosted-glass front over blank doors with cryptic signs that said things like "PVR SLD II (9)" and "OUT—Z99-over."

I went through one of the doors and was in a narrow chute like the bull comes out of, with a turnstile blocking it. There was a slot at one side about the right size for a silver dollar, but I didn't have a silver dollar. I leaned on it and it leaned back. There was nobody around to ask questions of, even if I'd been in the mood to attract attention that way. I braced a foot against the crossbar and tried again. Something inside made little tinkly sounds and it spun free.

Ten feet beyond it, the passage right-angled and I was looking at a blank screen dazzling with little points of light. There were a lot of buttons beside it. I pushed a couple of them, as instructed, and said: "Routing for West Bore."

The screen blipped red and white and blanked. So much for the kind of cooperation I get out of inanimate objects. I opened my mouth to ask the question again, louder, and something clacked behind me and I did a fast turn and a female came out of a doorway. She had a hard, good-looking face with no paint except a green dot on her right cheek and dull silver on her lips. Her figure looked good enough, what I could see of it under a gray overall.

"Passengers are restricted—" she started her pitch.

"I'll bet they are, gorgeous," I cut it off. "I asked it a question and it gave me a smart answer. Maybe you can do better." Her expression slid sideways a little, not quite as cocky now, but ready to be, as soon as she got the lie of the land. "The entry monitor indicates an all-categories tag," she said in a tone that had shifted a couple of points toward civil. That would be a reference to the sounds of breaking metal that had come out of the turnstile when I leaned on it.

"Right," I gave her a significant look. "You know what that means."

She didn't meet my eye. "You're with the Commission?" she tried to sound brisk but there was just a hint of a quaver in her voice.

"Would I be here if I wasn't?"

"If I may record your credentials—as a matter of routine—"

"We're dispensing with the routine, Miss—what was that name?"

"Gerda. I. L. Gerda, nine-three, Second, provisional."

"All right, Gerda, let's not waste the Commission's time."

"If you'll give me your authority reference—"

"This is hush-hush," I said. "Off the record. If it wasn't I wouldn't need you, would I, Gerda?" I sweetened it with the sort of smile her turnkey personality seemed to call for.

She twitched a couple of cheek muscles at me and said, "If you'll come this way. . . ."

I followed a nice hip action along the corridor to an iron gate, and about then I noticed a bell dinging somewhere in the distance.

"What is it, Gerda, a cross?" I grabbed her arm and she tried to kick me. She was looking mean enough to bite, now.

"You entered on a forged tag," she'd gone shrill on me. "Don't try to leave!" I pushed her out of the way and she went for my eyes, and I slapped her, hard. Her nose started to bleed. Something clanged back of the grill and a red light went on. Another bell racketed, nearby.

"Don't dare leave here," Miss Gerda squalled. "You're under criminal arrest!"

"Sorry," I said. "As it happens, I'm late for a Ping-Pong date at the YW. Better open it, Gerda."

Her eyes hated me, but she pushed the right spot and the gate snapped back. There was a sound from back the way I'd come and the girl twisted and threw herself down and something went *ssstt!* and a gnat's wing brushed my cheek and kicked a chip out of the wall. I got a quick flash of two men in tight black coming through the door twenty yards back along the passage. I cleared the gate just as a second shot whanged off, kicked it shut, and ran like hell.

14

An hour and a half of fast travel later I stepped out into a concourse crowded with people looking like travelers have looked ever since home got to be a place to get away from. I saw a few lads in dark uniforms standing here and there eye-balling the scene, but the uniforms were gray and had MVNT CNTRL lettered on their pocket patches. But they packed guns, just like real Blackies.

There was a railing on the right, and below it a spread of pavement with a rank of big torpedoes lit up like Christmas trees. Little cars like U-dodge-ems were ducking around between them, ferrying passengers. I went along the gallery, took the down escalator. Two of the men in gray were standing at the bottom looking at faces; two pairs of eyes lit on me. I felt them all the

way down and across the tarmac, but it must have just been my
conscience bothering me. They let me go.

I crossed the big glassed-in concourse full of people and flashing
lights and noise, went down a sloping ramp and was outside, under
open sky. There weren't many people here. In the distance, the city
lights were a jeweled wall.

The signs here weren't much help. Over on the left, beyond half
a dozen sets of what could have been roller-coaster rails, something whooshed and a low-slung vehicle riding on two fore-and-
aft-mounted wheels came slamming down the track and stopped
and the lid popped up and a fat man and a thin woman got in.
It racketed off and another one came down the line and curbed
itself.

There was a low rail between me and the cars. I jumped it, went
along a narrow strip that looked as if it might not electrocute me;
I went around the back of the car and put a hand on the door
and behind me a cool voice said, "Stop there."

I turned around, not too fast. Two gray uniforms were coming
over, relaxed, taking their time. One of them said, "Movement
control," and the other one said, "Step over here." No pleases and
thank-you's for these boys.

I came around the car and across in the indicated direction. The
one on the left went past me toward the car, which put me between
them and a yard from his partner. I doubled my fist and hit him
low in the stomach and grabbed the front of the gray blouse and
swung him around. The other one had heard something; he came
around, reaching for his hip. I threw his friend at him and socked
him in the throat and vaulted into the car and slapped the big red
button and the wheels screamed and I was off.

For the first hour I drove with my shoulders tight, listening for
the sirens or whatever they might have thought up to replace them
in this new, improved-model world. Then I had a thought that
cheered me some. This was an Autopike; the coppers probably had
ways of pinpointing any vehicle operating on it anywhere—as long
as he was locked into the system. But I was on manual. As long
as I stayed with the pack, there was no way to pick me out—maybe.

I held the car at 200 mph for five hours. About a hundred miles
northwest of where the little map unrolling on the dash screen
said the sprawl of light called Chago was, I pulled off on a lay-by

marked with big arrows of luminous rose paint. Inside my left jacket cuff there was a plastic button Minka had put there to fool the scanners. I ripped it loose and tossed it on the floor. Then I flipped the controls to AUTO and hopped out. The car jumped off from the rail and curveted on her two wheels along the metal strip in the road, angled out, and joined the main lane, picking up speed fast, running empty. She went over the rise howling, with her controls pegged at top emergency speed. I went over the guard rail and down a grip on the edge and felt for a toehold and started down.

By the time the sun was an hour in the sky, I was five miles north of the pike, working my way through a swampy patch toward higher ground north and west of me. The years had made a lot of difference in what had been farming country and tame woods back in my hunting days. Now it had the look of a forest prim- eval. The oaks and elms and maples were four feet across at the base, and there was a new tree I'd never seen before, a tapered, smooth-barked conifer that probably all started from a salted nut dropped by a tourist along the roadside. It was late in the year, later than the temperature would make you think. Leaves were already turning red, and the smell of fall was in the air.

This part of the route was easy; I steered by the sun, stayed away from the right-of-way of the few roads I came to that had cars on them. It seemed that the national passion for touring the country in the family station wagon had finally worked itself out. People either stayed in their hives, close to the buttons they needed to push for life's necessities, or did their traveling by air or cross- country tube. I saw a few high contrails, and once a copter whiffled past a mile away at treetop level; but whatever the boys used to sniff out fugitives wasn't geared to a guy without the little tell- tale set in the bone back of the ear. I was an untagged man, and as invisible to them as an Indian was to General Braddock.

Just before noon I crossed a strip of broken concrete with a rusted sign fallen on its face that seemed to say US 30 A. As well as I could remember the map, that would put me somewhere to the east of Rockford. I had a full set of blisters, but otherwise was holding up swell. The leg gave me a little trouble, but Minka had told me that I was walking on the best permanent-oil titanium alloy hip joint money could buy, so I let that thought console me.

Late in the afternoon a pair of copters came pretty close, crisscrossing the country to the north. They seemed to have a general idea where I was, and that worried me some; but maybe it was just coincidence. They worked their way on to the east and I had the world to myself again.

Just before sunset I came up onto a clear stretch covered with concrete foundations and broken-down chimneys and a few walls still standing, well blacked by a fire. Letters cut into a piece of cornice from what would have been the town's best building said BRODHEAD NATIONAL BANK. That put me over the line into Wisconsin, about thirty miles south of where I wanted to be.

I spent the night there, on the back porch of a brick house at the north edge of town. It wasn't that it was more comfortable than a nest in the woods, but maybe by then I was getting a little lonely. And even in ruins, the little town was something that was almost familiar.

I went on before the sun was up, hit a little stream west of the town, followed it northwest. About noon I saw an airplane, a short-coupled job with vertical jets that made a big noise and curled leaves in the tops of the trees. It went past, a quarter of a mile north of me, moving slow enough to make me stand under a tree and pretend to be a natural formation. A few minutes later, I crossed another road trace and was into rising ground. I picked a route along a ravine between wooded ridges and in the next hour hit the dirt three times when little one-seater aircraft came whistling over at low altitude. It began to look as if the Blackies were closing in on me. How, I didn't know. There didn't seem to be any posses combing the underbrush with dogs so far; that was something. I went on, keeping to cover now. But I was starting to feel hemmed in.

By midafternoon I had crossed three ridges and was coming down into a valley that had a half-familiar look. The trees were a hundred years bigger than they should have been, but otherwise it all looked just the way it had the last time.

I couldn't exactly place the last time.

I went on down to a gravel strip that had been a road, thought it over and tried the left-hand direction and ten minutes later recognized the turn-off that led up to Musky Lake.

Things got a little more rugged after that. Twilight was coming on, and it was chilly up here on the high ground. There was a lot of loose shale that made the footing tricky, and the light was no help. It took me an hour to reach the top of the ridge. The growth was heavy here. I picked a route back toward where the road sliced through and saw a light through the trees and hit the dirt. It seemed that Musky Lake wasn't the unspoiled wilderness it was in the old days, after all.

I counted the lights shining through the dusk. There were eight of them, spaced at regular intervals on the other side of the rise of ground ahead. I was still admiring this view when something big and dark with lots of blue and red navigation lights whiffled overhead and disappeared over the ridge. The place I was heading for seemed to be a popular spot with the airborne set—and the look of the jobs I'd seen spelled military.

In front of me, a deep black shadow angled across my route, the same gully that I'd bridged once with a pine log. The log was gone, and I had to go down through a healthy growth of brambles to get across it, but up ahead was the ridge, and on the other side of it was the spot I was aiming at. I made it in another five minutes and pushed my face out between broken rock to take my first look at what had been the prettiest spot this side of Wales, with the lake in the center like a star sapphire laid out on green velvet.

It wasn't like that now. In the late twilight I could see trees that thinned out for fifty feet down the rocky slope to a stretch of open ground a hundred feet wide and a cluster of buildings beyond, all of it lit like a prison yard on hanging night.

It was full dark now, with no moon. A couple more copters had flitted overhead, and a big VTOL job had made a noisy descent a couple of miles away, on the other side of the valley.

I backed off below the ridge line and started around. An hour later I was on the east side of the valley, looking up at a tall building with lots of windows with lights behind them, and fenced grounds all around. The rest of the enclosure seemed to be nothing but virgin forest. Somebody had gone to a lot of trouble to wall in a patch of woods no different than the seventy miles of the same thing I'd traveled through for a day and two nights getting here. Maybe the place had been converted into a private resort for the big shots of this day and age. The big building would be the ritzy hotel, and the blockhouses over on the other side were the servants' quarters. And the air traffic wasn't looking for me; they were ferrying the rich tourists in to enjoy a rustic weekend back of a wall that kept the peasants out.

It was a swell theory, but I still kept my head down and looked for the angle.

It took me half an hour to find a route in the dark. The old drainage ditch, choked level with weeds, was it. It wasn't over two feet deep where it went between the lights. I hugged the dirt and did it with my fingers and toes, an inch at a time. Fifteen minutes of this put me far enough inside the lights to risk sticking my head up. The coast was clear. I moved off in the cover of some deep grass to take a closer look at the big building.

An eight-foot fence made of black iron spears with big barbed heads was only the first obstacle. Beyond the bars a sweep of manicured lawn broke like green surf against a line of tailored shrubbery, and back of every clump a light was placed just right to cover a section of the perimeter. There were Blackies here— squads of them, pacing around the grounds like a bunch of but- lers looking for the duchess's lost diamond choker. They had packs clipped to their belts with wires leading to the sides of their helmets, and I didn't need a set of technical specs to tell that these were something that worked a lot better than leashed bloodhounds. I stepped on a dry stick about then and two of the boys turned and started drifting my way. I backed out softer-footed than the time I stumbled into a cave that had a sleeping cougar in it, and moved back a couple of hundred yards into deep woods.

It took me an hour to scout all the way around the fence. It enclosed about fifty acres of park with the fairy palace in the middle and a nice little pad for short take-off aircraft at one side, well stocked with everything from one-man hoppers to a deep- bellied heavyweight big enough to carry a full battalion complete with artillery. Nothing I saw gave me any encouragement.

About then I noticed some activity over on the left, not far from where I'd made my first approach. A section of fence swung out and a small air-cushion car came through it and moved along in a puddle of yellow-white made by its bow and stern lights and the gate closed again. There was nothing in that for me.

The car came along my way, and I faded back along a sort of trail until it dawned on me it was using the same trail. I did a fade into the brush then, and lay flat with my cheek in the dirt while it whirled its dirt cloud past and snorted on off toward the barracks across the valley.

I stayed there for a while and told myself I was watching the lights moving beyond the fence. After a while my chin bumped the ground and woke me up. I got up and moved back deeper into the woods, with a vague kind of idea of finding a nice dark spot to hole up in and nap until the next brain wave hit me.

The going was easier in among the big timber. There was a slight downward drift to the ground, and not much in the way of underbrush. Then I saw a gleam ahead that looked like riffled water with moonlight on it and came down the last slope and clear of the trees and was looking at Musky Lake.

For a long, timeless minute I looked out across the water and listened to the old voices, whispering to me over all the years, as if no time had passed at all. From here, you couldn't see the barracks or the fenced-in tower; just the lake, stretching to the far shore with the rising wall of big pines behind it, and over to the left the point where the cabin had stood, the one Frazier and I built barehanded one summer just after the war. I looked toward it and at first the shadows there under the big trees fooled me, and then I blinked hard and was still seeing the same thing. The cabin was still standing, right where we'd left it.

I took the path along the soft ground at the edge of the water, and had the feeling that if I blinked again, it would go away. I came up on it from the left, the way we used to come down from shooting in the woods, and even the melon patch was still there, a little overgrown, but clear enough in the moonlight. The dock was off to the right, and the old flat-bottomed skiff was tied up at the end of it, with the bow offshore, the way I'd always anchored her. I had the damnedest impulse to yell and see if Frazier would come out the door, waving a jug and telling me to hurry up, the serious drinking was about to begin. . . .

I came up with the little gun in my hand, skirted the place at a hundred yards, then worked my way in, ready to drop or shoot first, whichever way it worked out. Fifty feet from the cabin I lay flat and watched the back windows. Fifteen minutes went by, with nothing but a few mosquitoes whining around my head to prove I wasn't a ghost. Part of that shrewd calculating machine that was what passed for the Dravek intelligence was telling me I was taking chances, wasting time leafing through the faded gardenias of my yesterdays; but another part didn't give a damn. This was a place I knew, that was part of my life, the life I remembered. From here, strange people like Jess and strange places like the slum they called dirtside and man-eating corporations called ETORP seemed like something you'd think up in the dark hours of the night after too much lobster and fruitcake.

I made my final approach standing up. If anybody had the place staked out they could nail me as well creeping as walking, as long as I was coming their way. But nobody jumped out and put a spotlight in my eyes. I came around the side of the cabin and heard a bullfrog say moo, like a cow, down by the water. There was a small window to the left of the door. I came up to it and looked in, saw nothing but some reflected moonlight, went on past it to the door. It opened without an argument. The hinges squeaked; they always squeaked.

Inside nothing had changed, not even the dust on the floor or the soot on the ceiling above the fireplace. I tucked my toy gun away and started in to search the place.

An hour later the sky was beginning to gray up and I had covered the one-room cabin three times and turned up nothing.

I sat on the edge of the bunk and chewed my teeth and tried to be as smart as the note-writer expected me to be. He said as soon as I got here I'd know where to look.

The cabin was a lousy place to hide anything. The walls were plain one-inch ship-lapped redwood, with open studs, no paneling inside. The ceiling was bare rafters and boards. There was one cupboard, with a few chipped plates and cups in it. The fireplace had a liberal drift of ashes and a few chips of charred wood. The bathroom had nothing but what you'd expect, and the flush tank hadn't yielded any secrets suspended by a string from the float, or inside it. And if there were any compartments under the floor, they weren't anything I'd had a hand in. The trick drawer back of the strongbox in my office had been the extent of my instinct for conspiracy.

A little pale light was coming in past the red-and-white checked curtains that had been some short-term girlfriend's idea of woodsy atmosphere. I went over to the door and eased it open and stepped out and looked out across the lake and just like that, I had it.

15

It was one of those days that stick in your mind down through the years; a hot day, with a breeze on the lake that riffled the surface just enough to bring the bass out of the deep hollows and up from under the sunken logs to snap at the big juicy flies the wind was bringing out over the water. Frazier and I had landed half a boat full before the wind died and they stopped hitting. The two girls—Gwen and Rosanne—had laid out a nice table while we cleaned the haul and packed what we couldn't eat in the freezer. After dinner we went down to the shore and sat under the trees and finished off the bottle—the third bottle of the day. We had a big laugh with it: the third fifth on the Fourth of July.

There'd been a big pine stump outside the cabin. We counted the rings; two hundred and forty-seven. Then we buried the dead soldier under it, with full military honors. . . .

It took me under ten minutes to find the stump, grub away enough packed leaves and hard dirt to find the gap down among the roots and pull out the bottle. The label was gone and the metal screw cap had been replaced with a hard, waxy plug, but it looked like the same bottle. I held it up to the light and made out something inside it, pale through the brown glass.

My mouth felt a little dry and my pulse was rocking my hand a little, but otherwise there was just the feeling of unnatural awareness you get when all the days of anticipation focus down to the second you've been working toward. I made a couple of tries to get the sealing wax loose, then cracked the neck off the bottle and reached in and teased the paper out.

It was just one sheet, folded and rolled, and all it had on it was two words:

COUGAR CAVE

16

It was a stiff half-hour's climb up through dense timber to the escarpment on the east side of the valley where the bare rock pushed up a hundred and fifty feet higher than it did anywhere else along the rim. There were boulders there as big as London buses, piled where the glacier had left them; and in among them there were a lot of cozy little caves where Frazier and I had flushed everything from weasels to a mothy brown bear. The one where I'd met the cougar was up high, with an approach across a rockface that made it too hard to get to to interest most critters, or most hunters. The time I'd gone up there I was chasing a wolverine with a 30-30 slug in him who didn't know when to lie down and be dead. It wasn't the kind of chore that was any fun; I did it because if I hadn't, a long line of hunting Draveks would have come out of their graves spinning like roulette wheels. I went up soft and easy and my carcajou was there, a yard inside the over-hang, dead. I had one foot up to make the big mistake when I smelled cat and saw him, curled up in the back, logy after a kill maybe, just starting to move. I faded back and slid all the way to the bottom and spent the next week growing new skin on my palms and the seat of my pants. I'd never been back.

The sun was making rose-colored patterns up high on the rockface. I went up fast, not being any fonder of the climb than the last time, but even less fond of doing it in broad daylight. I made it to the ledge in ten minutes and came up over it and went flat, and looked back into shadows. It was no different than the last time, except for no kitty.

Inside, there was the same smell of wet rock and animal drop-pings that all these caves had. I had to duck to get in past the outer vestibule where the wolverine had died, and was in a big-ger chamber, about right for garaging a VW, if you could get it inside. The floor here was the dirt that had drifted in during the last few thousand years, more or less smooth-packed; the walls slanted up to a craggy ceiling with air spaces with roots showing in them. That gave me enough light to show me that things were just like I left them, without a hiding place for anything bigger than an aspirin. If I was hoping to find a ten-volume journal telling me what it was all about, I was out of luck.

The trip in had taken forty minutes; the search consumed another thirty seconds. I prowled the cave again, used up that odd half minute. This was the end of the line. It had been a swell chase up to now, but it looked like I was going to go back to the frat house minus the motorman's glove after all.

I went back into the outer cave and looked out over a view

of pine tops down to the sparkle of the lake a mile away and tried to think like a guy sitting in the dark beside a coffin writing notes to a stranger about something that he had to do that he knew was going to kill him; but all that got me was an attack of claustrophobia.

I looked over the anteroom, went out and studied the front porch and wondered how many little men with binoculars were watching me, went back in and scraped my foot across the spot where the devil cat had used up the last of his chips, and saw the shine of metal. . . .

It was a stainless steel lock box, not locked; all it had in it was a heavy plastic envelope, sealed. I got that open and took out a sheet of paper with typing on it and read:

> *In the back room. Look up high, on the left. The opening looks too small, but you can make it. About fifty feet.*
> *Brace yourself.*

17

The hole was there all right, and it looked too small, just like the man said. But I got up there and got my shoulders in and twisted over on my side and started in.

The tunnel slanted down after the first couple of yards, tight going but just on the right side of possible. In a couple of places I felt smooth clay where somebody had done some excavating.

Twice I thought I'd been stopped, and had to back off and try again, at a new angle; and once I got my head through into a pocket my shoulders wouldn't pass and I was stuck there for a minute, feeling the weight of a mountain crushing me flat before I worked an arm up and pushed a fallen stone out of the way and went on through.

It was pitch dark once I was below the broken rock level and into the solid stuff. This part of the tunnel was wider. I did it on my hands and knees, using my head for a bumper. Even in the dark I could tell this was a man-made shaft now. It dropped at a thirty-degree angle, after about twenty feet cut hard to the left, then left again and down twenty feet, and there was light ahead.

I stopped there and felt of my gun for whatever good that did me and listened hard, trying to make up my mind whether I heard a faint sound coming from down below or not, decided it was just a ringing in my ears, and did the last few feet to another right-angle turn and was in a room.

It wasn't a cave. The walls were cut smooth and faced with concrete. The floor was natural stone, ground smooth. The ceiling was high enough that I didn't have to duck. The light was coming from a strip down the center of it that shed a pale green light on something bulky that almost filled the little room. It was a cylinder, ten feet long, five feet in diameter, looped and hung with plastic piping and wires. I'd seen something like it once before, in the sealed wing under my old plant. That one had had a corpse in it. This one felt different.

I came up to it easy, as if there might be something there that I didn't want to startle. I put a hand against the side of the big tank and felt a vibration so faint that if I hadn't been alone under forty feet of solid rock I wouldn't have thought it was there at all. The curve of the top of the thing was a little above my eye level, but there was a platform there for me to step up on. I did, and looked down at a clear plastic plate about a foot square, set in the top curve of the tank. It was misty, and I had to lean close to see through it and when I did a big hand as cold as death closed on my chest and squeezed.

The face behind the cloudy glass was that of a child, a little girl no more than six years old, pale and translucent as a china doll.

It was the face from the dreams.

I found the letter lying on the platform and got it open and by holding it three inches from my face I could read it:

> She's here. Number Three was right; a billion dollars' worth of security systems, but our route slides under all of it. Frazier built it when he was building the Keep, right under his nose. He knew him; too tough to know when he met a man that was tougher.
>
> There's just one place more to go now. I think I've got a chance, maybe even a good chance; but I'm leaving what I've got for you, in case I slip. Maybe I was a little too tricky, feeding it to you in pieces, but it makes a broken trail that

can't be cracked by an outside man with one lucky find. Except the one man, and I'm counting on the trick paint to take him out. What I planted in the box for him to find should make him happy enough to call off his dogs, at least long enough to give you your chance, if it comes to that. He knows I'm here, somewhere, and I don't know how. He knows how I'd figure the play; but I know his touch too, so maybe it will be OK.

What's on the next sheets cost a lot of lives and years to get; it's the genuine article.

Now I'm going to take one more look, and remember some things, so when the choice gets tough I'll know which one to make. Then I'm going in, and I won't be back this way.

The drawing on the sheet tacked to the back of the note showed me the valley and the lake and a spot on the north side that matched the town, labeled "Keep." There was an X marking the cougar cave. Another sketch below showed the details of a door and a shaft cut to below the valley floor, and a tunnel down there that crossed to the Keep and then some more detail on a hatch that led out into a false wall behind a furnace room. Another page had the layout of the Keep, including more dummy passages and double walls than Canterville Castle. They led all the way to a big spread on the top level, with a couple of alternates and a few question marks, just to give me the feeling it hadn't all been done for me.

I read it through again, looking for some useful clue I might have missed, but I didn't find any more details of what I was expected to do. There was just the chart and the map, and the note, full of confidence that all I lived for was the chance to go where he'd gone and not come back from.

He was quite a guy, was my letter-writer, and he expected a lot of me. More than he was likely to get.

I was supposed to know a lot of things I didn't know, and maybe those were the things that would have made me hot to tighten my belt and go looking for the kind of trouble that would be waiting for me at the end of that cute tunnel and those neat rat holes in the walls.

I thought these thoughts for half an hour or so. Then I went over to the door that was cut into the wall behind the big tank and got it open and saw steps and started down.

18

There was enough water in the tunnel to make a spotty reflection of the glow from the ceiling strip and show up the rats that moved away ahead of me just out of BB gun range. I stopped a couple of times to listen, in case somebody was waiting for me up ahead and making noises. I didn't hear anything. That made me feel lonelier than ever.

The tunnel ended at a stair like the one I'd come down. The steps went up forty feet and ended in a landing just big enough to stand on. There was a wooden panel in front of me, with something chalked on the back of it in block letters: HINGES AT LEFT. WATCH FOR TRAFFIC FROM KITCHEN.

He was still with me. The thought didn't help much. From here, with all he knew, he'd gone on to get killed, an item that had probably netted two inches on an inside page; I felt over the panel, put a little weight against the right edge, then a little more. Nothing moved. That meant I could go back home and forget the whole thing. I gave it one last push and it swung out and dust sifted down and I could see a light coming through a vertical space at the end of a passage about a foot wide between the wall and a slab of sheet metal that would be the back of the heat plant. Past that, there was a big room with long tables and cabinets built in along one wall and a half-open door into another big room with a light and men in black sitting around a table. Just then something behind me made a *clack!* like a round sliding into a chamber, and I went as stiff as Automat Jell-O. Then a blower started up and sheet metal around me started to thrum. I let some air out and got my mouth back over my teeth and moved out along the wall. From here I had a better view of the room beyond the door. There were four men in there, with cards in their hands. A clock on the wall over their heads said seven-twenty-eight. It was well into the morning, but there was no sunlight shining in, which meant no windows. I filed that observation away and one of the men laid down his hand and stood up. So did the other three. One of them said something and they moved out of sight, acting like fellows remembering a missed appointment.

I worked my way along the side of the walk-in reefer and located three bolt heads that looked like the other ones but which turned, with a little persuasion, and let a piece of solid-looking wall ride straight back on oiled rails. I rushed in past it into a tight space and got it closed behind me. What I was in now was a tight vertical shaft thirty inches in diameter with six-inch rods going up in a spiral and a smell of old dust. The wall of the shaft and the rods both had the soapy feel of a high polymer plastic. I checked to be sure my gun was riding around front where I could get at it, and started up.

It was a nice easy climb for the first few dozen turns. Then my back started to ache from the bent-over position and my arches started to feel the rods and my hands were slippery with sweat and it was a long way down. All the light I had to see by was a creepy pale green glow that came from the plastic itself. I reminded myself of one of those restless corpses that grandpa used to tell me about before the DTs got him; the kind they had back in the old country that used to come out from under tombstones on the night of the new moon. Only this time I was the spook. I decided to give up that line of thought before I scared myself to death and just then somebody tapped me on the shoulder.

19

Now, maybe you think a tough Hunky with a gun in his pants can absorb that kind of surprise with no more reaction than a curled lip and a reflex move toward the hip. I made the reflex move OK: I jumped so hard I bent one of the rods an inch out of line with my head and one foot slipped off and I was hanging by my hands looking up at bones.

There was enough light to see a set of fingers and a wrist joint and above that what was left of an arm leading up to some less clearly defined anatomy. There was no flesh there, just the clean yellow-white skeleton, glowing a little, like old neon, in the dark. I made out the skull with the lower jaw hanging wide open as if it was getting ready to take a bite, and the other arm, and the torso and legs, just sort of folded down against the spine, which was broken in two places and doubled back on itself and jammed against the rungs.

I held on there for a while and then got my feet back on the rungs and made three tries and swallowed and felt sweat drip off the end of my nose. I got one hand unglued and reached up and got a grip on Mr. Bones above the wrist and pulled. The forearm came off at the elbow and flopped back and broke at the wrist and small bones made a light clatter going down the shaft. I dropped the ulna and went up a step higher and my face was in front of the spot where the hand had been and there was something on the wall there: a stain in the form of a couple of lines that made a straggly "T". I touched the lines and a dry, brownish powder crumbled away. Dried blood. Before he'd died, the skeleton with the broken back had tried to write something, and almost made it.

T. T for Treachery, or for Too late. I couldn't think of anything good that started with a T. T for Trouble, T for Turn back.

T for Trap.

I looked up and the empty sockets met my look. Number Four; the letter-writer. The letters that had still been there, left there for me to find—like these bones—warning me to look out for trouble ahead; tipping me off that I was walking into ambush. But why hadn't the man that killed him taken the dead mouse out of the trap and dusted off the cheese and set it, all ready for the next one?

Or maybe I was building it all on a set of cold feet. Maybe the skeleton was just a careless carpenter left over from the construction phase. Maybe he was the guy who designed this back stair, tossed in on top of it after it was finished, to seal his lips. And maybe I was a fan dancer.

It had to be the fourth man, because this was his route, and nobody had used it after him, because he was blocking it solidly with his bones. Yeah, maybe that was it. He'd gone up, walked into the trap, taken a load of slugs in the stomach, and then instead of lying down there to die, he'd made it back to his rat hole and fallen down it, so the next man would find him and think what I was thinking.

I looked up past the bones and saw the faint cylindrical shine of the tube, leading on up to the place I had to go, to find the man I had to find.

"Thanks, pal," I said to the skull. I pushed at the bones and they fell away into darkness. The rungs led upward another hundred feet and ended at a door that opened into a small, dark room.

✧   ✧   ✧

I crossed the room without falling over anything much, put an ear to the door. That told me nothing. I eased it open half an inch and looked out into a lighted hall.

There was a Blackie standing with his back to me about twelve feet away. He had a gadget like a stopwatch in his hand and he was aiming it at the wall and his lips were moving. I waited in the shadows until he worked his way close enough. Then I stepped out and he came around fast but too late and I hit him up under the angle of the jaw, the one that breaks the neck if you do it right. My aim was OK. He started his dive and I caught him and took him back into my lair.

It took me ten minutes to get him stripped out and tucked away in the closet, another five to get his pants and coat on. They were a lousy fit, and hadn't been out to the dry cleaner lately. I had to pass the boots; the ones I had on were close enough. I checked his gun, but it had too many colored buttons I didn't know about. I ditched it and tucked Minka's little one in the holster and headed for a door down the hall. I was almost there when a foot scraped behind me and a heavy voice said, "OK, all you culls are wanted up to Comsat on the triple."

I kept going, reached the door, had it halfway open when the voice yelled after me, "OK, Wallik, that means you, too."

I slid inside and was in a tiled room with a dirty window and plumbing. Great. Trapped in the john. The window was two feet high and a foot wide, with obscure glass in it. A light-and-shadow pattern on it looked like bars. It didn't give much light. I got behind the door and palmed the gun and waited. A minute went by. It was quiet outside now. Then feet came across and a fist hit the door and a heavy voice said, "OK, it don't take that long," and the feet went away.

I gave it another five minutes and came out, cautiously. The hall was all mine again. Faint sounds came from the far end of it. I went the other way, found stairs, went up them to a landing, listened, went on up and came out in a wide corridor with lights and open doors and crossed the hall and went into another door. Somebody was arguing with somebody, saying, "I don't care if you've replaced all of them, check them again, high and low scale. . . ."

I could see the foot of a wide staircase along the hall. It didn't attract me. I went to the right, checked a plain door that might have been a service stair, was looking at a vacuum cleaner and a shelf with cans and bottles. Maybe it was a good find at that. If the chase got hot I could hide in there and pretend to be a broom.

I went on to the end, turned left, smelled breakfast cooking somewhere. It made my jaws ache. There was a carpet here, and the lighting was recessed and muted, the way it is when there's money around. A Blackie came out of a room and started my way. I took the first door to the left and was in a room with a couple of easy chairs and a divan long enough to sleep two in-laws. A window looked out on a garden with flowers and another wing of the building on the other side. The steps outside went by softly. I waited and then opened up and looked out. He was standing at the intersection, looking back at me. For a long second we stared at each other. Then I winked. He staggered back a step as if I'd hit him in the gut with a wet towel and whirled and disappeared. I came out and went on and a few doors farther found an open elevator door and stepped in and palmed a panel full of buttons and started up.

The car went up one floor and stopped and two men got in. I got my fingers over the gun and one of them gave me a hard look and said to the other, "By God, things have changed since I pulled the duty." The other one did some noisy breathing through his nose.

We rode along in silence together and the car stopped and a woman with a pale doughy face got on and the two men got off without looking back. The woman gave me a look and patted her back hair. At the next stop a girl got on and stared at me. She stared at me through two more stops. At the next one a man in a gray coverall got on and she opened her mouth to say something and I said, "Excuse it, kid, I was up all night, and I don't mean walking the baby," and patted her hip going past. Her mouth was still open as the door closed.

There were more people here, moving up and down the hall, which was neat and clean and full of that office smell. Nobody seemed to see me. I went along fast to the end of the hall and found the service stair and went up two flights and dead-ended at a landing that needed sweeping. There was a small window here that showed me a nice sweep of early-morning lawn and the fence in the distance, inconspicuous behind the screen of shrubbery.

There seemed to be a lot of Blackies out on the grass. I was estimating my altitude at ten stories now. From outside it hadn't looked that high. The lonesome feeling was back, strong. I hadn't met any live people, to talk to, for quite a few days now. I pushed through a narrow door and out into the whisper of air conditioning and the dead white of artificial light. It was a big room with chairs and tables with magazines on them, like a room where you wait for one of those dentists who hate to talk about money. A hall led away from the other side of it. There was nobody in sight, in the room or in the hall. Everything seemed quieter than it ought to. I looked at two plain wood-slab doors with shiny hardware, and another door with a used look around the knob. It looked friendlier than the others. I went over to it and tried it. It swung in on a swell storeroom full of sealed cartons and a fat voice behind me said "Hey!"

I came around fast with the gun all set to go and a big fellow with eyes bugged behind lenses like biscuits pointed toward the door I came in by and said, "I've warned Alders about you people intruding here!"

"Sorry, chief," I said. "I guess maybe I kind of lost my way—"

"I heard you'd staged another of your ridiculous false alarms—the third this week, wasn't it? Every time a bird flutters over the building looking for a worm it starts bells ringing and lights flashing! You don't delude me with your show of activity! It's all an excuse for prying here in Tabulation!" He grabbed his glasses and pushed them back into his head, like coal eyes on a snowman. With his kind of vision, contacts wouldn't help.

"Yeah, I'll just be on my way. Guess we can't fool you, Doc—"

"Mind your tongue, you! You're aware that I detest that flippant epithet! Has Alders instructed you to add insolence to your other offenses?"

"Sorry, Doctor. I was just on the way out—"

"The other way!" He pointed a finger that was just a little longer than it was thick. I went the way it pointed and had a choice of up or down on a narrow stairway with dope-stick butts. I went up past a little landing with a couple of empties parked in the corner, up six more steps, and was stopped by a black door with panic hardware on it. I tried it and it gave and I came out into brilliant sunshine. I was on the roof. The tower apartment I was looking for wasn't here.

20

In the next five seconds a couple of things happened. The first was that I looked across seventy feet of open space and saw a second tower going up thirty feet higher than the one I was in, with a wide terrace tacked to one corner. The other was a noise off to the left that made me fade back behind the monitor and slide down flat against hot tarred roof.

"What was that?" somebody said.

"What?"

"I thought I heard Waxlow come up."

"You got ten minutes yet."

"I heard—" The door I had come through banged open and feet stepped out.

"Yah! Waxlow, you're early!"

They moved off talking. I sneaked a look. There was nothing on the roof but a platform with what looked like an ack-ack gun except that it had a set of cooling fins along the barrel, and some heavy cable snaking off to a big panel with dials, and on to a standpipe by the parapet. There were three Blackies, all wearing helmets and side arms. They jawed for a few minutes and one of them came back over my way and went through the door and it closed behind him. The other two settled down by the gun and squinted at nothing. One of them yawned. The other one spat. A bird flew over and dropped guano in a white streak and went his way. A fly came and checked me out. I stayed where I was and waited for the big break.

An hour later I was still waiting. Another man came up and relieved one of the Blackies and the other man took a couple of turns around the roof, but I was pretty well hidden in the shadows between the stairhead and a ventilation intake. Another hour went by. All I wanted was ten seconds with both boys in sight and looking the other way so I could sneak back inside, but it was no go.

Lunchtime came and went. The sun beat down and the roof soaked up heat and I sweated inside the black suit, and the tight seams galled me under the arms and around the neck.

The sun came over on the other side and made the boys shift position a little, but not enough. I tried to move a little to get back in the shadow and touched hot roof and raised a blister on my knee.

About midafternoon an NCO came up and poked around the gun and squinted up at the sky and came over and stood four feet from me and belched and went back inside. More reliefs came up. The sun went back of the high tower and I started catching dinner smells from below.

The roof had cooled some by then, and I shifted and got into a better position and could see the terrace across the way. A man's head showed over the edge once, bobbing around as if he were doing something fussy like weeding a flower box or laying a table. A little later lights went on up there and some music floated down. It was twilight now. The sky was a silent pink explosion. The pink deepened and scarlet ships flying purple banners sailed away toward the west. Then there were stars and a chill in the air and a mosquito bit the back of my neck. Over by the gun I could see little red and green and blue lights of instruments that could probably pinpoint a nosy aircraft at fifty miles; but none of them pointed at me, lying doggo twenty feet away.

A bell dinged down below and the watch changed again. When the door opened, a blaze of light shone out. Not much chance of a quiet sneak through that.

At a rough estimate, I'd been pinned in this spot for twelve hours now. The chances for improving my position didn't seem to be getting any better. Another few hours and I'd be too stiff to move and too weak to go anywhere if I did move. It was time to make a play—any play.

From my spot back of the stairhead, the gun emplacement was off to the right, near the parapet. To the left of that, the line ran straight back for thirty feet and then went into a series of setbacks and angled across behind me. The other tower was over that way, just a set of lights floating on the night now. I slid backward and got up on all fours and did a little silent groaning and made it to my feet, with the stairhead and the ventilator between me and the gun crew. The roof surface was smooth but gritty; I took off my boots and shoved them inside my blouse and went over to the parapet and had a look.

What I saw wasn't encouraging: A sheer drop of fifty feet to a ledge where light shone out on plants growing in a box and below that another drop of a couple hundred feet to the walled court, looking the size of a postage stamp. Off to the left, a connecting wall went across to the other tower, at the level of the planter ledge. To the right there was a swell view of the string of lights in the distance along the perimeter of the reservation. None of that gave me any ideas. I backed off, feeling that vulnerable feeling that high places give me, and heard a sound that made me spin and grab for the gun and then lights went on all across the roof. They were big dazzlers, mounted on six-foot poles. The air around them looked like blue smoke and they highlit the shape of every pebble on the roof like a die-cutter stamping silhouettes out of sheet steel. There was one patch of shadow, as black as a chimney-sweep's T-shirt, cast by the doorhead; and I was in it.

The men on the gun were shielding their eyes and swearing and other men were coming out on the roof and fanning out. There was no talking; the guns they had in their hands told me all I needed to know.

They formed up on the far side of the roof and started across. I had maybe thirty seconds to think up a scheme, check it over for flaws, and put it into execution. They were almost over to the stairhead. I backed away, which put the parapet against the back of my thighs. I didn't think about it; I swung one leg over and found a toehold in the rough stonework and ducked and heard feet walk past and stop and come back. That was enough for me. I got a grip on the ledge I was squatting on and let my legs down and felt around for a place to put them, and started down.

Two minutes later I was on the ledge I'd seen from above. It went straight on for forty feet to the fancy corner. The cross wall to the other tower joined there. I put my cheek to the wall and went along to the end. Then I turned to put my back to the wall and jumped for the cross wall. I was prepared to fall on the roof side if it worked out that way; but I landed square, went forward on all fours, and headed for the deep shadow at the far end. The light went past behind me. I reached the wall and pushed my face hard against it and breathed with my mouth open. The light traveled back along the ledge and up the wall again and went out. I sat up and felt around in the dark and found a heavy stone balustrade, got over that and was on a narrow terrace with a row of pots big enough for Ali Baba. Vines were rooted in them, growing thick and black up the wall. Up above I could see a little light on the railing of the higher terrace. The vines grew there, too. It looked like it might be possible, for a trained athlete in top condition, with spiked climbing shoes and a Derby winner's luck. I stepped up on the stone railing and got a fistful of tough vine and started up.

The first few feet were as easy as getting into trouble. The main stems were as big as my wrist, and clamped to the wall like British plumbing. Then they branched and I started hearing little ripping sounds. I stopped there for a few minutes with the night breeze blowing across my face and thought about what might be waiting for me up above, versus what I knew was down below. Then I unclamped my hands and tried for new holds higher up.

Half an hour later I got a hand on the bright-plated railing of the upper balcony just as the pencil-thick creeper I was hanging onto let go. There were a few seconds of fast living then, while I grabbed for a two-handed grip and waited for my life to flash before my eyes. Then I was hanging on by a knee and an elbow, looking across polished tiles into a deep room full of subdued light and oiled teak paneling, and a desk no bigger than a Cadillac with a man sitting at it, facing away from me. He was leaning back in the chair, smoking a cigarette. He had a wide back and a solid neck and a little gray in his hair. As far as I could tell, he was alone. While I looked at him, he reached and stubbed the butt out in an ashtray hewn out of a chunk of glass the size of a football. Then he pushed a button and a drawer slid open and up and he lifted a big decanter and poured dark brandy into a glass; while both hands were busy stoppering the decanter I came up and over the rail and slid the gun into my hand and went over to the open doors behind him and said, "Don't even breathe, pal."

He checked, just for an instant; then he hit the stopper with his palm and put the jug back in the drawer and swung around to face me.

The man I was looking at was me.

21

For about ten seconds we stared at each other; then I saw that he wasn't so much looking at me as he was giving me a chance to look at him. He was something to look at.

I've never had a delicate look, but this face was hewn out of the earth's primordial rock, weathered to a saddle brown and lined a little by time's erosion, then polished with a hand finer than Cellini's to a portrait of power held in restraint. He could have been any-where from a tough forty-five to a smooth sixty. He was wearing a wine-colored dressing gown with a black collar; his neck projected from it like the trunk of an oak tree. His expression was somewhere between a smile too faint to see and no expression at all.

"All right, you got here," he said in my voice. "Come in and sit down. We have things to talk about."

I moved a step and then remembered I was giving the orders. "Stand up and move away from the desk," I said. "Do it nice and easy. I'm not good enough with this thing to try any near-misses."

He pushed the corners of his mouth up half a millimeter and didn't move. "I tried to find you before you took the risk of coming here—"

"Your boys are second-rate. Soft from too much easy duty, maybe." I motioned with the gun. "I won't tell you three times."

He shook his head; or maybe my eyelid quivered. He wasn't a guy to waste effort on a lot of unnecessary facial expressions.

"You didn't come here to shoot me," he said.

"I could change my plans. Being here makes me nervous. Not having you cooperate makes me even more nervous. When I'm nervous I do some dumb things. I'm going to do one now." I raised the gun and aimed it between his eyes and was squeezing and he came out of the chair fast. He gave me a big smile. You could almost see it.

"If I'd meant to hurt you, I could have done it any time since you crossed the line," he said. "It's wired—"

"The perimeter fence, maybe; not inside. Your own troops would be tripping it a hundred times a day."

"You think you could have gotten this far without my know-ing it?"

"You can't lock the world out unless you lock yourself in. Eighty years of waiting could make a man careless."

He gave me a little frown to look at. "Who do you think I am?"

"There are some holes in the picture," I said. "But the part that's there says you're a guy I used to know. His name was Steve Dravek."

"But you're Steve Dravek." He said it the way you tell a kid his dog died.

"I just think I'm Steve Dravek," I told him. "You're the real article."

He frowned a little more. "You mean—you think I'm the original Dravek, born in 1941?"

"It sounds a little funny," I said. "But that's what I think."

He tilted his head a quarter of an inch and did something subtle that changed the frown back into a smile.

"No wonder you're nervous," he said. "My God, boy, put the gun down and sit down and have a drink. I'm not Number One; I'm Number Five!"

I moved around him to a chair and waved him to one and watched him sit, and then I sat, and rested the gun on my knee so the shaky hand wouldn't be so obvious. I wanted a drink the way Romeo wanted Juliet.

"What happened to Four?"

"What you'd expect. He was past his prime—over fifty. I tried to talk to him, but he wouldn't talk. Why should he? He owned the world."

"That would be how long ago?"

"Over forty years. As soon as I'd established myself here—there was a certain amount of pretty delicate maneuvering involved there—I tried to find out if there were any more of us. I drew a blank." He almost blinked. "Until you turned up."

"Tell me about that part."

"The tanks were rigged to signal when they were opened from the inside; just one quick squawk on the microwave band. You'd have to know just where to listen to pick it up. Unfortunately, there was no R and D feature; just the signal saying you were on the way. I tried to find you, but you dropped out of sight."

"It seemed like a good idea; even if your Blackies are lousy shots."

"They were instructed to fire anesthetic pellets."

"Some of those pellets packed quite a wallop."

He nodded. "It was too bad about that little man, Jess Ralph; when the men surprised you there, they jumped to a couple of conclusions—"

"Somebody tipped them. They were waiting."

"Naturally the ETORP reserve is under close guard—"

"Pass that. If you wanted to talk to me, why didn't you leave a message where I'd find it? You would have known where. And it would have been simpler than telling your Blackies to wing me with a needle full of dope."

"Would you have trusted me? As I remember the final instructions Frazier added to my 'cephtape, they painted a pretty black picture of the Old Man. I thought it was better to handle it as I did, let you follow the same trail I did. And it had the added advantage of bringing you here in secret. I think you can see it might complicate things to have the word get out that there were two of us."

"Uh-huh," I said, "maybe. By the way, let's see your wrist."

He looked thoughtful. Then he turned back his right cuff and showed it to me.

"It was the other one, remember?"

He showed me that one. The skin was perfect; there was no sign of the scar that only Number One would have.

"Satisfied now?" He was looking a little more relaxed. Maybe I was, too.

"Suppose you're telling the truth," I said. "How does that change things?"

"It ought to be pretty plain. The Old Man was nuts, power-crazy. I don't share that part of his personality."

"You took over where he left off," I said. "Nothing's changed."

"The world he built wasn't something I could rebuild in a day. It all takes time; if I tried to reform the whole thing at once, I'd have chaos on my hands."

"I got the feeling things were getting worse instead of better."

"It's not surprising you had a few wrong slants, considering the company you were keeping."

"What company would that be?"

"The little man, Jess. I thought you knew. He was Frazier's grandson."

"There seem to be a lot of things I don't know," I said. "Maybe by the time it got to be my turn the brainwashing machine was slipping its clutch. Maybe you'd better give me the whole story, right from the top."

His face tightened and his eyes looked at me and beyond me into the past.

"The first part of it, I remember myself, as if it was really me it happened to—the tapes Frazier took were good ones. Every detail is there, as if it had happened yesterday. . . .

"It started like any other morning. I had breakfast out on the terrace with Marion, drove to the plant, spent some time going over some tax figures with Frazier; then we went down to the new basement wing to see how things were going. It was a big pilot rig for a new process that was going to make us a mint. A new principle that would put us years ahead of anything else on the market.

"It was about half past ten when it happened. Marion was on the way into the city to do some shopping. The kid was with her. They stopped because she had some flowers she'd picked for me. White daisies, the first of the year. There were a lot of them down by the pool. . . .

"They went to the office and when I wasn't there some damned fool told them I was down in the new wing. They came on down.

"Frazier and I were over by the big cryo tank, watching Brownie stitch a plate in. Something slipped, and a piece of quarter-inch got away from the lift and it dropped and cut the high-tension lead from the portable welding rig. There was a lot of arcing and smoke—and right in the middle of it they came in.

"I started over there and waved them away and yelled to them to go back, and she saw me wave and started across and before Marion could grab her, she got into the smoke and lost her bearings, and I yelled to her again to go back and she heard me and turned my way and put a foot on the edge of the plate that was carrying sixty thousand amps.

"I was the first one to her. I grabbed her and yelled for the plant doc and the son of a bitch was off playing golf and there wasn't anybody else near enough to do any good. She wasn't breathing; there was no pulse. I knew five minutes of that and her brain would be gone forever. . . .

"I did the only thing I could do. We had a liquid nitrogen setup running in glass. I took her in there and told Frazier to get the top off the big receiver tank. He argued and I knocked him down. They all thought I'd gone nuts. I got it open myself and came back and Marion was holding her and wouldn't let her go. I had to take her. I carried her in and injected her and got her wrapped and put her inside and closed up and charged the coils and watched the plate frost over. In less than a minute it was done. Then I came back out and they were waiting for me, with guns and a cop they'd gotten in from somewhere. I could have torn 'em apart with my bare hands, but I knew I couldn't afford any mistakes now. She was in there, frozen, at six degrees Kelvin; but it was no good unless I convinced them I knew what I was doing, that it was the only chance.

"I talked to them. I kept calm and I talked to them and told them the kid was dead, and that what I'd done hadn't killed her any deader; and that as long as they left her where I'd put her, she'd stay just the way she was then. If any damage had been done, it was already done, and if it hadn't—well, if it hadn't, it was up to the medics to find out how to bring her back. And that meanwhile she stayed where she was.

"Frazier was the first to see it and side me. He'd been crazy about the kid. He got them under control and cleared the cops out and got a bunch of big-domes from Mayo over there and I went back home and drank a year's supply of booze in the next week. I didn't know where Marion was. They said I'd hit her pretty hard. But I wasn't thinking about Marion. I was only thinking about the kid.

"Some sob sisters got hold of it, then, and the newspapers got into it, and I was indicted for everything from murder to grave-robbery. There were laws that said a body had to be buried within two days, and a lot of other junk.

"Well, I beat 'em. She was underground. The research wing was twelve feet down. And I had witnesses that there was no pulse and no breathing. The papers kept playing the story for a few months, but after a while that stopped, too.

"I had the room where it happened walled off. I never wanted to see it again.

"We went ahead with the new process, and it worked out like I said it would. Food quick-frozen to under ten degrees K would keep forever, and come out as if it had been fresh that morning. Even the leafy stuff, lettuce and potatoes; everything. In a year we had a hundred licensees. In two years we'd stopped licensing and had our own plants, in forty-two countries. I poured every dime back into research, and the more we learned the quicker we learned. I didn't give a damn about the business; all I wanted was the money and the know-how to push the medical program. I went on working like six demons and waiting for the day the docs would give me the go-ahead.

"But they were a cagey bunch. In a year they told me they thought they were on the right track. In two, they were talking about breakthroughs. In five, it was unanticipated complexities in the mechanics of submolecular crystallization. By the time they'd been at it for ten years, to the tune of a hundred million a year, they were doing a lot of cute tricks with frozen mice and cats and lambs and telling me about critical thresholds and optimum permeability mass-ratios and energy transference rates and all that other gobbledygook their kind use to keep the laymen shelling out.

"I called for a showdown, and they said, of course, Mr. Dravek, certainly. Mr. Dravek, whatever you say, Mr. Dravek. But we won't be responsible. . . .

"What could I do? I hired and fired medical directors like baseball managers, but they all gave me the same pitch; wait another year just go be on the safe side. . . . Five more years went by, and another five, and meanwhile Draco Incorporated had grown into the biggest international combine on earth. We were in foods and medicines and the equipment that went with them, and had sidelines that were bigger than most of the world's industrial giants. The government had tried to step in ten different times to break us, but by then I'd made some interesting discoveries about politicians. They bribe easy, and a lot cheaper than you'd think. And for the big boys—the ones who would have laughed at money— we had some other little items. Those sawbones hadn't been just rolling pills; they'd come up with tricks that could make a man look and feel twenty years younger; and the Draco Foundation had been doing a lot with grafts and regeneration. We didn't publicize all this. It was strictly hush-hush, behind-the-walls stuff. Only our friends got in on it. And by then we didn't have a lot of enemies. So they left us alone, and I waited, and now they were talking about next year, maybe, and then a few more months and we'll be ready to take the chance. . . .

"You see, by then they had the techniques for deep-freezing and thawing. Hell, they were doing it on a commercial scale. But we were doing it under controlled cryolab conditions, with everything from tissue salinity to residual muscular electric charge controlled every step of the way.

"But with the kid, I hadn't had time for anything fancy. I'd just injected her with an anti-crystallizer we used in vegetable processing and put her under. That made it different. It gave them an excuse to stall. Because that's what they were doing. Stalling. They figured as soon as I had her back, I'd pull the rug out from under their operation. The damned fools! As if I'd sabotage the program that had made me the richest tycoon that ever lived—and with the power to appoint the whole damned Supreme Court if I'd wanted to!

"So they stalled me. And I was getting older. By then I was over sixty, not that I looked it. Like I said, the pill rollers had come up with some tricks. But I knew I couldn't last forever. And I had a board of directors who were looking ahead, jockeying for the day when one of them would take over where I left off. I knew if I dropped dead the day would never come for the kid. They'd leave her there. But she was my heir, you see? If she was alive, she'd own it all, and they'd be cut out of the pattern. So I had to do something. I had to work out a plan that would carry on after my death, so some day she'd come back, and find her inheritance waiting for her.

"I thought about it, and worked out one plan and then another, and none of 'em were any good, none of 'em were foolproof. Because there was no way to be sure there'd be a man there I could trust. Frazier would have done it, but he was my age; he wouldn't outlast me long. And anyway, the only man I could really trust was—me. And that gave me the idea.

"I called in my Chief of Research and told him what I wanted. He told me I was out of my mind. I said, sure, Doc, but can you do it?"

"He was a long time coming around, but in the end he had to admit there was no reason it was impossible. Illegal, maybe—we'd had some trouble with a bunch of fanatics and we'd had to let a few token laws get on the books—but it wasn't any trickier than what we'd been doing for some of our chums in Congress.

"It was simple enough. We'd been using test tube techniques for growing livestock for a long time; our brood plant in Arizona covered ten acres and produced more beef in a year than the State of Texas used to in ten. They took germ cells from me and started them growing, then planted them in automated life support tanks, like the stock brooders, only fancier. I gave Frazier the job of picking the spots for the vaults to be built out of indetectable nonmetallic material. I gave him orders not even to tell me. That way nobody could squeeze the secret out of me, or step in and act in my name and break up the playhouse; because I didn't know myself where they were.

"The first duplicate was rigged to mature in twenty years. I figured to be around that long. I'd brief him myself, and he'd take over from me, and they could scratch their heads and say that the Old Man was holding up a lot better than anybody figured; and when he'd run his time, the next one would be ready; and so on down the line, until the medics were ready to unfreeze the child. They could stall a long time, but they couldn't stall forever. And when they quit stalling, I'd be ready."

The man behind the desk took a deep breath and looked at me.

"That's where my tape ended. I came to in an abandoned mine shaft in Utah. The tank was set back into a side passage and covered over. There was information waiting for me, food, a full briefing up to the time Frazier had last been there. The rest of the story I had to put together from the Old Man's records.

"It was a swell plan he'd worked out; practically perfect. Just one thing went wrong. He got a hurry-up call from the Old Lab one day. He went over and they told him all bets were off. There'd been a freak power failure and the special tank she was in had lost its chill and the body had been at about a degree Centigrade for a couple of hours when they discovered it. So now Duna was just a corpse like any other corpse. She looked the same, but that little spark they'd been keeping alive all those years—or trying to— was gone.

"It hit him hard, but not as hard as it had the first time. Over thirty years had gone by. He'd learned to live with it. She'd been the biggest thing in his life, once; he could still lie awake at night and remember her voice, the look on her face when she'd come running to meet him when he came home. But that was all it was: just a recollection out of a fairy tale that he'd had once, a long time ago, and lost forever.

"He gave orders to Frazier for the body to be embalmed and buried; but by then Frazier was a little nuts on the subject. He didn't believe the medics. He wanted them to go ahead with the thaw, and when the Old Man wouldn't, he said some things to him that he'd have killed any other man for. Then he left.

"The Old Man went on with the funeral. And just before the grave was closed he had a thought and told them to open the box, and they did; and it was empty. Or almost empty. There was a little scale model of some kind of Indian temple in it, made out of solid gold. Frazier's idea of a joke, maybe. He'd been a good man once, but he was getting old. The Old Man tried to find him, but couldn't. He'd made some plans of his own. He was quite a boy, was Frazier. A billionaire in his own right. He knew how to cover a trail.

"So the Old Man called off the hunt. Frazier had been a good friend for a lot of years. It was too bad he'd gone off his rocker in his old age, but the thing to do was to let it go and forget it. As for the body—well, it was just a body now; in time Frazier would realize that and bury it and it would all be over.

"Meanwhile, there was a business to run. In a way, it was a relief to the Old Man to have the other off his mind. He'd been living in the past too long, trying to hold onto a dream that was a long time dying. Now he could put all his efforts into the important things.

"By this time the food processing empire was the tail that was trying to wag the dog. The sidelines were the big business. Rejuvenation methods that could keep a man looking young at ninety; artificial organs that he manufactured under his own patents— and some he didn't patent, because he didn't want any information leaks through the Patent Office. That was where the money was—and the power.

"After that things moved fast. The Old Man was already running the United States; he branched out then, took control of the French Assembly, then the Scandinavian Parliament, most of South America, Africa, Southeast Asia. He changed the name of the company, and reorganized it along lines that took control out of the hands of the board and put it where it belonged—in his pocket."

"You said you changed the company's name," I butted in. I already knew the answer, but I wanted to hear it from him.

"The Draco Company was all right for a small food-processing firm," he said. "When the outfit grew and moved into the life sciences field, the Old Man decided he needed something with a little more *élan*. He came up with Eternity, Incorporated."

"Commonly known as ETORP," I said.

He nodded. "He had it all in the palm of his hand; and then one day a man came gunning for him.

"The Plan; the one he'd worked out to insure that things were done his way, even after he died—was backfiring on him. Frazier's work. He'd been the one who set it up; he was the one the Old Man trusted. He'd matured the duplicate Dravek in an LS tank and briefed him to kill. It was a clever scheme. Who else was tough enough to kill Dravek—but Dravek?

"But it didn't work. Dravek Number Two found the Old Man; but the Old Man was too smart for him. He shot first. He had the body dumped where it would be found, so Frazier would hear about it and get the message.

"But Frazier was stubborn. Eighteen years later, another killer made his try. He went the same way. This time the Old Man knew Frazier had to go. He spent three years and a billion dollars, and he found him. But the medics weren't quick enough, and all he got out of him was the one fact: That each vault was set to signal when it opened. He got the details on that and nothing else.

"But when Number Three came out, he was ready for him. He was well over a hundred years old now, and still vigorous, but time was running out. He wanted an heir. So when Three showed, he knocked him out with a sleep gun; and when he came out of it, he told him the story. And he took him in and treated him like a son.

"A few months later the Old Man died in his sleep and Number Three went on where he'd left off.

"But the machine was still grinding. Twenty years later, Number Four came along. There was an accident. Three was killed. And then I showed up.

"I guess Number Four was a little greedy. He didn't try to talk to me, just took a shot at me. But my aim was better.

"Things ran quietly for quite a long time. There were problems, but what Dravek Number One could do, Number Five could do again. I had an idea there'd be a Number Six along, about twenty years back, but he never showed up. I figured the Draveks were all used up. And then you came."

"And where do you figure we go from here?"

"I'm not quite as greedy as Four was, Steve. And like the Old Man, I'm getting along to an age where I'm thinking of an heir. I don't have a son."

"Make it plainer."

"There's plenty here for both of us. In a way, you have as much right to it as I do. I want you to stay; share it with me. The whole world, Steve—and everything that's in it. . . ."

He leaned toward me, and some of the deadness had gone out of his eyes, and the smile he was playing with was starting to be a real smile.

"I've got a lot to show you, Steve, a lot to tell you. . . ." His hand went out to a little table beside him and dipped into a recess under it, and I brought the gun up from my side and shot him through the chest.

The shock half-spun him, knocked him out of the chair. I went after him fast, ready to fire again, but his face already had death written across it. His hand opened and the little silver-framed picture in it fell to the rug. The sleeve that had slid back when he reached was still pulled back almost to the elbow, and I could see the faint white line that ran all the way around his forearm six inches above the wrist.

"Whose arm did you steal, Old Man?" I got the words out. "Number Two's? Or weren't your boys good enough at their graft techniques back then?"

His head turned half an inch. His eyes found me.

"Why. . . . ?"

I stooped and picked up the picture he had reached for. "I thought you were trying for your gun," I said. "But it would have ended that way anyway, as long as we had this between us."

A light crossed his face, like a cloud shadow crossing a field of grain.

"Dead," he gasped out. "Dead. . . . long. . . . ago. . . ."

"She's alive, Old Man."

His eyes were holding mine, holding back death.

"Why did you do it, Old Man?" I gave him back his look. "Afraid a living heir might get in your way, after you'd learned how to make yourself immortal?"

He tried to speak, failed, tried again:

"Searched. . . . all these years. . . . never knew. . . ."

"Frazier outsmarted you after all. You ran the world, but in the end he took it away from you. I wonder what your boys did to him, to try to get him to talk. But he never did. He was loyal to you, Old Man, even after you'd stopped being loyal to yourself."

His face was the color of old ivory under the tan. His mouth opened and moved. I stooped to hear him.

"Tell Duna I said. . . . hello. . . ." His eyes were still on mine, dead eyes now, claiming their last wish.

"Sure," I said. "I'll tell her."

Epilogue

They brought Duna up from the vault under the ridge where Frazier had hidden her, and for forty-eight hours the best brains in ETORP's cryothesia lab worked over her. Then they called me in and I was there when she opened her eyes and smiled and said, "Daddy, I brought you some flowers."

That was twenty years ago. She's grown now, and a member of the first Mars Expedition. All the programs that had been stalled for a hundred and fifty years are moving ahead now, pushed by a force of nature that's like the grass root that cracks open a mountainside: population pressure.

I released the immortality drug for general distribution, free, the same day I opened the Ice Palace and started bringing the Old Ones out. Some talk has started up that I ought to reconvene Congress and hand the reins back over to the politicians, but I've got a theory that the world's not ready for that yet. I've set up a system that makes education tapes available to everybody, as many as they can absorb, on any subject. Some day I'll see signs that the race is growing up, and that there are men around who are wise instead of just smart; when that day comes, I'll retire and take that trip to Alpha, if I'm still around. Maybe that's arrogance; or maybe it's a sense of responsibility. Sometimes it's hard to tell the difference.

The Old Man kept a journal. It gave me the answers to a lot of questions that had been on my mind. The skeleton in the shaft was Number Six. He'd been shot, but managed a getaway back into the shaft via a fake air intake in the top-floor equipment room. It didn't look big enough, but it was. He killed two Blackies on the way out, and no one saw where he went; so he kept his secret.

The reason the Old Man hadn't closed off the route in via the tunnel was the easy one: he never found it. Frazier had concealed it so it would stay concealed.

The dead boy Jess and I had found was Number Two. He'd killed him and left him like that, as a warning to the next one; if there was a next one. By that time, he was a worried man. And then he had another idea: he meant what he said about taking me in. He wanted somebody else to do the sitting up nights, while he had a brain transfer to a new body—a young, anonymous one—and settled back to enjoy owning the world.

I brought Minka to the Keep, and married her. She and Duna got along swell. They should have. She was Marion's great-grand-daughter, which made Duna some kind of great aunt. She told me about Jess and his Secret Society. It didn't amount to much, after being handed down by word-of-mouth tradition for four generations. Most of it had been forgotten, and anyway, Frazier hadn't tried to saddle his descendants with a load of fossilized hates. But he'd left them the job of fighting ETORP, any way they could. Jess' way was hunting Blackies in the park. As I said, Jess was a guy who was full of surprises.

There was one thing that stumped me for a long time: how had Frazier gotten the jump on his boss, gotten the frozen child away from him? But I finally worked it out. Back in the early years, when the Old Man had had about the same life expectancy as the rest of the race, he'd set up a corporation to take over his affairs after his death, and operate it in Duna's name, hold it in trust for her until she was revived. He'd used all the pressure he had to set it up so it couldn't be broken, and to hire the best brains he could buy to run it.

It was a good idea—until the day when his top medical boys told him they'd cracked the Big One, and that now a chosen few could go on living as long as ETORP and its labs held out. That made a difference. He didn't need an heir, then.

By that time, there was a power struggle going on inside the organization that would have made the battle among Alexander's successors look like a pillow fight. That charter—and Duna, alive—was all the opposition needed to take over ETORP, lock, stock, and freeze tanks. And he couldn't have that. In the end Frazier realized the Old Man wouldn't be content for very long to have that small body waiting in the vault, hanging over him day and night; in the end he'd have turned the switch himself.

So Frazier set up the fake equipment failure, the phony funeral, and took Duna to a place where she'd be safe. The Old Man had really believed Duna was dead.

Oh yeah, one other thing. Yesterday a bell rang in a private alert station that's manned twenty-four hours a day, just down the hall from where I sleep. Number Eight is awake and moving—somewhere. I've sent my men out to try to find him, but he seems to be an elusive character.

I'm waiting for him now. When he shows up, I hope I can convince him that what I'm doing is the right thing. If I can't— well, I've got all the weight on my side, but Steve Dravek at twenty was a hard man to beat.

We'll see.

Afterword

by Eric Flint

The stories collected in this volume are rather unusual for Keith Laumer. As a rule, despite his sardonic and often downright grim view of the world, Laumer was not prone to writing dystopias. His interest as a writer was generally on the struggle of the individual against adversity, not the adversity itself.

To a large degree, that's even true of most of the stories collected here in *Future Imperfect*. Only one of the stories—"The Walls"—ends in sheer despair. In all the others, there is at least the element of heroism: the hero has done what he could as an individual to deal with the situation, even if the end result remains bleak.

In the next volume of this Baen reissue of Laumer's writings, we'll be returning to more familiar territory: adventure stories, pure and simple. The volume will start with *A Trace of Memory*, one of Laumer's best novels, and will end with one of Laumer's few collaborations, a novel he wrote with Gordon Dickson entitled *Planet Run*. Included also will be such varying stories as "The Choice," "Three Blind Mice," "Mind Out of Time" and "Message to an Alien."

Mind you, Laumer being Laumer, things will remain grim

371

enough. *Planet Run* has something of a comic flavor to it. The others . . .

Well. You'll see.